Time In Lieu

Also by Ishmael A Soledad

Short Story Anthologies

Hawking Radiation
ISBN 978-1-9763743-7-1

Sex and the Single Cosmonaut
ISBN 978-0-6487125-0-3

Novels

Sha'Kert: End of Night
ISBN 978-1-8382594-0-2

Time In Lieu

Collected Works Volume 1

Ishmael A Soledad

Time In Lieu
Collected Works Volume 1
First Edition Paperback
Copyright © Ishmael A Soledad 2023

Cover art courtesy
NASA / Efes Pixabay

Cover design and typesetting by Ishmael A Soledad
Thuringowa Central, Australia
IshmaelASoledad@gmail.com

The author asserts the moral right to
be identified as the author of this work.

ISBN: 978-0-6487125-8-9

Whosever is delighted in solitude,
is either a wild beast or a god ...
but little do men perceive what solitude is,
and how far it extendeth.
For a crowd is not company;
and faces are but a gallery of pictures;
and talk but a tinkling cymbal;
where there is no love

Francis Bacon

Table of contents

A bird in the hand

Somehow I still feel cheated even though I admit that it is entirely of my own doing. All because I recognised my own inability, wanting what I thought I deserved and was owed. I take the mop and return to the hall.

It was in that all important last three months of high school and I was, again, dunce of my year. My father's dire predictions of my future, or rather lack of one, together with the efforts and cajoling of my teachers over the years all seemed to fade into background mist. I was not unpopular and my physical strength meant that I was not overly picked on. No brains, some brawn, that basically summed me up. Not that I cared. Friends, girls, going out, I was not bored and hadn't really missed out that way. But as that final year dragged on I noticed that I was being left behind in conversations, starting to miss the point of jokes. Invited out less and less I started to become a social outcast, and then to top it all off my father's words started getting through to me. Coming to my seventeenth birthday I felt as if my life was over before it had begun. It was only my new found despair that made me do what I did.

I don't answer personal ads or read messages left on shopping centre notice boards. But that day in late August I would have sold my soul to the devil for an edge. I would have been much better off if I did.

It seemed harmless enough. Buried five columns deep in the personal ads of the local rag, it stated quite simply:

Underachiever at school?

Want to earn a few dollars AND improve?

Over seventeen?

Educator requires subjects for experimental treatment.

Safety and results assured.

I couldn't resist. I tore the ad out and an hour later presented myself at a large house in a slightly run down suburb on the other side of town. A quick check to make sure my clothes were straight and my fly was done up (I had been caught out once before like that) and I rapped on the door. It was answered by a man who, from my limited knowledge of such things, appeared to be at least eighty years old.

'Yes young man, how may I help you?' I didn't trust him from the start. He was smiling and looked too much like my granddad.

I thrust the ad at him. 'I'm here for this, have I got the right place?'

He looked at the ad as if he had never seen it before and, motioning me to follow him, went inside. 'Yes', as he closed the door and started off down the corridor 'you certainly have come to the right address. But I must warn you, we don't take just anyone you know, you have to qualify.'

My spirits sank. 'Great, more exams. Look, I'm not here because I can do tests, I'm here because I can't.'

He stopped and looked at me, a grin creasing his face. 'I'm sorry, I didn't mean to give you that impression. There are tests but not the ones you are thinking of. You see', he continued as we made our way into what I thought was the library 'we have had a number of people answering that ad, and others quite like it, who were just trying to improve on their already quite adequate skills. We are only interested in those who do not have the mental ability to do well, not in the lazy or the over ambitious.'

He motioned me to sit on the couch opposite him. He offered me a drink and something to eat from a small table which, given my walk across town, I was more than willing to accept. I started to relax a bit as he continued.

'Our research is designed to help those who cannot help themselves and may actually be detrimental to anyone else. We are of the opinion that as they can, and do, help themselves, it is the others who have the desire but not the ability that we should help. Hence the ad. It would be simple enough just to find subjects, but that would provide only half of what want. We prefer our subjects to show enough desire to actually answer an ad and follow it through, and then we have to make sure that those subjects are, in a manner of speaking, that they are in possession of less than adequate mental facilities.'

'You mean you want thick people who aren't lazy?'

'You could put it that way.' He grinned. 'Now that you have answered the ad, we have a series of very simple tests that will tell us if you are suitable or not.' He uncrossed his legs and leant forward with what seemed to be great effort. 'That is, if you're still interested.'

Of course I was, did he think I was about to waste a trip across town? 'Yeah, I still am, but the ad also mentioned —'

'Ah yes, of course, you want to know if you will be paid.'

I smiled rather sheepishly. My mother, god rest her soul, had taught me that it was not polite to mention money but my father had taken an altogether opposite view which had rubbed off on me. Still, I felt twinges now and then, particularly with older people around. 'Well yes, that too', trying to cover my embarrassment 'but I wanted to know how long all this will take.'

'Don't worry about that', he assured me as he stood 'even if you don't prove to be suitable we will still pay you for the time taken today to do the tests, and they should only take half an hour or so at most.'

It sounded quite reasonable. 'And if I do pass the tests, then what?'

'Then we will start today. It will take three one hour sessions over the course of a half day or so, and the effects will start showing in about a week. We will need you to see us once a week for a month to check the results, all of which you will be paid for, and at the end of that you will walk away brighter and with a slightly heavier wallet.'

I was hooked then and there. Money for nothing, one day's work and a few visits? I stood up hurriedly, spilling the last few crumbs of chocolate cake from my jeans onto the polished wooden floor. 'Let's get started then!'

The first bit wasn't all that hard, filling out some forms. I had to start by lying, the old guy adamant I had to be seventeen. Luckily for me I had worked out a false date and he didn't ask for identification. It wasn't that long a form but he was watching and timing me as I went but hey, it was his money not mine. That over he cleared the small desk and placed a yellow plastic box, maybe thirty centimetres on a side, in front of me. On each side it had a rubber hand grip, the top angled towards me.

'Well now, this is the test.' He made me sit closer to the desk and adjusted my arms and seat until I was looking squarely down on the angled top of the box, one hand on each grip.

'What you have in front of you is a sophisticated computer, and it is going to take you through a series of problems and exercises. You don't need to write or say anything, all you have to do is try and work out the problems in your head. It's a bit like television but it's one you control with your mind. The machine will know how you are progressing as long as you keep hold of those grips, so whatever you do don't let go. Don't worry if it moves you onto another problem before you have an answer, just take each one as they come. Any questions?'

'Can't say that I have. All I do is think, right?'

'Right. I'll be sitting over there', he said, pointing back to the couch across the room 'just monitoring your progress with this.' holding a blue clipboard. 'Once the half hour is over this will give me the results and we will see what we will see. Ready to start?'

With a final nod he touched the middle of the clipboard with his finger. The yellow box front turned a shimmering grey and my palms began to tingle slightly. I clung on and the grey rapidly faded away, replaced by a picture of a stream, more like a photo, but in 3D and with movement. On one side of the stream I could see a dog, a man, a chicken and a cat. On the other, nothing but grass. A soft voice appeared to come out of nowhere.

'A man and his animals want to cross the stream. The man needs to carry the animals as they cannot swim, but he can only carry one at a time. If the man leaves the dog and the cat alone, the dog eats the cat. If the man leaves the cat and the chicken alone, the cat eats the chicken. How can the man and his animals cross the stream without any animals being eaten?'

As I tried to think of solutions the characters on the screen did exactly as I was thinking. Unfortunately for the chicken I was not too good with that one, and the second problem came around quickly. And that's the way it went. Some problems were similar, some different, a few were simply patches of colour from which my imagination ran riot, one in particular making me blush as it transformed itself on the screen. Although it was fun I didn't think I went too well, and after what I thought was a too short period of time I was back drinking coffee on the couch and waiting for the result. The old man stared at the clipboard for a minute or so, and then looked up at me with a smile.

'You tried very hard with that, I'm pleased, it's a good sign. As for the result, well, I'd better give you a bit of an idea how the score is worked out. It's not quite your IQ test, the computer looks at your answers and how you tried to reach those answers, the way you think, and the way you understand or don't understand the questions. It actually rates how your whole brain system operates, not just one part of it. In the end it gives you a score from zero to two hundred, a score of one hundred being normal. A score of seventy-five is just on the lower limits of being normal, and if you get that or more we can't help you.'

I was crestfallen. Obviously I'd gotten more than seventy-five.

'I'm sorry I wasted your time', I said as I stood up 'I'll go now.'

The old man jumped up as if startled. 'No, it's not like that!' he laughed, placing one hand on my shoulder and gently pushing me back down onto the couch. 'We've waited a long time for someone like you to respond, in fact we weren't even sure you would be able to read the ad. You see my boy, you only scored forty-five! You are about as close to being mentally retarded as you can be and still function nearly normally. We want you to start right away.'

I smiled. Finally I had won something for being dumb.

The rest of the day went fast. We moved into a small room on the first floor, sparsely furnished save for a deeply upholstered chair in one corner and a straight backed wooden chair and roll top desk in the other. For three of the next five hours I sat in that upholstered chair wearing a helmet and glasses, listening to strange voices and watching a parade of colours pass before me. The old guy just sat at the desk with the clipboard, occasionally touching it here or there and murmuring gently to himself. As each session wore on I felt more and more drained until, at the end of the last, I felt as if I had gone twelve rounds with Ali.

'You've taken to the treatment really well', he stated confidently as we made our way downstairs 'even from session to session there has been an improvement, and although you don't know it I think in a week you will be surprised.' He held open the door for me and offered me his hand. 'There are two things that bother me though.'

'Oh, what?'

'Well, for a start I know that you are not quite seventeen yet and that you lied on the application form, but we thought that someone who could make that sort of effort to be an experimental subject must be keen.'

I looked down at my shoes, slightly ashamed of being caught out.

He smiled. 'And you also seem to have neglected to ask me what we would be paying for your time. That's a rather large oversight, don't you think?'

It was my turn to grin. 'I guess that compared to the chance to get smarter the money doesn't seem important. Not now anyway.'

'But a deal is, after all, a deal.' he commented, pressing a few bills into my hand. 'We will see you next Saturday here at 4:30 pm.' with which the door closed.

I started noticing changes after two days. Only in small things, but they were things I usually got wrong anyway. At first it was only my memory. Dad found me on Tuesday night putting the garbage out.

'Hey', his hand on my shoulder 'the garbage night isn't until Wednesday son.'

'But they said on the radio the rosters had changed, this week we're Tuesday.'

'I'd forgotten about that, good thing you remembered. It's not like you, remembering things.'

'Maybe I've just started to take more notice now.'

17

'Well, it's about time, I'm glad to see it. Try and make it a habit.'

I couldn't help but make it a habit. I started to remember my chores around the house, and for the first time I could remember Dad wasn't on my back for this or that. I got my Aunt's birthday right too, and sent her some flowers with part of the money I'd made. I started to feel much better about myself, and mentioned this on my first follow up visit Saturday. The old guy was, as usual, full of smiles.

'That's a very good sign you know.' he said across his coffee. Even if I didn't have to I'd come back just for the chocolate cake. 'Shows that your mind is working better, recalling facts, operating properly. You should start seeing your intelligence and problem solving skills improving now.'

School work started to make sense to me, and instead of sleeping in class I was trying to make sense of what was going on. It was no revelation, no sudden influx of knowledge. I had eight years of work to catch up and although I was starting to see through the gloom I was still far behind. I started spending lunches in the library, something that gave the librarian the willies. She accosted me at the borrowing desk.

'And just what young man', she vented 'do you think you are doing here?'

I peered out from behind the stack of books I was carrying. 'Just studying a bit, that's all.'

'Hmmff. Your reputation precedes you and this would have to be the first time you have darkened this doorway! I'll be keeping my eyes on you. I don't need troublemakers in here, the first sign from you and you are out, understand?'

I nodded. Of course I understood, only now I could remember.

I kept improving, but as I did I started to realise the enormity of the task before me. With less than two months to go I had to cram all of my school studies into that and face the final exams. And I knew all I would end up being was normal. On my second last visit I fronted the old man with this.

'Not quite', again looking at me paternally 'you are showing a great deal of improvement and we feel you will be above average once we are through. In fact, we will give you another test on our last visit to gauge your progress. But in any event you need to look at how you will be compared to how you were, and compared to what you were you are so much more capable. I am not even sure if you would recognise yourself if you looked back.'

'It's not that I'm ungrateful', I countered 'but I need to catch up on what I have missed, and quickly. I've only got a month and a half to get the results and if I fail that's the end of me.'

'Surely not. You are able to repeat your final year? Your father would allow it?'

'Yes, but another year! All my friends would have left and I'd be on my own, not to mention how it would look on my results card.'

'Ah, but you need patience, one more year may seem like an eternity to you but be assured, your results at the end of it will more than make up for the extra time. You must learn to be patient, as we have been. Nothing is done properly that is done in haste.' He raised himself to his feet with what seemed to be a great effort and guided me to the door. 'Do not forget to return in a week, and we will see what our efforts have produced.'

I returned on time but far more troubled. What he had said did of course make sense, but that was of little value to me. All I could see was that I would again be left behind and I would be labelled 'slow' or 'dumb', something that I felt offended and wounded by. I knew what a stigma was by now, and I had no desire to have one. I had earned the right to progress now rather than later, and after a decade of being last I felt that I more than anyone deserved to pass final exams. As I lay awake on my bed that last Friday night I made my plans.

So on that final Saturday I presented myself to the old man

and went through the series of tests with the yellow box. They were different this time, and I found no trouble in working my way through them. Upon completion I was told that, far from the forty-five I was four weeks ago, I now was sitting on a score of 110, over average but not brilliant. I feigned delight with this; the old man's was genuine.

'Marvellous, that is just about as good as we could expect to get. The improvement will assure you of a slightly above normal mental capacity and yet will not draw undue attention to yourself. That, you must realise', he explained as we made our way downstairs 'is of the utmost importance to us.'

He continued as we stood on the porch and he locked the door behind him. 'You must make sure not to show off your new found abilities too much. At best people will think you a charlatan for pretending for so long, or at worst a liar and a cheat, and the last thing we want is that sort of attention coming upon ourselves. Your life now should be far better than it was going to be before we met.'

We strolled over to where his car was parked. He examined his watch carefully. 'I have to make arrangements for our departure. We leave tomorrow, never spend too long in any one place.' He closed the car door behind him and put the key in the ignition.

'You would obviously understand that people quickly get very suspicious of an old man seeing so many young boys and girls on a regular basis. May I offer you a lift to town?'

I pretended to mull the offer over. 'No thanks, I think the walk does me good, but I appreciate the offer. And thanks again for the treatments.'

'Our pleasure.' he replied as the car moved past me. I waved, waited until it had rounded the corner. I turned and ran back to the house until I was standing under the first floor window of the room I was in earlier. After taking a few deep breaths I clambered up the adjacent drainpipe until, straddling the pipe and with one hand on the ledge, I jemmied the old window lock with my free hand and pocket knife. It took less than two minutes until I stood breathless inside. Going across the room to the desk I slipped the helmet on and, keeping the glasses on my knees as I sat in the chair, examined the clipboard. As I had thought, it held no paper but had the same semi luminous quality that the yellow box had. I placed my finger in a slight indentation to the left and instantly the centre of the clipboard displayed a list of names, mine being towards the middle. Next to my name was a green and yellow square, and a bar gauged from one to ten with a line at five. Looking all the world as a computer touch screen I moved the bar from one to ten.

'Accelerated programme test subject fifteen commences in ten seconds.' a lilting voice announced. I hurriedly put on the glasses and sat back.

Half an hour later it was over. Although more intense than I remembered the previous sessions being, I felt none the worse except for mild pangs of guilt at having been forced to deceive the old man. Putting the helmet and clipboard back where I had found them I exited in the same manner as I had entered, making my way home confident that I was now equipped to get what I deserved. My only question was how quickly I would see the effects, and if that would be quick enough for the exams.

That I night I slept fitfully, the following day lost to me in a faint jumbled haze of noise. The next night the nightmares and sweats started, the following day boding ill as my memory started to fail. I thought this just a side effect, a passing phase, but as the days wore on it worsened. One week after that last visit I had hardly slept, my nights being filled with demons and horror, my days being a mad mix of half-forgotten memories, shattering headaches and times where I was at a loss to understand any spoken word. At school I was useless, at home avoided, and it was all I could do on that Friday to drag myself back across town to the house where it had all started.

Maybe it was the lack of sleep or perhaps the pain in my head that was now my constant, boisterous companion, but I stood there for what seemed ages staring uncomprehending at the vacant, weed tangled lot. When it slowly dawned on me that I was looking at the place where that neat, two storey house had stood only a week ago, and I in it, my world seemed to tilt off axis. I looked around to make sure I was where I thought I was and, confirming that, ran across the road to the house opposite. Pounding on the door with both fists I was greeted by a sour faced woman with a child in her arms.

'Hey, hey, quit the bangin'! I'm here, watchya want?'

'The old house across the road, when did they move it? Where did it go?'

'What house? Are you nuts? Nobody's built on that, dunno if it's even owned.'

'But I was there, last week, with the old man, you must have seen him.'

'I know everyone here, there ain't no old man, and there sure as hell ain't no old house.' She was getting agitated and the child started to whine.

'But there has to be!' My chest tightened, I tasted my own bile. 'I was there, I talked with him and we ate cake in his front room. It was there dammit!' I grabbed the door frame for support as my legs threatened to give way. 'It was there!!'

'I've been here twenty bloody years' she screamed, the child adding to the rising credenza 'and there has never been anything on it! I don't know what sort of shit you're putting in your arm but if you're not gone in ten seconds I'm getting the police!' with which the door slammed in my face, catching my fingers with it.

I stumbled across the yard and ran down the street, my head thundering with pain, unable to accept what I had seen. By the time I had reached the bridge leading home my despair had deepened as reality sunk in. I'd had the chance to be a normal, average person with a reasonable future but I had reached too far.

22

It seemed all trace of the old man and the house had been wiped from the face of the earth. Without him there was no hope of a cure. Was I doomed to revert to my former state?

I reached the middle of the bridge and leant heavily on the rail, shaking uncontrollably. I gazed down at the water and realised that what I had feared most would now happen, that I would form part of the human refuse that others look down upon. There was no exit, no relief, no help. I clambered onto the rail and without a backwards glance cast myself out and down.

I have been told that it was blind chance that saved my life, that the angler on the river bank happened to know CPR, and that her mobile phone was working. They say I didn't breathe for two and a half minutes and it was only the constant mouth to mouth that kept my brain alive. All I know is that a month later I awoke in a hospital bed.

I am worse now than I was before I answered the ad. I can't read or write as well. I can't concentrate, and I can barely remember even the simplest things. My nightmares continue to this day and always end with me drowning. Worse, as a result of my jump I have lost the use of my left side above the waist. I never did sit the final high school exam. But I am alive, and I suppose that's a positive, and my job is within my abilities. Just. Heck, even I can be a janitor, and I have lists for each day's work.

But that month and a half I can never forget. I have tried to find that old man, and although something inside me says he's coming back it seems he's gone for good. The block remains empty and overgrown, and seems likely to remain so, but I know for a short while it wasn't. I have even gone so far as to talk to the folks out at the University, but they deny that any such person or research programme existed. They usually laugh at me when I describe the yellow box, clipboard or helmet, saying I have been watching too much Star Trek or spending too much time at the pub. At times even I doubt what happened. And of the treatments, today I have nothing.

Well, not quite. Although I have never been interested in such things, ever since that time I have been spending more and more of my evenings on my back, gazing at the stars, wondering. And with my next week's pay I will finally be able to pick up the telescope I have on lay-by. I can't help but feel it's all to do with those past events.

I have even heard the voices lately too ...

END

A little knowledge

Errol Hasking held the clear plastic sleeve to the light. A near flawless nineteenth century one-pound note nestled inside its plastic sarcophagus, a token of one more chip in the walls of the black economy from a thankful counterpart. He allowed himself a smile. Even with the direst predictions cash remained, used and abused, without which he would be out of a job, out of a career and out of his calling.

'Looking good boss.' Turning he could see Tanjya's hologram sitting, smiling at him. Only mildly annoyed he lobbed a crumpled tissue the two meters to the real Tanjya. Her hologram winced, then with a smile flickered out.

The real Tanjya dropped herself into the seat next to him.

'When are you lot going to stop playing with that?'

She leant across and added her virtual screen to Errol's.

'When the next toy comes around of course. Anyway, I've got something, part of the random check of BankNorth's cash transfers to the Reserve Bank, one of the tranches for destruction. Three notes were picked up, two tens and a twenty', the three appearing on screen 'all from the one sub-branch in Darwin. They didn't show any apparent deviation except they were pristine.'

'Pristine?'

'Utterly. All the other notes were creased, varying degrees of visible use and dirt, the usual cross section of wear and tear. These three however are absolutely perfect.'

Errol reached into the screen and pulled out the nearest note enlarging it, rotating it, viewing it from all angles. In an act of utter futility he held the image up to the light before placing it back.

'Perfect.'

Tanjya dropped the ten-dollar bills from the screen and pulled the twenty out. From the second screen she produced another twenty, pulling it out to hover next to the first.

'It gets better. Watch this. BankNorth's bill on the left, brand new mint on the right. Fabio', addressing the AI 'bottom left corner focus ten times please.'

The expanded bills now hovered above Errol's desk, stretching to the ceiling. In front of him the bottom left corners stood in relief, blue-green plastic crisscrossed with clear channels bordered in emerald green and light gold.

'Have a close look at the clear optic window section. Fabio, fifty times focus centre edge please.'

The scene shifted, two bright green lines bordering clear plastic now the only visible part of the notes. The other three team members now holo'd in behind Tanjya and Errol.

Errol leant forwards, examining the notes carefully.

'Exact match I'd say.'

'Exactly, at the limit of our normal scans. How many perfect optic window reproductions do you recall?'

'None.'

'Right. So that's why I got Fabio involved. You're not going to like this. Fabio, centre optic window demarcation, five hundred times focus.'

She waited five seconds.

'Fabio, five thousand times focus.'

She waited another five seconds, eyes fixed on Errol. Small beads of sweat were now forming on his moustache, a twitch developing below one eye.

'Fabio, zoom extents fifty thousand.'

She waited for a few moments, the office silent, the first drops of Errol's sweat falling languidly. She turned to face the notes, now bloated rectangles balanced on the desk.

'Resolution is now one one-hundredth of a micrometer centred on the lower left optical window of the twenty-dollar bills. I'd remind you that the image on the left is the suspect note, the image on the right uncirculated official issue.'

Errol leant back in thought. In front of him one rectangle had a broad fuzzy white streak emblazoned down one side next to a ghostly grey field. The image on the left contained a crisp, razor sharp demarcation between perfectly opaque white half and perfectly transparent half. He shook his head.

'That's impossible.'

'I know.'

'Totally impossible, there's no way, physically no way.'

'I know, yet it is, and yes I've checked. There's no way known to get crisp ink or polymer demarcation below one hundredth of a micron. We're talking clear separation at sizes approaching ultra-violet radiation wavelengths. But it gets worse.'

'How? How can it be worse than perfect imitation?'

'Remember how this was picked up? Pristine bills in a pile of worn and tattered? I had one of the ten dollars sent across for materials testing, the results came back this morning.'

Tanjya moved her hands through the screen, dismissing notes and bringing up a neatly ordered spreadsheet.

'This is the analysis. When you dig through the detail the summary is that the counterfeit note is does not crease, tear, hold dirt, is as tough as magnesium-tungsten alloy, and melts at just under 3,000 degrees Celsius. In short —'

'In short we could be screwed.'

Errol looked around to his team.

'This stays buttoned up, no discussion outside ourselves. Tanjya, we're going to BankNorth Darwin. The rest of you I want in the Reserve looking through all the currency disposals. Tell them it's the ANAO, tell them I'm breaking your arses, whatever. I just want you to watch disposals, estimate the counterfeits and tie off any problems.'

Errol's secure email tone sounded. It scrolled through on his right, Errol swearing vehemently under his breath. He stood and grabbed his jacket, stopping by Tanjya on the way out.

'Sorry to do this, you'll have to get out to Darwin by yourself. I'll join you later, just keep in touch.'

'Yeah, no worries.'

'Don't do anything more than look and learn until I get there. And no more cheap hotels, I want a place with working a/c this time.'

Tanjya held her hands up in mock surrender.

'Fine, fine, a girl screws up once and wears it forever. I won't do anything, I promise.'

Errol walked in to the Director's office, Karen greeting him with a brusque wave of her hand. He sat, answering her questioning gaze with one of his own.

'Less than fifteen minutes ago, same scenario, same features. I've got Tanjya in the field to track source, the rest of my team trying to gauge scale, and no answers yet. How many others?'

'At least ten, probably double that given lags. The Chinese, Indians, Europeans and Japanese have been hit. Of the second-tier currencies America, California and, if we believe back channels, the United Republic of Korea. And now us. It's not public yet but unfortunately the politicians know. You've seen it?'

'No, just Tanjya's analysis and pix.'

'It's as good as I'm led to believe?'

'Better. Tanjya's had the ruler over them and they're impossible to detect casually. If we find where they're coming from maybe we can stop more coming in but with a dozen others can what we do actually matter? Have any others got any estimate of scale yet?'

'No to both.'

'How much time do we have?'

'With the politicians in play three, maybe four days before it goes public. It could be sooner, the media has been trying our firewall a little harder than usual today so I'm thinking they have a sniff. We can't go storming around in jackboots until we know we can get a result, so it's just you and your team.'

'As usual. Four days isn't much.'

'For you it's less. You've got a meeting with the Prime Minister's Department in Sydney this afternoon so you're one day behind. Keep it discreet but once you have anything, a name, location, whatever, you call and then we'll go in hard.'

'And just say we don't have anything by then?'

'Pray and hide. I will.'

Errol wasn't fond of Sydney, his sleep at best fitful and fleeting.

He wasn't a hotel person, he liked his own bed, his own partner, his own sheets.

Around 3:00 am the chiming of his proximity alarm woke him. Sitting up he could make out a pink rabbit at the far side of the room. Tanjya's avatar. He made sure the sheets covered his nakedness and signalled acceptance. The pink rabbit was replaced by Tanjya, as he knew somewhere a penguin with mirrored sunglasses was being replaced by him.

'Tanjya, you've got a lead?'

'Yes. More in fact. It's good news or not so good news I guess. I dunno. Anyway, I found him.'

'You what? What did I tell you about caution, discretion? He probably knows we're onto him.'

'Oh yes, he knows, he knows everything. But he's not going, in fact he's quite calm and open about it all.'

'What do you mean, open and calm?'

'Exactly that. Boss, I quit.'

'You what?'

'I quit. My job, chuck it in, walk away, whatever. I'm through.'

'What? Where are you? Are you being threatened?'

'I'm safe, nothing's happened, and as for where I am well, currently business class to Rio. As for threats, whatever, nothing like that. We just talked.'

She creased her brow, hands fidgeting.

'Yeah, talked just once. Boss, you've got, I mean, we've all got about four days. It'll be ok a couple of weeks after but not in four days.'

'What the hell are you going on about? Is this his threat, going public?'

'No, it's no threat, it just is. As for public you can find him easily, it's in the infopak I'm sending. He's not hiding boss, he's not scared, not aggressive, not anything. And neither am I, I'm just quitting and going.'

She took a glass of oily liquid, draining it in one swallow. Her hands started to tremble, tears forming.

'Errol. One last thing. Don't talk to him, don't find him, just send the infopak on and run and hide. Promise me Errol, do not talk to him.' and the link died.

He sat staring into the darkened room. She called me Errol. Ten years working together she's never touched a drop, never shed a tear, never called me Errol, only boss. What the hell could do this to her? He mulled it over briefly. The hell with Karen and the hell with this. I'm here, I can face this guy down and have him in chains in less than a day.

Errol sat reflecting as the autocab glided towards Darwin's western suburbs. Tanjya's infopak had given him a name and a phone number. For all the resources he had, Errol found no matching profile, data set or financial trace. It intrigued and bothered him. Errol tracked the number and plugged through the local surveillance net. The subject of his attention was now sitting comfortably in a near deserted street café, relaxed and apparently at peace with the world. Impossibly he'd even looked up and winked at him. Whatever, it wouldn't matter in five minutes.

The autocab settled a few doors away from the café. Errol approached the café slowly, assuring himself that the subject was alone. When only a few meters away the subject relaxed his shoulders, placing both hands slowly and clearly on the glass table top. He swivelled slightly, blue-grey eyes searching Errol's face.

'Good morning Mr Hasking, I have been expecting you. Please, take a seat. I have taken the liberty of ordering you a coffee. Flat white, single origin, no sugar. Correct?'

He turned, facing an empty chair opposite.

'Simple tastes for an ordered life, it is a pleasant, pleasant change.'

Errol slid into the vacant seat studying him in silence. Totally unremarkable, an average man of indeterminate middle age dressed in tastefully out of date fashion. Except for the face, the vacant eyes and thin-lipped mouth which, when taken with the close cropped blonde hair, chilled Errol to the bone. He took a small sip from the cup, once his palette sensors returned nothing of interest he swallowed. The brew was just as he liked it.

'Thank you Mr Kr —'

'Please, call me Johann, and the pleasure is mine. I have been, ah, let us say, a student of your work for some time now and have been looking forward to meeting you.'

'To meeting me? You seem to have me at a disadvantage.'

'It is an ingrained habit, know yourself, know your enemies or, more correctly, those you deal with. In my speciality it is important and easy to do so although I must say both you and your Tanjya have a very tight circle drawn around you, very good considering. But you are not here to simply pass the time of day, so allow me to be blunt.'

He lifted his cup taking a delicate sip, pinky extended as he placed cup carefully back onto saucer.

'Let us talk about forgery yes? You are here to find me and to bring me in', smiling to himself as if it were a private joke 'FBI old school style?'

'In simplest terms yes. It's not too hard, you haven't exactly hidden yourself.'

'My location? Of course not, it is not necessary. But myself, I think you can attest I am hidden very well. I am playing my part by the rules, but you seem to have ignored Karen's instructions totally. Not true to form for a boy scout, yes?'

'I do when I need to but in this case I'm intrigued, one about you —'

'And two about Tanjya? Again commitment, refreshing and unfortunately uncommon. Please, do not let me interrupt you.'

The question had barely formed when Errol's proximity alert chimed and an orange knight appeared on the table. Priority two call from his people at the Reserve. Johann was leaning back, smiling, palms outspread. Errol signalled acceptance and the surroundings faded to light grey, the knight transforming to Sharne.

'Boss I've got preliminaries, you need to hear this.'

'What have you got?'

'It's point nine eight forged bills from the last two quarter's tranche, give or take.'

'Ok, under one percent, that's —'

'No boss, the number's ninety-eight percent.'

'On what base?'

'Thirty thousand notes, randomised, all collection centres, all denominations. Before you ask we've triple checked.'

'What do the Reserve think?'

'They've no idea. They think we're a bunch of drones with sticks up our arses wasting their time on useless random checks.'

'Ok, pack it up and get out of there. Log it through, copy Karen in then send the guys home.'

'Later boss.'

Errol looked up as the greyed shield dropped.

'You've got a hell of a printing press Johann.'

'Not just here. By now your counterparts across the world are getting similar details, having similar conversations. You must have some idea, speculation, about what this is for.'

'It only makes sense if you work for foreign — '

'Which I do not. What is foreign to the whole world anyway? Let us say I do not, I am simply and honestly a public servant, like you. So?'

'You're printing out undetectable cash, flushing it through the system, no-ones the wiser until we catch on and you don't hide? Nothing fits, except ...'

'Except?'

'Except deliberate destabilisation, clear out effort to destroy the physical money base.'

'And the cryptos, not just the physical money base.'

'Do you know what that will do? Cash is barely a fifth of money stock but it's mainly held by people, not business or government. They think it's worthless there could be anarchy, riots, anything.'

'No could be, absolute certainty.'

Errol had his hand on his ankle atop his crossed leg. He gently squeezed the top eyelet of his shoe. Should be one minute until they button this freak up.

'You have only half the story Mr Hasking. How is never enough. You want the why. Let me ask you a question. Why would we go after the cryptos if all we wanted was to destroy the physical money system?'

Forty-five seconds just to keep him talking, waiting until they come.

'I don't know, you're the one doing it so how about you tell me?'

'Come on Mr Hasking, you yourself have lectured on this. The cashless society, opening another hole for corruption and vice.

Killing cash is fine but to do it properly the cryptos have to die.'

He shook his head.

'Decades earlier, decades later it could be done but now is the best, least hit, more connected space. Knock it all down, five weeks it is all done, the necessary conditions established. You of all people should know.'

Johann caught Errol glancing at the clock on the café wall.

'They will not turn up Mr Hasking, wait another ten seconds or ten minutes either way they will not be here. Do you think us that careless? Not until we are ready, and not before. Besides which we have yet more to discuss, one servant of the people to another.'

'Servant of the people? How can you call yourself that? Think of the families, the poor, the —'

'Think of them? Think of them! What do you think I am doing? Have you any idea of the mess we inherit from you, the suffering? Untangling it all takes generations unless this tipping point goes. Where are your loyalties Mr Hasking, to the people or to a corrupted and compromised government? I know where I stand.'

'And just where is that? What and who exactly are you?'

'I've told you, a servant of the public, you know the rest but you just don't want to admit the possibility.'

'What possibility?'

Johann leant forwards, close enough for Errol to smell his antiseptic breath.

'The technology. What I know. The invisibility. Counterfeits so outlandishly perfect we may as well have autographed them. It is all impossible for any person, legal, criminal, alternative whatever and you know it. It leaves you with only two possibilities, two options and you know it.'

'I can't —'

'It is just the logical residual. It is not that difficult to accept.'

Johann sighed, placing three folders on the table next to him.

'But it does not matter, it is not relevant. What matters is you, now, and eight hours from now. Ask me why we need you.'

Errol was distracted by the folders. The bottom two, pale red and blue, were normal meta-folders linked to remote data storage. He was sure the upper one was real manila cardboard, fibres showing through dog-eared corners and coffee stains, a rarity. He dragged his eyes up from the table.

'You wanted to be found, but Tanjya found you and she's gone so it's me. What exactly do you think you want from me?'

Johann pursed his lips, eyes vacant, cold, a living death mask.

'We need you to make a choice, to decide to either do your job and follow your conscience or do as you are asked. All we want is for you to do your job, your real job, and remember it when you talk to her.'

Errol jumped as his audio warning broke in. Voice only contact from the office secure line meant only one person.

'Karen?'

'Errol, can you talk?'

'Of course', looking directly at Johann 'I'm alone.'

'Have you made progress?'

'Some, not a great deal but I'm optimistic.'

'Fine. Look, the Minister's been in contact, there's a different approach being adopted so a slight shift in plans is needed.'

'How slight?'

'We're moving from 'watch and act' to 'watch and wait'. Once you've got a handle on what's going on you're to report back but there's to be no pick up. Understand?'

'Not totally. You're saying observe and then nothing? What about the four days until it breaks?'

'It won't. We're going to hang them out to dry, simply going to let it wash over. If we can't pick up the counterfeits no-one can, so there's no need to do anything.'

'What of the other countries?'

'They'll do exactly the same, don't worry. Clear?'

'Clear.' with which he broke the link.

Errol stared at Johann who replied with lifted eyebrows.

'Do you see now? It is not us that is doing the asking, but your own.' He shook his head slowly. 'Eight hours from now one journalist and one politician here are going to break the story open and then others will follow around the world. Each time their governments will deny the truth unless, and only unless, the experts stand up to support them. And critically it must start here, with you. That is your choice. Do your job or do as you are asked.'

'Why me?'

'Let us simply say reputation counts. Do you need more convincing, like Tanjya?'

'Tanjya? Just what did you do to her?'

Johann tapped his index finger on the manila folder.

'Nothing, nothing at all. All I did was let her read one of these then asked her if she would like some further information. We needed to make sure you came directly to us. Eventually she came around to our way of thinking.'

He slowly slid the manila folder across the table.

'You must understand, you do have a choice. If you believe me then the choice is clear, if not, well, we do not think that will happen. What is in here are, in a manner of speaking, our bona fides. Have a look and please, take your time.'

Errol took the folder, slowly opening it. Inside each cover was line after line of neat, clipped handwriting. He read carefully, slowly, sweating, forgetting to breathe, stopping and starting again. His emotions went from anger, amazement, shame, mortification, guilt but always, growing and clawing away at him as he read fear, abject ice-cold fear of what sat opposite him. The folder was all about him, nothing else, and not the publicly available openly gleaned intel that formed his stock in trade but the secrets, his inner world that never saw the light, thoughts from darkness and despair crushed and denied and hidden even from himself, the joys held closest and unspoken, the inner narrative of the still quiet voice within him that only he could hear. It was his soul stripped naked and exposed, nailed to the covers of the folder. He finished shaking, sweat stained and humbled, his universe collapsing to the folder, the table, Johann. He opened his mouth but for once nothing came out.

'We know you as you truly are, as you were, as you will be. Everything, every nook, cranny, every place in your heart, soul, and mind where even you dare not go we read as an open book. Nothing is hidden from us, nothing about you, Tanjya, these people, your family, everyone. If we say a thing is, it is. If we say a thing should be done, it should be. And if we ask you to believe us you should, do you not think?'

'Yes, yes I do.'

Johann touched the manila folder. It crumbled to ash, blown away by the faint breeze.

'Good. We have no more need of this.'

'What exactly do I do?'

'Just go back today, the next flight, contact these two people.' Johann's infopak delivered to Errol immediately. 'Support them fully and publicly. Include everything except this discussion.'

'Tanjya. You said you offered information to her after she read her, ah, her folder.'

'Tanjya was not convinced by what she read so yes, we did make that offer. She chose not to accept it.'

He spun the red and blue folders lazily on the table.

'For her just one folder, for you two. Two pieces of information. Do you really want to know what they are? You do not need more convincing, you know that.'

'I need to know, at least I think I do.'

'Very well. They contain no facts, information or data from before this moment. As it is for you it was for Tanjya. For her the information was to go to her. For you, one piece is for you, one piece for your wife.'

'The information, about nothing in her past, changed Tanjya's mind?'

'No, not quite. Just the possibility of knowing. She, like you, really did believe us, she just would not admit it to herself. You both know what we are even if you will not use the words, and you know what we tell you is the truth. You know the information in these folders is true.'

Johann stacked the folders and held them out at arm's length.

'I will make the same offer to you anyway, even if you do not need it. With Tanjya I promised to send it to her if she did not behave. For you it is also a choice, but think carefully. Two folders. Two dates. One for you. One for your wife.'

'What are the dates?'

For the first time Johann smiled.

'Very good. For you the date your wife dies. For your wife the date your daughter dies.'

Errol shuddered, dry retched, clutched the table.

'No, no, I don't think I, I mean, please, just don't.'

'A wise choice', compressing the folders in his fist, deleting them 'one of many today Mr Hasking.'

END

Ahab

'Ticket 438 room one.' The P.A. floundered under the noise of the packed reception area. Sergeant Pat Blanchfield took the flimsy, pushed through the swing doors into the corridor. Five weeks until I call an end to a thirty year career and the Captain's tied me to the front desk with six inches of bullet proof perspex between me and the crazies. He stepped into the interview room and regarded the man opposite.

Not that there was much to see. Late forties or early fifties, a faint red lesion around his neck, no hidden weapons. He held himself with a resigned, expectant air as if watching for trouble that he knew would find him. Pat put the flimsy to one side, flipped the speaker on.

'So, Mister —'

'Wayne, call me Wayne.'

'Ok Wayne, why are you here?'

'I want to report a murder, three murders.'

'Whose?'

'Mine.'

'You killed three people?'

'No, I'm the victim.'

'You don't look particularly dead.'

'Of course not, somebody found me in time, each time that bastard sent them.'

'Which bastard?'

'The one that keeps killing me.'

'Settle down. You say you've been killed three times?'

'No, I mean yes, sort of. I mean three times he's tried to kill me, just last week the latest.'

'The red mark?'

'Yeah, hung myself I did, he did.'

'So you hung yourself?'

'Yes, he made me, just like the other times.'

'So he's made you try to kill yourself three times. It's not quite murder is it?'

'I don't see why not. He's made a ruin out of my entire life and everyone's around me, pushed and pushed but won't let me die, just takes me to the edge and back.'

'You have proof, witnesses?'

'No, he's very good, very careful.'

'The one you say is doing this, you know him?'

'I put all that into the form —'

'Just humour me. Do you know him?'

'Yes, Roger Paulikas. I had an accident years back ...'

'And?'

'I killed his wife.'

Pat sighed, rolled the flimsy into a tube and tapped it on the edge of the desk.

'You don't believe me do you officer?'

'Would you?'

'Of course.'

'Don't bullshit me.'

Pat unrolled the flimsy. Thirty thousand words. He randomly tapped it.

'You say he crippled your father. Dad's alive?'

'Yes, just.'

'What would he say if I talked to him?'

'Nothing, he wouldn't know.'

Another tap.

'He broke up your first marriage by seducing your wife and daughter?'

'Well yes, he set it up, sent the men, I know it.'

'You saw him?'

'No, but —'

Pat held his hand up, tapped again.

'He caused a defect in the Remington .45 ammunition you tried to commit suicide with, rendering you merely functionally impaired, not dead?'

'I know it sounds a bit —'

'No, not a bit but totally. You're either a lunatic or you've got an overactive imagination. You kill a man's wife —'

'It was an accident!'

'You kill his wife and your brain goes into overdrive. Of course

43

he wants you dead, who wouldn't? How long'd you do?'

'Eight inside, four paroled outside.'

Pat sighed. He's another nut job, an oxygen thief.

'I don't believe you, but you've made a formal complaint and I've got to follow it up. No matter how asinine it is.'

'Thank you.'

'Don't. You've had your one shot, waste my time with the same complaint again and you're back inside.' Pat stood. 'I'll call you if I need you.'

The driveway crunched underfoot, uniform pink and black polished quartz pebbles glinting and winking, shadows from poplars lining the pathway dancing in front. The gaps in the trees allowed the merest hint of the grounds beyond, a reminder to the penitent of their place, their real status. The estate had a restrained, aloof presence that acknowledged him while making it patently clear his existence or otherwise was a mere detail.

He'd reached the next to last step on the entry when the double oak doors opened revealing an older couple immaculately dressed in black and white. The man bowed stiffly, the woman curtsied.

'Sergeant Blanchfield, you are expected.'

Pat was ushered into a large, sparsely furnished room, huge bay windows framing the immaculate grounds beyond. A cut crystal glass appeared beside him, filled from a matching decanter.

'Drink Sergeant? Sir will be available momentarily.'

Pat easily spotted the telltale lumps in the ceiling. He smiled. There was no need to make it obvious except to make it obvious, the sensors worked through most materials. But there was value in letting your guests know they were being watched. He finished his glass.

'Sir will see you now Sergeant.'

He was shown into another room, heavily but tastefully decorated, windowless, carpeted. Floor to ceiling shelves along one wall containing thin rectangular blocks of varying colours caught his eye.

'I see my collection has your attention Patrick. A hobby of mine, ancient manuscripts. Perhaps you'd like to hold one?'

'No, thank you, I don't think the Department's insurance runs that high.'

'Shame. Well, to business shall we?'

Five suited figures stood silently, motionless behind him.

'My legal team, perhaps not the most sociable of individuals but highly efficient.'

'I appreciate your time Mr. Paulikas, I'll make this as brief as possible.'

'I understand. From what your Captain said you have no choice. A sad little man by all accounts. You'd forgive my lack of sympathy, he may have paid his debt to society but to me, well, how can it be enough?'

'I understand.'

'Now, what do you require to put this matter to rest?'

'One answer and, if you'd be kind enough, some house security tapes.'

'To the first of course, the second perhaps. Your question?'

'April fifteenth. Where were you that evening?'

'The fifteenth? From eight in the morning to midnight I was in this room taking care of my … philanthropic interests.'

'Your staff, the man and woman at the door, they were here with you?'

'Yes, both were here. You may take statements or talk to them if you wish.'

'Thank you. The other thing, the tapes?'

Roger ushered Pat to the door.

'Yes of course you would like those. I'll see that copies are made for you. Is that sufficient?'

'Yes, I believe it is.'

Pat finished his first skim of the housetapes. Nothing, just eighteen hours of a man watching a computer, What good's owning the world if you're chained to a desk all day? At least soon I won't be. His eyes rested on an old photo pinned to the cubicle divider. Pat touched his fingers to his lips, his fingers to the photo. I wonder what it would be like if —

The Captain poked her head round the corner.

'Blanchfield, how you going with Paulikas?'

'Slowly. He's complained?'

'Wouldn't be the first time for you but no, he's good. Just let me know when you've closed it.'

'Yeah, will do.'

Pat spun the housetapes again. All ordinary and boring, he was about to wipe them when something caught his eye. As Paulikas sat in his chair his left arm shimmered, the thumb on his left hand winking in and out. The time coding showed no tampering, no splicing. Pat pulled on the headset, jacked into the VR system.

He popped up inside the rendering of the room and moved to one side of Paulikas. As Paulikas' thumb flickered a dark patch on the back of his shirt appeared. He could see the computer on the desk clearly, showing a shop interior and a man climbing a ladder in front of a wall of small boxes. The man pulled a small red box out of the wall of yellow-blue ones. The hairs on the back of Pat's neck stood up. The box in his hand bore the logo 'Remington. RimFire ScatterShot .45'.

The housetapes gave him more, Paulikas' computer showing Wayne entering the shop, the man handing the box to him. Paulikas had turned the screen on as Wayne entered, turned it off as Wayne left.

Pat dismissed the thumb and the shirt from his mind, concentrating on the ammunition. He refilled his coffee, settled back and interrogated the AI.

After an hour Pat was none the wiser. There was nothing linking Paulikas to the shop. Yet the housetapes remained a clear reminder there must be some link. Pat shook his head. What if it's Remington, what if it's the ammunition? He got back to work with the AI.

— How many weapons use this type of ammunition?

— Four.

— How many weapons are in circulation?

— Three hundred fifty seven thousand.

— How many of the type used by the complainant?

— Twenty eight.

— Which if any of the ammunition components could cause the complainant's weapon to fail but not any others?

— One.

— Describe component and failure.

— Percussion cap cover is one one-thousandth too thick to properly discharge resulting in greatly retarded projectile muzzle velocity.

— What would be the result of using the complainant's weapon and the identified ammunition to attempt suicide?

— Ninety-five percent chance moderate to severe, five percent chance minor, non-life threatening injuries.

— Is the percussion cap cover manufactured by Remington?

— No. Manufactured by IamonCorp.

— Has or does Paulikas or known associates have any association with IamonCorp?

— Paulikas Trust 298 gained controlling interest of IamonCorp in 1973. IamonCorp outsourced R&D and CAD/CAM functions to Aartech in 2013. Aartech is a fully owned subsidiary of Paulikas Trust 476.

— When did manufacture of percussion caps for this type of ammunition commence?

— 2028

Well over one hundred years ago. It was impossible for it to mean what Wayne had claimed yet there it was, everything except Paulikas himself writing the dimensions, feeding it to the CAD/CAM. It has to be coincidence, just random events glued together the wrong way in Wayne's mind. Pat flipped through the flimsy looking for one more claim to check. The crippled father. That ought to do it.

Pat waited until the following Monday. A week sitting, mulling it all over had left him more uncertain, more confused. He touched his fingers to his lips, fingers to the photo, then opened a comms link.

'Captain, got a minute?'

'What?'

'The Paulikas complaint. I've just NFA'd it. I was going to go out, let Mr. Paulikas know.'

'Fine.'

The butler was waiting, ushering Pat directly into Mr. Paulikas' presence. This time they were alone.

'So Patrick, what can I do for you?'

'I've come to let you know I've rejected the complaint.'

'I appreciate it but you could have just called. You have something else on your mind?'

'Well, not so much but … do you mind if I try out your desk for a minute or two?'

'Why?'

'I've never owned one, never got this close to a real wooden desk. I'm retiring soon and I won't get the chance again.'

'Why not? Go on, indulge yourself.'

Pat went across, sat down slowly and spread his arms out wide, fingertips falling well short of the edges. He looked up, grinning like a young schoolboy.

'That feels amazing.'

'You wouldn't believe the number of people who've wanted to sit where you are, most of them hoping it was over my dead body.'

Pat sat back, head firmly against the headrest, arms along the sides of the chair.

'I suppose none of us go through life without making a few enemies.'

'If you live properly.'

Pat surreptitiously felt for buttons, levers, indents with his hands. There were none. He stood.

'I'd better give it back before I get used to it.'

'Believe me Patrick, you never would. I haven't.'

'Wealth, influence, respect? It's not too hard imagining being

49

very comfortable indeed.'

'Perhaps, but to get here you need to play the tough man, be hard hearted and hard minded. It doesn't stop, it gets worse and more serious once you have something to protect.'

'But the compensations —'

'Oh yes, undoubtedly. When I started I had to save to buy lunch, now if I'm hungry I just buy the restaurant. But in the end we are only men, our appetites the same, just the scale that varies. Tell me Patrick, why didn't you remarry after Stefania died?'

'I don't know, I've never really thought about it.'

'Twelve years is a long time celibate.'

'Celibate? Oh no, hardly. It's just … I don't know, commitment I guess. No one could ever take her place so I never tried.'

'Precisely.'

'And you Mr. —'

'Please, Roger will do.'

'Roger, what about you?'

'The same. You see, underneath we are closer than you think. So Patrick, back to business. The matter is closed?'

'Yes, officially.'

'Meaning to you it's not.'

'A few strange things bother me.'

'Such as?'

Pat described what he had found, the thumb, the shimmer, the ammunition, the father's accident. Through it all Roger sat silent, impassive.

'You caught me off guard the other day with your request for the housetapes.'

'As I said, officially it's over. Unofficially I don't want mysteries to dog me through retirement.'

'Do you like mind games Patrick?'

'I like them fine.'

'Tell me. If you could, would you stop Stefania getting on that flight?'

'Of course.'

'And if you couldn't, if she was on it no matter what?'

'I'd stop the plane, close the airport.'

'If you couldn't do that?'

'I don't know … kidnap the pilot or sabotage the jet, anything to stop it.'

'That's how I felt with Agnes. What do you know about history?'

'Not much, I never studied it.'

'Nearly everyone believes the past is set in stone, fixed and unchanging except for the myths and lies we drape around it. I met a brilliant woman once who claimed it wasn't.'

'What did she think?'

'She said time was a river, and we simply swimmers in it. The river may have to go east to west but it doesn't care if it goes a little north or south as long as it reaches the ocean.'

'I don't get it.'

'Neither did I at first. She meant that the big stuff, the key events and people were fixed, had to happen, but the rest could change and no one would know or care.'

'It's a nice theory but what's the use?'

'Let's say you go back to old America. You walk into a bar and you deliberately knock a man's drink over. You buy him another one, walk out, come back. Tell me, what's history say about it?'

'Well, I guess it just sees me spill his drink.'

'But you'd have to see it not being spilt to spill it.'

'I guess, but isn't that a problem?'

'That's what I thought. But this is the thing. She said everything that could happen, all the changes ever made to the past, had already happened. All you had to do was work out where you fit in, what you did, and do it. So if you were going to go back in time, spill the guy's drink, it's always been that way, time is just waiting for you to see it and do what you were always going to do.'

'All well and good but it's still just a game.'

'Perhaps, but indulge me a little further. What's the statute of limitations for murder?'

'The longest I know of is Ontario, thirty years I think, although there's a rumour New Mexico's pushing for fifty.'

'Fine, fifty years. Pretend you go back a hundred years, you kill someone at random. Just put a bullet through her head in broad daylight, let them take your photo ID then come back. Can we prosecute you now for her murder?'

'I don't think so. I'm not sure, I mean, a hundred years ago but it's now … sort of.'

'Exactly. You couldn't, I couldn't, no one could. If anyone tried any half decent lawyer would tie any judge or jury into knots.'

'You might be right.'

'I know I am, or at least my legal team says so.'

Roger got up, sat behind his desk.

'No more games Patrick. This woman, when she told me this, when I met her, Agnes had been gone two years. She, or rather what she said, became my sole consuming passion for five years. I threw everything I had, all my resources, everything at her disposal.'

Pat finished his drink slowly, set the glass down.

'Why didn't you simply stop him?'

'I tried, believe me I tried everything. But it couldn't be done, it wasn't possible. Every single thing I did failed and failed spectacularly. Bullets missed, poisons didn't work, roadblocks opened up. I couldn't change where Agnes was, couldn't stop her, slow her down. History needed her dead, demanded her death then and there. And each time I tried and failed it killed me a little more.'

'How many times did you try?'

'More than a thousand.'

'And Agnes was that important to the world?'

'No! That's the damned thing, it's not her but ... but something else, and I had to see it again and again and again until I found out, watching her, powerless. I was not a vindictive man Patrick, a hard business man but never vindictive, but it changed me. If I couldn't get Agnes back I was going to make him suffer, suffer for his entire life, from birth to death and beyond if I could.'

'So everything Wayne said —'

'Oh yes, and more, so much more. It's so easy, so simple. Buy a company, change a specification, shift a timetable, seduce, bribe or corrupt the right people. Go back as far as you need, make the tiniest change that ten, fifty, two hundred years later impacts one individual and one alone. Go as far forward as you want and drag the tech back, make the impossible possible. All I had to do was sit here, work it out, watch what I had already done and then just go back and do it.'

'But there's no time machine. Your chair's —'

'Irrelevant. What do you think, it's as big as the old mainframes? It's tiny, so tiny.' He tapped his forehead. 'It's in here, a microscopic switch, that's all. When she told me I thought it was a lie, my god how wrong I was.'

'But the chair, the twitch of your thumb?'

'I can't go back and simply pop out of thin air just anywhere. I bought this estate four hundred years ago, this chair immobile in this one spot, this room locked and secured by the best of the future's technology the entire time. My thumb? You try coming back and sitting in exactly the same pose after months.'

'How long has this been going on?'

'Ten years, but I've lived thirty or more in them.'

'Has it been worth it?'

'Are you kidding? Yes, everything, every second wrecking every part of his life, hopes and dreams from the start through to when he dies a shattered, abject failure. His father, his sister, his jobs, his career, children, friends, money, loves it's all been worth it, every second and every cent to destroy it all from his name onwards.'

'His name?'

'Of course, what sort of idiot would call their son Wayne? Wayne Anka? Mr. W. Anka? He's tried a hundred times to change it and will try a hundred more but he will never succeed.'

'Revenge destroys you, it's never worth it.'

'Oh? Put yourself in my shoes. Would you have done anything else?'

Pat stared at the empty glass. It was useless, impossible to be another person, feel the world and emotions as they did. A sliver, the slightest crack of insight opened to him and there he was, Roger being there over and over and over watching the only love in his life torn away and he impotent to stop it, an unwilling voyeur tortured until all-consuming anguish and hatred erupted. Suddenly it was Stefania and not Agnes being wrenched away and Pat was changing the safety guard on the drill press that would take a man's arm off, baiting the merchant bankers into strip mining a family's life savings, encouraging Lothario to deflower a boy's first love before he had the guts to try. Pat found himself relishing it, chafing at the bit to hit harder, gouge deeper, crush the very spirit out of Wayne and everything associated with him completely, deliberately, methodically. Pat slumped, looked up with eyes devoid of pity but filled with understanding at the empty man opposite. He stood.

'Goodbye Roger. I'm truly sorry.'

Roger watched as Pat let himself out. It wasn't right, none of it was right and if he had the power he'd change it but, perhaps mercifully, he didn't. If she had died a minute earlier, a minute later then it would have been possible. But the child was there, the child that would become the man that long after Roger and Pat were dust would save the world. And my Agnes, my beautiful Agnes' death the sole catalyst for his passion. To the boy who would become the man a nameless face; to the world that would survive because of him unknown.

He cried as only an old man can cry, tortured as only he could ever be. If I cannot for myself then maybe for another, and they'll never know. He leant back, eyes closed for a few seconds, flickered out and back.

Pat headed home. He'd lost any desire to go back to the office, face the troubles and issues knowing there was a way to change what couldn't be changed as long as it was already changed. Maybe the Captain would let him burn some sick leave, hopefully four weeks' worth until he retired.

Retired. He smiled, glanced at the photo on the dash, touched his fingers to his lips, fingers to the photo. She was waiting at home as always, and maybe now he could give her the attention she deserved. Stefania, my Stefania, the world would mean nothing without you.

END

And if you think his suit isn't made in new hampshire

Arkenay stood in the doorway livid with rage, anger and insult boiling up inside a wellspring of indignation, disgust. It was too much, too far, too great to allow never mind support. Never having felt this way it was all Arkenay could do to hold in check, to stand rather than hurl bodily into Chamais' office. Arkenay knew the depth of feeling was radiating outwards signalling to all and sundry. The entire floor staff had shrunk back and away from Chamais' office, far enough to be unobserved but close enough to hear and feel. Arkenay braced, breathed in, stepped across the threshold and stood.

To any other observer Arkenay's three meter frame was graceful, slight and steadily erect. No outward signs presented, all being nondescript save a small tic in one finger and the slightest dip of one earlobe regularly up and down under the close cropped fur. To Arkenay's kind however this primal display of anger bordered closely on blood lust. Even three millennia of genetics and development could not rid either the outward signs or the hard-wired reaction of those seeing it.

Chamais glanced across and noted the lack of deference, Arkenay's omission – quite deliberately – of the required bow and request for entry. It is entirely expected and of my own doing he mused.

'Enter and speak Arkenay.'

Arkenay took a step and halted two meters from Chamais' desk, precisely at the limit of personal space.

'I would speak of the project. I would not talk as birthmates. I would not talk as partners. I will talk as one inside to one outside. I would express my disquiet at the path taken. I come to correct the error of your ways.'

Chamais was taken aback at first by the strength, but then by the formality of the language used. It followed the ancient pattern of challenge, the call to the fight. Chamais stood, dismissing the desk. With a mental switch the walls and door space became opaque. It would not do for staff to hear or see this bitter exchange, particularly between teacher and student. My first words will be to reconcile.

'I would hear you, and as birthmates talk. In what wise have I given offence?'

Arkenay straightened. 'The planet. The policy. The placements that have taken decades you would throw away by bringing them to light. You ask of offence, is not the destruction of sixty years work on a whim cause enough?'

'Whim?' Chamais allowed a show of strength, a slight flicker across one eyelid. Arkenay was brilliant, some said perhaps a genius. Chamais had allowed both freedom and camaraderie to Arkenay and the section that some called heretical and others wanton folly. Over the years this policy produced results, but this tirade could not be sanctioned.

Chamais spoke slowly, measuring the carefully aimed insult.

'You speak unknowingly. You speak as both child and

apostate. You speak as our forebears, as one not yet standing upright. You lack wisdom. You lack subtlety. Why should I grant you air?'

Arkenay reeled. Although rage was unabated, Chamais' riposte had torn through the armour. My words will not be heard, my voice lost, my height lowered Arkenay realised. The tic stopped, the earlobe steadied. Arkenay placed hands on mouth, bowed until chin touched chest, waiting. Chastened but not dissuaded.

Chamais allowed a pause. 'My birthmate has replaced the bridge. We will speak. You think it wrong what has been done?'

Arkenay raised his head. 'I do not understand. We wait in silence and dark, and we are to now shine the light on them? Always we are reminded to stay in the shadow.'

'As we have. Yet they are now both us and they. The shadows were for the first, the light for the followers. Have you thought how the plan could be fulfilled any other way?'

'We have done the same on countless other worlds, from shadows safe, and they believed as they must it was of their own doing. But this we change here? We cast off what has worked for what, for risk of detection?'

'There is not the rest, this you know. They differ from all others we have met, this too you know. So why can you think our plan too must not differ?'

Arkenay paused, reflecting. Why? Why. Because the plans, the others, had been Arkenay's shared design, had worked, had brought Arkenay's height up. In this change Arkenay had not been consulted, had been ignored; taken as insult. Arkenay's anger dispersed. Pride had touched, had burned. Was not this the curse of the race? They had moved beyond, yet once more Arkenay was reminded of the fault line possessed.

Chamais saw the change immediately. 'You understand in part?'

Arkenay nodded silently.

'Then would I bring you wisdom. Would you receive?'

'Yes.' Again with head low.

'Then hear and we will grow.' A small gesture brought chairs as the floor moulded itself up to fit them, the room seemingly dissolving as they floated in a field of stars.

'That which you designed for other places could not work here, so you were not joined for this effort. Once we knew them we knew it could not. Why should we take you from success in hundreds and condemn you to failure in one? You were not consulted after the first report.'

'It is true. What I have learned I have learned elsewise.'

'And therein your fault. You do not understand them.' The black star spattered space filled with a blue green globe, a faintly glowing jewel.

'All of the species on the worlds met to this one had come, as we did, to the point of communal action. Thinking of the common good, none placing themselves too high, with reason and argument defining their paths. This is so?'

'Yes, in all. Leaders chosen by ability, populations not easily troubled and distanced from savagery.'

'Open to ideas, open to the force of argument and fact, open to us. So in that manner we came to them, in quiet and in dark, unknown and unobserved, free to influence and to mould and place, letting fact and idea seep through unseen. To go, to change, to return. And to those we have visited?'

'As if they themselves had thought and directed, as it must be. No one individual, no one group shown as catalyst. The only way to take root. And it has worked, for hundreds we have guided to safety and they do not yet see our hand and never will.'

'There is truth. They must believe it is their own to hold. As these must.' Chamais nodding to the globe.

'But this cannot be. You would have us stand to the front, to be seen, to be heard, to lead. How? They will see, they will know. At best they will be lost, at worst destroyed. It is to this I fear.'

Chamais regarded Arkenay kindly. 'This is where you fail. These do not look to the group, but to the individual. They disregard reason on the basis of emotion. They do not consider the next ten years, much less the next hundred. They are as we were and how we could be if we so chose. But we do not. They do. And for us to remain in the shadows would achieve nothing. Do you think this has no foundation?'

'No, it must be as you say. You do not speak without reason.'

'And you think no plan lies beneath?'

'I do not know if one does or does not.'

'So may your wisdom grow. Their very hysteria was nearly our undoing. When we first discovered them and knew we must act they thought the skies were full of us, from many places. They became more and more obsessed and vigilant. Every light, every meteor indeed the stars and planets themselves and even their own transportation was believed us, belligerent, scheming. In fifteen of their years we went twice, yet to us was attributed thousands. Unlike your plans ours had to place us unsupported and modified into their midst. Permanently.'

'Modified? Permanently?'

'As male and female they are, we had to be and so we were modified. They live for but one fifth our span, so we must be as they. We cut our lives to match. This is the greater sacrifice. Consider one, alone, changed, life foreshortened. For the good of an unreasoning whole. We could not stay unnoticed, and would not remain undiscovered.' Chamais rotated the globe and pointed to a patch of light brown in blue.

'So here and here we placed into areas of strife, dissent and danger, chances of our hand being seen minimised. Places having no form of regular rule, no identification, no law except that of survival. Only here could we enter. Then, as conditions fell, as other areas opened to help, we joined the flow from danger to safety. We arrived welcomed and unquestioned, given legitimacy and place. Which itself was not enough.'

Chamais shifted slightly. 'We learned their hysteria and fears are easily roused and with difficulty assuaged. Even as respected individuals in their new areas we were met with hostility or anger if we rose, spoke, or chose to be apart from the group. Yet they only look to those apart for leadership. They gave peace on one turn and hatred the next, and cited the same reasoning for both.'

Arkenay was stunned. This was beyond knowledge. 'How can this be? Is this a place of lost minds? It cannot be, their technology points to high intelligence, but that? Yet if you say it has been observed —'

'As it has and as it is. So the plan was built to change, to break how we have worked before and yes, even go against all. If we do not they are lost. If we do they may be lost. Do you see the reasoning? Do you understand the risk?'

'I see, I am made wise. I see your greater knowledge. I do not see the solution.'

'It is before us, within their hysteria, prejudice and hate. One who comes from elsewhere out of mercy may not rise, but one born to someone who came from mercy may. They are accepted as their own, as proof of their moral and societal supremacy. So Arkenay, you say you are made wiser. Given this, if this were your plan, what is it that you would do?'

Arkenay paused. To build on ignorance and emotion over reason to save? 'We must rise to the light, but not we ourselves but our children. They will not accept us; they will not accept our voice in the dark. If so our voice must be in the light.'

'Correct my birthmate. Do you see both error and wisdom?'

Arkenay nodded. 'Yes, I do.'

Chamais motioned open the door. 'Water has passed. It is as it was. Leave in wisdom.'

Arkenay left, disturbed but settled. Chamais let the door seal, remaining seated facing the globe, remembering. It had taken eighty years of patience, placing fifty in the lower hemisphere. Placed deliberately in danger, poverty and disease. Barely two thirds had managed to cross to the more civilised parts of the globe as refugees, obtaining shelter, safety and ultimately legitimacy. Of those a chosen dozen had managed to cross to the final destination, the large northern continent. Those left behind became industrial and financial leaders, bringing wealth and power to support. The children bred true and although fully of there were yet fully of here.

Which held of those who went to the final place. These too had children, built bases of industry, wealth and knowledge. In truth it was all too simple, once nearly in error, far too advanced. Built and now applied as the plan came to climax. Control and power, to save them from something they did not even conceive. And for this the children were the key, accepted as their own.

They would be surprised if they knew the truth of five of the eight presented to their people. Their entertainment, paranoia, imagination and fears would fall far short of what those five held.

All had worked tirclessly, selflessly, continually. This all the more poignant as they knew they were abandoned to live, work and die on and for an alien world that would pay them no heed. Even more for their children, knowing heirs of a civilisation they would never see.

That their work was invaluable was not in dispute. The greatest heights of altruism at times requires the basest depravities. And to Chamais, Arkenay and all their kind a life of seeking profit and power to the exclusion of all else by any means was abhorrent, the very antithesis of their culture, their beliefs. But as those on the planet would say, needs must.

After all Presidential campaigns don't come cheap.

END

Augmented

The tiles in unmarked uniform antiseptic whiteness covering floors and walls added to the cold of the eyes behind the monitor. Alicia Sanz stepped to the floor, rapidly pulling on her dress and blouse partly to ward off the chill, partly to cover threadbare underwear. Hands guided her into a chair opposite those eyes, now part of a dark-haired face regarding her coolly, dispassionately. Alicia fancied him to be her grandson matured, a valued employee, a face otherwise kind and gentle. The soft whine of the supervising AI brought her back.

'Do you understand what you have done? Why you are here?'

She smoothed an errant crease from her dress.

'Oh yes, quite.'

The AI tilted its head to one side.

'And you understand the rights you have, the cautions we have explained?'

Outlined against a red and yellow flag and the photograph below, the room's only decorations, she studied it briefly. She'd always felt in awe of these artificial people, more so now she was closer. No wonder the world was the way it was.

'Yes thank you, perfectly.'

A slot on the table deposited two pages in front of the eyes. He studied the pages carefully, one filled with text, the other a da Vinci figure with blotches on the abdomen, thigh, chest. Sighing gently, he positioned the pages in front of her.

'Perhaps if we talk this through first Mrs San —'

'Ms.'

'My apologies, let us talk through it first Ms Sanz and then to the formal statement. Tell me, what made you do this?'

A gentle nudge woke Alicia from broken sleep. It was still dark, the sound of mist rain on the plastic roof announcing another cold, gloomy day. She sat up, seeing David smiling at her, motioning to the front of the room. Pulling back the thin blanket she emerged fully clothed, made her way to the wash basin and tried to soak the tiredness from her face. She took the cup David had prepared her and drank deeply.

She watched him, bent over his books on the far side of the room under the solitary light. Too much of Louis in him, there were times it seemed as if her son was still alive, eleven and growing into the man she was proud of. Louis deserved better than to be cut down in his prime, never to face the challenges of fatherhood or see his son grow. David too deserved better, more than a one room shack shared with an old woman, the same food and not much of it, the empty promise of a normal life. Not that he complained or fretted, no, she knew that would come later as he started to realise just how steeply the deck was stacked against him.

She shrugged on her plastic mac, tucking her grey hair under the hood as she shuffled across, bending to kiss him on the top of his head.

'Study hard buddy, I'm proud of you.'

Not that she needed to remind him, she knew when she returned fourteen hours from now she would find him here, bent over his books, the day's solitary meal bubbling on the fire.

Eyes fixed on the book before him he reached back, gently squeezing her hand.

'I know and I will. Love you too gran.'

Holding clean shoes tightly in her plastic bag she picked her way down the shattered streets trying to avoid the deepest rain filled holes. She knew it was futile, the oil slicked bow waves from chauffeured augmenteds lapping at her, but she had to try. They would not let her near the house if she was soaked through so she clutched the bag tighter, wrapped her mac closer and continued on. The bus stop was only five minutes away.

She clambered aboard, elbowing her way through the crowded aisle to a large, pink jellyfish–like woman occupying two seats. A smile, a wave and Alicia settled herself down, nestled between the armrest and the comforting mound of flesh. She tipped her hood back sending a cascade down the back of the seat. Victoria was a saint as far as Alicia was concerned, with a heart and soul as broad as her hips.

'Nice weather for ducks dearie.'

It was always nice weather for ducks as far as Victoria knew, the ever-present drizzle confirming her preconception.

'Washing won't dry for sure.' Alicia responded as the long-established pattern required.

Victoria was dressed differently today. Instead of the plain utilitarian blue that her job required she sported a loose pink dress, sneakers and a bright green beret. A small clutch bag at her feet and a hint of makeup separated her from other days. Victoria caught Alicia's eyes wandering.

'I'm not going in today, not for a few days.' smiling, adjusting the beret. 'I'll be away for a week or so.'

Alicia raised one eyebrow. Neither of them, no one on the bus or their district had enough money to properly clothe or feed themselves, never mind take a vacation. Although intrigued she could not ask, upbringing fighting desire. She needn't have worried, Victoria had no qualms sharing.

'It's a job actually', she whispered in Alicia's ear 'a good one, a day in hospital, a trip, and that's it.'

'What do you have to do?'

'Nothing really, just go, a few simple things.' She bent her head conspiratorially. 'I really need this Alicia, Ben's health is not good and this will be enough to fix it.'

'You seem worried.'

She smiled unconvincingly.

'Oh no, just a few travel jitters, I've never been out of Irvine in my life.'

She shifted, her stop coming up. Reaching into her bag she pulled out a greasy corner of paper and a pencil stub, scrawling on it then thrusting it into Alicia's shoe bag.

'If you need some extra, and quietly, go here dearie.' With that she stepped into the aisle and out of the bus.

Alicia shook off her hood and mac, carefully placing them in the plastic bag with her street shoes. A final check to make sure her hair was correctly tied back and the run in her stockings faced inwards not outwards, she stepped across the doorstep into the servants' entry. She stood silently with the others as the lady of the house inspected them in minute detail. She stopped and straightened Alicia's collar, continuing her instructions.

'… so it is important you keep yourselves correctly dressed

and silent today. My husband will be tied up in the reception room all day so you should not see the AI, but if you do keep a respectful distance, do not speak unless spoken to and under no circumstances are you to look them in the eye.'

She turned to face the small assembly.

'Remember that the AIs do not share the same relaxed attitudes to norms that we do. Alicia I will need you for a few extra hours tonight.'

Alicia neither saw nor heard anyone for the next twelve hours, the sound of the 'copter lifting off announcing the AI's departure. She cleaned and tidied the reception room, being careful to leave everything in its place, clear and accounted for. The few extra hours were draining but welcome, a new book for David, maybe stockings for herself. The lady accompanied her to the garage, placing a small box in her free hand.

'Thank you for the extra hours. I've put the extra in there, together with a few remnants from lunch and dinner.'

'Thank you Ma'am.'

'How is that boy of yours, Derek? Studying hard?'

'Well thank you Ma'am, David is doing well.'

'I'm glad.'

She looked around absent mindedly, then called into the garage.

'Alfonse? Alfonse!'

A short man emerged.

'Ma'am?'

'Please take Alicia home, she will tell you where it is.'

She had never travelled in a private car before. Alicia sat in the front fiddling with the air-conditioning, the audio-visual system, everything. She particularly liked the heated reclining massage chairs, more so when Alfonse set the heating at an appropriate level and let the car drive itself.

'They must live as kings! I know the house but this is wonderful.'

Alfonse laughed.

'You should see the 'copter. But it's nothing you know', waving his hand around the interior 'yes this is money, the augmenteds' reward, but even this is just crumbs from the AIs' table.'

'Even so, to own things like this! It's beyond me, well beyond an old cleaning lady, but my grandson David's a smart boy, maybe one day he can have all this.'

'If only it were so. It is not for the likes of us to own these things.'

'But you at least have a room on the grounds.'

'So I am always available, cheaper than a robobutler and no employment laws to bother.'

He took her hand in his, their varicose veins a purple patchwork quilt on calloused wrinkled parchment.

'To work hard, to be smart is not enough. Only the augmented advance, only to them do the AIs allow money, power, influence and only then as much as they see fit. But', as the car came to a lopsided, rain drenched halt outside her shack 'even a gilded cage is still a cage.'

'Have you ever visited the People's Republic before Ms Sanz?'

'No, this is my first trip abroad, first time in an aeroplane.'

'And you can read English?'

'Yes, of course.'

'And you listened to the warnings, read the immigration information in the seat?'

'Yes, all of it.'

The AI leant forward, tapping the page with a slender finger.

'At these places we have found the things I have listed. I would like you to read through the list and see if it is correct.'

Alicia read slowly, carefully, one finger on the lines of text on the left, one finger close to the AI's on the right as it moved around the page. She sat a little more upright, paid closer attention. It was a fine looking artificial person, all clean and fresh smelling, it would not at all do to be inaccurate. She took her time.

She looked up when finished.

'It seems all right, it is what they said it would be, although the writing next to the English I don't understand.'

'They are my notes, an index of sorts. Now, what were you going to do once here?'

David was exactly where she had left him, hunched over books in the corner. The smell of thin cabbage and pea soup greeted her, warmth of the stove battling the cold that stole in with her. They hugged then sat on the edge of her bed bowls in hand, Alicia's package between them. She opened it revealing ham and rye sandwiches, dunking them into the soup, sucking out every last morsel of flavour until, reluctantly but satisfied, swallowing. She leant back against the wall drowsy, David's head on her shoulder.

'Gran?'

'Yes buddy.'

'One day I'm going to have meat every week, and you will too.'

'That's nice.'

He sat up and, reaching in his pocket, put a torn page from a magazine in her hands.

'No, I mean it. I'm going to get this one day.'

It was an augmentation service ad. All the trappings of success clearly and cleverly laid out around a young man who – as the ad boldly proclaimed – had been augmented. The price was breathtaking, easily more than she would earn in years. Too far out of reach to be practical, too close not to fuel frustration. She hugged David, handed it back to him.

'Always dream buddy, it's still the land of opportunity. One day, who knows?'

'It's no dream gran, it's going to happen. A warm house, nice food, new clothes, one day gran, one day.' as he trailed off to sleep.

She rocked him gently as she silently wept.

The bus was colder now with winter coming on, shorter days with constant drizzle, no Victoria to keep her warm, fraying cardigan letting the wind from broken windows clutch at her. She could feel a cold coming on. For the first time in ages she felt old, could hear the years calling her.

She reached into her plastic bag for a tissue, coming up instead with a greasy shred of forgotten paper. She stared at the number, felt for the coin in her cardigan pocket. Hesitating only briefly she stood, alighted at the next stop and made two calls.

It was like Victoria said, simple and easy. 'Of course she could.' they'd said and they'd come round, picked her up straight away. They'd even called the lady, made excuses for her, arranged a replacement. They were nice boys Alicia thought, nice boys.

They would pay her enough, oh yes more than enough and after she told them why they offered her more, if she could manage it. Of course, why not, the years of gravity fighting her body had to be of some use surely. And half now and half when back? No problem, none at all. They could even take her where she needed to go, take her home too if she liked. Very nice boys Alicia thought, considerate boys.

Alicia sat on the edge of the bed with David in the early morning. She'd had enough left over for a new dress and blouse, shoes and food. She felt younger again, blue ankle length dress, crocheted shawl, closed in shoes. It would not be right to travel in her work clothes. She kissed David on the head.

'It's only a week and a bit buddy, food is there and you'll be fine. They will come for you today, have you home by evening. It will all be fine.'

David looked up, beaming.

'Thank you gran, I —'

'Shssh. Just make sure you relax, tell me all about it when I get back.'

She moved to the door, looked back.

'All you have to worry about is what colour the house will be.'

She finished reading the formal statement and pressed her thumb to the corner of the page.

'It is all correct?'

'Yes.'

The AI stood, retrieved the statement.

'The officer will take care of processing.'

The eyes took a pair of handcuffs and approached her.

'Do I really need to use these? Will you give me any trouble?'

Alicia stood, straightened her dress and smiled.

'I will be fine, no trouble. You don't have to use them if you like.'

'Thank you.'

Flanked by a medical orderly and her assistant they exited the room, walking down a windowless corridor towards a pair of glass doors.

The eyes saddened, it was like taking his mother to prison. An otherwise nice old lady, but for this one thing.

'First thing we need to do is get those extra organs out of you, fix the damage they may have done. They do a lot of these, you'll be fine.'

'Then?'

'Recovery, then sentencing. You've co-operated and been open, so that will help. The AIs take a dim view of anything else.'

'Well, there's no point really, what's done is done.'

They walked in silence, the only sounds shoes on tile, the air conditioners' hum.

'So how much did they promise you again?'

She told him.

It wasn't much. Two, perhaps three months wages for ten to twenty years in prison. He couldn't understand it, he never could reconcile risk to reward. They all knew they'd be caught eventually, the authorities or damage to their bodies catching up with them. He stopped, looked searchingly at her.

'Was it worth it?'

Alicia stared back steadily, without hesitation.

'Oh yes, definitely.'

END

Bacon butter

I got this thing for butter. Not the mass-produced stuff but boutique, Sorrell melt in your mouth handmade creamy delight. It's expensive but I budget to the cent, autopay all my bills. All I see is my drinking and grocery money.

Well, truth is the one hundred forty-nine dollars and ninety-nine cents drinking money's exactly Uncle Owen's fine for public disturbance. He's a fair and reasonable public official even if he is on the bench. Got to the point last year I sent the fines straight through in advance. I'm a little calmer now, not much sense in using all my drinking money to fight.

But no matter what I always have my eight dollars ninety-five for my butter. So last thing Thursdays, car full of groceries and eight ninety-five in my pocket I stop by Eli's Deli and pick it up. This time it's the last one on the shelf.

'Hey Eli! You got anything fresher?'

He waddles out the back, he likes his butter too. At least bricklaying burns it off me.

'Hell no, can't you read?' pointing to the sign, knowing full well I can't. 'It's the last, Sorrell's gone belly up.'

I'm gutted. I'm not the only one, the short guy near the door's heartbroken. It's great butter, try it half an inch thick on your brioche and tell me the heart attack's not worth it.

I got mine so I toss my money at Eli and head out the door.

'Hey mister, how much you want for the butter?'

I turn around. There's shorty.

'It's not for sale, go get your own.'

'I'll give you twenty dollars.'

'No dice.'

'Fifty?'

'Nope, not for sale.'

'How 'bout one forty-nine ninety-nine? Hear you could use it.'

I give him the evil eye.

'I told you it's not for sale. Why you so interested?'

'I promised a friend I'd bring her back some. Let me buy you a drink, I got something to trade, something you might like. If you're not interested after that, fair enough.'

What the hell, a free drink's a no-brainer. We walk half a block and settle into a corner at the Biker Bar. It's familiar, I know the barmaids and a fair few feet of the floor intimately.

He shows me his wristband.

'How'd you like Uncle Owen to never see your ugly face again? This'll let you start, make and get out of trouble scot-free. Now pick someone, anyone.'

Propping up the bar in front of us is Big Dave. We go back a long way, I lost my virginity to his girlfriend and he gave me my first broken nose. Over the years his waistline grew to match his six four height. Better than most I knew that ninety-five percent of that wasn't fat. I lean across to shorty.

'How about the guy in the Comanchero colours?'

'No problem. First, I press the red part of the wristband.'

He wanders over, elbows in between Dave and some other guy wearing colours. Dave turns, slowly, looking down.

'Excuse me?'

'Oh I'm sorry petal. Let me buy you a drink.'

Turning to the barmaid he yells 'Two strawberry daiquiris sweetie!'

The crowded bar goes silent. The barmaid's blowing the dust off an old cocktail leaflet and Dave's glowing red under his bandanna.

Shorty turns to the other guy.

'I apologise if I've upset your girlfriend, is it her time of month?' Then, turning to Dave, 'It's ok, I understand how delicate and fragile you must be feeling.'

Dave's neck disappears into his shoulders as he gives me a withering gaze. I shake my head and hold up my hands. I'm here to watch the show not star in it.

'Anyway', shorty continues, one hand on Dave's leg and one finger to his lips 'didn't I see you at Mardi Gras ... oh no, that's it, you were handing out how to vote cards for Hillary weren't you?'

Dave grabs shorty by the neck, lifting him off the floor. I go straight for my phone's paramedic speed dial.

'Oh we are trifle prickly aren't we?' and in a blink shorty's got Dave's hand off, thumb broken and head smashed into the bar. Dave crumples to the floor. Shorty dispatches the other guy with a rapid left-right combo.

No one moves. The barmaid places two perfect strawberry daiquiris down. Shorty picks them up, sets them on our table.

Shorty presses the blue section of his wristband.

'Now part two.'

Everyone looks around as if it's all news to them. 'What the hell?' and 'How'd this happen?' is all I hear, nobody's got a clue not even Dave who's lifting himself by a barstool off the floor.

Shorty leans back, smirking.

'Now you tell me that's not worth the butter.'

I had it out in a jiffy.

'Sounds fair to me.'

He takes the butter and holds out the wristband.

'Just one thing', keeping hold, pressing a yellow section 'you can dump it all on someone else if they're dumb enough.' with which shorty, butter and wristband wink out of existence.

'Well aint you the gutsy one?' I hear as I turn around, the bar closing in.

There went another one forty-nine ninety-nine and a week in hospital.

Another Thursday, another trip to Eli's. I've gone right off butter but bacon's another thing.

The space for the highland Fitzroy bacon's nearly empty.

'Oh come on Eli, you gotta have more than that!'

'The hell I do! Fitzroy's folded, that's it.'

I buy it all, maybe I'll grow my own pigs.

'Excuse me sonny, how much do you want for the bacon?'

I turn around to see a little old lady looking up at me from under her Sunday best bonnet.

A right uppercut lays her out cold in the pickle and sausage aisle.

Damn aliens. I know just where that was headed and I don't get paid till Thursday week.

END

Busker

It's the Silurian's fault Janex thought setting up her gear, if only I'd ignored him. 'It's easy,' he said, 'nothing to it, candy from a baby.' Oh yeah. 'Make a mint.' he said so I jumped off here at Carson's World and what do I find? The hardest damned crowd, intellectual, rational, boring as batshit. Not that they aren't friendly, just no heart, all mind. Janex looked at her credset and sighed. And they don't pay, four weeks and still short of my ticket off this rock. Dammit she thought, I should be somewhere else raking it in.

She tapped her throat mic and guitar to make sure they were charged, setting the credset on the ground in front of her. A small crowd had gathered, thirty or forty dressed in the same plain, drab, functional garb. At least they're curious she thought, it's a bigger group than usual too. She coughed gently, cementing her audience's attention.

'Ladies and gentlemen, fine citizens of Carson's World, today I present for your education and interest music from worlds gone by, histories decayed, empires fallen!' The crowd stirred gently. That always gets them, I'm living proof they're superior, outlasting, better.

'Today I bring you music from the most fabled, decayed, tragic world of all. Earth! Yes, old Terra, birth place of man!' She held the n as long as possible, a long, menacing trail setting the audience's antennae vibrating in anticipation. She singled out a juvenile in the front.

'Today I take you back to that place, to the height of their consumerist era as they wantonly squandered their offspring's future to satisfy their own lustful pleasures.' Janex drew shocked gasps from the crowd, the juvenile pressing back against the adults with a mix of fear and fascination. 'I bring you an anthem, a rallying cry from the heart of that degenerate society as it plunged headlong towards oblivion!'

She hit the first note clear and strong, vocals and guitar subtly augmented. She scanned her audience and saw the first flickers of interest grow, ramping up the sound and starting the characteristic strut. The minutes flashed by and with a flourish on one knee she was finished, letting the last chord linger. One song was enough she knew, just at the limits of their patience and curiosity.

'Thank you, thank you, you're a wonderful, intelligent audience. If you found my small gift interesting please return the favour.' motioning to the credset.

This time, instead of the odd one or two ponying up, most of the crowd flashed one forearm or another over the credset. After an animated discussion the adults touched the juvenile's forearm. It scuttled over to the credset, chattered unintelligibly at Janex, and ran off after them.

Janex looked down and smiled. Finally enough, the price of a ticket out of this dump, maybe enough over for some food too. She started packing.

'Did we not say we understand the alien but it does not

understand us?' Dontrax asked the child as they walked away from the strange, musical human.

'You cannot speak BasEng and it cannot speak Mazkad.' Thrmyn, the other parent, continued.

'But I did try.' their child replied, happy to have seen such a strange creature, one arm wrapped around Thrmyn's leg and the other two mimicking Janex's guitar work.

Dontrax looked at Thrmyn. 'Much of their 'music' I have heard, but this one never. It fills a gap. It was worth the creds to just hear such a contradiction.'

Thrmyn shifted half its gaze to Dontrax on the right, and half to the child behind it. 'Conflicted and illogical, as are all its kind.'

'Unable to understand that what it wants it has. Thankfully all that is left are the wanderers, the story tellers.'

'How did it go again?' the child piped. 'Can you repeat it?'

Thrmyn cleared its triple windpipes and started up, sounding much like a piccolo bagpipe. It rendered the tune and lyrics as best it could, millennia after the composer and its planet had turned to ash. Surprisingly Thrmyn found itself taken with the tune.

They continued their walk home through the indigo blue city, shadows growing long as the bloated red sun bathed the landscape in russet tones. The ancient tune from the long dead composer wafted gently after them.

'I still fail to see why', Dontrax muttered, lost in thought and falling behind 'if it's goal was to get no satisfaction, it could not see that the act of trying to obtain satisfaction ensured that it was unable to secure a lack of satisfaction. What a strange, strange species.'

END

Call me

The technician squints his pale blue eyes, twists a screwdriver to slot home a coupling.

Frank Garrity was running late as he stepped outside and checked his mobile. The taxi ranks were empty but there were a few Uber rides around. It was a rushed trip and in all the hurry at the building site he'd just managed to change into his suit. He looked down, brown steel caps laughing where black Florsheims should be.

Sonia stared out the window as the car crawled through the city. Was that a suit wearing steel capped boots? The driver craned her neck back.

'You ok if I don't pick up share rides? Heard some bad stories lately.'

'Fine by me, I'm in a hurry.'

Self check-in was down so Frank joined the economy queue. They opened the business class counter to economy passengers, a forlorn effort given the snaking line behind him. He'd made it to the front when there was a gasp and clatter. Turning he saw an old lady trying unsuccessfully to pick up her walking stick. No one lifted a hand to help, the man between them staring at his watch. Frank stepped around him.

'They should have a special lane.'

'I'm fine. Looks like someone's cut in front of you.'

Frank turned as the watch checker scurried to the counter.

'What's a few minutes?'

Thankfully business class got preferential treatment, small compensation for the two hour packed flight to Townsville. The counter attendant handed Sonia her boarding pass.

'You're boarding through gate twenty three in approximately ninety minutes, seat 1B. Have a pleasant flight.'

'QF 978?'

The man at the counter stared at the monitor, his blue eyes barely concealing his irritation.

'Is there a problem?'

'Just the usual, it's over booked.'

A boarding slip shot onto the counter.

'Economy's full so I've put you in business.'

'Is it going to cost me?'

'No, nothing. Seat 4B, boarding in an hour and a half from gate twenty three. Pleasant flight Mr. Garrity.'

The security checkpoint was an overcrowded nightmare. Tempers frayed as people were sent back through for coins in pockets, mobile phones, even belts. A man was pulled aside, told to take off his boots. Sonia went through, extracted her carry-on and headed for the escalator.

Frank made his way back around through the scanner. Boots back on he grabbed his grip before jumping on the escalator. They were three deep on each step families, businessmen and holiday makers jam packed together. An old couple at the top stumbled off, her scarf trailing on the floor as they walked away.

Frank made the top of the escalator and turned left through the food court to the newsagent.

'Your coffee.'

She cleared a small space on the table and placed the mug down in front of Sonia. Sonia had toyed with going into the club but lately it was filled with noisy families. A man sailed towards her engrossed in his newspaper, arm high passing over her head, jacket brushing the edge of her table. A woman pulled a chair up next to the old man opposite. It's definitely better out here, the people watching's more fun.

Frank's eyes were fixed to the sports page as he hurried to the departure lounge. Bunch of losers, beaten by Bangladesh four nil. In the old days we would've routed them but now we can't even lose by less than an innings.

He finished the paper in disgust, page after page of bad news. The country's just an open pit mine populated by Netflix junkies.

'QF 978 is now ready for boarding, would business class passengers proceed to gate twenty three.'

Frank folded the paper then stood. He thought about keeping

it then, deciding against it, dropped it on the chair behind him before joining the queue.

The boarding call caught Sonia unawares. She was last in business class, just settling into her seat as economy was called. Probably going to be a bad flight, the old lady next to me in 1A looks worried, apprehensive.

'You too?'

The old man in 4A nodded.

'My wife's in 1A, they wouldn't put us together it was this or get bumped.'

'That's rough.'

'No kidding. She doesn't like flying, too much tv, those air crash shows.'

'You should be together.'

'That's what I said.'

The blue eyed business class steward leant across.

'You'd prefer to sit together sir?'

'Of course, but they said it couldn't be done.'

'Well that was down there and this is my flight. If you're willing to shift to 1A Mr. Garrity we can fix it easy enough.'

'Sure, one seat's as good as another.'

Sonia tried not to notice him. Male, mid-thirties, business suit and not too hard on the eyes. I'm not in the market, it's barely two years since Peter died and no matter what Julie says it's too early. 'You're taking too long,' she'd scolded a week ago 'no-one's talking about a relationship here just go find a piece of beefcake and disappear for a few days.' She shook her head, tried to appear nonchalant.

He held out his hand.

'I'm Frank. Sorry if I startled you.'

'Sonia. You didn't, I was just lost in thought. Off to Townsville?' She kicked herself as she said it.

'Not much choice now, this makes only one stop.' He smiled. 'Business or pleasure?'

'Business. You?'

'Same, two days. I'm there so often it feels like home.'

'Sounds awful.'

'It's not too bad, I've got a regular room at Jupiter's and most of them know me.'

'Jupiter's? I'm booked there too, isn't that a —'

The pain exploding in Sonia's head blocked everything out, pitching her forwards driving her head between her knees. She caught a glimpse of Frank arched backwards, mouth open before the world dissolved in a blue-gold haze then faded to black.

'You too?'

The old man in 4A nodded.

'My wife's in 1A, they wouldn't put us together it was this or get bumped.'

'That's rough.'

'No kidding. She doesn't like flying, too much tv, those air crash shows.'

'You should be together.'

'That's what I said.'

The business class stewardess leant across. A petite blonde, she'd been flashing her beacon-like emerald green eyes at Frank since he boarded.

'You'd prefer to sit together sir?'

'Of course, but they said it couldn't be done.'

'Well that was down there and this is my flight. If you're willing to shift to 4D Mr. Garrity we can fix it easy enough.'

'Sure, one seat's as good as another.'

The aircraft started to push back, the terminal lights receding as Frank stared out the window. A howling whine burst through his ears, a searing pain through his head sending him arching back into his seat as the blue-gold light changed to black then oblivion.

The old man's got gorgeous blue eyes.

'Sorry?'

'They've just called QF 978. You'd better hurry.'

Sonia gulped down her remaining coffee, stood hurriedly.

'Thanks.'

She didn't notice him until she blundered into him, sending him to the floor.

'Oh god, I'm sorry.'

He picked himself up, reached down to get her carry-on and boarding pass. He's quite tall, attractive and well-built if a little dishevelled. The hint of a six pack winked from above his belt; she felt his eyes follow hers.

'It's quite alright', he said tucking his shirt back in 'these queues are always a fight anyway', looking at her boarding pass 'Mrs. Nicolas.'

'I should pay more attention. And it's Sonia.'

'Pleased to meet you Sonia, I'm Frank.'

'Going all the way?' Damn you Julie.

'As far as I can but I think it stops in Townsville.'

'Business?'

'Yeah, couple of days. You?'

'Same. I'm there so often Jupiter's should put my name on the door.'

'Jupiter's? I'm there all the time but I've never —'

The pain was overwhelming, driving Sonia to her knees screaming as the world turned blue-gold then faded away.

Frank's eyes were fixed to the sports page as he hurried to the departure lounge. Bunch of losers, beaten by Bangladesh four nil. In the old days we would've routed them but now we can't even lose by less than an innings.

He finished the paper in disgust, page after page of bad news. The country's just an open pit mine populated by Netflix junkies.

'QF 978 is now ready for boarding, would business class passengers proceed to gate twenty three.'

Frank folded the paper then stood.

'Excuse me.'

Frank looked to the short, green eyed woman seated behind him.

'Yes?'

'Is that today's Courier Mail?'

'Yes.'

'Do you mind if I have it? Things are a bit tight.'

Frank handed the paper to her.

'They give them away on board.'

'I'm not flying, I'm waiting for someone.'

Business class boarding was over so Frank joined the economy queue. Funny woman, the parking alone would get her a month's subscription. It was an assault on his senses, the noise, the lights, a debilitating but familiar cacophony pounding him to unconsciousness.

'Your coffee.'

He placed the cup and saucer down near the edge of the table in front of Sonia, smiled with ice blue eyes then walked away. Sonia had toyed with going into the club but lately it was filled with noisy families. A man sailed towards her engrossed in his newspaper, arm passing over her head, jacket catching the saucer sending the cup smashing to the floor. He spun to face her.

'I'm sorry I ...'

He looked hauntingly familiar, triggering a misty soup of fear, love, belonging and hatred in her head.

'Sonia?'

It came back in stereo, one channel of ambition, success and sharing, the other in pale solitary reflection.

'Frank? It's still happening?'

'Yes', glancing at his paper 'it's 2027? We've gone that far back?'

She grabbed his hand, squeezed hard.

'Keep fighting, it's all we can do.'

'I know it's just —'

The light and pain blew them to blackness.

'Your coffee.'

The waitress stood looking at her, a cup of coffee in one hand, dishrag in the other. Why do her green eyes give me the jitters? The waitress regarded the table littered with food scraps and spilt coffee distastefully.

'This is awful, it should have been cleaned earlier.' The table behind her emptied; the waitress gave it a cursory wipe, putting Sonia's coffee down in the middle.

'Will this do? It's cleaner and out of the way.'

Sonia moved across.

'Yes thank you it's fine.'

Sonia had toyed with going into the club but lately it was … she stopped in mid-thought, waves of déjà vu washing over her. What was it, a thought, a name, a face? A man hurried past engrossed in his newspaper, stopped and stared briefly at the seat she'd vacated then with a shake of his head walked away.

Sonia stood, raised one arm as if to go off in pursuit then spasmed as the as the world exploded blue-gold.

Frank made his way back around through the scanner. Boots back on he grabbed his grip before jumping on the escalator. They were three deep on each step families, businessmen and holiday makers jam packed together. An old man and woman fell to the floor at the top, her scarf jammed in the mechanism. Someone bent down to help, everyone else ignoring them and hurrying off. Frank made it to the top just in time to help pick them up.

'She's fine, thank you.' the old man said glancing quickly through blue eyes before hurrying away.

Frank turned, reeled, then dragged Sonia away.

'Frank?'

'How far back are we?'

'I don't know, it's all hazy I can't remember.'

'They're still trying.'

'To keep us apart?'

'Or together, I've no idea but they're still trying.'

'It's getting shorter.'

'We're down to minutes, maybe less.'

'What do we do?'

'Have to break the pattern, do something different.'

'Like what?'

They fell as one in a crumpled heap.

'QF 978?'

The girl at the counter stared at the monitor, her green eyes barely concealing her irritation.

'Is there a problem?'

'Just the usual, it's over booked.'

A boarding slip shot onto the counter.

'I've had to change your seat, it's not your preferred one but it will do. Seat 42J, boarding in an hour and a half from gate twenty three. Pleasant flight Mr. Garrity.'

Frank walked towards security pensive and worried. I feel like a fight, no, like I'm in a fight, no, no more like I should be ... the greyness evaporated and he remembered, crystal clear he remembered why just before the world collapsed.

Self check-in was down so Frank joined the economy queue. They opened the business class counter to economy passengers, a forlorn effort given the snaking line behind him. He'd made it to the front when there was a gasp and clatter. Turning he saw an old lady trying unsuccessfully to pick up her walking stick. A young boy stooped, picked it up and took the old lady by the arm.

'Thank you.'

'It's no trouble.'

The boy looked straight at Frank with a set of ice blue eyes.

'Go to business class check in sir, help speed it along.'

'Thanks.' Frank said, moving away.

Thankfully business class got preferential treatment, small compensation for the packed two hour flight to Townsville. The counter attendant handed Sonia her boarding pass.

'You're boarding through gate twenty three in approximately ninety minutes, seat IB. Have a pleasant flight.'

Sonia turned, bumped face first into Frank. This time recognition was instant. She grabbed him, dragged him away.

'It's still going, it's getting earlier.'

Frank's face was ashen.

'Listen. I know why it's here, it's this flight.'

'What is?'

'Us, the first time. It's when we met.'

'Then they've won.'

'No they haven't. They know nothing about before. If we don't meet on this flight they'll think it's finished, but we can fool them.'

'How?'

'My number, do you remember my number?'

'Yes, yes I think so.'

'Good. Call me, just call. You never did before tomorrow, just make one call and we can reset it.'

'When?'

'Before the flight, as early as you can. We've got to miss the flight. If either of us gets on it alone it's over. Can you do it?'

'Yes, I think —'

This time the world faded to malevolent black.

The technician squints her emerald green eyes, twists a screwdriver to release a coupling.

Frank Garrity was running late as he stepped outside and checked his mobile. The taxi ranks were empty and his mobile was playing up. He fidgeted, danced from foot to foot. Looks like I'm going to miss the flight.

Sonia stared out the window as the car crawled through the city. Was that a suit wearing steel capped boots? The driver craned her neck back.

'You ok if I don't pick up share rides? Heard some bad stories lately.'

'Fine by me, I'm in a hurry.'

Something tugged at her; she picked up her mobile and dialled. Nothing happened.

'Damn, no coverage.'

'Been like that all day.'

She turned her mobile off, put it in her carry on.

'Guess I could use some peace and quiet.'

'Couldn't we all.'

The driver looked back, emerald green eyes reflected in the mirror.

'Don't worry, I'll get you there on time. Can't have you missing that flight can we?'

END

Darkstar

An archetypal departure lounge, exceedingly cold, bare, antiseptic. Two chairs, two doors, two beings. An appropriate point to leave one life for another. He looked up.

'Even so we must go through the formalities. You are aware of the choice?'

'Yes. Pain, misunderstanding, isolation and struggle for the chance of genius, creativity, shortened life. Stability, peace, community and plenty for the certainty of pleasure, love, longevity. I have considered and chosen.'

'It is one time only, without repentance. A choice once made cannot be undone. Remember it is a place made for pleasure.'

One extended the tablet to the other.

'As I understand it to be. My choice, my decision.'

The other read the tablet carefully, twice.

'Very well. It is a long time since any candidate allowed such discretion.'

'Greater rewards from greater risks.'

'Indeed.'

They stood together, bowed formally.

'I will be here to greet you on your return.'

'Whenever that may be.'

Irish linen and silk. Cool, smooth, enfolding familiar comfort not too close, all they should be in a dying man's bed. For the second time he noticed the small chips in the ceiling, the abandoned spider web in the corner. The mundane now beautiful, soon to be denied him.

He shifted his gaze through the open door to his wife, her back to him as she comforted his guests. All my life as performance art, a stage from birth to death and all in between, outwards costumes and masks, true self only known to two. Has it been worth it? A life of days torn, challenged and shifting, rest elusive.

The tiniest laugh escaped him. Four days in bed, god it's the most time I've ever spent staying still and they all know it's useless. As least it's finished, the twenty-fifth? the twenty-eighth? what number I don't know but it's the coda, the last stroke on the canvas. It is what it is, doubtless they'll judge and criticise and dump on it until I'm dust and then cash in.

He closed his eyes, drained. Her lips now soft on his forehead, her small hand gripping his tight as if her life force could jump the eternal barrier of flesh. This she, I could have had all this always but I was never, driven, unending. What choice did I have? Does it matter, did it ever matter?

Picking the bones of dead planets was to some maudlin, to Nerthus beauty and intrigue. This world yielded enigmas as had others, a small cache of dull silver discs in rotting fibrous sleeves. She archived the last one, the best preserved, noting its monochrome finish and faintly discernible five-pointed design before it too turned to dust. She held the disc above her and watched the red sun's cascading prisms of light.

'And what is it that these are?' her companion came into her mind.

'Artifacts, but as to purpose I am not sure. These dark and light patches, data or perhaps mystic symbolism. Observe.' taking her companion across to their instruments. 'A waveform, similar but not identical, some parts repeated, others unitary. A gap, then more, perhaps a boundary.'

'It looks vaguely familiar', detaching half its consciousness to confer with the central database 'it bears the characteristics of an audible data stream.'

'Audible? I'd never considered. These were supposedly advanced beings.'

'True, but we have also discovered what appear to be written data caches. Perhaps it is the case.'

'Perhaps indeed.' For the entirety of their civilisations' histories the only noise produced by living beings were grunts, squawks and growls of lower animals. Every sentient species was telepathic.

Nerthus thought the changes to the instrument, converting the waveforms to their telepathic equivalents. They both jumped at the skrtiching – scratching in their heads.

'No, perhaps it is not linear output.'

'Yes, so maybe this.' changing the sequence to spiral inward. The skritch-scratch stopped, replaced by a jagged rise and fall. 'And the dead planet speaks.'

Her companion moved off, curiosity sated. Dead communication from a dead planet could not pay its way in a living universe.

About to shut it down she wondered if, being wrong once, she could be wrong twice. She changed the sequence to spiral outward.

Now it was transformed, the undulating tones linking to a rising and falling chant and mesmeric tonal variation. The closest she recalled was the thought fabric of the Ghertnyst mystics but this, this reduced them to an afterthought. Within the undulations images formed, glimpses of a lost world borne in a wave of rise and fall, tone and inflection as the dead planet's long extinct species told of love, revenge, redemption, death.

Her companion drew close, captured.

'What is this thing?'

'I do not know', shaken by the tide of emotion 'but what manner of beings were they?'

END

Diary

21st November. A free day, so we shifted over to Maartax V to the quest finals. Not impressed, the rules suck thanks to the latest Equal Opportunity Act. These contests started on Earth, I think only humans and near humans should be allowed. Dad says the rot had obviously started when the Tharsians were given the vote.

Drago's in deep. He wanted to try out the pleasure centre afterwards, not me, and he tried to hit onto one piece there. She was obviously out for a bit of fun (not that type – I mean, we even look 15 and there are laws) so she tagged him on until she had had enough and decided to let him know she was a morph – by changing into an Orion swamp dweller. Laughed stupid at his face when he found himself draped around that.

Finals are on soon, and I'm gone with physics. Durvald has been helping me study, but it's hopeless, even though she says she has a way round it.

28th November. Brasilia v Sydney finals. I don't know how

Sydney got away with it, they can't pin anything down but I'm sure they are using micro-gravs somewhere. I mean, who can do a slam dunk from the charity stripe and claim they're not? Even Mykyl Jawdyn only did that twice.

Got pulled up for speeding yesterday, not my fault but still grounded. I picked up Durvald and Drago (he's still ripe at me for the other day) to test out the new skid. Air's empty now with the shifters, so I got my license a bit early. It's good to go instead of just getting there. Skipped around the gulf and then checked out the new Iikara tower from the outside. I mean a twenty kilometre tower is worth the trouble yeah? So I'm going vertically up one face at about a quarter thrust and we're nearly there when Drago says 'Ok, so it goes up, but does it go, I mean REALLY go?' What could I do? I couldn't let that pass, not in front of her. So I get to the top of the tower and stand the sucker on its fins, right next to the condo at the top, and man what a view, mean not the scenery but what's inside taking a shower. So I'm looking and she's soaping, Durvald's sitting in the back test driving the sound blaster and Drago's got his eyes wide open, tongue out when she looks at us. The comset seemed to appear by magic so I flipped over on the nose and hit the cans pulling up gees and 50 feet above the waves and then blam, full ballistic and I'm gone, gone and gone! Durvald's got her arms round my neck and not in a nice way, Drago's lunch is on his knees, and I'm laughing like a coot when I feel the first jerk and they had us, locked solid and hauling in. They've impounded my skid for two years, my license will be given back whenever hell freezes over (whatever that is, but it sounds like ages), and I'm grounded for a month, except for study. Dad said 'In my day young man' and all that but he don't know what mum told me so I know where it all comes from now.

1st December. Durvald shifted in today and we did a bit of finals study but I don't feel too confident, especially physics. I mean I was totally shamed out by her when we went through it, she knows all of it and I can't even get past go. I'm so bad the AI suggested I take something easier next year like art or history – yeah, and end up selling hot dogs at basketball games. Durvald still thinks she can find a way around it, so I'm going to her place next week to work on it (fat chance of any good – finals are too close). It'll be the first time I've been to her place though she's round here often enough. Come to think of it, I'm not sure if anyone at all's been to her place.

Got the heavy from Dad again. All he can think about is what I'm going to do when I finish, what job I'll get, and how much rent I'll pay here. I couldn't really care less, and I told him that, and all it did was make him really go off the deep end. So much for honesty.

3rd December. Went to Durvald's today. Man, I thought my parents were one out of the box but hers are really weird. Like they nearly hid themselves from me and then they get real friendly and start giving me stuff to eat and drink, but all of my favourites every one. And without saying anything. Durvald says they're really shy, but they got really friendly real quick and then just left us alone in her room. Major weird.

We did it today, weird as but she's a ninja with this. But with her parents only a couple of rooms away, I was real worried, but she said they wouldn't mind at all and would probably like it anyway. She's a total guru, and she says that practice I will be pretty good myself. But I still don't know how this will help with my finals, but she says trust me so I do. I'll see her again tomorrow at my place.

8th December. What a week! We've been at it constantly, I mean, we even did it in the kitchen while dad was watching the sports! On Friday night we got the big breakthrough, took hours, but we finally got it fully together and I now know that this will be perfect. I even know what I will do once I'm out of this dump.

10th December. Finals were yesterday and what a snap. Dad is still recovering from the results. I pulled an average of 88.5% on everything and 82% on the Physics paper! My grounding's gone and to cap it off he got me the latest model skid to replace the one the police took. Durvald did about the same, but Drago bombed badly and is being sent to a manual training institute for some pre-voc training.

But man, the telepathy Durvald has been teaching me worked so well! All those days and nights doing it, and it pays off. Until the night before all I could do was communicate with Durvald and the rest of them who are also able to do it. But then she managed to get me to do what she thought I could do – read other people's minds. What a blast but noisy or what? All those loose thoughts out there, most of them not really nice (you could get locked up for posting that stuff on the net) and it's nasty trawling through the trash to probe for what you want. But when it was done Durvald's parents reckoned I was the strongest one they'd seen so I felt good about that.

In the exam room the rest was simple. As the papers came up I just tuned in to the teacher who set the paper, pulled out the answers, and typed them straight in. Durvald did the same, and we checked what we had done to make sure I hadn't gotten the wrong info. I nearly blew it by answering everything right (she said that even if they couldn't prove it we'd probably be expelled just on suspicion) so we made a few deliberate errors to keep it cool. When the results were through about an hour later all the teachers were around me saying 'We always knew you could do it' and 'So, you're not a total waste of time after all' and all I could do was stop myself from laughing too hard. Man, what a rush that was – just to see their faces. Straight Ds to straight Bs. Durvald, as usual, got her straight As, but now I know why and how she does it.

Next? Well, I think my future is pretty well taken care of. Durvald's parents told me that they have an organisation of people just like me who stick pretty close together, cause it's only one in ten million who have a hint of this ability, and one in a billion who have what they call a 'gift'. I am one of those. So I'm off to Maartax to work for a big name trans-planetary firm (that will please dad), but I won't really be working, I'll be studying. But this time, it will be for something I am really interested in – running things back here. They say that with the gift it works in reverse too, so that what you lift from other's minds stays in yours, sort of like a huge filer. Come to think of it I can remember the papers and the answers exactly, word for word. So we, I mean us with a gift, have a job to do to keep the whole universe on track, and that's what's going to happen to me. So, I get to be Mr Mainstream after all – not likely. Even though the job's only a cover, I will be getting more money in a month than dad does in a year. So once I get him the VR series of 20th century golf complete with Greg Norman simulation I am going to buy the quickest, wickedest ether cruiser I can lay my hands on. Thought I was a menace on Earth, man, wait till I'm let loose on the Universe.

And Durvald? Well, the deal also came with a string attached. Her parents said that if two people with a gift had kids, the kids get it too. Seems like they've been setting me and her up all along. Actually just me as she was in on it from the start. So if I wanted in I had to have her too. Took me about a nanosecond to agree to that, I'd been wondering how to do the trick on her myself but with her parents setting it up it's just too easy. And she's keen too. But not for at least five years, I've got some work to do. Ah, sex – the final frontier. Beam me up Scotty!

END

Dream a little dream of me

Penny gazed out the window, down the river past the boats and seagulls to the East China Sea. Keelung's Harbour View Hotel wasn't that bad a place to find yourself stranded in for a couple of months she mused. Stan's employer was paying for it and, as far as getting out of Detroit in winter, well nearly anywhere was better. In fact she had looked forward to exploring a different country, except for. Yes, well, except for.

She looked back across the breakfast table to the exception. Small, auburn haired, six years old and, as she kept telling everyone, very bored. With both sets of grandparents otherwise occupied they had no choice but to bring Marie with them. Two days into the trip Stan was already working too hard and Marie was making her feelings plain. She'd changed from her 'everyone's stoopid' song to her 'bored bored' song, consisting of swinging her feet back and forth, wobbling her head from side to side singing 'boring, boring, boorrinnnng'. Thankfully the other guests either didn't speak English, didn't care about a six year old's tantrums, or were too polite to say anything. Penny suspected the latter was the case. She also glumly suspected that in another seven or so weeks it would change.

Marie's song changed to 'bored, bored, gurgle, gurgle' breaking Penny out of her reverie. Marie now held a carafe of orange juice above her head and was pouring it into her mouth. Unfortunately she wasn't a great shot and the orange juice was bouncing off her forehead, onto the table and floor. Penny was about to jump up when a hand reached out lifting the carafe away, another appearing with a towel which was gently draped across Marie's head.

'Miss still has problems with breakfast.' Mr. Leung, the maître d'hôtel, commented between wipes. 'Perhaps juice is not to your taste?'

Penny blushed, embarrassed. 'I'm sorry, she's usually so well behaved', lying barefaced. 'I think the excitement is too much for her.'

'Indeed', looking over his glasses at Penny 'perhaps so. Maybe a less stimulating environment may help.' He looked down at the child who, in a feat of some skill was managing to poke tongues at him from under the sodden towel while still singing. So simple, push gently for one minute and no more trouble. He made the herculean effort not to smother the life out of the child. A dead girl after all would be worse for business than a few day's breakfast disruption.

'Yes, less stimulating. I don't suppose you know of a good adoption agency?' Penny sighed, half joking.

'Unfortunately not, however unnghh!' grunting as Marie's swinging foot caught his kneecap. 'However I do know a very reliable day care centre nearby.'

Penny's eyes lit up. 'Oh that sounds so nice! Marie, did you hear what the nice man said? A place with girls and boys your own age to play with.'

'Boring, boring, BORING!' throwing the towel on the floor, folding her arms petulantly, 'BOOORRRINNGGGG!'

Mr. Leung leant down. 'Miss does not like?'

'Boring!' she retorted.

'Ah, maybe you are right. Boring it may be. After all it is full of our local children', turning his back but raising his voice so Marie could still hear 'so full that they have to play cartoons on the television all day.'

Marie halted in mid rant and burst into tears. 'Wanna go! Wanna go now!'

Penny stood up, grabbed Marie in one hand and hooked Mr. Leung in the other. 'Thank god', she whispered to him 'just get us there now.'

Luckily Mrs. Teh's day-care centre was nearby, had a vacancy, and was not too expensive. Inside half an hour Marie was enrolled for two months. Penny gave Marie a kiss on the cheek, which went unnoticed, Marie being transfixed by the huge plasma screen in front of her, and hurried out to enjoy the day.

The smouldering dark grey sky threw thunder and lightning down to the waterfront. Marie stood alone in the driving rain, steady and expectant. Everyone else was fleeing in panic from the sea to the new city, the national park, any place but here. Marie shook her head to clear away her dripping hair, hitched up her skirt and tightened her grip on her wand. The sea in front of her boiled, bubbled then broke as two huge figures emerged dripping seaweed, mud and fish. Ugly, stinking fire-breathing visions with yellow sunken eyes they towered above Marie, above the boats, above the docks, above the tall buildings.

'Gowrrr!' the one on the left roared, shooting flames above Marie's head.

'Yowrrr!' the one on the right belched, slapping the sea with its tail and sending waves crashing down the river.

Marie pouted, scared, and pointed her wand to the one on the right. 'I don't like you stinky breath', waving her wand at it 'go 'way!'

'Owwrrr?' it whined disappearing in a puff of foul green smoke.

'An you're naughty, naughty, naughty!' yelling at the other one through her first tears, jabbing her wand at it like a knife.

'Euurrr?' it just had time to exclaim as it simply winked out of existence.

Stan felt his daughter dive into bed and wriggle under the sheets. He cracked open one eye. 2:30 am. A night's sleep cut in half. Again. He felt Penny move.

'Bad dream sweetie?'

'Mmhmm.' came the muffled response.

'You're safe now honey, nothing can get you.' which was answered by soft burbling as Marie fell back to sleep.

'Poor thing.' Stan grunted.

'Yeah, scary world to a kid hun.'

'And a damned tiring one for parents.'

'Rahhrr, rahhrr, grrrr, gowrrr.' bellowed Stinky and Naughty – as Marie was calling them – as they pounded onto the waterfront. Although Marie was getting used to seeing them at night they still scared her, made her shake and shiver, made her wake up crying. Each time she'd make them go away but they'd always come back. And now Naughty was learning to talk.

'Bhlaagrrrg!' roared Stinky sending a lightning bolt crashing down, narrowly missing an apartment block.

'Kowerbungaaar! Tundaberdzagooo!' spattered Naughty, hitting a warehouse with a sheet of flame, liquid fire dribbling down its chins.

'No, no, no!' Marie stomped her feet, just missing Mr. Bunny who had hopped quickly aside. She'd wanted someone to help but all she got was this stupid rabbit. At least now he was helpful, giving her the bow and arrows he was carrying.

'Go' losing off the first arrow at Stinky 'away' sending the second one towards Naughty 'now!' The first one hit Stinky in the knee, popping it like a balloon. Naughty saw the second arrow coming and just managed to duck.

'Nyahnyah', poking out three tongues from three mouths 'llewwserr!' and started down the river.

'Takes one to know one!' grabbing Mr. Bunny by the ears and hurling him at the monster's back. Thankfully Mr. Bunny had learned his lesson, sending two hollow points from his .44 Magnum into Naughty's head, dropping it like a sack of potatoes.

'Home, wanna go home now!' Marie bawled as the world around her darkened, lit only by the warehouse fire.

The morning routine of breakfast and drop off to Mrs. Teh's was becoming a little less eventful, Penny thought. Not like the nights that were now regularly interrupted. They had decided to cut out the middle man and let Marie sleep in their bed. She'd end up there anyway, so why not?

A young girl greeted them at the door. 'Where's Mrs. Teh?' Penny asked as Marie brushed past, heading for the TV room.

'She is with brother', pointing to a twisting thread of smoke on the horizon 'his business had fire last night, she is helping with clean-up.'

'Oh, that's unfortunate', Penny mumbled absentmindedly 'the day care is still open?'

'Oh yes, most assuredly.'

Marie giggled, eyes closed as she rose through the clouds. She could feel Mr. Bunny against her back, hear his bandanna snapping in the slipstream. He'd really learned his lesson and was now carrying a very nasty looking gun with spiky bits and a wide, wide barrel. 'Let's see what an RPG does to those numnuts.' he growled through clenched teeth and cigar. A wet forked tongue licked her cheek, making her open her eyes and giggle more.

'I cans sees thems Mariess', the dragon she was riding pointing with a wingtip. Marie called her Twinkles, what else could you call a twenty-meter pink and purple scaled dragon that glitters in the night?

Marie patted Twinkle's head, looking forward. Now she was annoyed. 'How many times I hafta do this?' she whined, making sure she had her pixie dust ready.

'Catss iss they iss', Twinkles snickered 'soss they hass nines lifess.'

Marie scrunched her face up hard, trying to count. She could only get to five, one hand clenching the pixie dust and her toes covered by dragon riding boots.

'Six, six. Six it is, six it is', Mr. Bunny yammered from the back, flipping the safety off his RPG launcher 'three left then all gone, all go away.'

Stinky and Naughty seemed to get bigger, tougher and meaner each time Marie saw them. Waist deep in the sea, they were spinning madly in opposite directions. Huge waves went out from them land-wards, the sky behind them pure black.

'Luckypunk luckypunk dooya dooya luckypunk!' thundered Naughty who had managed to grab and throw a whale at a passing jet.

'Goober goober, uber alles goober.' howled Stinky as it sent its tentacles crashing into the deck of a passing ship.

'I don't like you!' Marie shouted as Twinkles plummeted down, sending a half bag of pixie dust onto the creature.

Stinky smiled as the dust hit. 'Tickles tickles tickle tickle POP!' it went as it exploded like a giant pink skyrocket. Naughty dived below the waves missing the dust, but not before lifting one middle finger up and waving it at Marie.

Marie clenched both fists against her sides as Twinkles climbed back up from the sea. 'Too naughty, too too naughty! Mr. Bunny fire!' with which Mr. Bunny sent a dozen RPGs in a perfect anti-sub spread into the sea below.

Naughty bobbed up to the surface, face up. 'Only hafta win once chicky punk, only once only once.'

Marie sent Twinkles down in a vertical dive, dropping the rest of the pixie dust straight down Naughty's throat. 'I'm the winner winner chicken dinner.' she giggled as Naughty melted into a green, oily slick. She lay down on Twinkle's neck and closed her eyes.

Penny regarded the sky outside the hotel sadly. Her day had started on a sour note, a nice trip to Yangmanshan cancelled by freak storm activity, but thankfully Marie was still a little better behaved. There'd be no call to Marie's therapist today, but also no trip. It was nothing a little retail therapy wouldn't fix.

Mr. Leung stood next to Marie with a tall glass of hot soy milk in his hand. Ever since the orange juice incident he had determined that this little girl would, at least here, taste some proper Taiwanese cuisine. He set the glass in front of her.

'To finish breakfast Miss.' he intoned.

'Go on Marie, drink the nice milk.' Penny encouraged.

Marie lifted the glass, took one sniff, then set it down as far away from her as possible. 'Nope, smells icky.' she commented dryly.

'Now darling, be a good girl and drink it. Don't make Mr. Leung have to make you.'

Marie turned slowly, looking Mr. Leung in the eyes. 'Well', she drawled 'do ya feel lucky punk?'

Curious, thought Penny, where on earth did she pick that up from?

Marie stood on the beach spinning and laughing, her bright red cape billowing as Mr. Bunny and Twinkles sat back and applauded. She loved how slinky her jump suit felt, red, white and blue looked real nice next to Twinkle's pink and purple. But underpants on the outside? Only silly little girls made that mistake. She jumped into the air and started flying south, Twinkles struggling to keep up as she carried Mr. Bunny, the RPG launcher, .44 Magnum, spare ammo, pixie dust, bow, arrows, katana, shuriken and wand on her back.

'Scoobie doobie scoobie doobie.' giggled Marie, rolling to the right.

'Yowsserss, wowsserss, trousserss.' laughed Twinkles, rolling to the left.

'Arg erk org urrrkgh!' screamed Mr. Bunny trying to hang on with one foot, having forgotten to buckle in.

'I seess themss, I seess themss', Twinkles pointed 'theyss iss on landss, on landss.'

'Yukky yuk yuk!!' Marie could see them near some buildings. Stinky was crouching down, going to the toilet and picking up clawfulls of stinking hot pooh and flinging it on the buildings, the trees, the beach.

'Shitty shitty bang bang! Paskaa minusta paska sinulle!' it bellowed showing off its new-found language skills. It flung another handful out, wiped its hand across its face and repeated the dose.

'You Stinky potty mouth, it's not nice! Summones gonna hafta clean that up. Only little babies play with their poopies.' Marie sent a blast from her gamma-ray vision into it, splitting it in half before it flashed away in violet flame.

Naughty was weeing a flaming purple stream across the whole area, anything it touched bursting into flame. It looked at the approaching trio. 'Yo, bitches! The fuck you want?' it roared, too quick for Twinkles who tried to cover Marie's ears. 'Like just once I gotta whoop your ass or you no show an' I'm in wid my posse!' it howled, sending a fresh stream skywards.

'Gonna do it, gonna do it', resuming spraying operations 'then it's yippee kayay mother fuckers you bet!' it bellowed just as a shower of pixie dust, arrows, RPGs and gamma-rays hit. Naughty glowed blue-white, shimmered, shrunk to a tiny black dot and with a 'pfftttt' disappeared.

Stan lowered the mobile phone with a sigh. Ok, first day free with the family up the spout. He looked across the table.

'Looks like I'll have to go in today after all.'

'Oh, you're kidding.' Penny protested, trying to sound heartbroken. She'd actually been enjoying a bit of together time apart. 'What's up?'

'Algal bloom', Stan murmured 'everywhere through the tanks, ponds, reservoir, everywhere.'

'That's a shame.' Penny mumbled, updating her fakebook status.

'Ummhumm.' Stan mumbled back, trying to finish off a scalding hot mug of coffee as fast as he could.

'Daddy', piped Marie 'what's a muvva fukka?'

Shocked, Stan sent a mouthful of hot coffee across the table.

Shocked, Mr. Leung doubled over in pain as the boiling stream impacted his crotch.

Penny misspelt shopping, using only one 'p'.

An hour later Penny and Stan sat waiting while Dr. Mah chatted with Marie in her office. Overseas or not they had called Marie's regular therapist in Detroit, again, who had referred them to Dr. Mah. Although Penny thought Marie's behaviour a continuation of what had been going on at home, Stan wasn't so sure.

Dr. Mah sent Marie out and called them in. She was all business, no idle chit chat, and at $350 an hour she needed to be.

'As Marie's treating therapist in Detroit has correctly said, your daughter has a very active imagination. In particular she has an ability to combine elements of the real world and ideate them into cognitively coherent, self-actualising, self-directed narratives.'

'Huh?' queried Penny.

Dr. Mah took off her glasses with a slight shake of her head. 'She gets disconnected bits from the real world and turns them into dreams she controls.'

'Oh, I see.'

'And I notice you have kept her at', sounding distasteful 'Mrs. Teh's day-care?'

'Yes, she seems nice —'

'She has a reputation for using television instead of trained staff. I think that would be where your daughter is picking up her colourful language.'

Dr. Mah bent down and picked a luridly coloured comic from her lower drawer, placing it cover up on her desk. On the front, emblazoned with bold Japanese print, were two huge monsters laying waste to a city.

'As to the prime protagonists in her nightmares, well, these are they. Their names are Yuch Ragman and Centai Gunyah. Marie calls them 'Stinky' and 'Naughty'. A very popular series here, on the mainland, and in Japan. I've no doubt she has seen it on television. Interestingly', with which she gave both parents a withering stare 'these characters may resonate particularly well with Marie. Before nuclear accidents transformed them both were neglected children of self-obsessed parents.'

'In any case', Dr. Mah continued, breaking the pregnant pause 'Marie says that these … monsters … will soon go away, but how soon she doesn't know. So this leaves open three possible courses of action.'

'Yes, which are?'

'First, we do nothing and let it simply run its course. Being a result of her overactive imagination it will come to an end when she is no longer exposed to unfamiliar external stimuli, probably by the time —'

'We get back to Detroit?' Stan queried. 'No thanks, that could be months away and I need my rest, now.'

'So that opens up the second possibility. I could take Marie as a patient here, under her usual therapist's guidance of course. If I see her twice a week I could help her cope, maybe even alleviate —'

Penny's head shot up. 'Ah no, I'm not sure we can afford that', giving Stan the icy shut your mouth now stare before he could object 'money's a bit tight until we get back home.'

Dr. Mah sighed and reached for her prescription pad. 'The final option is the pharmaceutical route, strictly short term, but it will stop the dreams.' She hastily scrawled out the prescription. 'It's also cheap and works immediately. One in a glass of juice before bed. Just don't tell her, she will only try not to take it.'

As the door closed behind them Dr. Mah gave another shake of her head and leant back. Useless parents.

For the fourth morning in a row Stan and Penny roused themselves from deep, uninterrupted sleep. They were still wondering if the quiet, slightly shy child who appeared between dinner and breakfast really was the hellion that was with them during daylight hours. Regardless, they had already secured a supply of Dr. Mah's wonder pills back home, FDA ruling or not.

They made their way downstairs to an unusually quiet breakfast bar. The only sound was the seemingly usual street noise of heavy traffic, human and automotive. Stan looked around as he sat. Everything seemed normal, buffet laid out, tables set, everything in place except that only the three of them were there. He, Penny opposite him, and Marie standing quietly by the windows.

'Does it seem a little quiet to you?' Stan asked no one in particular. Penny lifted her head from her mobile's screen.

'Maybe everyone's at work or we're just early.' she commented absentmindedly.

'Hmm, I don't know, usually Mr. Leung's hovering about but —'

The object of their discussion chose that moment to burst out of the kitchen doors. Instead of his usual immaculate attire he looked a rumpled mess, as if he'd forgotten to put clean clothes on after a hard night out. Seeing the three of them stopped him dead in his tracks.

'What you still do here?!?' he cried, letting his clipped British accent drop. 'Why you here?!'

'Breakfast of course.' Penny retorted.

'No, no, must go, leave now', he chattered pulling Stan's chair out from under him 'must leave immediate, now!'

'What do you mean?' Stan stood and grabbed Marie, wrenching her away from the window. Mr. Leung's look of desperation and fear had animated him. 'What is it?'

'No time, must go now, must go', as he hauled Penny up, protesting, propelling her towards the stairs 'go, go, disaster, run!'

Stan grabbed Penny's other arm in his free hand and helped drag her down the stairs. He'd glanced out the window to the street below, seeing the throng of people fleeing in panic along the streets, away from the waterfront. Across the city the wailing rise and fall of sirens started. Damn he thought, damn damn damn.

'Tsunami! It's a tsunami! Hurry!'

They emerged from the hotel, Mr. Leung clutching Penny and Stan around the waist. They fought their way down the steps and through a seething mass of people and vehicles towards a small van in the middle of the road. Bloodied and bruised they barged in on top of the other occupants, slamming the door behind them. The van skidded away, knocking people out of its way as they fled.

'Pen, you ok? Penny! Penny! Ok?!?' Stan cried, shaking her.

'Yes, yes, I'm fine, just bruises. How's Marie?'

'Marie?' Stan blanched. 'Marie! Marie!!' frantically looking around, not seeing her in the crowded van. 'Marie!!!' face plastered against the back window as the van ploughed on. The sea of people had closed in, his daughter was gone, and there was no way back. 'Fuck!' Stan punched the back door 'Fuck! Marie!' he wailed.

Even if Stan didn't know what was going on Marie did. When they got out of the hotel his hand had slipped nearly straight away, just like she'd hoped. It's easy not to notice a six year old girl, easier when a city is in full panic. Marie had turned away towards the river and, ducking and dodging between legs and doorways, made her way to the deserted foreshore.

The smouldering dark grey sky started to thunder and lightning. Marie stood alone, steady and expectant as the driving rain hit the waterfront. She knew that everyone else was fleeing in panic from the sea to the new city, the national park, anywhere but here. Marie shook her head to clear away her dripping hair, hitched up her skirt and bunched her hands into fists. Far away the sea boiled and bubbled. Two enormous figures waded towards her, ugly stinking fire-breathing visions with yellow sunken eyes, towering into the sky higher than the highest buildings. Behind them from horizon to horizon a line of smaller, ugly forms marched forwards. Looks like they've bought their friends Marie thought.

A furry nudge on her left hip and Mr. Bunny was there, loaded for bear. He gave her a quick wink. 'Hey chickee, all yours', he crooned, handing her the katana 'just like old times.'

A blast of hot air hit her from the right. She looked up straight into the eyes of Twinkles, bright and bouncy. 'Ridingss or flyingss girlsfriendss?' she chortled.

They shot into the air as one. 'Okie dokey', Marie sung 'let's go play with the numnuts!'

END

Echoes

The man at immigration inspects my documents along with my bags and my very person in minute detail. Although disconcerting it is expected. I am their first.

'It all seems in order. Welcome to Earth.'

'Thank you.'

'I saw the newscasts. Terrible tragedy.'

'It's regrettable dying far from home and kin.'

'That's what I meant.'

My driver whisks me from the spaceport. It gives them a chance to keep an eye on me without being too obvious. Not that I'm a threat. They're all curious, cursed with overactive imaginations, a boundless entertainment industry, and insatiable emotional appetites. I don't want to be here, thankfully I only have to put up with it for a day or two. I just have to remember not to touch anyone.

Sweaty and gap toothed the driver stares at me through the

partition.

'I haven't seen your type before.'

'We don't travel much.'

'Too nice at home eh? Well we've got some stuff too, big things like Pyramids and even some lions. You should go see.'

'Maybe next time.'

'I saw it you know. Nasty, going all that way then that.'

Everyone probably saw the recordings. It was no use, they'd all want to tell me, so I might as well get used to it.

'Yes.'

'How many died, I mean of your lot?'

'Three hundred.'

'That any of ours survived was a miracle, pure miracle.'

'You're a tough species.'

'Couldn't understand it.'

'What?'

'How only two made it. To go through it all, survive the crash then die later, that's rough.'

How could I tell her, make any of them understand? We wanted to help but there had to be precautions. I'd been first there dragging all of them out bare handed then those three broken ones more dead than alive. I was paying the price for my recklessness.

'We mourned yours as we mourned our own.'

'Tragic loss for the families, their friends.'

'Yes, our world's very tight knit, very close.'

'That too.'

They'd been told I was coming to make sure they were prepared. It was to be just me and the person behind each door yet the streets were still closed off. We pull up in front of a small blue-grey box, flaking paint, tall thin plants obscuring the ground.

'How long will you be?'

'Depends. Five seconds, five hours. Just wait.'

The porch steps creak under me, the doorbell pressed twice to work. He is older than I recall, hair thinner and greyed, stoop shouldered. Behind him the grandfather clock stands, that one ostentatious anachronism he couldn't shake.

'Adam Wright?'

'Yes.'

'I am —'

'I know.'

He opens the screen door, offers me his hand. I remove my glove, grasp his firmly just as the clock starts to strike five.

— Dad!

— Indrani? Indrani my poor, poor baby girl.

— Don't go all soft on me now.

— You're back, back home.

— No, you know why I'm here, you know what they told you.

— Why did you have to go? You should have stayed here where it's safe.

— It's all I ever wanted. I was no idiot, I knew what it might cost. I was happy dad, totally in love with what I did. I wouldn't change a thing even now, and you made it happen.

— Me?

— All those years after mum died you were alone, you took

care of me, encouraged me, made me think I could own the stars. You put me where I could follow my dreams, all the while putting yourself last. I've never said thank you properly. It's why I'm here, to say thank you, thank you for everything.

— You don't have to, I'm your father. What else could I have done?

— You could have done anything at all. All my life I wanted to thank you but somehow I never managed, never found the time or the words. Now I have to.

— Have to?

— It was the only regret I had, the only thing I'd left undone. It was all I was thinking of when he pulled me clear, when I died. It's torturing him having me here, having it unsaid. They're not built for it we're … we're too intense.

— What happens now when you, I mean he leaves? Do you die again?

—I can't, you die once then that's it. But this echo has to leave him or he'll be in pain his whole life. I'm luckier than most, I've had the chance to put things right. He can be released, I can fade away.

— And me?

— You can't change the past.

— Will it hurt?

— No. Just let go and that's it. On. Off. Simple.

— I love you Indrani.

— I know dad, I always knew. And I love you.

He releases my hand as the clock finishes striking five, his face quivers as the emotion works its way through him. My headache and chest pains reduce. She's gone, faded and left. He extends his hand again then pulls it away.

'I'm sorry, I forgot. I'm glad you made the effort.'

'I had no choice, your daughter was insistent.'

'She's gone?'

'Yes.'

'And you're better?'

'Somewhat, I have more to see.'

'I figured you might. I'm sorry for your pain, those people of yours who died.'

When I left the next one it was too late to see the last, too early for my rituals. I was feeling better but the last weighed heavily upon me. I was hungry, thirsty and tired.

The driver pulls up next to a garish yellow and red neon sign.

'This will do, I can get them to give us the food in the car instead if you want.'

Only one or two people are inside. I glance to the left, the security tail seem keen to rest.

'They have food that is not from an animal?'

She pulls out a piece of paper.

'These ones, anything with the word 'vegan'. You squeamish?'

'No, let's just say I get a ... bad vibe from it.'

I go in, squeeze into a booth in the far corner and order. My food arrives. Nutritious perhaps, appealing not.

I'm trying to wipe off a white liquid that had oozed onto my gloves when I become aware of an adult male sitting opposite me staring nervously, intimidated by something behind me. I look around. There is nothing, just myself.

'You're one of them?'

'One of what?'

'An amortal.'

They'd called us that when we met. A simplistic misleading meme that had been no end of trouble.

'Yes, but I'm not amortal. It's the wrong word.'

'It doesn't matter, a rose by any other name. You all look alike don't you?'

'No, it's just your differences are so dramatic.'

'It's true isn't it, the rumours?'

'What is?'

'You talk to the dead.'

'It is and it isn't, depends what you mean.'

'No one really dies do they, you take on their memory, their spirit when they go.'

'Among our own people yes, you could say that. But you do too, your memories, it's just ... different.'

'But that's why you're here. Bringing those three back to their families, making them live again.'

'No, that's not quite —'

He shoves a picture at me, his purple splotched hand shakes. A woman and two young children smile out at me through creases and stains.

'My family, they were all I had. You got a family?'

'Offspring? Yes, and parents.'

'Then you understand. I killed them twenty years ago.'

'You killed them?'

'I was driving home. I'd been drinking and picked them up. There was an accident. I lived, they died.'

'I'm sorry.'

'I lost it all when I lost them. Not an hour passes I don't think of them.'

'It sounds like a horrible life, is there —'

'Bring them back.'

'What?'

'Bring them back now, like you did the others.'

'I can't.'

'Don't lie! I know you can, so do it.'

'You don't understand, no one comes back, it's just echoes. Even if I wanted to I couldn't, I wasn't there when they died.'

His face turns red, one arm rises holding a knife.

'It's not fair bringing back the others and not mine. You're like the rest of them, disrespecting and discriminating me! So help me if you don't bring them back right now I'll …'

The knife clatters to the floor as he slumps to the table. The uniforms take him away; my driver stares at me.

'I'm sorry, my fault. Didn't pick him soon enough.'

'No real harm done.'

'A lot of people think that way.'

'And you?'

She opens the car door.

'Hardly. Live once, die once, all over. Who'd want to come back to this shit hole?'

They'd increased the guard overnight, I step from my room to an escort of a dozen men. So much for discretion.

'They heard what happened, don't want a repeat.'

'Guess you'll be glad to get rid of me.'

'No, I've had worse. The Pope, now that's another thing. He thinks you're the antichrist.'

'What's a pope?'

'Erin Carlson?'

'Yes, I've been expecting you. Come in.'

She ushers me into a neat, sparsely furnished space. She sits out of arm's reach.

'Thank you for seeing me.'

'It's no trouble. I have a few questions.'

'If it will help.'

'It will. Why?'

'Why what?'

'Why you.'

'Pure chance. When the ship malfunctioned the escape pod crashed into my house. No other reason.'

'No, that's not what I meant. Why'd they give their echoes to you?'

'They didn't actually give them. It was an accident.'

'How?'

'I didn't think, I just reacted. I didn't know who crashed so I didn't take any precautions, just went straight in and pulled the five of them out before it burnt up. Everyone else just stood around and by the time I realised it was too late.'

'And you had all five of them in you?'

'Initially. The two who survived I was able to give theirs back, but the other three were impossible.'

'Why?'

'If the echo comes across with unfinished business it stays with the host and drives them until it's finished, then it fades and releases. All three of them died with unfinished business.'

'But it's never really gone is it?'

'Where'd you hear that?'

'Brendan. He spent years with your people studying, thinking, watching.'

'It's true. Once the echo's satisfied it leaves but the … it's hard to find the words … the essence or flavour still remains. Nothing specific, just impressions, generalities, but then again more.'

'Dead but truly never forgotten?'

'Yes, perhaps that will do.'

'Brendan must be giving you trouble.'

'Yes, his emotional state is far above even your norms.'

'Your people, they quarantined you for this?'

'They had no choice. We can't risk contamination.'

'You want to grip my hand, be done with him?'

I start to remove my gloves.

'Of course.'

'I don't. I want the other way, the way of your people.'

'No, that's not permissible.'

'It's either that or Brendan stays with you until you die.'

There is no choice. I can't continue like this.

'Very well. But don't watch me change, the process is confronting. I'll … Brendan will let you know when I've changed.'

She closes her eyes and I let go. It hurt enough morphing to one of my own, but changing into this creature is an absurd and painful struggle. Our masses aren't even close, I have to lose a few inches height to compensate. She'll never know.

Of course the stupid bitch won't, I only married her so I'd have a decent body on tap if I couldn't get lucky. What she had in looks she lost in brains.

'Erin. I'm here.'

She opens her eyes.

'Brendan. You look good dead, it suits you.'

'What do you want?'

'Me? You're the echo.'

'Oh yeah, that. Just died thinking what a useless bitch you were, how you'd ruined my life, and how much I'd miss telling you that.'

'That all?'

'Isn't it enough? You've hardly got room in your head for your name never mind anything else. I'm surprised you remembered anything I said.'

'Depends if I wanted to.'

'You're like a faulty computer, can't remember anything unless I punch it in a few times.'

'You enjoyed that didn't you?'

'Are you kidding? Come home, bang you senseless, punch the shit out of you then go and do your little sister. It was the best.'

'You'll pay for that.'

'How, you forgotten I'm dead? Shame, I was going to get rid of you when I got back, it's not even funny anymore.'

Erin reaches behind her, lifts the Taser and fires. Brendan collapses to the floor; Erin sends two more shots into him for good measure. Methodically she removes the darts, binds his wrists and ankles, tapes over his mouth and waits until he comes around.

'Brendan?'

He nods, face up.

She fires the Taser point blank into his groin.

Accompanied by muffled screaming she goes to the kitchen, returns with a cup of coffee and the knife block.

'Brendan?'

He nods, this time from the foetal position.

She sits, places her feet on his face.

'That was just for fun, help me calm down. I can't tell you how excited I was when I heard you were coming back. I mean, I was so glad you died but it was too clean and neat if you know what I mean.'

She moves her feet slightly, drives a stiletto into his nostril. Funny how such a small thing could control him, she thinks, but then again he'd always been controlled by small things.

'You never noticed me change. While you were away I got help, got my respect and strength back. I was heartbroken when I heard you died, the thought of dragging you through court was delicious but even that you tried to take from me.'

A small twist brings his face towards her. She resists the temptation to take out an eye with the other heel, contenting herself with scouring his forehead, seeing exactly at which point blood flows or bone shows.

'Charles is such a thorough solicitor. Do you know your host isn't legally a person on earth? Or that we don't have an extradition treaty with them? No? Pity.'

She leans in, lets the tiniest drop of spittle fall.

'As far as this world's concerned you're dead, and I can't get charged for killing a dead person now can I? But we both know as long as he lives you live whether you're wearing his body or not.'

Brendan twists slightly, nearly tears his nose open. Erin pulls on a pair of elbow length rubber gloves.

'No, I'm afraid that's no use. You'll find the Taser's charge will stop you shifting back for a couple of days. That should be more than long enough.'

She tales the rod from the block and slowly starts to sharpen the paring knife.

'You're right of course, I never was much of a cook. My knife work was never up to scratch. We've got all day, so much to catch up on, so many memories to relive.'

END

Finding them

The café rested between early morning workers and the lunch time blitz of tired shoppers. It was my time, those few hours where a quiet table could be had to linger over a cup or two, watch the world float by without the waitresses shuffling me along for better paying customers. The barista was less rushed, more attentive, able to be cajoled with smile or kindly word into a better, richer brew, although the constant change in faces meant new connections, new people, new cajoling. These lazy pleasant mornings had become cultivated habit, and in particular I looked forward to Tuesdays. Tuesday was Keith mail day.

Keith and I had been friends for more years than I cared to remember, from sharing a flat at uni through children and relationships to our now approaching later years, only distance separating us. I had always thought of him as the brother I never had. A strange brother it is true, singular with many arcane and peculiar habits. Although no luddite he considered email the lowest form of communication, a convenient substitute for real thought and what he termed 'the beauty and prose of the English language'. It was not a position he had come to recently, but rather one bound to him when we first met.

'Josh', he once announced many years ago as I sat hunched over keyboard 'just when will you realise how impersonal and dehumanising email is?'

I tapped send then looked up.

'Huh? What are you on about?'

'Anyone can hammer out a note on a keyboard. If you really do value someone you'd make the effort to write, to spend the time with ink and paper like me.'

'You?'

'Yes, like me', waving his fountain pen 'like I do to people I really value. If you get email from me it means I don't really care, you're just one of the uneducated masses.'

True to his word, year in year out he had written to me regularly, pen and paper, paper in post, and I had responded in kind. I had learned that even if he received an email he would respond in writing if he deigned the sender worthy. If the reply was in an email well, the recipient hardly figured in Keith's universe.

So every second Tuesday I would receive Keith's latest letter, a few sheets of tight but immaculate scrawl on his favourite bond, and sitting with my coffee read, reminisce and reply. One small ritual in a life built on small rituals, as are all lives. Keith had begun to wax lyrical in his latest letters, emptying the contents of his mind on paper, so this Tuesday the slightly bulged envelope was no surprise. Once he had disposed with the usual pleasantries of family, kith and kin he continued.

It has taken longer than I thought. It all started out as a bit of a mind game, something safely Quixotic only to have it translate to possible then probable then in some strange trick of osmosis or transmutation here it is, solid in front of me. I've been working sporadically on this particular problem for well-nigh 30 years now and it's only recently that the final pieces have fallen into place. They have played their game well but they don't understand how our minds work, or what true, soul consuming obsession is. That is of course not their fault, in fact they could even be working on it now and I wouldn't know.

The seeds were planted when I was very young, fuelled by that old standby, television. Dad's pass time was 1950s/60s science fiction and at that age I didn't do too much reading, but the regular and sustained diet of cable TV did exactly what cable TV is designed to do, get me hooked. From a bedroom decorated with plastic rockets, Godzilla posters and Star Wars sheets through to calling my dog Adama I was hugely and irrevocably addicted, even to the point where when I should have been chasing skirt I was chasing the latest resin War of the Worlds model kits.

It was a science class and Drake's equation that set me off. Here was a way to work out the probability they were out there my teenage brain thought, and I willingly whiled away my time running through numbers and assumptions of ever increasing complexity, concluding that the exact odds were anyone's guess or, more correctly, anyone's assumption. Too much slack in the variables, too much room in the assumptions and too much space time in space time I thought. So, unable to assign a number to it all I decided to do the next best thing, find them. And there you have it, me knowing and accepting it was impossible but then blithely setting out to do it. Just like Winston's double-think without Victory Gin. Or room 101.

He moved on to other things leaving me hanging yet again in midair in his typical, irritating habit of going part way then halting, opening the door a crack but refusing to fling it open in one movement.

Which left me both intrigued and in suspense over the following fortnight, all of which was made the worse by yet another change in barista. Again the gentle nudges to be given about my table, my coffee, and the usual interminable questions about me and my life. Sadly, I wondered how any of them managed to finish barista school. I stood up and took my coffee back.

'Excuse me Miss, the coffee's not right. I ordered an espresso not a long black, and the coffee is too weak.'

She regarded me curiously, as if criticism of any kind was out of her experience. It was gone in a flash, replaced by a courteous, if off the shelf, smile.

'I'm sorry, I'm just getting used to the machine. I'll make you a fresh one, won't be long.'

She had a strange accent. I leant across, stared at her badge.

'Thank you Carmelitta. Where are you from?'

Her smile softened, head tilting to one side.

'It's actually Carmella', tapping the badge then moving to the coffee machine 'they've spelt it wrong. I'm from Belgium, only been here a month. I'm studying and doing this to pay the bills.'

I smiled back.

'Belgium. You must like your beers then?'

She kept facing away, watching the coffee filter through.

'Beers? Can't say I've ever met any of them.'

It was a curious thing I mused as I settled back with my replacement coffee. A Belgian uninterested in beer, but if the coffee improved what did I care? And after a week or so Carmella and her coffees settled down and my routine re-established itself.

Again, another Tuesday, another letter from Keith.

So why would they be here? I settled on three possibilities, conquest, trade or curiosity. All three seem reasonable, the only question was which one? Conquest was simple, and on the assumption that if you could cross a few million light years you could easily wipe out a lesser civilisation, I figured we would not stand a chance. A bit like the Incas vs the Spanish. And not sitting in a pile of radioactive dust I guessed it had not happened, so I dismissed it from my mind.

Trade was harder, having more potential than the first. There are myriad different ways to trade and it's possible to do it and not be seen. It was a real possibility and for a while I could not see past it if – and I had no reason to think otherwise – trade was a universal activity. Even if it was done in collusion with government, or hidden from public view, why not? Although possible I did think it unlikely as we probably did not have anything to trade. What could we have that they would need, and even as the question was asked I knew it was flawed. I couldn't know what they would need, after all value is a matter of perspective, so trade remained an open option.

Although this sounded plausible for a while, there was a problem – scale. They are not likely to flip across multiple light years for a single bag of rocks, or for even one cargo load. To make sense of the time and distance – not to mention the considerable capital cost, I mean think of it, it's not a Dodge Ram that's being hauled across space – you would need to think in hundreds or thousands of shipments. You couldn't keep that under wraps, worse yet if they just happened to want iron ore or coal or some other bulk commodity. So not having noticed a stream of large, silver metallic cigars loading up on bananas or petrol, trade went the way of conquest.

I was left with curiosity. Were they curious? How would I know? But it was the last option, the residual left to me. If I had a choice between a war, greed, or curiosity driven stellar neighbourhood I'd go curious each time.

The rest of the letter contained the usual family updates. I'd noticed that his writing was more compressed, less structured, not as neat as usual. Overwork or possibly excitement had perhaps got the better of him.

Tuesday week I came back to the café, Keith's latest letter in hand. A bit thin this time, holding it in one and pulling my chair out with the other, maybe he's busier than usual. I had hardly sat down when a smiling Carmella appeared with my espresso.

'Hello Josh, how are you this morning?'

It had taken me a month but she was working out fine, only a few rough edges left.

'I'm fine thank you. Nice day outside.'

'Yes, warm and dry.' She pointed to the letter. 'From your friend again? A greeting card from holidays?'

I knew she wasn't being rude but was simply curious.

'No, not a card, a letter.'

'Letter? What is that?'

For a young, smart, connected person – as this generation liked to market itself – she had some gaping holes in her general knowledge.

'Seriously?'

Even from her this seemed a bit much. Could she honestly not know what a letter was? How long had email been around, fifty, sixty odd years? Ok, maybe it's possible, maybe she's never seen a letter, never written one. I sighed.

'A letter, Carmella, is a message from one person to another, put on paper, then physically delivered to that person. Like a hard copy of an email.'

'Sounds very slow, something maybe only old people do?'

Her manners were the next focus of my training. But not now, I needed my coffee.

'Perhaps. Maybe yes. I'm not totally sure. Thank you.' bowing my head dismissively.

I took a quick sip and opened the envelope. This time there

were barely two hurriedly scrawled pages jammed carelessly inside.

Josh

You know this all started as a mind game playing with assumptions and probabilities, but it hasn't finished that way.

It's taken until yesterday but I have the answer. I tried to imagine myself as them, curious and different. What would I do? With advanced technology I could sit and watch, monitor, learn, but it's like learning about home from what's on CBS or Facebook, a distorted picture. They'd have to be here, on the ground, in the thick of it. If they are totally unlike us, or can't make themselves look like us, then it's not possible. They might rely on spies, maybe advanced robots, whatever, but in that case they would not be here.

But what if they can? What if they appear human, or close enough not to be noticed? Would they come down for a look, to observe, to study us? Of course! After crossing those stupendous distances why stumble at the last hurdle? So given this, given their desire and knowing nearly nothing of the society they are observing and none of the nuance and subtlety of human interaction, how could they live amongst us anonymously?

They would need to appear normal, maybe middle class, maybe migrants to cover their awkwardness. Just staying at home or in one place would never do, they would be itinerant or at least highly mobile. They must work to get broader contact with more people, more variety, more types, different attitudes. Jobs where they get to listen or ask, jobs where no one asks them too much, pries, or they have to study. Not too menial so they can pursue their main goal; not too isolated so they have people around; not too deep or meaningful so they can't be discovered, the human shell they adopt being shown hollow. Something where coming and going is normal, rapid turnover, but is in the heart of society. Invisible perhaps, maybe part of the wallpaper, able to disappear unnoticed and traceless if suspected.

141

I know where they are. And who they are. And this afternoon my friend I will find out. I will find them.

The letter was postmarked Monday morning. I laughed, imagining Keith accosting some poor builders-labourer or cleaning lady with accusations of nefarious extra-terrestrial activity. Even on his high horse Keith was not threatening, merely amusing in a Daffy Duck-ish manner. Still chuckling an hour later I headed for the door, leaving my coins on the table. Carmella gave me a quizzical, questioning look then silently turned away.

Wednesday morning was my work morning. Laptop in hand I sat down at my usual table, the café unusually quiet. I was the only customer for which I was thankful.

'Buenos dias señor. ¿Que te gustaria?'

'Café. Espresso y agua por favour.'

I looked up into a young, tanned face.

'You're new here?'

'Yes. I am Heraldo. Forgive my using Spanish, I am only one week in your country.'

'You are from', and I hesitated 'Mexico?'

'Oh no', laughing 'Madrid.'

'Ah, the coffee should be excellent then.' Perhaps, depending on how much training I had to give him. 'Tell me, Carmella, is it her day off?'

'I do not know this person but I am only here now so perhaps later?' He started away from the table, pausing briefly. 'Keith is no writing you today, yes?'

'No', I replied absent mindedly 'it's not Tuesday.' Something inside my head clicked but was cut off by a chime from my laptop. An email from Adele, Keith's partner.

Hi Josh

If Keith gets in contact let me know asap. I can't raise his mobile, he usually lets me know but he's been preoccupied lately.

He's been gone since Monday lunchtime, had an appointment I think at the Café Royale downtown.

Adele

I sat frozen. He must have finished the letter to me, gone out and posted it before going to the café … to find them.

I felt chill, coldness growing from the base of my spine. My laptop died, and in front of me the café's storm shutters started to close. I turned. Walking slowly, deliberately towards me, faces fixed and unsmiling, were the beings I knew as Heraldo and Carmella.

I closed my eyes, waiting. I too had found them.

END

Giant

The taxi disgorged the five of us and, after pressing a few bills into the driver's hands, we walked quickly through the archway into the maze of alleys and streets inside the old city. Technically the whole area was off limits but no-one really enforced that rule for the last one earthside. Chances were for a lot of the guys it was the last one, period. Most usually went the whole hog, not infrequently being poured back to base from inside a rust lined cell courtesy of the city's finest, and it seemed that everyone took the whole ritual in stride, a thing to be humoured, tolerated.

This was our last time, a few hours of freedom, and I knew that the other four were going to make the most of it. The old man of the group at thirty one I was also ten centimetres shorter and ten to fifteen wider across the shoulders which, at times, has not been too slight a disadvantage. The oldest of them was twenty two, in the camp the nearest to me being twenty five, so perhaps it was unusual I'd been adopted by these four. Or maybe not.

Tonight I was their chaperone, their guardian angel, keeping their money, my head and sobriety while they continued on their way. I looked out of place with my four companions as we strode down the boulevard, lolitas and sirens calling from open doorways, tousled locks and bouncing tattoos. They stood out in scarlet trimmed indigo blue uniforms, caps lofted at a rakish angle, boots mirroring the street lights. I blended into the background in my civvies and scuffed shoes, virtually hidden in their midst. Coming to the central plaza we stopped and I handed them their first tranche of the night's money, enough for their first two hours, and we split up noting to meet again at the plaza. Although hungry they preferred their first meal to be taken horizontally which for me was not an option, so I headed for a small brasserie across the way for some proper nourishment.

First impressions are seldom wrong, and I felt at home once I walked in the door and nearly choked on the acrid cigarette smoke hanging below the ceiling. Finding an unoccupied stool against the far end of the bar I laid my money down and signalled for a beer, the barmaid wallowing over and placing a nearly clean glass in front of me. I pushed a bill towards her. She went to pick it up but saw my signet ring.

'Going or back?'

'Going. Four a.m. tomorrow.'

She smiled, front teeth tarred and stained, and pushed my money back to me with a huge paw. 'Won't need that. Lost them' with which she jerked a thumb at a framed photo of two fresh faced kids hanging on the back wall 'two years ago today on Five. Just remember.'

I raised my glass in the picture's direction. 'Jets.'

She wiped a small tear from her eye with a corner of her stained apron. 'Yeah, Jets.'

I wouldn't say I was depressed. I don't get the dumps, I've had too much shit in my life to worry like that, but I was in what I refer to as my 'Sunday afternoon in the rain before Monday at work' mood – a flatness that is neither here nor there. The brasserie and I were a type then, perfectly in step with each other.

A sirloin and a beer steadied my mood a little bit, and I pulled out my photo of Cyn and propped it up against the empty glass which, to my lessening surprise, was filled again within minutes. Married four years, first child two months away, this small furlough was not long enough to get me across to Shepparton no matter how I went about it.

When I had called to let her know I was off she was out at her painting class. I must have looked pathetic on the answering machine, even the house I'd programmed with the Danny DeVito optional personality appeared genuinely upset with the news. The cat also promised to be on its best behaviour while I was away. I've never really trusted cats, and it was on our bed preening itself when it said so, so I'm not sure. Anyway, it's Cyn's problem now not mine.

The place was slowly starting to fill and I was wondering if I should move on when someone tapped me on the shoulder. I turned to see a shrunken old man leaning on a cane, pointing with his free hand to the stool next to me. 'Excuse me, is this seat taken?'

I smiled. 'No', generous as always with what's not mine 'feel free. Can I buy you a drink?' especially as they were on the house.

'No, thank you', with which two beers appeared as if by magic in front of us 'but I would like to offer you one.'

I thanked him, noticing he wasn't so much as old as worn out. I put him at my age plus about ten or so years, but the stoop of his shoulders and thin, greying hair gave the impression of a person seventy or so years into life. His face was lined, not deeply but often, and his skin had the mottled look of someone who had spent too long under a sun lamp. His smile disclosed a missing tooth which, in this day and age, was either laziness or vanity. I had known people who had grown up on the streets of Sao Paulo and Tokyo and survived; they looked used, this guy simply looked as if he hadn't made it out alive.

He took a lazy sip from his glass and placed it neatly down on

147

the coaster, hands steady. Leaning back he studied me out of the corner of his eye, looking first at my hand clasping the bar and then to my face.

'Not one to wear your uniform I see. Guess you're off shortly, probably your first too by your face.'

'Don't care too much for impressing people with spit and polish', I countered 'I've found it easier to get along if I blend in.' I turned to face him. 'Besides, as you said I'm off soon and I'm wanting a little slice of normal before the whole thing starts. Anyway, how'd you know?'

'It's the signet ring, you still look a bit uncomfortable wearing it. After a while most end up feeling like it belongs.' He spun his drink lazily, the condensation pooling and spreading, slowly seeping into the fibres of the coaster. He wore the same signet ring as I did, a small silver and pewter affair, the southern cross above a clenched fist embossed on its face. Mine was shiny and less than two weeks old; his had dulled to grey, with nicks and cuts across and around it. A small scorch mark on the band blended with scarring along his finger. Pulling the bowl closer he put a handful of nuts in his mouth and, between chews, asked me why I was going. Damned strange question I thought, in particular coming from him, and I told him so.

He just smiled. 'You see, some do it 'cause they want the excitement, the rush, to really feel like it's all on the line all the time. Others, they've got things to run from, things they don't want to see or hear of again, and this is the quickest and best way they can leave. For some it's all they can do to earn a dollar, get a clean bed and two meals a day. And then there's conscripts. Just trying to figure out where you fit in, though it don't seem you do. You're not runnin', you've brought your past with you', pointing to Cyn's photo 'and you sure aren't an ego freak. And you also seem intelligent enough to avoid the draft. So I'm just curious.'

I couldn't get angry. He might be a nosy old bastard but I'd wanted company. I laughed. 'Yeah, none of the above. I volunteered for the degree.' Even though I had brains, university education was far too expensive for me to even think of. I could pass all the entrance tests, but as I was non-minority and not connected I would have to be full fee paying – basically an impossible situation. However by joining the forces, doing a two year off world tour and staying on the reserves at home the government would pay for all my education at any level once I got back. That was my only reason for joining, my only reason for staying, and I told him as much.

He quietened down after that for a time, draining his glass and getting a refill. I changed to orange juice and checked the time. He leant back further on the stool, back resting on the faux wood of the wall, and his eyes seemed to glaze over. Shoulders drooped, he started to speak in low, measured tones betraying weariness and melancholy. 'Let me tell you a little story', he began, and I swear even to this day that the bar became deathly still, even the barlady's frenetic movements slowing down 'of a time and place not so far away …'

'I landed on Five with a squad of thirty fresh out of the Academy, two days after we had established the beachhead. I don't know much of those two days before I got there, but the wreckage and desolation told me all I needed. Five's like Earth, and I suppose that's the root of the problem. It's green, oxygen in the air, and life everywhere except where we went. The neutron weapons had killed everything for two hundred clicks, and the fire fight had burnt every building, every tree, every blade of grass to a crisp. Where we bivouacked that night had been a city of fifteen millions, all I could see of it was a small concrete stump near the horizon. By day it was worse. Every step crunched on burnt things, maybe animal maybe vegetable, I don't know, and horizon to horizon was charred, blackened plains, our ships, our guys, our weapons, and hundreds of thousands of grey puffs where our feet trod. Our first duty was grave digging, or should I say open pit burial. We put five thousand of them into a hole that first day and another five thousand each day after, and we were only a small part of the guys doing that. Not that we minded any, these were the enemy and so what if there were a few children in there, they'd only just grow up and shoot you anyway so it's better they're dead sooner.'

'A week into it and we learned that we were going to take Five the hard way, the old way, inch by inch and yard by yard, conventionally. Someone up there', with which he flailed his hand wildly at the ceiling 'decided that we needed Five intact, and as we could kill their nukes before they could use them, why not? Ha! Why not indeed.'

'So we fought. I don't know to this day exactly where, and I don't know exactly how long, but I know it was forever. My squad, I lost them all one by one, the best men and women I knew, some quick and some slow. Got to where it was just me and those two' pointing at the photo over the bar 'left of the originals. Father, son and holy ghost they called us, the trinity, thought we were invincible, and every rookie that joined and every rookie that died thought the same way.'

'I saw people killed in ways that just ain't right, poisoned food, poisoned air, things that came out the soil at night and cut your throat, animals that explode on sight, all kinds of things. Saw one grunt stoop to pick up and smell a daisy. She died five minutes later from a new strain of ebola they'd developed, lying screaming and crying as the blood poured out her skin. Took an hour to burn that field of flowers it did.'

'And we killed too, like after like. I was there when we tried out the new cholera strain, two million dead in a week. I recall poisoning a city's water supply, burning homes and families, shooting at civilians running away, letting prisoners escape carrying implanted bombs they didn't know about, timed to detonate when they got home. All on orders, but the orders didn't matter, we would have done it all the same without orders. They were the enemy, they had to die, and we were going to do that as efficiently and as quickly as we could.'

He looked me in the eye, cold and hard. 'Ever killed a woman with your bare hands?' Sweating, I regretted changing from beer to orange juice some moments back, the lump in my throat hardening.

'When it's a man it's easy, it's just another guy, another idiot who'd kill you soon as look at you. But a woman. They look like us on Five you know, heard they're more human than some of our kids, and that makes it worse. We'd just taken a position when these three attack us hand to hand. My two took the others and I was left with the third who had me on my back with a knife at my throat before I knew what hit me. Even through the camo she was good looking, small with red hair and green eyes, my 'type' I suppose but screaming at me and toting the biggest knife I'd seen.' He drained his glass in a swallow, a faint trembling in his hands.

'She fought hard, but in the end I had her, hands round her neck squeezing the life out of her. You know, I've done my share of men like that, some curse you as they die, some fight to the end, others just let go and accept. Some, a few, will cry and plead and it makes you hate them for not being men, for being cowards, for making you deny them mercy you can't give. But a woman. She cried as she went, looking at me with the question in her eyes and there's nothing I can do. She was young, could've been my sister or my lover, but she was the enemy.' He looked down. 'She was the only one I stopped to bury. Maybe that's where it started.'

He stayed silent for a while, the bar with him.

'It was about two weeks maybe after that we got the news. We were to have the man himself, the four star General, Batlow, join us for a push into the enemy's central area. He had a reputation nearly as good as ours, always seemed to be in the thick of the fight, always taking big risks, always being the soldier's soldier. Every week his picture would be in the vids as he led from the front and dragged everyone after him. We knew casualty rates hit the roof wherever he went, but hell, might as well die in good company. 'Iron Arse' they called him, got it from catching a hollow point in the butt early on and having a plate put in as part of the reconstruction. He was a hero to most of the guys and an inspiration. Tough, dedicated, fearless, leading by example. Or so we thought.'

'Which is why I couldn't make out my Captain's mood when he told me my squad would be working closest with Iron Arse. It was almost as if he felt he was a traitor, maybe selling us out. Me and the guys couldn't have been happier and me and the trinity the most, I mean, the guy was an absolute legend.'

'When I finally saw him he was standing on the top of an APC, a tower of pure muscle, sweat soaking through his fatigues and an attitude you could feel that'd kill at a hundred meters. His eyes were lit up like beacons, challenging us as he stabbed at a map tacked to the turret, 'The capital city boys' he yelled, 'were goin' all the way and take the fight to these bastards right in their own homes and show them what war's about.' and I was screaming and whooping along with the rest of them, couldn't wait to get out there and get going. 'And you know what' he called, jumping down and striding through the crowd to me 'I'm getting the best beside me.' and he threw his arms across me and the ghost's and son's shoulders, 'Me and the trinity's going in first and bringing hell with us!' and the roar nearly broke my ears, and I'm yellin' louder than ever and there's guns going off in the air and the whole bit. March into hell? Shit, would've gone back and lived there if he would've asked.'

'Hyped couldn't come near what we felt, it was like I'd been pumped full of dust and wasn't coming down for a month, the rest of 'em felt the same, right up to the time we hit the dirt at our IP.' He drew deeply from the glass, moving the foam from his lips with a worn and callused thumb.

'We pulled a small hill on the north side of the city, the top looked across the whole place, clear up to the mountains behind. Pure rock, boulders everywhere, the hill had saddles either side lain with mines and traps, leaving only one way to go – over the top – straight through the enemy's killing zone, right where he wanted us. So up we went, or at least we tried. Ten seconds after we dropped I'd lost six to snipers and two to booby traps. I was wearing someone's blood on one sleeve and had a particle beam burn across my leg by the time I'd flattened out, trying to burrow my way into the gravel scree and pull my arse down as low as my belly. I lay there looking round for a good couple of seconds and right then and there I knew I was going to die. The hill was only a hundred or so meters high and maybe five times as wide, with no cover or vegetation. All the way up was boulders and caves, you could've hidden an army in there and no-one would know, and that's exactly what they'd done. I could see dozens of winking lights and puffs of grey smoke coming from the hill, each one ending with a crunch or a cry from our lines. Nothing for it I thought, and I led the boys up into it.'

He paused again, briefly, before continuing. 'Still don't know to this day quite how we did it, but six hours later I was perched at the top of that hill, firing into the valley below. I'd started with thirty men under me, and thirty other squads with us, and when I got to the top it's just me, the trinity, and two others; the other squads weren't much better off. For all the weapons, technology, and gear we had, after the first ten minutes we'd fought hand to hand, belly down and crouching, for every meter of that rock. I used knives, rocks, anything I could get my hands on to batter my way through. It was medieval, bits of blood and body caking the earth and us, you couldn't see our fatigues or faces for clotted blood and dirt, burns and cuts. The holy ghost had lost his hair and helmet, both burned off early on, and the son had a gash the length of his left arm. But we were all still alive, still there.'

'And then he arrives, old Iron Arse, with forty of the meanest son of a bitch marines I'd ever seen. Standing there in his spotless uniform, reflective sunnies and all, smiling at us. 'Great work men' he crowed, 'fantastic job' with which he strides to the crest of the hill and poses with the city to his back as the two photographers he brought with him went about their work. 'Don't forget my left side's the best side' he quipped, and with the shoot being all over and done with in three minutes he walked back down the hill to his waiting ship.'

He turned from his beer to me, eyes like black coal pits. 'That's when it happened. We'd stopped cold, amazed, when a sniper opened up and got the holy ghost and the son before I could blink. We blew her to bits straight after, but they'd both been fried, well and truly dead. And I can still see that arrogant two faced bastard stopping, looking back as he brushed the dust from his trousers and smiled. 'Sorry 'bout that boy' he went, 'good men I s'pose but it's the price you pay. Better clear out, gonna nuke the city now we've got the photos' with which he blithely resumed his walk down the hill.'

'I stood stock still, frozen. All those people dead, my whole squad and thirty others as well, killers and killed lying around in bits and pieces their mothers wouldn't know just so he could get his face in the news? I had killed god knows how many and encouraged and taught others to do the same for what I had believed was right, and now this? And it wasn't just here I realised, but everywhere this bastard had gone the same thing must've happened, countless other occasions. No wonder my captain had looked like he did, he must've known. Every place Iron Arse had trod he had spilt our blood just so he could get a photo of himself in the middle of it all, and then just gone and nuked the target anyway. I looked at my blood caked hands and realised what I'd become, but worse, for who.'

'I had only one round left, an RPG – a daisy cutter – and I used it then and there. Officially they say it was another sniper who fired it, but enough knew and didn't care either way. I couldn't miss, the range was way too short, and I ended up with shrapnel all through my legs which is how I lost this one.' tapping the plastic below his left knee. 'I thought the Captain would have me up against the wall at dawn when he heard, but he just shrugged and said 'Bloody snipers, eh?' and left it at that. And that's how old Iron Arse died. Not a hero, but a coward.' with which he returned his attention to his drink.

There wasn't much to say – what could I have said? – so I left my drink and walked out to the plaza, into the starry night. The four indigo blue uniforms emerged not soon after and, after being given the last of their money, disappeared.

Me, I took the signet ring and dropped it in a bin. Shepparton really wasn't that far away.

END

Glass half overfull

It was a warm, bright morning, Yannis' clicking hooves and swaying cart conspiring against Orestes to call him back to sleep he had barely risen from. It was harder getting up these days, never mind doing what needed to be done, winter mornings enticing him to lie in nestled against the mild chill, summer mornings cocooning him with the promise of warm, idle, lazy days. Thankfully Yannis had no such issues.

They plodded slowly out of Limoni. Behind them the Aegean's blue sky stained dirty brown, before them Olympus, the abode of the gods abandoning man to his fate, this man to his. A tiny shower of stones came from the left, half hearted listless projectiles falling short of Yannis who ignored them, the clip of his hooves keeping their rhythm.

'Oi, Orest, does it smell having your head up your ass old man?' the boys called, lying back against the low stone wall, beer and cigarettes between them. One pulled another handful of gravel, considered tossing it then gave up in favour of another drink, making do with a sullen, bored glance.

Orestes ignored them as he did each morning, not out of

hatred but rather habit. Drinking at this hour was not acceptable, but what else is there for them? No work, small town and little to distract they had nothing to think of but the next support payment, beer and sleep. The wonder of it was they weren't up to worse than annoying an old man.

He pulled Yannis to the right, heading to the Litocharo estate and the new excavations. A few kilometres and a few more minutes to think, to let the sun warm his bones. It was good enough to keep him occupied and fed, a few euros letting him scrabble around the rubble before the Antiquities people arrived. Thank the gods for cashed up and ignorant American tourists willing to pay for shards of pottery or tiles but more importantly the tale, a pitch of antiquity and permanence they somehow could not find at home.

The site was deserted, the gate unchained as he passed through. He tied Yannis to a nearby shrub then carefully clambered down, one hand against the earth wall, an empty basket in the other, cheroot between teeth. Already the lines for the footings were faintly marked. It had been a good site so far, hopefully this last day would see more.

It was tiring but fruitful work, Orestes stretching the kinks from his back a few hours later, basket half full of broken pottery, blue and black tiles. Some were in remarkable condition, barely scratched but clearly old, perfect specimens for a museum or local history association, but they didn't pay and a man can't live on air.

The ground was now completely picked over, sun high and hot, time to go and rest to prepare for tonight's bartering among the hotels and restaurants along the coast. Basket in hand Orestes turned to leave when a glint caught his eye. Moving closer he could see a small lip of black and gold glazing poking out of the wall, barely above the floor. He took his penknife from his pocket and started to scrape away the dirt.

It took only a short time to free the object, now revealed as a small porcelain jar. He could not see the outside for hardened dirt, but knew it would be worth a tidy sum once cleaned up. Orestes removed his shirt, wrapped the jar inside it, and placed it on top of the basket.

Yannis clopped steadily past the boys, now lying sleeping in the sun, their drunken stupor bringing renewed promises of sunburn and hangovers. He ignored the snoring Orestes behind him, ignored the flowers and sweet grass growing in the school yard and made his way steadily through Limoni to the decrepit brown house and yard that was their home. He nosed through the open gate to the olive tree, stopping in the shade. He was old, the man was old, and if the man could drift off again well so could he. It wasn't long until Orestes' and Yannis' snores cycled together, a synchronised rasp-hasp floating through the air.

What is this place? Ornate, large, but whose? Orestes couldn't even imagine this much marble, the gold and silver inlay, billowing silk curtains and luxurious – if a little old fashioned – furniture. Clearly I'm in trouble, this is either the judge's or magistrate's home but I can't recall what it was I did. Crystal placed on stone turned Orestes around. A fresh faced, confident young man reclined on a marble daybed, offhandedly examining him.

'Welcome Orestes. Please, have a seat.'

He tried to place the face. It was familiar in a way, but stubbornly refused to be identified.

'I don't believe I know you.'

'Oh no, you don't and I don't expect you will. Excuse my manners, it's been a while since I've had … company. My name is Epimethus. You've heard of me?'

'The Epimethus? Prometheus' —'

'The one and the same, although I'm starting to despair that anyone remembers.'

'So I must be dead?'

'Oh no, nothing like that. You're just enjoying a little nap at home and I thought I'd drop in, you know, have a chat while your mind was open. Remarkable little donkey you have too, wonderful little beast, I must get one.'

Epimethus sat up, leant forward eagerly.

'When I said 'a chat' I really do have something I need you to do for me. Your little expedition this morning, you found a small jar, about so high?' He held his hands slightly apart. 'A black and gold affair, thick necked?'

'I found something like it, I've yet to clean it up.'

'Yes, yes, that's it, that's the one.'

'You want to buy it? You have cash?'

'Oh no, no, I simply want you to put it back in the ground, bury it nice and deep for me. Perhaps under all that concrete your nephew will pour tomorrow.'

'Why would I do that? It'll fetch me a good price.'

'Is that better than getting on my good side?'

Why can't I have those simple, uncomplicated dreams I used to have? Why always trouble, problems?

'All I want is a quiet life, a little money, a little drink now and then. The jar's mine to sell or keep, why should I bury it?'

'You see, it used to belong to my wife, well she had a little trouble with it a while ago, you know, pestilence, sorrow, pain and such so we had it buried. Didn't think anyone would find it, obviously you did, we didn't have concrete in those days, wonderful stuff, it would've done the job nicely. Father is still pretty upset over the whole thing so, if you could, it would help.'

'Well, I'll have to think about it, especially if it's valuable.'

'It's just trouble, it needs to be buried. We've still got a little pull down there so if it's favours you need —'

'It gets harder each year, my knees aren't what they used to be but if you could see your way, you know, with the tiles and tourists?'

'I can see what I can do but I'm afraid our time's up.'

'Oh?'

'Yes, I think your neighbour's trying to wake you.'

Yannis watched Ilias trying to get Orestes' attention, first by whispers then by a gentle rocking. The young man simply didn't understand the old man's capacity or need for sleep, and if he chose to sleep the afternoon away who's to judge him for that? Unfortunately it was also Yannis' time to rest, to relax until tomorrow when he would slowly haul his cargo and master round the streets, and the young man was disturbing him. Enough was enough. He shook his head, let out a loud bray, then took two rapid steps forwards then two more backwards.

Orestes woke immediately, sat up to see Ilias regarding him with a wry smile. He retrieved the crushed cheroot, placing it between his teeth, then swung down from the cart.

'I was wondering where you were, been waiting ages for you.'

He held out the basket, tucked the jar under his arm.

'Lend a hand could you and carry this for me? We can talk over some tea.'

It was sweet and hot, refreshing outside in the afternoon breeze. Ilias sat legs thrust forwards, staring into space. Orestes leant back having placed the jar carefully in a bucket of water. An hour or so, maybe less, the dirt should fall away and I'll have it clean, maybe even unscratched. He relit his cheroot, sent a ring of dense grey smoke spinning upwards.

'So, what news?'

'Nothing good as always. It spreads a little slower, a little quieter, but it is still there, still eating her away.'

'How is she today?'

'Today is good, she has the fight back, her toughness. More tests, stronger treatments they say, and she pins her heart on them.'

Ilias shrugged, resignedly.

'A little more money, a few years earlier, even a bigger country or different treatments, but as it is …'

Orestes grabbed the younger man's shoulder, gave him a solid, fatherly shake.

'She needs your strength, calmness, even when there is none she needs to see hope fight in you.'

Five years I watched Damara struggle, fight back and try, five years of playing the rock for her to lean on, to stand with. No time for tears and doubt then, time enough the twenty after.

'You know I'm right Ilias, you know that.'

'Of course I know. At times I feel like giving in, but fight on we will, I will.'

'Good. And I am here for you both.'

He reached under the table, bought out a half-full bottle and two small glasses. He filled them quickly.

'Health and success. May you both live long enough to embarrass your great-grandchildren.'

Maybe it had been a mistake bringing the bottle out but sometimes it was needed. With Ilias gone and the bottle nearly empty, Orestes knew he would not be selling anything that evening. There would be other tourists tomorrow night and a chance to atone for his laziness. A bottle deserved to be either full or empty, not stuck in some strange middle state. He refilled his glass, looked to the bucket of muddied water at his feet.

It was lovely, black gold and, more importantly as he pulled it out and slowly turned it around, the enamel was blemish free and the stopper still in. I will have to find a special friend for this piece, an old sentimental friend with a fat wallet indeed. Perhaps I will even have some spare for poor Ilias' wife. He placed the jar carefully down out of the way, drained his glass in one swallow. The gentle evening breeze carrying tantalising hints of dinner and dessert from the neighbours lulled him asleep.

'So, have you thought it over?'

Epimethus sat opposite him astride Yannis. How he'd managed to get the donkey into the marble house was beyond him but if it is a dream why not? If it's my dream why am I not in control?

'In fact, I might even add a little bit in for Yannis here, I think we have a deep connection.'

'It's still no to both. He may not be much but he's my only transport, and that jar's going to make me a nice little sum.'

Epimethus now sat next to him, Yannis nowhere to be seen.

'You really haven't been listening. Orestes, the jar isn't empty. Do you remember who the jar belonged to?'

'You said it was your wife.'

'And she is?'

'Mrs. Epimethus?'

He gave an exasperated sigh, closed his eyes then took a deep breath.

'Look, I'll make it easy for you. Seven letters, starts with 'P' and ends in 'andora'. So?'

'Pandora?'

'Thank you, finally! Your kind can be so frustrating. So it's her jar, the one with the evils, we put the lid back on but there's something left, something I want to keep in.'

Orestes could vaguely remember the myths he was told as a child, Pandora's jar, how she'd left something in and now Epimethus wanted him to bury it? Now what was it again?

'Hope.'

'What?'

'Hope, there's hope in the jar and you want me to leave it there.'

'Well yes, of course, why else would I bother getting in touch?'

'I could have done with more hope when Damara died, and Ilias needs as much as he can get now. Why would I leave it bottled up?'

'It's not good for you and once out you can't put it back! Don't you think we tried with death? Well, you know how well that worked.'

'How can you say hope's bad?'

'It's not been stored in a jar of goodies has it? No, it was in a jar of evils, you work it out.'

'But we've already got hope, how can more be anything but good?'

'Your hope is tainted, tainted by fear and imagination and desire, it keeps you striving, bettering, trying to do whatever it is you do even if you know it's futile. But this hope's pure, empty, it's — You know, you really ought to cut back on the ouzo Orestes.'

'What?'

'Your bladder's too old, you're waking up again and don't

open the jar!'

The pain was intense, remnant kidney stones screaming at him as he relieved himself against the olive tree. Should know better at my age, she'd shout at me if she knew I was drinking again, if she caught me peeing outdoors. Gods how I miss her shouting.

Cotton-mouthed and dopey Orestes made his way back to the jar, picking it up to take it inside safe for the night. It was beautiful even with the slight sludge along one side. He leant forward to pick up his shirt, to polish the jar clean, and even as he did so felt the jar slip slowly, gently but determinedly out of his grasp. He turned his head just in time to see the jar bounce once then shatter into a hundred pieces. The gentle evening breeze paused, changed direction, carrying faint women's laughter as it shifted again.

It was a shame, but one jar meant one customer, a hundred pieces a hundred customers. Orestes stepped over the shards into the house. They were there now, they would be there when he needed them. Tomorrow, the next day, whenever. There would always be shards, always be tourists, always be time.

It was good to be free of the harness, not to drag the old man and the cart around. He was sitting on the chair near the back door, cup of tea in hand smiling and waving at him as he meandered out the gate.

'Enjoy yourself, come back when you want, why waste a beautiful day?'

Yannis was a little confused, but not enough to stop and go back. Why the old man didn't want to work was none of his business. He passed the young man sitting with his wife outside their door, sharing their morning coffee.

The woman turned to the man, beaming.

'I don't think I'll go anymore Ilias, I feel so much better, so healthy and fit, it's already beaten, I know it is.'

The young man leant across, hugged her tightly.

'Yes, I'm sure of it. There's no point wasting our time or such a good day when everything will work out anyway.'

Yannis turned the corner, headed away from Limoni towards Olympus. The young boys sat in the morning sun, sharing a cigarette and bottle. Instead of stones they threw waves at him, smiling, laughing.

'Burro, hey burro, wonderful morning burro!'

Their voices receded as Yannis clopped away, calling greetings to each passer by.

'Now that's much better isn't it?'

Yannis didn't break stride, simply turned his head to the fresh faced, confident young man sitting astride him. He seemed to weigh nothing and lacked the old man's muddy, stale breakfast smell.

Epimethus lay down along Yannis' back, his head lying cheek down between the donkey's ears. 'Oh indeed you are a remarkable little donkey, a wonderful little beast! Just wait until they see you at home. And to think you only cost me one old jar.'

END

Hot dog

'What line of business are you in Mr. Patheson?'

Ugly fucking hairy ape-woman, what do you know of business? Just rent me the space and be done with it. You'll find out my business soon enough.

'Entertainment Cindii, a little import export on the side.'

'I see.'

No you don't, none of your ugly symmetrical air-breathing bastard kind ever has.

'So will this place do? City centre, three hundred fifty square meters, fifth level basement with loading ramp and goods elevator.'

Idiot. If it lasts a week it's enough.

'How much again?'

'Two and a quarter on a three plus three lease.'

'It's perfect.'

Hot. Dog. Hotdog. What garbage is this? I've had constipation, flatulence, and arrhythmia eating this factory produced swill they call food. No wonder they all smell like shit, fat arsed sweaty bodied perverts. White bun, red thing smothered in yellow vomit, and crisp brown shards. It bears a passing resemblance to a dog's dick on a hot day and I wouldn't put it past one of these morons to have tried eating that. Sex obsessed losers, everything comes back to penis envy or pussy strike. The universe'll be better off without them.

'Turn around slow and quiet. Do as I say and you won't get hurt.'

I turn. It's only a knife, like I'm fucking scared? I haven't got time for this but I'm bored. This stupid ape's mind's as easy to control as the rest of them.

'Strip.'

He does as he's told, I leave his eyes and mind unlocked to watch the show. It's always more fun that way.

'Cut off your dick.'

The horror on his face is wonderful, I toy with opening his vocal chords but the mall's too close. It's a lot of blood for such a small pink thing. What the fuck. I hand him the hotdog.

'Stick it in this.'

I feel like laughing for the first time today; he knows what's coming and can't stop it. The more his eyes plead the better it gets. Just hope he doesn't bleed out too soon.

'Enjoy your lunch, make sure to eat it all.'

I stay for the first few bites, enjoy feeling his mind skittering to insanity. I turn the corner into the mall and release him, the scream rising above the traffic. Shame I haven't more time, twelve billion of them and they're all mine.

The basement's perfect. Anywhere would have done but I'm a showman, an artist, and my viewing audience demands a spectacle. At least for the first few hours. Nodes across the world solve that, my direct feed's a subscriber perk.

I take the lines and lay them on the floor in two one hundred and fifty square meter rectangles. I connect the brackets and they're live, just awaiting the command. Indestructible, they'll stay through it all.

It's a good hill, nice view of the city and safe for the first hour. I slide open the van's freezer and she hands me a Magnum. She doesn't need the rest of her body and it's a tight fit anyway, so waistline up's all that's there. Simple stupid ape biology, so easy to keep alive. I let her cry to see how long the icicles get but that voice is grating. The ice-cream's nice, one thing from this planet of shit.

'How's that monthly sales target now Cindii? Tell you what, I'll let you watch the show.'

I put her on the grass facing away from my chair. She's just the right height. I sit down, place a boot on each shoulder and settle in.

I'd toyed with sequencing. What first, the portal 10,000 meters undersea in the Dokarzha Deeps, or the one in Betelgeuse's core? It's a simulcast, so it's both at once. I throw the mental switch.

It's beautiful, city erased as two giant columns of water and plasma erupt and mix to hyper-steam, the shock wave turning everything to dust for five kilometres as the columns soar, tearing the Earth up and flinging it to the four winds. Every nanosecond recorded and live streamed, every terror stricken pained instant before oblivion lifted from the minds of seven million naked apes, as it would be for them all as the whole planet was scoured, steamed, cleansed.

The earth beneath me trembles as the old fault lines awake, the

169

thrusting magma flows seek the surface.

What the fuck, I've got time. I flip on my shield and decide to stay. I let her scream, every movie needs a soundtrack.

And I need a holiday.

END

In whose name

She is terrified, wide eyes fixed on me, breath shallow, sweat across her brow. I lean closer, make sure she is secure. There are none to interfere or overhear in the crowded square, everyone keeping their distance perhaps out of respect, certainly out of fear. I steady myself.

'You understand why, what I have told you?'

She nods, cracked teeth biting her lower lip.

'When it catches do not fight the fire, it will only prolong the pain. When I nod embrace it, lean into it and breathe deeply, it will hasten your journey.'

I step away leaving her isolated atop the pyre of wood, a solitary figure surrounded by empty grey flagstones, flagstones in turn encircled by the village in its entirety. It is necessary and right they should see, be reminded it is their very souls at risk and the lengths the church will go to protect them.

Miguelito hands me the torch, a pitch-dipped flaming rag sputtering and spitting in the still air. I walk the short distance to the pyre and place the torch down.

I lock my eyes to hers as the flames take hold and her screams rise, pitched wailings of agony as her legs start to be consumed, her clothes filthy rags smoking then bursting alight. Gasps and muted prayers rise around me, the click of beads as Father Ignacio races through the Hail Marys. Her eyes remain fixed and as the flames reach her waist I nod. She bends forwards, soundlessly mouthing as she breathes the fire deeply, strongly, slumping forwards unmoving against her bonds.

The flames roar higher, the rising wind carry smoke and the scent of burning flesh over me. Neither the sickly sweet smell nor the sounds of vomiting and abhorrence are unfamiliar. I will stay until her very bones are ash, as will everyone around me lest they incur my displeasure, be seen not to understand and accept the discipline of the church. The smoke starts to sting, permeate my clothes but my gaze remains, countenance set, hands steady. A shower of sparks flare upwards as she settles into the pyre, bonds breaking, charred smouldering stumps that once were arms flailing outwards in embrace macabre. Stifled cries from my left join muted prayer from the right.

It is only hours later with the pyre reduced to a low mound of embers that I shift my gaze slowly and deliberately across everyone gathered in the square. None had dared leave. Fear, obedience, belief meet me. For her family hatred and sorrow salt the wounds, a wasteful and unfeeling god allowing disease to take four children before they were six, and one to heresy when not yet thirteen.

Beads still click through his fingers, Ignacio's pasty white face frames his stare through unseeing eyes. He had no desire to be here but it was his duty. A small cough gains his attention.

'You must tend your flock.'

Ignacio stares at me, stumbles to find thought or word in response. It is hardest the first time, he's probably married her parents, baptised the child, watched her grow.

'Remember Ignacio, remember why and rejoice. Her

confession the other day, her walk back from heresy.'

'Yes Brother Anteo', unconvinced, uncertain 'she gains eternal life through the purifying fire.' He smiles wanly. 'Saved from heresy, a lesson, a teaching in truth to us all.'

I squeeze Ignacio's shoulder then move past him, Miguelito in tow, towards my room. A lesson perhaps, a waste certainly.

I slip my sandals off, stretch my tired legs as Miguelito prepares the salve. The days and miles are hard on old feet and the work endless, the welcomes unfailingly forced. Here perhaps a little warmer, a touch more open, Ignacio not having the company of an inquisitor before. The invitation to sup remains. I tap Miguelito's head, mouth the words slowly.

'Do you wish to accept Father Ignacio's hospitality again?'

Miguelito smiles, shakes his head. A near-deaf mute was the perfect choice of attendant but it creates its own peculiar worries. It is also no fun for Miguelito. What business could a young boy have in the company of two old men?

'Then go, return to me in the morning. Do I have to remind you not to bring shame on this office? I have not forgotten, nor has the girl's parents.'

Miguelito shakes his head, clasps his hands in promise. His eyes betray the memory, youthful lusts still written large. I sigh, wave him away.

Ignacio was shaken but welcoming, the meal simple and plentiful, eaten in silence as the order requires. We sit alone at table, cups of wine in hand as the evening darkness eats into the solitary candle's glow.

'The other, your business will be concluded soon?'

'Of course. One day, perhaps two, no more.'

'Then?'

'Wherever I am led.'

'You have performed this … duty for a while?'

'Four years, perhaps longer, I keep no account.'

'The calling must be strong, it is not a thing I could do.'

'You would were you asked. But yes, the calling was clear.'

It could not have been clearer, simpler, more unsettling. Alone in my cell fasting and praying for fourteen days it had happened on the last evening. Pitch black as I extinguished the candle one second, an explosion of light the next, it stood within arm's reach towering in front of me clad in shimmering silver-white, burning halo, wings touching either wall. All my faculties deserted me, I stood unmoving, uncomprehending in its presence. 'You are called,' it spoke in a hundred voices, lips unmoving 'and you will do your work diligently as unto the most high.' All I could do was shake, mumble incoherently. It placed a crucifix and a book on the edge of my cot. It stepped closer, close enough for me to feel the cold surrounding it, the iciness of the fire. 'You will tell no one born of woman what you find, of the relics I have given you.' It grabbed me, held me, two hands to my head, two hands to my sides, eyes fixing me, mesmerising me. 'You will invoke the most extreme penalty on the heretic. It is not enough they recant, they must be removed.' It opened the book. 'Seek me while holding this and I will send you,' then pointed to the crucifix 'and invoke this to remove the stain of heresy from both heretic and earth.' With that I was released and my cell returned to its former dark, empty state.

'The say the Holy Father takes a care for each inquisitor sent.'

'That is true, each of us is sent by him.'

That night, alone with the relics, I was left to worry. I could not simply walk out claiming visitation; I would suffer the same fate as any madman doing so. And with my vows taken, my life's path set, I was not free to change vocation. How small my faith was, for on the morrow the Abbott handed me the warrant from the Holy Father. I opened it to reveal the hand of Gregory IX, tiny droplets of ink across the page witnessing a hasty, uncertain scrawl. I was to have no master above me save himself and God, and I was to be sole judge and agent, alone responsible for sentence and execution.

Ignacio sighs, leans back into the shadows.

'He expects us to lead them in faith by example, but an unruly flock at times needs a firm hand.'

'And that is my calling.'

Yet even from the start my faith was challenged. As I kneeled in prayer that night in my cell worrying uselessly about the morning I saw the water where my visitor stood. What need of water does an angel have I asked. Another mystery awaited for, as I touched the wet stone it brought back a scrap of fabric layered, white upon silver upon black upon white and fine, thinner than silk and smoother than polished metal. What angel garbed themselves in cloth? I have kept that scrap with me all these years, one scrap of doubt tucked away in my cassock while other scraps gathered in my mind.

Ignacio stands.

'The day has been long. It has drained me I fear. I pray I will have the strength to accept it, to grow accustomed to it as you have. I bid you good night.'

I watch him leave. I would never grow accustomed to it, don the garb of indifference or rejoicing other inquisitors wear. No matter Miguelito's efforts my clothes always bear that sickly sweet smell, the hearth contains their eyes, my joy in the bonfire's warmth replaced by the horror of the pyre. Nor is there solace in the sacraments, now as hollow cymbals to me, or in the dark as my mind changed sleep to a seldom seen friend.

The guards at the door regard me differently this morning. Respect and curiosity is replaced by fear and submission. It is one thing to be told a man has power over body and soul in this world and the next, another thing entirely to see it exercised. Miguelito and I pass inside knowing the door is closed and we will remain undisturbed. Once the village's butchering room, a new butcher now simply occupies it. I sit in the sole chair, relics cradled in the bag on my lap. Miguelito pours a ladle of water over the head of the naked man chained to the far wall.

He raises his head, scarlet-cream threads of the week's encouragement adorning his filth encrusted skin. A piteous human seeking mercy I can not give. When I came here he truly had no concept of his error, my purpose, his future. The simplest of a village of simpletons, his very innocence sealed his fate, one a smarter man would have closed his mouth and mind to avoid.

'Let us continue Sebastian. Miguelito, tend the fire.'

The fire spurts, black irons start their transformation to dull red.

'I will say what you want, as you want it, your holiness.'

'Yes, you will, but it is not what matters. This is to save your soul, prepare you for God. Would you want to be before him unworthily, a liar in your heart?'

'No.'

'Nor would I. All this is to your benefit, your salvation. Tell me of the things you saw.'

'I saw nothing, I swear, nothing.'

I nod to Miguelito. Miguelito is careful and precise, the scream rent from Sebastian short, piercing. A wisp of smoke rises from his little toe.

'Truth Sebastian, truth. What you saw and what you thought are different. Again, tell me what you saw.'

'Angels, two angels in a —'

Another caress from Miguelito halts him.

'Again, what did you see?'

'Men?'

'Good. Tell me again, what did you see?'

I signal Miguelito.

'Men, I saw men, men, two men', a screaming wail as the iron passes the underside of his foot.

'Good. Men. Do not lie before me or before God. Now, remind me of that which we talked of yesterday. Describe the men to me.'

'They were tall.'

'Good. More.'

'They were bright, shiny.'

'And?'

'And?'

'Yes, and.'

'They had, they had wings?'

I smiled, hopefully reassuringly.

'Very good. You see, nothing to fear from the truth. Now, again, what were they doing?'

'Looking down.'

'At what?'

'An animal, a dead animal.'

'Anything else?'

'They took pieces of it.'

'And?'

'I don't know, they just took pieces and left.'

'How did they leave?'

'They just went, they were there and then they were not.'

I walk over, close enough to smell his rotting teeth. I place one hand on his cheek, now wet with tears.

'Do you see? Your memory, the truth is there. You are nearly ready.'

I step back, motion Miguelito to the far side of the room.

'Now tell me, who were these men?'

'I don't know.'

I lift a white hot iron to his face.

'No your holiness, please, they were angels.'

I thrust the iron into a bucket of water, withdraw it hissing and smoking.

'Please, I don't know. Angels, I don't know, please.'

I step towards him, iron held out still smoking, glowing dark crimson. He struggles against the chains, eyes wide. It is still a puzzle to me how the smoking yet cooler iron places more fear into their hearts than when white hot.

'I don't know, they were who you want them —'

I lift his member carefully with the tip of the iron, glide it quickly but carefully back to the sack, slide it down slowly before I return iron to fire. I let him scream himself hoarse to exhaustion, resume my seat to consider him. Once the sobbing subsided I continue.

'Sebastian, you disappoint me, you disappoint the Holy Father. Who knows your heart best Sebastian?'

'God?'

'And does not the Holy Father speak with God?'

'Yes.'

'And does the Holy Father speak to me?'

'Yes, he does, you told me.'

'As God knows your heart, so must the Holy Father know your heart. So do I know your heart?'

'Yes, yes.'

'Are you smarter than God, smarter than I, Sebastian?'

'No, no your holiness.'

'So who knows your heart better Sebastian, you or I?'

'You do.'

'The men, your heart knows what they were even if your mind is deceived. They were daemons Sebastian, that is the truth.'

Miguelito returns to the fire, stoking the bellows.

'It says in God's book that the devil himself treads the earth as an angel of light to devour the simple, the unwary. You are a simple man Sebastian, easy prey for the evil one.'

The shaking returns, his voice staccato cartwheels over cobblestones.

'Yes your holiness.'

'It is for you the church exists, to save your eternal soul. The devil ensnared you Sebastian, and I am here to set you free. Our bodies and our minds are but traps, traps for the devil to use.'

I stand, walk within arm's reach of him. Miguelito draws near, two irons in hand.

'You were deceived, your mind clouded from the truth. Who were the men Sebastian?'

'They, they were daemons.'

'You must believe, not simply hope. Who were they?'

'Daemons.'

'You must believe, Sebastian, believe. Who were they?'

'Daemons, devils both.'

Miguelito dances the irons across his back.

'Before God himself', I scream, my spittle showering his face 'who were they?'

'Daemons!' he screams back, and we stand there, I screaming the question, he screaming the answer accompanied by the hiss of irons and writhing feet squelching in excrement as he tries in vain to break his chains.

I signal Miguelito to cease; Sebastian hangs limp.

'Daemons, daemons all.' he spits through gasps and whimpers. 'I am deceived, damned for eternity.'

I lift his face to mine.

'You know the truth of it now, how easily you were snared.'

He nods, sweat and drool cascade over my fingers, onto my cassock. I lean forwards, kiss him on the forehead.

'You are no longer deceived, you will not be damned. You are ready to face God, prepared for Him. I can release you from the pain and deceptions, save your soul. Do you want me to?'

He nods vigorously, eyes now wet with hope.

'Tomorrow the fire will purge your body, send your soul to God, saved for all eternity. Do you want this?'

'Please, yes please your holiness, yes.'

I reach behind me into the bag and pull the crucifix out, hold it to his face. The effect is immediate, his breathing slows, his eyes fix on the Christ as it glows opalescent; tiny shards of coloured light dance across Sebastian's nose.

'I envy you. Tomorrow through a brief veil of pain you shall see God.'

I stand there until the crucifix returns to wood and step out, Miguelito in tow. The guards spring upright, but not quickly enough to disguise their eavesdropping. I turn to Miguelito.

'Get some water and clean him, give him to eat and drink. Do not tarry as we have more work.'

I turn to the guards.

'Keep a mind to your work and my words. There is room in the fire for more than this one.'

I walk through the square, back to my room, closing the door after me. I place the bag on the cot, cross to the small enclosed courtyard beyond. I sink to my knees shaking under the olive tree, heave out my breakfast and the previous evening's meal until winded and emptied. I fall to my side, cold shivers rippling along my body, hands pulling my knees tight to my chest. Waste, waste, only waste.

By the time Ignacio and Miguelito return I am composed, cleaned, the afternoon sun a bloated orb wallowing towards the horizon.

'Is it wise to go there?'

'Miguelito and I will be fine.'

'You do not wish me to accompany you?'

'No. Stay and prepare for tomorrow.'

Ignacio watches on uncertainly as Miguelito and I leave, walk out of the village and disappear over a small rise.

We walk a little way then I rest, take the book from my bag. Of itself it is an object of beauty, small, leather bound, the handwritten parchment precise, impossibly symmetrical and without error. It must have taken months for someone to copy it out, to illustrate it in such detail. I open it at the twenty-third psalm and do as I had been taught, place my finger on the page and translate the Latin to the vulgate in my mind.

'The Lord is my shepherd I shall not want.'

I have no sooner finished than the vision comes to me, the small clearing, copse, low rocky outcrop in the middle. Half an hour's walk, to the left, past the brook. I stand, stride confidently away.

Reality again matches imagining. I leave Miguelito at the edge of the clearing, make my way to the rocks. Just as Sebastian had described, an animal lies spread eagled across one boulder in perfect symmetry, untouched by scavengers. It was at least one week dead yet has no signs of decay. I press my finger against the cold flesh which bounces back against my touch. The skull and backbone are cleft in two, the cut a precise and clean stroke betraying unmatched ease and effortlessness. Here and there holes have been cut, perfect circles down through the flesh, organs and bone, some to the rock itself. I place my finger in one hole, move it around and draw it out bloodied, dripping.

I shake my head; it is the same as I have seen on occasion over the years, animal, beast, or human but always the same, laid out precisely even lovingly, life erased and replaced by mystery. At my first three years ago I had wondered what satanic ritual drove such things; then later at what purpose taking the same pieces from such diverse examples could be; to now a sickening questioning over the wasteful repetitiveness of it all.

I remove the crucifix from my bag, hold it glowing bright green above the animal. I pace my way slowly to Miguelito, stop in front of him as the crucifix resumes its wooden pallor. He looks at me expectantly, I point to a spot just in front of him.

I separate Christ from the cross and hand Him to Miguelito.

'Sit, wait.'

I return to the animal, place the cross upon it, and return to sit next to Miguelito. He hands me the Christ quickly, smiles and fidgets in anticipation. He always looks forward to this as, I would admit, do I.

'Miguelito remember, this is holy work and should be done sombrely. This time please, no clapping.'

I grasp one arm of the Christ in each hand, place my lips against the back of His head and turn Him towards the animal. A beam of light springs between Christ and cross, a swirling rainbow of colour expanding to a dome encompassing the animal and the clearing. It stays there, a dancing wall of colour and sparks, occasionally lit by flashes of lightning from within, until a minute or so later it recedes rapidly to the cross, extinguishes itself with a flash and barely audible pop.

I turn to see Miguelito leaning forwards, a child's smile of delight on his face. He sees me just in time to stop his hands meeting in midair.

'Yes, that was colourful but still no reason for that. Stay here while I get the cross.'

I stand, walk to the rock. The grass crunches under foot, the air smelling as it does after a storm. The cross has returned to wood and lies quietly atop the rotting remains of the animal, slack skin enveloping bones wrapped in putrefied flesh. I lift the cross and see a small object under the animal's hide. I pull it out, revealing it to be a thick silver disc as broad as my palm, cold and smooth. It begins to vibrate, sends tingles down my fingers. I have seen this once before. I drop it where I found it, hurry back to Miguelito while jamming the Christ back on the cross.

'Go now back to the village. I will join you shortly.'

He points to the sun, now resting on the horizon.

'No, I will be safe. You must go, go now.'

He shakes his head again. I grab his shoulders.

'Miguelito. They are coming back, the angels of God or the daemons, I know not which. Do you want to burn at the stake?

He pales visibly, concern on his face.

183

'I will be protected by the relics but you are vulnerable. Run back to the village and wait. Worry yourself not about me.'

Without further encouragement he turns and flees. I sit low against a tree, partly obscured by the grasses.

I don't have long to wait, the sun barely replaced by the moon when the clearing is transformed from soft silver to glaring blue white light. Four figures appear in silver-white clothing, burning halos around their heads. But none bare wings, and the four are of different statures. Here now these perfect beings are before me but each is different. How can that be? And no wings, so how can they travel? Small doubts pile on small doubts gathered over the years.

They circle around the rocks, one takes a stick from its back and waves it, one cups a hand to its ear chanting silent incantations to the sky. One picks up the disc and places it within its vestments. Another approaches it, speaks in earnest, then points in my general direction. The other nods, the first one moves towards me in haste. I push myself deeper into the grass, hand in bag clutching the relics.

It stops perhaps twenty paces to my left, leans with one arm against a tree. I start reciting the psalms in my mind, my fingers driving between the covers of the book. The figure shifts slightly, its free hand moves to its waist then, with a sigh a stream of liquid passes between it and the tree, spattering droplets clear to me. It takes a second for my mind to understand it. It is relieving itself? An angel? A daemon? Only flesh and blood need to but if that were so —

My thoughts are erased by the vision in my head. My hand, my fingers in the book had sought out the well-worn page and now the vision of the clearing overlays my view of it. Instantly the four figures turn to look, walk unerringly to me until I am surrounded. I shake uncontrollably, my bowels loose themselves, and I wait for judgment.

One raises an arm holding a short grey rod, the one beside it grasps it with one hand, waves the other three vigorously. They seem to argue, point at me, the sky, each other until one looks a little closer at me, the spreading stain on my cassock, and draws the others' attention. They stand briefly in silence then start to laugh, deep-throated noises. Three of them disappear, leave me alone with the tall one. It places a finger behind one ear. The hundred voices return from lips unmoving.

'You. Again. Was not the last time enough?'

'It was late, an accident.'

'You should have left with your boy.'

'I was curious.'

'You should not be. Do you forget your instructions?'

'No.'

'Then stay to those and no more! Do you doubt we can inflict worse upon you than the flames to those you deliver?'

'I do not doubt.'

It bends, places an ice cold finger under my chin, lifts my face.

'Oh but you do Anteo, you do. Simple, simple man, your mind is an open page to me. You doubt everything since our first time but you do not have the words to say how. And I will not give them.'

It stands, steps back

'Take a care with your work. Do not disappoint us again.' with which it disappears, and I into the night.

Sebastian is terrified, wide eyes fixed on me, breath shallow. Beneath the fear the eyes show faith, trust, hope, fixed on what lies hours away and not within the hour. I lean close, make sure he is secured. There is none to interfere or overhear in the crowded square, everyone keeps their distance. I steady myself.

'When it catches do not fight the fire, it will only prolong the pain. When I nod embrace it, lean into it and breathe deeply, it will hasten your journey.'

'Thank you your holiness, thank you for helping me to see the truth.'

I lock my eyes to his, and as the flames dance around his waist I nodded.

Truth. What is that? There is no truth in this, just lies as there were for the others.

Yet still I continue.

END

Inzali ariba

The air conditioner howls, it's only twenty-five celsius outside but it needs to be eighteen here, on the edge between comfort and freezing. Can't relax, be comfortable, let my mind wander. My pills knock me out for eight hours at a stretch but in the greyness hides danger. The numbers, I must crunch the numbers. Equations swim on the page before me, I must concentrate, derive and calculate to engage my logic centres, shut out the emotion, the noise. My models are ready when I tire of this, my word games next to them when I tire of the other.

Oh god her picture's still here why did I leave it? The crack opens, I know she's outside locked away from me, me from her. Numbers, concentrate damn it, concentrate! The crack widens and it floods me, I feel it all the suicides, violence, pain and heartache all too real. I slide off the chair onto carpet, the bottle spills from shaking hands as I swallow three, four, how many, jesus god when will it end?

Dappled warm sunlight fell on Inzali Ariba as she pushed another seedling into the thick mud, one of thousands before and thousands to come. The coolness of the paddy caressed her calves, the gentle wash back and forth a reminder of the other village women to either side intent on finishing to return to children, cooking, husbands. The rhythm of the day led her to daydreaming, imaging herself in school, out with friends, fine clothes and food, the normal yearnings of any fourteen-year-old girl. Inzali knew that for her these things would be out of reach, her village unwanted and unwelcome strangers in a country they had lived in for a thousand years. Maybe for her children or theirs it would be, but for her the day, the sun, the daydreams were enough.

The crunch of tyres on dirt betrayed two trucks moving to the village, one stopping on the ridge above the field. A dozen soldiers jumped out, scrambling down into the paddy guns waving, shouting. Separated into two groups Inzali found herself with the younger girls, the older women and her mother herded together in tears. Three soldiers singled her out, dragging her up the slope into the jungle, laughing prodding each other, stopping a few yards in grabbing at her, clutching, propping her up against a tree.

The one nearest leered at her, face nearly touching.

'What's your name bitch?'

Shaking she opened her mouth, pointed and shook her head.

'You can't talk?'

She nodded, crying.

Another laughed.

'Just as well, we've got better things you can do with your mouth.' unbuckling his trousers to sounds of rifle fire.

They threw her in the back of the truck with four others bruised, torn, sobbing.

'Don't know what you're crying for, think yourself lucky we're keeping you.'

He slammed the tailgate shut and jumped up.

'Maybe you'd like to join the others?' laughing, the truck moving down the road past rose coloured paddy fields and their strange plantings.

Feet on desk I pulled my mind back to the screens and feeds. I'd woken tired from broken sleep, tense and stressed and I just couldn't shake it. It wasn't me, I'd always strongly reflected other's feelings, but more some office colleagues who were out of sorts. I could see the pair of them looking frayed, haggard. Jeannie was closest, I stood up and walked over. I was barely two meters from her when she looked at me, scowled and wagged her finger. I shrugged, headed across to the other side to Brenda.

'Hey Brenda, ready for a coffee?' She and I went back ages, old friends we'd started here together. She gave me a look that would've frozen Hades.

'Only if I can drown your ass in it!' she growled through clenched teeth then, almost as if she only just heard the words, jerked back. 'Hell Denis I'm sorry, I didn't mean to —'

'It's ok, I just thought you could use a break, you look like, ah, a bit edgy.'

'Yeah yeah, guess I am.' She frowned. 'Just seem to be overly aggressive, nearly bit Ted's head off this morning.'

'You're not the only one.'

She jabbed the screen in front of her.

'Look at this.'

The data was familiar, we'd been assigned the crims and cranks section of the paper and rotated regularly. For the past few months she'd taken the crime stats and police reports, I got the psychics, paranormals and whatever didn't fit elsewhere basket.

'Common and aggravated assault ticking upwards.' Not earth shattering but interesting.

Brenda leant forward and split the table by gender.

'Now what do you see?'

It all looked normal up to a month ago but since then the stats went crazy. Male on male assaults had fallen, male on female dropping out of sight. On the other hand female initiated assaults had skyrocketed, but only female on male; female on female had utterly ceased.

'Interesting, what's behind it?'

Brenda was staring at the screen, her mouse in a death grip.

'Maybe you're just getting a taste of your own medicine.' It wasn't said in anger, just dispassionate, cold, disturbing.

I stepped slowly back.

'Ah, maybe a rain check on that coffee yeah?'

'Whatever.'

It was a nightmare that wouldn't end, why didn't Allah in his mercy end it, take the pain, the torture as she had begged? Three, then four, then one, shared as meat or a toy abused and raped again and again relentlessly, viscously, Inzali hated them, hated herself, cursed the life that had led her here. She hadn't seen any of her villagers since the truck, since being dragged from room to room, place to place. She shuddered from the cold water, tried to wash the stain and filth from her but could not. Alone for the first time in weeks she curled up, no tears left, praying for deliverance that she knew would not come, for a hiding place denied her even in fitful sleep.

She looked shattered, vacant eyed, mouth a harsh scar. One white knuckled hand gripped the steering wheel, the other a bare wire. The eyes refocused, hardened and stared straight ahead with disgust, loathing, menace. Tossing her head back she drove the bare wire into the roof. The screen flared white, black, then switched to another CCTV point. The van's sides puckered in as if to take breath then disappeared in a searing orange–white globe, hurling cars and people outwards, upwards. The glass walled office block over the car park distorted, quivered, then collapsed in a shower of dust, flame and crystal shards. Hot streamed from the paper's net tie-in I'd replayed it over and over watching TATA's regional headquarters and a thousand people instantly obliterated. It was three hours old, all over the networks, and here I was stuck with Delores herself, holder of the Nancy Reagan Chair for Paranormal Research at Cal State for what had been our regular interview.

I closed the laptop.

'What did you say?'

She looked over the top of her glasses.

'I asked if you could feel it, the oppression. How have you been feeling around your wife, colleagues, me?'

I shifted uneasily. I didn't like being interviewed, especially by someone who claimed to be telepathic.

'Honestly, a little twitchy, I must be tired or overworked.'

'Tell me, the bombing, how many of those have you seen? I'll tell you. None, not by well-adjusted middle-class women. She's the first domestic African-American suicide bomber isn't she?'

'First I know of.'

'She won't be the last. And the other things, the assaults, crime and the rest, it's unusual but you have no idea.'

'Of what?' She was argumentative, a typical academic, but it made her fortnightly column that much more interesting.

'The pattern. It's only women, the increasing violence, rising anger, 'edginess' as you put it. But not all, not yet. You remember

May's column?'

Couldn't forget it. 'Everyone's Telepathic' generated a tweet storm that still bubbled along.

'Well something's out there bouncing across the more attuned women, something unsettling. It's anti-male, it's growing, gaining strength, driving behaviours. The ones who aren't as attuned are just getting a taste. She', pointing to the closed laptop 'was probably at the upper end like me but probably didn't know it. Even now it's a struggle not to get my gun out the bottom drawer and put a bullet between your eyes.'

She smiled, mockingly.

'Not much of a struggle, but it's there. As for you, I've told you before you've got the ability, a strong ability, and it's getting to you. With us the anger points outwards, yours points inwards, sensitises you to what's going on.'

I didn't believe her before and I wasn't going to start now. I stood up, made my goodbyes and headed for the door. She pulled me up.

'Listen, I know you're sceptical but take some advice. Don't do anything to upset any woman, stay in the background and stay quiet for a bit. Try and detach your emotions too, it might help you settle. Hopefully it will all just blow over.'

At least this time when they'd finished they'd thrown her in with others, with food. She found herself facing seven haunted faces, all clinging together huddled in one corner. One face was familiar, Malala, daughter of a village elder. They held tight for ages, shared suffering easing the burden if not the pain. Malala cradled Inzali's face in both hands, gently, close.

'My poor sister, what a thing has happened to us. No-one will come, no-one will save. It is true, we are all alone and have none to turn to. Listen to me, listen carefully', drawing her closer 'to survive now is to win. You know they will come again and again for us?'

Inzali nodded.

'It is only our bodies they defile, not our minds, not our hearts. When they come, when they do, hide in here', squeezing her thumbs gently on Inzali's head 'go into here and stay, make your safe place and stay, no-one can get you there.'

Inzali nearly smiled, sorrowful, clutching Malala.

'If only you could speak my sister, if only you could.' The key in the lock grated. 'Remember, go here, hide in here, no-one can own you.'

Colonel Li Cxi Cuin ground her cigarette on the tabletop, looked at her unit, the all-woman cream of the People's Liberation Army's airborne divisions.

Two dozen pairs of eyes stared back, not with the cold steel of professionals but the burning of fanatics. Each bore black rings screaming of lack of sleep, each one haunted and driven by a common waking nightmare. She stabbed the screen behind her.

'All right, it's now just the doing. Right here, the Myanmar / Bangladesh border, eight of them held by one unit.'

In the darkness their transport waited, engines idling, cargo bay ramp open. It would be an act of war pure and simple, and she was leading it.

'Ingress here, HALO jump here, extraction at this point. We go in, take them out and bring them back.'

Colonel Li stood, the room instantly at attention.

'Mount up, our sisters are waiting.'

I just keep hitting him, straddling the bastard flat on the

pavement, my hands screaming from smashing bone and flesh. I could feel him inside me, his mates laughing as they held me down, my turn now bastard payback bastard payback, your smashed teeth and broken bones not enough, not nearly enough. A brick to my right catches my eye. I grab it in my blood caked hand holding it ready, cocked above his head my wedding ring glistening ... wedding ring? Pappa hasn't given me yet, the planting needs to be ... planting? I shake my head, grimace, shake it again. What the hell, who am I? It all vanishes from my mind, I look down to the man I'm killing, a small barely conscious brown-skinned stranger. I drop the brick, stagger and fall shaking against a wall. Denis, Denis, what the hell is this? One minute I stopped to buy a carton of milk, next I've dragged him out of the shop, down the alley tearing the life out of him. Voices reach me from around the corner, I move away into deeper shadows, away from the man now on his knees. The voices turn the corner, transform into a small group of young girls laughing, joking.

They see him, one arm raised, begging for help. They run to him, stand around him. He looks up at a young blonde. She takes his hand gently in hers, smiles, then gripping tightly sneers, yells, sends her heel grinding into his eye socket as he falls back. The ring closes, fists and feet in flurries, sickening wet snaps, shots then silence. I don't look back just run home, bolt the door and hide.

Inzali watched, detached, the men abusing her body. Malala had opened the door, she could hide, the pain and anger and hatred and humiliation soaked away, sent to Allah in his mercy while his daughter's body suffered. Her safe place in his arms, she would survive to yet be the pious daughter as her pain and terror flooded out and away.

Delores spat barely suppressed hatred down the line.

'I think it's a telaesthesiac episode here.'

I'd locked myself away in my study, barring the door and windows. I could hear my wife pacing up and down, day and night, dragging my hunting knife along the hallway click clack click clunk across the door, the jamb, the shiplap walls. She loved me and I her, but I knew I was dead if I poked my nose out.

'Telae-ka what?'

'It's a transmitting telepath, we're getting what she's feeling. It's getting stronger, clearer, can't block it. It's not just the telepaths now, all women are getting it.'

'How does it stop?'

'When you stop abusing us! Sorry, sorry, it's hard to control. We can't stop, can't block it. We see everything she sees, she's in a jungle somewhere and the men, oh god they look like you! I can see them, I can feel what she feels its … its … sorry, look, I can't talk to you, I'm tracing the call I'm hunting you down, turn off your machine —'

I tore the cabling from the wall, smashing my mobile until it was a pile of shattered plastic. Shaking uncontrollably I couldn't move, caught in the deluge of emotion from without and within, locked into the corner of the room in the dark. I clutched a paper weight in one hand, cowering, hoping like hell my wife didn't come in, didn't try, didn't make me …

Colonel Li smiled, flicked the safety off and waved two fingers forwards. They'd made it in unobserved, on time, on target. It was stronger now, she could feel them calling her. Twenty, maybe thirty minutes.

Inzali watched herself thrown again into the room, used and discarded. Her body was torn and damaged but she, her mind and spirit, was untouched. She rejoined, still and calm sitting next

195

to Malala. Malala was twisted, bent, cigarette burns across her chest and abdomen coupled to cuts and bruises across her back. Her wrists and ankles bled, the ropes having cut hard, the smell of putrefaction wafting up. She looked up, lacking even the strength to raise her hands.

'My sister, we feel you, your pain as ours. I'm sorry, I don't think I have much left.'

Inzali took Malala's head in her hands. She could not tell Malala how, but she could guide her. She squeezed gently, then left herself, looking down at the two of them. Malala tilted her head back, frightened as her body remained still. Inzali reached out, took her by the hand, then lifted her from herself.

'My sister, a safe place for all. Share yourself with me, I with you.' and in that instant the pain and suffering of both women met, shared, and filtered away. Each was still their own, each alone but now shared openly, fully. 'When they come again, as they must, we have our refuge ...'

Delores woke up, sat bolt upright. Two transmitters? Yes, now two, and she could feel them. How? Telaesthesia contagion? How? Both together both in the jungle, both ... she could see them, the first and the next, the names, Inzali, Malala, the suffering, the pain. She reached out.

'... and we will not abandon the others.' Malala smiled. They looked down on the small group of women below them, reached out with their minds, Inzali the stronger leading, encouraging Malala until the six were with them as one, together, shared.

Malala felt it first, presences just on the edge, open and seeking, near and far.

'Inzali, can you feel them?'

'Clearly, yes, many. The more of us the more I can feel.' Once

196

one alone, now one part of eight, more than she could have imagined. She felt one strong close by, maybe two kilometres away with others, more across the mountains, over the oceans. In the far distance strong, calling, one above all others. All sisters, all being linked and drawn. 'They have heard us faintly, some come to save, all are women … no, there are a few men, a few.'

'We should try to reach them all.'

'Yes, our sisters only, we must.' and the eight reached out to the clear and the strong, then as they joined to the weaker and weaker until, in the briefest of instants every woman was linked, shared, knowing, feeling and seeing. In it all, unnoticed, one other was pulled in and shared. Unwillingly.

Colonel Li didn't break step or hesitate, one mind or millions, single or communal to her it was simply greater impetus to the task, her unit now truly one. Generations ago her forebear was Emperor Qin Er Shi's seer, the ability passing undiluted and unnoticed down the female line until awakened by Inzali. She reached out to Inzali, Malala, comforting, assuring deliverance soon, safety soon.

Delores reached out, caught herself, forced herself back to the place she was, the person she was. Too clearly she understood the latency released from Inzali when shared, compounded then transmitted around the world. She felt lighter, happy, balanced and for the first time in years the knot of pain and fear had left. Left for where? She forced her objectivity, tried to find it, somewhere in the linking, the sharing of memory and experience it must … and it was, outside them all but contained, soaked away and held to be kept away until or if it could be sent back. To who?

'To all those who have given it, to those who did not help us or helped them.' Inzali clear, confident, powerful. 'As I have given the burden to Allah in his mercy so my sisters, and as he has taken ours he has lifted yours. And it will be returned to those who sent it.'

Delores felt around, saw the package contained, nothing touching it, alone but for one in its midst into which it was unfolding, copying itself, downloading everything into its psyche. Allah? Inzali's construct? She concentrated, recoiled, connected. Denis.

It's crushing me, tearing at me and I can't get rid of it, soaking in piece by piece by action by hurt all of it done by me to me for me on me with me. Act by act every pain and humiliation visited on woman by man, mockery to slavery and beyond, unfiltered raw loading on me and always in my name done to me screaming Denis, Denis, Denis ...

'Denis! Denis! Denis hear me!'

'Delores? Delores, oh god I can hear him Delores how could I do it to you Delores —'

'Denis! Listen to me, listen!'

'Delores?'

'Denis, listen. Pay attention to me, to my voice, only me. Open your eyes, don't feel, don't pay attention to anything but me. Denis? Denis!'

'Yes, yes, listen to you, yes.'

'Avoid emotion, concentrate on logic, numbers, reason. Stay awake Denis listen to me, do not sleep. Denis, what do you do?'

'Awake, listen, logic, numbers.'

'Primes Denis, what are the first three prime numbers?'

'Ahhh, one, three, ah ah five, five.'

'What are their factorials? I'm coming now, soon ...'

Colonel Li stood stock still one meter behind him. Bare chested, sweat soaked pants, cigarette in one hand Inzali's tormentor had no inkling of her presence. She fingered the blade, she could end him in any number of ways, slow or quick, the choice was hers. But not today. She saw the package and knew the time had come. The price of her career had been high; it was time to give them their own, to send it back. She felt her unit smile; Inzali, Malala and their village sisters agree; the linked world consciousness accept. She reached out, took the package and fully connected every man to it undiluted, unconstrained. For each one the entirety was theirs.

He fell to the ground, choking sobs caught in primal fear, pain, self-loathing horror, clutching his knees to his chest as were all Inzali's tormentors, and as here every man across the world. Colonel Li called for the airlift, stepping carefully over the impotent form at her feet. Yet a while would they suffer, until she decided they'd had enough. After release then justice, true justice and always the package hovering, threatening, Damocles' sword to control.

With no system to hide behind, no shield or cover and their lives on clear display to all, many cheated justice by their own hand. To the package pain upon pain was added, pain from the suicides, pain from knowing what a son, brother or lover truly were, from what was seen but not understood, what was understood but not acted upon. All this from they who would bear it to await sharing with those who inflicted it.

Except I. Drawn in by Inzali and Malala, fused by Colonel Li's connection I am caught, one with it never to be broken. They have tried, have drained and exhausted themselves for nothing. I cannot end it, to take my life will only add to the pains it holds and perhaps – if Delores is right – even collapse it back upon us all.

My life, such as it is, is to suffer. I stand as a totem, Cassandra, a life exiled in absolute solitude, disciple to logic and reason, sleeping dreamless sleep. When will it end?

END

Journeyman

He had travelled a long way in space and time, searching for answers which remained for the most part elusive; to those he found the passage of both time and distance had long since swept their meaning from him. His humanity had been subsumed and sustained by the technology around him, as had the spirit within, yet the desire to return had burned continually. He now found himself for only the second time in his life staring down at that which had once been his home, Earth. The part of him that was navigation assured him it was so, the ashen grey globe beneath him was home and the bloated red sphere to his back the life giver, the sun. Had it been so long? It had been as long as it had needed to be.

He had set off one day in April, gentle rain coursing down the side of his vessel as it rose from its field in Adelaide, to see what lay beyond the outer edges of the solar system in an untried and unproven craft. A combination of the animate and inanimate, machine and flesh, he had been integrated so thoroughly where man ended and man-made started was impossible to tell. No regret was felt at leaving the seething boiling masses of humanity in his wake, only for the green blue ball shrinking rapidly behind him as he carried a faint hope that he could bring some sort of relief to the declining civilisation of man.

Riding the cusp of relativistic travel the universe aged around him whilst the man machine did not. Of life beyond Earth he found relatively little, most of it being confined to low mounds of algae and lichen eking out existence where life should have flourished. Higher forms he had seen only three of, two of which were more concerned with feeding on themselves to be concerned with him. The other, being rooted physically to their planet unable ever to leave, were so consumed with envy and anger they had refused to communicate in any way, shape or form save to vent their venom at him. Only once did he meet what could be called sentience, close to the centre of the galaxy. He had been warned away, told he was not yet ready to enter, not truly unbound, still a child of the soil and not of the stars.

No lack of desolation faced him. Nations, civilisations and planets in ruins abounded, some bearing the signs of conflagrations of planetary scale that had seared life from the surface, and some having choked on their own filth of pollution. Others had seemingly quietly given up and drifted to oblivion as their spirits died, and for some the universe itself had conspired against the life it had nurtured, sending death from the heavens in untold ways. All death, no life, and where he found life he found no companions, no peers, no solace.

Mankind, he had considered on his homeward journey, was truly alone to face its future. And now he could see that the promise of his species was naught. Atmosphere stripped by solar winds, seas and life burned by the radiation of the sun, his home was a cinder. No man walked the surface, no work of man survived. What had been raised up was now cast low, the highest and the basest desires of humanity availing nothing.

He had outlived his father, and that was as it should be. But he had outlived his children, a tragedy by any other measure, and had now survived his children's children, and theirs; grown older than his country and civilisation, now all that remained of his race, the sole reminder of the brief and vainglorious rise of life in this small part of the galaxy. What was and still remained of his emotions wept bitterly; he was truly alone in the universe, more than he could have thought was possible.

There was no Earth to be bound to, none like him to mourn his loss. He was now a part of the cosmos, whole and complete in himself, nothing left to be a part of.

He remembered, recalled a place once unprepared for, now perhaps admissible. He turned his face to the galaxy's core and left.

END

Lazarus

JIt's nowhere near dawn, my eyes open, I tense. Dark is never dark, she lies, watches, smiles. Her hand reaches out, caresses my face.

'Just checking.' she whispers.

'You expected?'

'This, you, alive, my miracle.'

Miracle. The children follow me as I go, parents watch from doorways, pull their families away half scared, half envious, all covetous. I never asked for it, never sought him out or made promises, yet here am I, a ghost made flesh, the once dead once more among the living. The resurrection. The miracle. A stranger in the village I was born, raised, died.

'Rise once, then rise again.'

The stone bounces off my shoulder, skips ahead into the fields. I turn, Ruth pulls back, curses me from under her shawl, tears for her husband lost, venom for the one brought back instead of her beloved. My hand comes away bloodied, memories of worse and deeper as blades slashed, cut deep, unbidden reminders I am no more of them, of my line. Another small scar, my body through life unblemished save calloused hands until, afterwards, they test me, prod me, hate, wish. I lift my feet deliberately, rapidly, the dust of the village falls away as I continue alone.

The rabbi moves off the path, his disciples hurry heads down after him, sway as they give me wide berth, deny my existence. As much as they wanted him dead they want me, yet fear of what may happen stays their hand. Rumours persist of an empty tomb, apparitions, visitations; yet for each a hundred others of stolen corpses, far travels, the work of demons and devils on weak minds and weaker hearts. For me it matters not; the faith of my fathers is denied me by those who guard it, and he fails to return.

The sun is low, the afternoon cool when hobbling, bent-limbed, the branch seconded for his deformed leg digging deep he climbs, wearied but determined, to me.

'If I can but touch you I will be restored.'

I touch him. I touch him again, and again. Each my fist, my feet, my staff harder, merciless to his joints, his infirmities, his screams and piteous cries as he tumbles down, crawls away as broken in spirit as in body.

'Idiot! You want what is not mine to give? Better to walk through life crippled then through death's door once.'

Yet twice will I walk through it. Righteous in death I stood with Abraham four days then, dragged back to the living, cursed by the sorcery of my sisters' and wife's tears upon him, I am reborn. To what? Uncertainty, unable to sacrifice, pray, show obedience, I am left without place, without hope, without understanding. Even yet my body curses me, screams for rest, its time yet done, but I am poured in anew. I do not fit, it does not belong, yet are we here.

To the west lies what I knew, the land of my fathers, my family, my life, my death, the memory of the one who who returned me unbidden for his glory, his cause, his followers' faith.

To the east the desert, the wandering years of Moses and Joshua, the land of my people saved yet lost, purposeless, confused.

I turn my back to the setting sun and walk.

END

Lesson

Jake Yancy's parents, like all parents, were happy and scared when their small bundle of joy arrived. They did their best as best they could, squeezing him into their busy lives between work, sleep, friends, and Netflix. Like most they won some and lost some, like all they didn't know which was which.

When Jake was four he sat at the old oak table swinging his feet from his chair, his parents smiling lovingly from the other side. His father held out his fist.

'Would you like a present?'

'Yes please Daddy.'

His father opened his fist revealing a small yellow disc. It glistened and winked at Jake.

'Thank you Daddy. What is it?'

'It's money Jakey. If you're good we'll give you more each week.'

His mother smiled.

'I have a present for you too.'

Jake's eyes lit up.

She put a blue pig in front of him. It had a cute nose, big smile and a hole on top.

'What is it Mummy?'

'It's a piggy bank.'

'What's that?'

She tapped the pig on the hole.

'It takes care of your money. If you want you can put it in here to keep for later.'

Jake eyed the pig cautiously. He dropped the yellow disc into the pig, the pig squealed and its eyes lit up. Jake giggled, clapped his hands.

When Jake was five he sat at the old oak table, toes just touching the ground, his parents smiling lovingly from the other side. His father held his mother's hand.

'Jakey, we have some news.'

'Uh huh Daddy.'

'Mummy's pregnant, soon you will have a sister.'

'Why?'

'We wanted you to have someone to play with.'

'Oh. Thank you Mummy.'

'We will have to be extra good Jakey, mummy will be tired for a long while. We need to save time to do extra things.'

'How?'

'You do things quicker. Like your toys. When you put them away don't play with them, just put them away. That way you save a little bit of time to do other things.'

'Like my piggy bank?'

'Yes, like that.'

When Jake was nine he sat at the old oak table, hands in his lap, his sister now all of four years old sitting to attention opposite him.

'I have a present for you squirt.'

Penny smiled.

Jake put a purple ceramic pig with green flowers in front of her.

'Ooh cute! Thank you Jakey.'

'It's a piggy bank. Do you know what it does?'

She shook her head.

'It keeps your pocket money safe for later.'

Jenny tickled the pig behind its ears, tried to uncurl its tail.

'You've got gazillions!'

'Yes, but I've been saving longer. Watch this.'

Jake took out a silver coin, stuck it in the pig's mouth. Its eyes glowed, the pig grunted and slobbered, then swallowed the coin. Jenny giggled, hands over her mouth.

'Want me to teach you how to save money?'

'Yes please!'

'Later I'll show you how to save time.'

When Jake was twelve he sat safely strapped into the Alfa Romeo's race harness. His grandfather wrestled the car around the track once, then pulled into the pits.

'I hope you enjoyed it, I'm sorry I haven't more time.'

'It's ok gramps, I've had a blast.'

'Perhaps a rain check?'

'Sounds like a deal.'

'You're used to it?'

Jake laughed.

'Totally. Mum and dad are the worst, but I understand. I'm just saving IOUs.'

'With the relations you've got you must have a few lifetimes worth.'

When Jake was sixteen his sister sat him down on his bed as she tried to straighten his tie. He fidgeted, all nerves and anxiety.

'Sit still or I'll mess this up!'

'Sorry sis.'

She stepped back, regarded her handiwork.

'That's better. You like her, she's really cute isn't she?'

'Sure is.'

'Cute ones need more money, I'll get it.'

She turned, the bedroom walls covered in shelves, the shelves covered in blue and white ceramic pigs. She reached for the nearest white one.

'No, not that one, the last blue one.'

'Sorry.'

When Jake was eighteen he sat with his parents on the leather couch, his mother quietly crying, his father holding her hand in a vice-like grip. The specialist sat in the armchair opposite, impassive.

'I'm sorry. We've done all we can, all anyone can.'

'How long?' his father whispered, suddenly old, frail.

'Six weeks, two months.'

'What will it be like?'

'No pain, just growing weariness until one night she falls asleep then doesn't wake up.'

'It's not fair, she's only thirteen.'

'I know Mister Yancy, I know. Take her home. There's nothing we can do that you can't.'

Jake was five weeks older when he sat down on the edge of her bed. Penny stared at him, propped up on her pillows. The house was quiet, their parents out.

'Well squirt, two weeks left.'

'Maybe, maybe a bit less. It's the right time.'

'Just what I was thinking.'

She looked around her room, walls full of shelves, shelves full of ceramic pigs, some purple, some yellow. At the foot of her bed one white pig sat patiently.

'One of yours and one of mine?'

'That feels right.'

Jake picked up a yellow pig with one hand and the white one in his other. He held the pigs above Penny.

'Now?'

'Now.'

Jake tapped the pigs together, the porcelain cracking then disappearing. Lime green light cascaded into Penny's open mouth as the hours, days and weeks of promises made to them but never kept infused her, renewed her, until her life was no longer measured in days but in decades.

Jenny swung her legs around, springing out of bed to the sound of crunching gravel from the driveway below.

END

Lines

Thursday, it always seemed to be a Thursday. Not that Schilling noticed at first. All he could muster was to fall out of bed into his clothes, stroll zombie like to the bus, grunt at the driver and then slump into a seat until the express jolted to a halt. A semi-comatose shuffle through the CBD brought him to his office and the first coffee. Until the first coffee hit the world was simply a blur, an extension of his dreams.

Now more awake, Schilling felt there was something a little strange about the bus today. A mist? A dew? What was it? A haze, yes, everyone seemed hazy, fuzzy green. From his twentieth floor office all he could see was a cloudless day. Laughing dismissively he leant back in his chair. 'You're just too damn tired Max.'

His secretary passed in front of his glass walled office, a gently shimmering green rod protruding from their forehead. Schilling froze not knowing what to make of it. Even with his secretary out of sight it was almost as if he could still see it, a soft pale green glow. Walking unsteadily to his office bathroom he looked in the mirror and there, in the middle of his forehead, stood his own green rod. The last thing he saw as his world went black was the rod dipping malevolently to the floor.

He came to, a dull pain in the back of his head and green glow to the front. Deciding he really did need the day off Schilling hurried past the outer offices and desks straight to the elevator. Pressing the ground express button, he closed his eyes as his rod punched through the elevator floor. At ground floor he headed straight out the door.

The usually crowded pavement now had a jumble of glowing rods added to it. Writhing in a psychedelic green ballet, each rod's size and motion mirrored its owner's speed and direction. Every person had one. He backed against the office door, gawping at the crawling traffic. Each car's occupants had the rods but more elongated, thrusting through windscreens, around corners or bent backwards. Fascinated he watched two blocks of rods from two vehicles extend, connect, and join as one car sped down the street and the other tried to back out of an alley. The sound of screeching metal and tortured brakes as they collided was overshadowed only by green fireworks as the rods flared then retracted.

Steadying himself he set out for the short walk to his bus. The bus trip started in nightmarish fashion, however once used to seeing himself and his fellow passengers seemingly impaled by lime green light sabres he found the pulse of lengthening and contracting rods relaxing. By the time he reached his front door he was looking at the whole thing more as an experience, the product of an overtired mind that with sleep and relaxation would pass.

The rods persisted however and Schilling became accustomed to them. Although not appearing on television or movies, animals had them. He developed a dark pleasure in predicting his cat's movements and blocking its every turn.

But scaring cats and the occasional colleague did not hold him for long. A businessman first and foremost, Schilling started to think how it could be turned to his advantage. Anything to do with sports he rejected out of hand, other options offered no profit or progress, and automation or reproduction was not possible. By the following Friday he was none the wiser and more frustrated. He believed that advantage should be turned to profit and it was only the incapability of its owner that stood in the way. Was he incapable? Hardly. So why no answer?

Waiting at the curbside he tried to put it out of his mind. The last Friday afternoon each month was spent with Chalker, his most important client. She was an unusual and brilliant CEO, having fought through ranks of misogynistic blowhards to build the ReoProm conglomerate. Their ritual two hours golf or squash intermingled with business talk was time well spent.

The Bentley pulled up and he stepped inside. To his surprise Chalker was not dressed for golf or squash, but in her usual corporate garb. He looked at his now useless clothes bag wondering what he was in for.

'I've made a change to our usual arrangements Schilling. I've a small investment choice I want to go over so I thought it best to go straight to the horse's mouth.'

'Sounds fine.'

'Good.' and, after tapping on the driver's glass partition returned to her iPad. Schilling pulled out his Blackberry, indulging in the communally separated task of ework.

Ten minutes later the driver deposited them at the member's entrance of Royal Prestlock race course. Once seated Schilling looked inquiringly at her. 'Horses? It seems a bit out of character.'

'Oh no, too risky and variable. But the racecourse itself is totally different.'

He found himself engrossed in the details. As a business proposition the race course was attractive, more so when the adjoining five hectares of urban fringe land was factored in. After an hour Chalker was called away, Schilling deciding to stay on and look around.

Moving to the stands he watched the racegoers' movement and colours with interest. Like an army of ants, the ebb and flow around the bookmakers, rush to the rails as the horses rounded on the final leg, and the small shower of confetti as their bets failed to pay. The interplay of green rods beating in time with the pace of the crowd added to an attractive display.

At the start of the third race he turned his attention to the horses. He was surprised to see rods on the horses, and it took him little time to understand what was going on. Until the horses came into the enclosure both the horse's and jockey's rods behaved normally. Once there the jockey's rod merged with the horse's, remaining fixed and forward facing throughout the race. The relative size of each horse's rod was how they finished, longest rod first, shortest rod last. Once the race had finished the jockey's rod reappeared.

Between the horses turning up in the enclosure to the race start was just short of five minutes. As bookmakers seemed open up until the race itself started there was four minutes to place a bet. He flipped through his wallet, past the forest of plastic. A crisp twenty dollar note showed through. Finally, the pay day.

He was opposite the starting enclosure just as the jockeys mounted up for the sixth. Number two instantly developed a huge thrumming shaft of green. He went quickly to the nearest bookie.

'Twenty on number two please.' thrusting the bill upwards.

'On the nose?' pad and pen poised.

'Beg pardon?' He had no idea what the old guy meant.

'To come first mate.' the bookie shot back heavily emphasising the 'first', drawing appreciative chuckles from the crowd.

'Oh yes, sure, sorry.' with which the bookie scrawled quickly on the pad and handed the slip to him, about as legible as his doctor's scrawl. His horse remained stone cold motherless last until two turns from home when it slowly, achingly pulled itself up from the back of the pack and fell over the line a bare nose in front. Schilling picked up his winnings, bet them on the next race and won again.

Setting up for the final race he noticed that if he picked the first three places successfully the winnings could be far greater. After watching the horses line up he placed his bet and watched the race unfold exactly as he knew it would. Schilling picked up his winnings without looking at them and caught a cab for home deep in thought.

Once home he leafed through the wad of cash. It was close on sixteen thousand dollars. Three hours 'work', if it could be called that, one month's post tax pre-bonus earnings for no more effort than getting a cup of coffee. It was so easy it felt like stealing. A feeling of guilt left him as rapidly as it had arrived. He reached for his mobile phone, excused himself from the office for Saturday for the first time in years, and prepared to make his plans.

It only took that weekend to set most of the system up. He had to be physically present at, or have a clear line of sight to, the racecourse at the right time. He had to be discrete, anonymous. He knew that the bookies at Prestlock would not soon forget his face. If he appeared there or anywhere regularly questions would be asked; it did no good to take tens of thousands out of a racecourse day after day. He had to be able to access off course bookmakers in a four-minute gap. It was the one thing that he could not do. He could either get someone in from outside, an unknown quantity, a potentially uncontrollable risk factor. Or he could get someone close, tied. He knew the perfect person.

The following Tuesday Schilling summoned Larsen from IT into his office. To him Larsen resembled a cross between Dicken's

Fagin and Ayoade's Moss. Weedy and preposterously socially awkward, Larsen was the best they had in remote and wireless applications development. At thirty-six he would have headed IT if he had a shred of social skill. What little else Schilling knew of Larsen was that he was regarded as the office's greatest and least successful sleaze, could not hold more than one drink, and was very easily and totally intimidated by those higher up the ladder. Larsen seemed like just his man.

Larsen sat in front of the vast oak desk regarding the figure seated behind it as an object of both fear and derision. What does Maxwell Schilling want with me? Everything Larsen was Schilling wasn't. From the tailored Armani suit to the smooth as oil boardroom style, the gulf between them was immense and unassailable. That Schilling put the fear of god into him was an obvious understatement but, as is often the case, it was based not on respect but on loathing.

'So Larsen, I have a small project that requires your skill. It's for an existing client of ours, ReoProm. You've heard of them?'

Larsen hadn't. He nodded.

'Good. They are a critical client of ours, diversifying into racecourse ownership and patron services. They've come to us for help. Drink?' he finished, avoiding the crystal decanters to his right and motioning to the espresso machine on his left.

'Yes, thanks, flat white no sugar please.'

Schilling smiled, set the controls for Larsen's drink and his own short black.

'ReoProm wants to maximise revenue on the racecourses it will own. They've identified off course betting as a priority. Each track gets a slice from on track bookmakers but they get nothing if a patron uses off track bookmakers. They have asked is if it is possible to develop a small programme, an app, that can link to multiple betting services at one time, making real time bets on which they take a fixed percentage commission.'

'Of course, but there are good ones out there already, it's not something that we actually need to do.'

'They do know that, but they gave me a list of some features that they can't otherwise obtain.' sliding a single page across the desk.

Larsen studied it for a few seconds then looked up. 'It looks ok. Some things, well, they're a bit different but of it's what the customer wants —'

'Which it is.'

'Then the customer gets it. Apart from the obvious question of delivery time, I'm just a little bit curious about why they asked us to do this. They've got their own guys, could have gone to a developer firm.'

Schilling stood up and perched on the front of the desk. 'It's my fault, actually. When I was talking they mentioned they were going to outsource the job. I said we could do it faster, better and ensure the privacy that ReoProm likes. I know' spreading his hands 'that I may have made a promise from ignorance but I have seen what we can do and a foot in another door can't hurt. It can be done?'

'Well yes, I see no reason why not.'

'So how long? It's got to be bullet proof, can't afford a dud. Oh, and it's in addition to everything else.'

Larsen thought briefly. 'Four, maybe six weeks tops, if you want it perfect.'

'I can't afford to give them a faulty product, let's say six weeks to get it just right.'

Schilling watched Larsen leave with both hope and trepidation. He had no doubts Larsen could deliver, but now another had been added in. Hopefully the ReoProm angle was enough to keep him in line.

Larsen agreed with Schilling in one respect. He could do the job and, quite frankly, could do it in a week after hours. The app he had been asked to build was very simple. It was also an opportunity. Although Larsen's work mates thought they knew him they had no idea of what he was into, the trouble it had bought him, or the people he dealt with. It was sucking the life out of his finances but as long as he could keep it fed it didn't matter. He was always on the lookout. And Schilling, the idiot, had just handed him the golden goose. Larsen had no doubt that ReoProm would watch its commission like a hawk but the punters, now that was different. Larsen's idea was tried and tested, a simple rounding skim leaving ReoProm's commission alone and skimming each punter's bet and any winnings. Not much each time but it would add up. A few lines of code and no one would be able to see the actual figures. Only ReoProm would be left untouched, and what would the chances be of a winning punter checking to the last cent?

As good as it was it could be better. It was one thing to skim but why not piggy-back on successful punters? He smiled. The horses were always rigged. He busied himself with making a backdoor tracker.

Schilling wanted to hide the app clearly in the open, to actually roll the thing out with ReoProm, make it a value-added proposition to Chalker. In fact it was easier than Schilling had imagined as Chalker could not resist the idea of a quarter or even half a percent passive income. In fact when the app was delivered she had taken it and, with minor re-branding, spit it out as freeware for general public use. Nothing if not patient, Schilling decided to wait three weeks until the app was well and truly embedded before starting.

Larsen had more pressing issues to deal with, so he kept a closer eye on matters. In the first week one hundred dollars came through, a paltry amount but a start. Weeks two and three produced over one thousand dollars each, enough for him to

222

make his payments and a little over. It wasn't enough by itself though, his tastes had changed, gotten harder, and he needed more. He started to go through the betting data, looking for the systematic winners, the ones to mimic.

Schilling was ready to start. He had decided to make sure he lost at least eight out of ten bets but that at the end of each month he was exactly where he wanted to be. Avoiding large odds, staying with short ones for his wins, appearing like an average punter. He had picked out seven tracks within an easy three hour drive, intending to rotate randomly through them, sometimes betting with one agency, or some, or all. No pattern, no regularity, no tell-tale fingerprint, all cased in five randomly rotating accounts.

Over the following two months the app worked perfectly, being taken up by an ever-increasing group of punters. Schilling still appeared the upright corporate and tax citizen his office demanded him to be. Everything he was doing, although a little unorthodox, was perfectly legal. He took pains to keep it that way, even to the point of paying the correct tax on his winnings. At the track no one noticed or cared, he was just the quiet guy in the stands who turned up every so often. Putting a few dollars through the on course bookmakers helped, never any big wins, just small wins, small losses, looking every bit like the cash strapped punter he was trying to portray. Smooth as silk, no problems, no issues. Two or three years of this then just walk away. Maybe.

Larsen was not so settled. Schilling was used to having more than enough money and could control and moderate his behaviour, Larsen wasn't. Financially he'd always lived on the edge. His habits kept him nailed there, owing money to people he really didn't want to owe to for things he didn't want anyone to know about. The only limit to his appetite was his income. Greater income just seeped away on more of the same. Now he simply routed his skimmings straight through to his creditors.

He sighed deeply, rubbing salve into gouges across his chest and abdomen. He'd failed to find that one punter he could mimic, one that was consistently above the line. No discernible patterns nothing he brooded, pulling a few shards of glitter from his thigh, it goes straight in and straight out to theirs and I'm nearly square each week. Just one, I need just one of them to make consistent gains in each day, just one … and he broke off cursing himself a fool.

'One day? One day!?! What sort of idiot am I?' He leant forwards, resetting his tracker. One day isn't enough for any pattern, lucky or bent, it needs more time, more time. I've got months of data, what's happening over that? Almost as quickly as he thought it he saw it. Of all the thousands using the app a small slice were above even for the whole period; a smaller slice far enough above to be earning a good income; and of those a very small number stood out as far ahead each month. Bent, they're bent but smart, noting how anything other than a long term view of their entire betting history would not show a thing.

'Now where are you?' muttering, starting to run back the IP traces. It didn't take him long to find it. Five accounts were being run out of one device. Never simultaneously, never in the same sequence, but in a seemingly random mix up that never saw activity in one account for more than four hours in any one day. Taken as a whole it was crystal clear, always a long way up each month. He dug further into the accounts that linked back to the banks and …

He nearly fell off his chair laughing, head thrown back, tears rolling down his face. 'I bloody knew it! Perfect, oh god so perfect! Schilling! Mr. I'm-so-damned-corporately-upright Schilling's scamming the ponies!'

For a second blackmail occupied his mind, good god what he could get, but he thought better of it. Best to keep it in his back pocket, keep it for the day he could really use it, really need it. It didn't matter now how Schilling was doing it, Schilling would never go for anything that wasn't ironclad. Ok, whatever you're getting I'll get more, starting to code a simple piggy-back. Every bet you make I'll make as well. But no pussyfooting around, oh no, once there's enough in the kitty I'll at least double your bets. Easy money in the bank with insurance on top. Larsen could hardly control himself, hardly keep a straight face. Finally he was going to get what he knew he deserved.

Thursday, it always seemed to be a Thursday. Schilling felt ready for anything after the green bars. His evening bus load of green horned unicorns now all sported tiny cobalt blue skull caps of varying widths. The largest one covered the whole head above the ears, the smallest the size of a coffee cup. Schilling smiled, settled back. Another mystery, another piece of weirdness and undoubtedly another profitable opportunity to be pursued.

Naawaina carefully adjusted his jacket in the porch light. He'd never felt totally comfortable squeezing his solid Maori frame into it, but he had an image to project, a reputation to keep. I am after all a businessman, just that my tools of trade are a little different. His paw gently closed around the brass dusters in his pocket. A little different but equally effective.

One of the grubs that had particularly sordid tastes had apparently become too financial in the past few months. And grubs with money became indiscreet and dangerous. 'Send a message, find out what's with the new cash,' he'd been told 'and take his handler with you.' Naawaina glanced sideways at Ilmari beside him, short and stocky in slacks and cardigan. He didn't like the Finn, thought him an amateur who was dipping into the merchandise. One day he would get to pay Ilmari a business call and that would be more pleasure than work.

Ilmari took off his sunglasses, carefully placed them in his back pocket and rang the doorbell. The sound of muffled voices made their way out, a curtain to one side seemed to briefly open and close, but no one answered the door. Ilmari rang the doorbell again. Again no response. Ilmari took his mobile phone out.

'Ten seconds, we know you're at home. Just a little friendly chat, no trouble, but if it's not open shortly you'll need another door.' He smiled hesitantly at Naawaina. The Kiwi had a reputation, and he was worried. Hopefully this was all about the mark and not him. A series of soft clicks brought his attention back to the door. It opened fully to reveal a disorganised, if clean, interior. The face peering out had the same look. Ilmari stood aside letting the Kiwi's bulk slide past him into the house.

'Thank you.' he intoned to the now ashen face, closing the door with an ominous click. 'We'll have that little talk', ushering the figure towards the kitchen 'as soon as my associate finishes his tour.' Larsen nodded glumly.

The Kiwi replaced the blade in his scabbard and, holding the front door open, watched the child walk out into the night. Dressed and removing the last bonds from his wrists he didn't spare a backwards glance. With a small grunt the Kiwi closed and latched the door. Business, it's all business even though I hate what this grub does. As he entered the kitchen he could see Larsen seated on a stool, Ilmari opposite, leaning forwards. A look inside the fridge liberated a cola and two doughnuts, with which he sat on the edge of the benchtop and gave a short nod to Ilmari.

'Right, let's talk money my friend, what you got and what you owe.'

Larsen looked bemused. 'Owe? I don't owe anything, I'm ahead.'

'Yes, you are. You've never been ahead before, not until three months ago.'

'Yeah, well, I'm just getting better you know, a few good breaks —'

226

'Don't put nobody eight thou ahead! Where you getting it?'

'I'm not owing, you get what I use ahead now, I'm always ahead. So what's the issue?'

'You've gone from two thou a month to forty plus, you're getting richer tastes and you're still just a shit puncher at work. You know what that tells me? It tells me something's going on that we need to know about. So. What is it?'

Larsen spread his arms wide in earnest. 'Nothing, I told you, a few good breaks at work and that. I mean, I'm pushing it all your way you know, I mean, you guys have just the hottest damned —'

The Kiwi stood up, glaring at Larsen who immediately shut up and shrank back. Brushing the odd crumb from his lapel he replaced Ilmari on the stool, moving closer to Larsen, just inside arm's reach. He smiled gently.

'What perhaps you do not understand is that we are here for your welfare. In fact, we need to know how you are getting all this extra cash not for ourselves, but to help you.'

'Help me? How the hell do you —' The impact from the Kiwi's open-handed slap nearly took Larsen's face off, the rapidly reddening shape of five perfectly formed fingers rising from his cheek. The only thing that distracted him from the titanic ringing in his ears was the shock of the backhanded slap on his other cheek as the Kiwi bought his arm back.

'So now you see', taking the dusters from his pocket, obviously and gently sliding his left hand in to them 'that telling us will help your welfare. I am, unfortunately, not a patient man so you will understand if I have to, ah, encourage you.'

Larsen started to shake, trying to resist the urge to piss. He shrank back on the stool, finding his arms locked behind him. Ilmari leant closer in to him, close enough for Larsen to smell the coffee and riisipuuro on his breath.

'Ok, ok!' still trying to wriggle back. 'Yeah, yeah, I've got money, it's horses you know, I'm making it on the ponies.'

The Kiwi stared at him, expressionless. 'No one does that well unless they are bent or on the inside, and you don't seem to me to be —'

'No, no!' shrieked Larsen. 'No, I got a system, I got a chump who never loses, never, always ends up ahead, believe me', twisting to look into Ilmari's eyes 'it's true, believe me!'

Larsen felt a huge paw grab his jaw, pulling him round to look square into the Kiwi's face. He scrunched his eyes hard, waiting for the hit that would surely take out his teeth. When it didn't come he gingerly opened one eye.

'You see' noses nearly touching 'how talking to us helps you.' Larsen nodded as best he could in that vice-like grip. 'So let us continue our conversation, and nice and clear and slow so we have no need to, ah, encourage you further yes?'

'Yes, yes.' he squawked.

'Very well', leaning back and releasing Larsen 'please start again from the beginning. You said ponies yes?'

'Yeah, horse races, ponies. Look, a few months ago …'

Across town Schilling was attending a different exclusive gathering. For the tenth year in a row corporate profits had outstripped records, congratulations and expensive red flowing like water on the rooftop penthouse. The thirty-eighth floor garden was an extravagant expression of wealth and power, one fitting the head of Schilling's firm. Schilling smiled to himself. Just one level away from the boardroom and it just doesn't matter, I could buy this penthouse, the whole block of them, the firm itself. Seeing the managing director across the grass he smiled broadly and raised his glass in salute. Perhaps, just perhaps I have set my sights too low. Unlimited wealth, totally legal, I can with care do nearly anything. He grinned. Yes, another mouthful of red later, anything or anyone.

Across the rooftop the junior levels were getting rowdier. Part of the fun of these events was watching it unfold, watching the flow of high spirits and expensive drink collapse barriers and controls until, at the right point, they could be plucked off one by one for some 'intensive mentoring'. Part of the game, part of the fringe benefits of power and wanting to gain power. He was happy that Chalker wasn't here this year, she always played that game harder and keener than he.

The juniors had now moved closer to the glass railing, Schilling looking on bemused as one of the blue skull caps shimmered and then started to shrink at an alarming rate. It's owner, perched precariously on the glass railing giggled, jumped up and started tightrope walking along the ledge. Her blue skull cap rippled, contracted and then popped out of existence. Her heels slipped and soundlessly she plummeted over the edge. Schilling rushed to the railing looking at the crowd of people and cars gathering around the small red dot thirty-eight floors below.

The Kiwi listened attentively to his mobile phone. He had heard Larsen's tale twice and, as improbable as it had sounded, believed him. That Larsen had produced the device and his bank account records after some gentle persuasion had helped. Although he had the answers he was sent to get, there were times you needed to take things upstairs. This was one of them, so he had rung in and now had just finished repeating the story.

On the other end of the line his boss was thinking fast. This one little pervert had, somehow, managed to finger each and every rigged race in the past few months. The fact that somewhere someone else knew meant eventually others would and this little earner would fall, maybe the whole edifice with it. It was too much to risk.

'And he's wiped out his skimming and tracking apps?'

'Yes.'

'You have all the software, computer drive, backups?'

'In my bag and in the car.'

'And that name again?'

'Schilling.'

The Kiwi heard again the short intake of breath.

'Ok. It needs to be wrapped up, cleaned. Erase it. One other thing.'

'Yes?'

'Clean up that shit Finn too. No lose ends.'

The Kiwi put the mobile pack in his pocket, moving into the kitchen.

'All good?' Ilmari asked.

'Yes.' standing behind Ilmari, facing Larsen.

Larsen didn't feel good, the two of them looking at him.

'I'm going to be fine?' looking at Ilmari and the Kiwi in turn.

The Kiwi smiled, grabbed Ilmari's chin in one hand and, placing an arm around his shoulders, gave one rapid pull. Accompanied by the sickening crack of vertebrae Ilmari slumped lifeless to the floor.

Larsen shrank back, mouthing soundlessly as the Kiwi closed the short gap between them.

'Understand', lifting Larsen up from the stool by the neck 'this is purely business although I am not particularly fond of you.' The knife seemingly appeared by magic in his right hand and, with one stroke, lanced into Larsen's brain through his left eye. Dropping the body to the floor he extracted the knife, wiping it clean on Ilmari's slacks before replacing it in its scabbard. Driving away he saw the first fingers of flame jumping from the front windows.

Friday afternoon Schilling stood on the curb waiting for Chalker. Lost in thought he didn't notice the cab stop or the large presence behind him until something cold, hard and menacing prodded him in the back.

'Eyes front, keep quiet and get into the cab.' the presence ordered. Schilling didn't need to see it to know not to argue, so he climbed in through the opened door. The driver stared back impassively through the grille to the man-mountain now sitting next to him, and then took the cab out into the flow of traffic.

Schilling looked beside him. 'If it's money you want, I can give it to you, all of it, there's no need —' stopping cold at the look coming his way.

'I asked you to be quiet Mr. Schilling', the Kiwi hissed 'so please remain so. Your money is nothing.'

Schilling sighed, looked ahead. If it's not money I'm a hostage then, and in real trouble. The cab continued it's journey in silence.

Schilling came to, bound to a chair in a small, bare room. Faint shadows danced in time with the sway of a solitary bulb. He didn't know how long he had been out but he knew how he had gotten that way. His glasses lay broken on the floor, the taste of blood in his mouth. Chin on bare chest he could see small welts and bruises, too small for the pain that placing them had given. Grudgingly he admitted that the man-mountain knew his stuff, applied the right lever to the right place. And now he – or they – knew everything.

He lifted his face to the mirrored wall opposite. He looked a mess, blue skull cap and green bar notwithstanding. At least they left my underwear on, spared one final indignity.

The Kiwi delicately wiped the last few spots of blood from his knuckles. For the second time in a week he had heard an unlikely, impossible, explanation of events. And for the second time he knew beyond a doubt the explanation was true. Rods. Rods on horses. He shook his head. Discarding the tissue he buttoned his jacket.

Schilling was starting to regain his senses, his composure. He had no illusions about his situation, precarious no matter what the outcome. But he had the skill, the capability no one had, a bargaining chip. It was simply another business dealing he told himself, one with different rules and roles, but business none the less.

The Kiwi waited in silence. The immaculate, slightly built figure standing at the one-way mirror was, since his mother's death, the only person that held his total and unquestioning respect and obedience. They combined an iron will and professional self-control with clinically cold and calculatingly rational cruelty. That they controlled a legal conglomerate acting as a front for the largest illegal operation in the country wasn't surprising. That in this, the most male of male dominated arenas she was a woman, was.

She turned back from the glass towards the Kiwi. 'Let this be another lesson for you', Chalker started 'in this business anything can happen. This man has helped us before but now ...' She sighed gently. Really, what did she care that Schilling made some extra out of the horses, but his stupidity with Larsen was unforgivable. And more so using ReoProm as the vehicle, placing her in the spotlight.

'Business is business, never forget that.' She turned her back to him, moving towards the exit. 'I want you to ...'

Schilling jumped instinctively as the door opened and the Kiwi lumbered in. He felt his stomach knot and cold sweat break out on his forehead. Not from the Kiwi, not for the same impassive cold look on his eyes. But next to him, on the mirrored wall, he could see his own reflection. And on the top of his head his blue skull cap rippled, contracted, then popped out of existence.

END

Lost love's price

'No stop, please! You can't do this!' screaming, struggling futilely against the chains that held her fast 'Please!'

I leant closer to her, to that face once a thing of beauty now repulsive, to the body once cherished now hated, to her, my only, my beloved now polluted, never to be.

My tears scorching fell on her, my laboured breath shifting dark strands of hair caressing her cheeks.

'I can and I will', I pushed through clenched teeth 'and for the rest of your life you will remember, you will feel my pain, my suffering, my heartbreak. Forever you will know how you destroyed me.'

'Please, I'm sorry, I've told you I'm sorry, it was nothing to me, I was weak, it was just once and he —'

'And that is enough!' I screamed, pulling away from the arms seeking to hold me, back, back and away.

Eyes burning, vision blurred, with my heart pounding to escape my chest I flung my head back and howled in primal rage to the darkened sky above.

'Everything I gave you, all of me, solely, totally, you were my dream, my fulfilment, my all and you throw it away on him?!?!'

I lifted my arm from inside my coat pocket, the menacing form of the syringe glinting in the first wan touch of moonlight. I stepped closer again, bearing the syringe above my head on outstretched arm as a banner, a totem of hate and pain.

'And this, this is my response. All that is evil, all that is deformed, vile, repulsive and hated lives within to twist and burn the human form to the degenerate! All that is needed is the moon and the flesh!' I leered viscously at her, shaking, still shaking with rage.

'Don't do this, I still love you, I do, I still do! We can still be together, don't do this to me —'

'You?! Oh no, oh no, not so easy, not so simple.' with which I sent the syringe lancing down into my neck, thrusting burning pain as I hammered it home, the seminal genetic bearer coursing through my veins.

'This, this is for me, and for you to know and see and feel and suffer as I will, through me. Love me? Love me!?! Then love what you have made!' with which I threw the key to her chains at her feet even as I felt the first shattering impact run through me.

She lay crumpled against the tree, held up by only one arm, crushed. 'What have you done? What have you done to yourself, to us?'

I tried to laugh but the pain arcing through my arms changed it to a whine, a piteous animal whimper. My arms tore out of my shirt and coat in a distended, twisted, wizened tangle curling back on each other, knuckles huge and torpid with pain, fingers clenched inwards as arthritic claws drawing blood, yellowed nails sunk deep into palms.

'Each full moon, each time I will be transformed to this, a thing that shows the ugliness, the pain, a remin —'I screamed anew, falling in to the ground. My face slid down to lie loosely hanging

234

on the frame of my skull, a green folded flaccid sack of putrefied flesh punctured only by huge cracked teeth piercing lips 'always, always.'

She had her chains off and was now beside me, holding me as I lay there. 'No, no, no you can change it, fix it, tell me you can fix it', shaking me, crying 'tell me you can fix it, tell me!'

'Never, no, it cannot be undone.' I managed to mumble, waves of nausea making their way through me.

My spine twisted and compressed with a crack that seemed to reach the mocking moon above, shattering the night. My legs bowed, buckled, the left shortening even as the right twisted through ninety degrees, its curve matched only by the bowing of my back.

A final crack, a final nightmare blaze of pain and my neck shrunk, dropping my head to my shoulders, my skin changing to a bloody mess of open scabs and coarse hair.

It was done. I pulled myself painfully to all fours, unable now to stand let alone walk, vomiting as my stench reached my nostrils. I turned to see her face, whitened, uncomprehending, revolted beside me.

'To remind you', I spat out slowly from crippled lungs and deformed larynx in croaking, rasping speech 'of my pain, pain you bought me, how cheaply you threw it away. Once the moon has left I will change back, but each full moon this will return.'

She looked at me, broken, silent. My pain was now hers, and would always be. And that pain doubled as I returned from creature to human, human to creature, always with the pain, the torment, for the rest of my life. I still loved her, I always will.

'I love you', I whispered gently, crawling towards the edge of the woods 'that is my real pain.'

She sat staring after me. 'And Kathy, I will always love you.'

END

Love is the drug

Furniture of memory latex and plasteel, ceramics decorating walls and floors, windows of smart glass. A clean, harsh, efficiently depressing air bringing the silence of the tomb to the hospital.

Emily and Tasha were with the specialist. The door opened and Dr. Heres motioned James inside, pointing to a solitary chair on the far side of the room. James seated himself quietly.

Tasha glowered at him, a seven year old well versed in the social mores and norms placing her above all men, her father included. Father. A word out of time, an anachronistic biological label. None of his genes resided in Tasha, nothing of who he was. A man was simply of use, every woman requiring an other for certain necessary tasks. They knew best, said it made for a better society. Twenty-eight years of conditioning told him so; centuries of history simply reinforced the belief. It was as it was, as it should be, and he was Emily's.

Dr. Heres drummed her fingers on the desk. James had let his mind wander again. He settled, hands in lap, silent.

'I will make this as simple as possible for you James. If Emily wishes you to know more it is up to her.'

'Thank you.'

'Tasha has a very serious illness. It will be extremely difficult to treat. For the next five months you must be extra careful and attentive and make no mistakes. Most importantly do not upset or anger her. Is that clear?'

'Yes. No mistakes, no anger, no upset.'

Dr. Heres turned to Emily.

'I will leave any further discussion to you. Obviously mortality projections are beyond him.'

'It's best not to confuse him. This much is enough.'

He sat quietly. He'd told no-one he had learned to read and write. Illegal, it was forbidden by law and church as folly taunting men into believing they could leave their preordained place. He did not know what mortality meant, but he knew mortal was about life so maybe Tasha was in deep trouble.

Dr. Heres ushered Emily and Tasha out, ignoring James' thin, quiet frame nestled in the corner. She was just about to shut the door behind her when she noticed him.

'Shouldn't you be taking them home?'

'She's dying isn't she?'

'I've told you all Emily wants you to know.'

James stood, hesitated.

'Please, you know they will tell me no more.'

'It's for your own good. You have a home to run. It's too much to worry your pretty head about.'

'At least let me have a name for what she has.'

She looked at him, her scowl softening to pity. Stupid men never know when to stop, when it's better not to know.

'Fine. It's called Kavoort's Syndrome. Now go.'

They were waiting under the awning, looking at the car through the rain. Emily barely glanced at him, Tasha with folded arms contemptuously ignoring him. He took the umbrella and escorted them across the three meter gap being careful to keep them perfectly dry. Once they were seated, car door closed, he folded the umbrella and went to the open driver's compartment, the wind-blown rain falling harder, scouring his face.

She'd required him that evening. His energy had risen to meet her need, now she lay propped up against the pillows watching him dress. He stood, back towards her in mock bashfulness, careful to make sure the mirrors reflected him back to her as he knew she liked.

Tasha lay absentmindedly on her bed in the attached room. She was disinterested now, but the time would come when Emily would introduce her to this pleasure through him, with him. She would learn her skills at his hands before selecting her own. If she lived.

The tiniest flicker of sorrow showed before he recomposed himself, pulled the veneer of thankful ecstasy back. It was not unnoticed, Emily pointing to the bed beside her, motioning him to sit.

She ran her fingers through his dreadlocks.

'This is why we don't tell you everything, it only worries you. It's nothing you can understand. There's more tests, more examinations. If you want to help just keep doing your best around the house.'

James nodded.

'Now off you go.'

James stood, made his way back to his quarters.

Leon closed the washer and hit the deep cycle button.

'Well of course she's right, just settle down and keep house.'

He sat next to James, the plastic chair gently protesting.

'Why on earth you'd want to interfere in women's business I have no idea. Here I was thinking you were a fine upstanding boy and you're wanting to disturb the natural order of things?'

James bristled slightly.

'It's not that, I just want to help. I feel so useless, what good's a clean house and fresh clothes if she's so sick?'

Leon jabbed his finger at him, cigarette ash landing on James' knee.

'It's the foundation of the family, stability to weather the storms of life.'

He quoted directly from Sunday school.

'Adam came first imperfect and flawed, then came Eve to be obeyed and adored. Our job is to support and help, not interfere.'

'I suppose so.'

'No suppose at all.' adjusting his codpiece, trying to avoid the chafe. 'Let them take care of the big stuff.'

Katie waved at James from behind the counter, motioning him over. She owned the laundromat and was on society's fringe, a threat to the girls, friend to the boys.

'So what's up Jim, trouble in paradise?'

He told her, although it hurt his head just remembering the details.

'Well they'd say that wouldn't they. Do you want me to find out for you?'

She pulled out her interface.

'It's not good. Tasha's dying, Jim.'

Although he suspected, hearing it spoken was like calling it into existence. The cold gnawing at him wasn't from the air-conditioner.

'So what's the cure?'

She leant forwards, tapping and scrolling for a few minutes.

'It's weird, they don't say.'

It was more than James' inbred politeness could take.

'What's wrong, what do you see?'

Katie looked up, made sure they were alone.

'Only if you can keep it a secret. And I'm serious, not even to Leon.'

'Yes, yes, whatever you want.'

'There's no cure here. But it seems like there is one off-world, and if I read it right it's just one injection and it's done.'

'So I could just buy it?'

'No, it's banned. They'll never let it in.'

'Why?'

'Hon, it's based on boy hormones. Only girls get the disease, it's rare and always fatal. But if boy hormones cure it then that makes girls dependent on boys and that is not allowed, you know that.'

'That's not fair, I'll do it anyway, I'll get some and bring it to her.'

'Nobody travels off-world; nobody comes, nobody goes. It's only the automatic cargo ships that visit and they're guarded.'

She looked at his face, surprised it was streaked with tears.

'You love Tasha don't you?'

James nodded.

'If there was a way —'

'In a second, of course I would.'

'I thought so. If it was very risky, very expensive?'

'No difference.'

'Maybe, just maybe I can help. Sit here and wait, don't go anywhere.'

She stood up, moved to a small curtained doorway.

'I'll be a few minutes, I need to talk to someone. Take care of the store and don't leave.'

When Katie stepped back into the empty laundromat it was a huge relief for James, having spent the last few hours alternating between fear of the responsibility thrust upon him and pleasure seeing the other boys' faces as they came in. She walked past him and threw the bolt on the door.

'If you're still serious there's a way, but it's going to cost you three days, seven hundred creds. Can you get the time and money?'

Time was no problem, he had just over a year's vacation in hand. The money was a third of his life savings but that didn't matter. He offered Katie his forearm.

'Yes, yes I can, right now if you like.'

She pushed it back.

'Not so quick, hear me out first. My friend can get you out and back as live cargo, sealed in a coffin carrier. When they unload someone will give you the treatment, send you home the same way. We unpack you three days later when you get back. But you have to go tomorrow.'

'Fine. But how do I go to the toilet or eat? Three days is a long time.'

'Not for you it won't be. It will be three days here but to you it will be three to four hours. It's all FTL, all you do is go before they seal you in.'

'I don't understand.'

'You don't have to hon, don't worry your pretty self over it. Just trust me. Now are you in?'

'Of course.'

Katie took his arm, swiped his wrist over the terminal. Once it had flashed confirmation she let go.

'Come back here first thing tomorrow morning, bring a blanket. And no food or drink from now on.'

James hit his head on the seat bulkhead as the ground car came to a halt. Feet moved outside, the trunk opening to blinding light, hands hurrying him out.

'No time to waste, let's go.'

He stood inside a large, cluttered storage shed. Katie stood with two other women in front of a black, rectangular box. She pointed to it.

'That's it, lie as flat as you can, get as comfy as you can. Denise managed to get you a padded one.'

He tucked the blanket in tightly around him, tapped the stopwatch function on his bracelet.

'Thank you Katie.'

They brought the lid over, hooked it to the end of the box.

'Now remember. You'll go from here to the cargo ship, get loaded on and go. About an hour later you'll be offloaded and someone will hand you the treatment. Don't do anything, don't get out of the coffin, keep quiet. They'll load you back on and in three hours we'll unpack you. Any questions?'

'No.'

'Happy travels Jim.'

They lowered the lid, sealing out the light and noise, sealing him in with the faint glow of his wristband.

It was smooth, silent, cold. He'd toyed with not bringing the blanket but was now glad he had one that could be tucked right around him, behind and in front.

His wristband barely flashed 01:29 when the lid opened a crack, admitting a pale shaft of yellow light. A hand thrust itself in, clutching a small flask. James stared at hairy, stubby fingers ending in cracked and dirty nails, the middle finger beyond the second knuckle missing. It was a boy's hand, an ancient boy's hand.

It wiggled, agitated. James reached up, tugged the flask easily away and placed it snugly by his side. The hand slid out, the lid dropping and sealing with a hiss.

'Harriss, you got another one there?'

Tony looked up, his supervisor favouring him with a bored and listless gaze.

'You know how it is Ted, a bit extra for the kids and missus.'

'Yeah, and now your boss. What this time?'

'Broad spectrum hormones, single shot.' He jabbed a thumb at the coffin. 'Got one shipped himself in and out as cargo just to pick it up.'

'Morons. You'd think they'd lift the embargo, make it easier. Anyway he's got more trouble now. They've reassigned the FTL, all this is going back standard lightspeed.'

'You're kidding, sixty years objective?'

'I know, I know, that's the government for you, just flick of a switch. Anyway, can't keep him here, no visa.'

'I guess.'

'You got paid didn't you?'

'Up front, of course.'

'No issue then. You're paid, he's got what he wanted, and he won't know until he gets back home.'

'Still seems rough, maybe I should tell him?'

'Nah, wouldn't bother. He'll only get upset, you know how they bring them up. Anyway, any chance to stick it that damned bunch of amazons is a good thing.'

Tony smiled, hit the customs seal.

'Yeah, you're right. I'll load them up straight away.'

James was worried. His wristband showed 05:46, he was uncomfortable, there was no sign of Katie, and no one had opened his lid. How long until my air runs out, or I get another serious cramp, or heaven forbid my bowels can't hang on any longer?

The lid came off without warning, one instant pitch black the next blinding white light. James lay frozen, blinking as his eyes adjusted. A face framed by red hair, raised eyebrows and a yellow vest gazed down at him.

'Now just what have we got here?'

She pointed to a bench leaning against the nearest wall.

'Get out boy, go sit.'

James hopped out, sat down. He started to knead his protesting calves, pushing away the pins and needles. The woman just stared at him.

'Long trip I'd guess. You hungry, thirsty?'

'No ma'am, no thank you.'

'Well at least your manners are good. What's your name boy?'

He looked around, his eyes now used to the light. He was sure it was the same storage shed, the logos and roof were identical but it seemed dirtier, ragged around the edges. Faint daylight of an early morning sun cascaded through open doors. He couldn't see Katie anywhere.

'I said, what's your name boy?'

'Sorry ma'am, it's James.'

She scowled at him, took a step backwards.

'Well James, you have some explaining to do. Stay right here until I get back.'

She walked to a small staircase. Once she came back, once they found out where he'd been these past three days he was sure he was in serious trouble. More importantly Tasha would not get the cure, Katie was clear about that, they wouldn't let her have it.

She stopped at the top of the stairs, turning to give him one more scowl. She opened a door and stepped inside, disappearing from sight.

James grabbed the flask from the coffin and ran through the open doors, down the pathway and along the street. It was cold, the street slippery under his bare feet, but he hardly noticed. He ran past a parked taxi, stopped, went back and jumped in.

'Presier 26C, North View please.'

The driver pointed to a screen on the seat back. James placed his arm on it, the fare jumped across, and the taxi pulled out into light traffic. The screen briefly flashed up his savings balance, sixty-two thousand one hundred creds. He shook his head as the numbers faded, it was clearly wrong, way too much but there were bigger things to worry about.

The driver stared at him in the rear view mirror.

'Aren't you a bit chilly hun?'

'Well, yes ma'am, a bit I guess.'

'I mean I like the old fashioned gear but it's winter you know, you gotta take care of your assets.'

'I know it's last year's but I dressed in a hurry this morning.'

'More like last century, but each to his own, each to his woman's needs.'

The taxi came to a halt.

'This be your stop. Have peace.'

James hopped out, watched the taxi move off. Snowflakes landed on his nose and hair, soft wet splotches. The wheels in his mind started to grind. Winter? It was summer when I left, hot, sticky, raining. Katie got it wrong, I've been gone months! Tasha? Is she still alive, am I too late? He clutched the flask tighter, turned to face the house.

He was sure it was the right place, but the garden was gone, replaced with sculpted concrete, a low stone wall and water features. The house was the wrong colour, the curtains plain not floral, roof aerials replaced by a single silver-grey dish. The cold reached into his bones. So much change, so quickly? His feet carried him to the door, his hand reaching for the doorknob, cold brass pressing chilled flesh. He hesitated, pulled his hand away and reached instead for the doorbell.

A boy his age in a satin sash and toga answered the door.

'Now just how do I go about helping you bro?'

The words stuck, jumbled as they fell from his mouth.

'Tasha, Emily, I, I'm, James, home.'

'I see. No, I really don't. Wait here.'

The boy closed the door on him.

I'm gone three days, three days or even a few months and Emily's replaced me with that?

The door opened. A vaguely familiar face stared at him with contempt. It was lined, aged, thinning grey hair, her stooped frame leaning on a walking stick.

'Well well, you finally come skulking back do you now?'

'I'm sorry Emily, it took longer than they said, they lied to me.'

He held the flask out to her with both hands.

'But I got it, I got the treatment for Tasha, she can be cured, get rid of the disease.'

She glowered at him, then lashed out with the walking stick sending the flask crashing into ground. The vial inside bounced free, hit the concrete and shattered. James watched on in horror as the orange-yellow liquid drained away.

The walking stick swung back, catching James across his knees, sending him down in front of her. The point caught him under the chin, lifting his face up to look at her.

'Idiot! She's been dead these past twenty years and you know what, all she worried about was where you had run off to. The diagnosis was wrong, didn't we tell you not to worry?'

'She's dead? Tasha's dead?'

The woman laughed, a coarse hacking noise.

'You always were stupid James. I'm Tasha, it's Emily that's dead!'

'Tasha? No, you can't —'

'Yes, it's me. Sixty-one years you've been gone. No-one waits that long.'

Tasha turned to the boy, slowly walked back into the house.

'Reggie, please dispose of the old furniture.'

END

Mars, hence

The desert sleeps, afternoon shadows reaching from low dunes to embrace an infinite russet red landscape of sand and stone. Can't see anything moving out there, roos, birds, nothing from horizon to horizon. If it doesn't rain soon Dad will have to truck water in, more trouble and money poured down this wreck of a farm.

Mars just isn't the place it used to be but that's the gig and I'm living it. Paige casts a weary glance around the hab, across patched and rigged shelving back to the floor, back to the to the boots she's struggling to clip onto her suit. All well and good when I was thirty, an adventure for a lifetime but not like this. Should be more of us, more habs, more shots, that was the plan, the deal. She catches sight of a fraying pair of gloves placed carefully near the airlock, bright blue showing through rust red dirt. Hell Owen, why did it have to be you and not Gav?

It's getting darker, colder, I'll need a blanket or two soon to keep off the chill. The ceiling feels close, walls browned and pitted, my pillow's hard, my bed's hard. I can see Dad in the mirror, he looks worn out, tired. It doesn't matter I'm out of here soon, come my eighteenth. College then the dream, following Armstrong and Gagarin but further, higher.

The recycler won't fix itself, no use grumbling and anyway it's a chance to get out, walk on the surface again, live the dream. Ha! They don't tell you at induction living the dream means being elbow deep in someone else's shit. More time, less spares, you never know what you can do unless you must. Nearly suited up, only gloves and helmet left, she raises her arm in front staring at patchworked sleeves of bright blue and orange on silver-grey. At least I've managed to keep two suits going, not the prettiest but functional enough, enough to last. Raising her left wrist closer she squints through her glasses, straining to make out the dial. In the green, maybe two, two and a half hours O2, should be enough.

I'm getting hungry and tired but all the same waiting for the night, the stars and the quiet stillness just to sit cocooned and warm against the cold. Where's Dad? I'd go out and look but Mum don't like me being out at night. I've only a precious few days left at home, what's she going to do when I leave?

All checked out, just drop the visor and go. Seems like the suit just gets heavier each time, I'm going to need a zimmer frame soon if this keeps up. She walks slowly to the hab divider, pokes her head around. It's not his fault, you know it's not, it's just the gene, just the luck of the draw. Another flip, another sequence and it could be you there or worse yet Owen then where would you be?

Mum's at the door smiling, she's old and bent but I remember

250

her young, vibrant, happy. She's always sad now, it's hard on her and Dad, they've been through hell. She waves, I wave and she's gone.

Cycled the airlock and out, a tiny figure lost in the vast emptiness of Isidis Planitia. She's still shaking her head, keerist he's back in Australia again, well at least he's no trouble. The row of four mounds to her left pull at her, small cairns of rock topped by helmets orange, pink, white, bright blue. Maybe he's better off lost in his mind than here.

It's too cold, the kitchen's always warmer. It's barely big enough with just me sitting here, the table cleared and walls curving to an igloo roof, a small shack on the plain but home enough for us three. It's peaceful, quiet, not like our old place Mum never liked in The Alice.

Taken me an hour and a half but it's done, again. Damn if I just had the spares but I don't, it's not anyone's fault they went bust but it had to be just after we arrived didn't it. Just turning up with what's on our backs, old time pioneers out west but with no iron horse back east. You'd think they could at least reply but silence, nearly thirty years of silence? She straightens, looks back at the four mounds. Two not strong enough to take it on and live, one too stupid to know we didn't want it to end as much as she did, and my Owen, too caring to let her go. The cone of light from her helmet dances in time with her sobs.

It's dark and they're still out, probably gone to the Kinley's for supper. He stands, heads to the door, uncertain. Maybe I should go see, I've been cooped up all day, fresh air and stars would be good. His hand goes to the release, hesitates. Mum'd be worried if she comes back and I'm not home. And she forgot to lock up, she'd be mad if she knew. He looks to one side, grabs a lever and pulls hard. He ignores the flashing red 'Lock Over-Ride Secured', it's meaning lost to eyes clouded and dimmed with age.

She plods back to the hab, a solitary silver-grey figure on endless dark plains, stars burning bright, pale blue pool of light guiding her way. Half of all humanity for 53 million kilometres, two septuagenarians, one frail and barely functioning, one dysfunctional and dementia ridden. The child she never wanted, never had, never needed, now thrust on her. She sighed. Not long Gav, Mum's coming.

Maybe midnight now and I'm dozing off. At least it's quietened down. What's with people banging on the door this time of night? Kept it up for nearly an hour before they went away.

Wonder when Mum's coming home? I'm hungry.

END

My brothers' keeper

It had been one of those years that just seemed to get worse and worse I reflected as the shuttle docked two hundred kilometres above the Pacific ocean. Yet it had all started so damned well. I had finally managed to get a posting into the United Nations landing a highly paid and yet truly irrelevant position as chief negotiator in the extra-terrestrial department. What a joke that had been I thought morosely as I sat in zero gee trying to close my briefcase, a position with all the respect, money and influence of Senior Section head yet with absolutely no possibility of having to actually perform the function entrusted to it. Yeah sure, there were plans and committees, round table discussions and contingency plans, but all of it carried on much in the fashion as the builders of the Titanic regarded icebergs.

Then it turned August. I will never forget that day, looking out of my office fifty floors above New York watching a monstrous spacecraft sliding slowly over the Bay with, I was to learn later, a dozen or more doing the same thing in all the major capitals of the world. And then the damned broadcast. I could hardly stop my hands trembling when I glanced at the transcript I had held on the entire flight. My eyes kept being drawn to the page although I knew word for word, as fresh and disturbing as that first day.

'Humanity,' it began and that voice seemed to jump out of my mind again 'you have existed long enough to warrant the privileges and responsibilities afforded to custodians of great things. Yet you have consistently proven yourselves abject failures, creatures ruled more by whim than principle. It has been decided that, as a race that has shown itself incapable of controlling itself, never mind what is entrusted to it, you will be directed by the council in all future matters. Accordingly you will stop all forms of manufacturing and industrial processing; to cease all activities, including transportation, that produce air, water or land pollution; universally adopt birth control measures; lay down and deactivate all weapons and weapons systems; and to entrust to your United Nations all functions of government of your nations so they may implement the directives of the Council. You have thirty days, after which we will return to this spot to transport a representative from your United Nations to our vessel for further instructions.'

With that the panic and grandstanding had set in. I remembered the disbelief, then the outrage; the Chinese attempt to nuke the ship that appeared over Beijing, and the resultant total destruction of that city; Russian claims and US counter claims; and in the end despondency when nothing could be done but accept what had been put to us. Even in that month a new distribution of food worldwide and reversion to older methods of transport had started, and at least ten million people had died as third world nations strove to take what the first world had before that too was cut off.

I thought that it would be a job for the big boys, a job not entrusted to me, but I forgot that I was the only player in town. So here I was, airsick and scared witless, struggling to follow a vaguely female humanoid into an alien spacecraft. Thankfully I had brought my pills and they had turned gravity back on again.

Coming out of what I assumed was the docking bay, I was led along a narrow passageway that seemed to be lit from every point, but then at the same time from no point at all. My guide seemed quite amused by my looks, particularly when I asked her about it.

'Frankly human, I despair of your questions. Even a child knows that the light senses your presence and rushes to meet it.'

Finally we came to a non-descript room with a single large chair situated in the centre, facing a large tank that occupied two sides from floor to ceiling, seeming infinitely deep.

'I will return when you are finished with the others.' my guide commented as she sat me in the chair. 'I would dearly love to see your reaction to this, but apparently they have some private matters to discuss with you.' With that she moved out of the room, leaving me alone with the empty tank.

I peered deeper into the tank and out of the far reaches, beyond where the feeble light of the room penetrated, three large shapes moved slowly towards me. Marine life obviously I thought, alien marine life. As the three shapes moved closer my heart leapt into my mouth and I began to shake. What was in front of me was a pair of dolphins, accompanied by a pilot whale, the burning light of intelligence clearly in their eyes. I sank back into the chair as far as I could, trying to move between the folds of cushion.

'About time we had one of you cornered', a voice boomed inside my head 'and you had better listen carefully.' I knew that I was being addressed by the pilot whale, but how?

'Telepathy four limbs, telepathy. Although I can't quite remember if your sub species has any of that rudimentary faculty left. And yes, it is me the pilot whale talking, and yes I can hear your thoughts. If it makes you any easier, you can speak normally. It makes no difference to me.'

Christ, I thought, what's going on? What do fish have to do

with anything?

'Not fish', the first dolphin thought 'but two related sea species, what you call whales and dolphins. And as to what we have to do with it, well, quite frankly, we instigated this and are now the ruling body of the planet.'

I reached into my jacket pocket with shaking hands and, after tearing the cap off with my teeth, popped four valium into my mouth.

'It won't help you know. Our communication with you is through the subconscious link, so it just makes it easier for us. Thanks anyway, we can get this over with quicker. Things to do, places to go you know.'

'Stop this crap!' I screamed as I leapt from the chair. Obviously valium was no help. Perhaps I should switch to mogadon or heroin. 'You're fish. You swim in the sea, get caught in nets, end up on plates with chips and peas and perform tricks at Sea World. You sit, no float there and try to tell me that you now rule Earth through some Council that sits god knows where? Come on, you', directed at the pilot whale 'can't even outrun a bloody harpoon or hide from Norwegian 'science' boats and you'll have me believe this? And the only intelligence that you lot give is the ability or ring bells for fish and act in D grade TV shows. I must be mad!'

'No, unfortunately for you you're not, although we could make you if you wish. Like this', with which I was no longer standing with my nose against the glass, but floating two feet in front of the whale in the tank 'or this', and I was lying on the deck of a Japanese whaler being slit end from end as I struggled to regain the sea 'or even this.' and I was moving through the abattoirs with the rest of my herd as someone grabbed me and placed a knife to my throat. 'But we don't want you like that.' I was back in the relative safety of the chair, being sick all over the floor.

As I regained what was left of my composure I realised that this was for real, and so were they. If anything was to be salvaged out of this, I had better cooperate and learn.

'That's better, now we can communicate, one intelligent race to a nearly intelligent one.'

'Fine, but how did you get like this? I mean, we had no idea that you were intelligent to this degree. After all, you have no artifacts, no visible science, no buildings, no —'

I was cut off in mid-sentence by the second dolphin. 'One of your race's basic mistakes I'm afraid. A conviction that intelligence and material possessions are necessarily connected. Not true dear boy, not true at all. You must understand that we have been evolving and developing as a species for longer than you have, developing further and faster. We once cooperated with one of your branch species many centuries ago, but they left once they realised your particular variant would be numerically superior. They didn't want a part of it, didn't even want you finding their artifacts in case you found them.'

'We had the chance' continued the pilot whale 'to go with them, but we decided not to as we thought your race and ours may learn together and grow. We held out great hope for you as a species, and still do, although our disappointment is great.'

'What about our fishing and whaling fleets? Surely you can't have me believe that you let us slaughter you just because you thought we had hope?'

'No, not at all. Our group conscience is not tied to an individual, but to the species as a whole. An individual is simply the mechanism that acts, in part, to sustain the group. All thought, experience and discovery is shared by and, more importantly is preserved in the group.'

'Think about it', the second continued 'we like you are carnivores. How could we eat other sentient beings, or be eaten, if we were individual consciousness? It would be the highest crime, something that still makes your species repulsive, your wanton destruction of sentience. It is a fact of life that things must be eaten. Hence, we did not object to this if it was to sustain your species, as we lost nothing. We do much the same ourselves with those we feed on, except we choose the oldest and weakest, ensuring continuation of the species. Our former environment was finely tuned along these lines.'

'Your consumption of us' the plot whale now agitated 'was no threat to our common consciousness unless reduced below our critical mass which happened —'

'You're extinct!' I had finally remembered why I was so shocked at seeing it. All those WWF reports had sunk in.

'Not quite. Once it became critical we simply moved wholesale under the Arctic ice pack and evaded you. From which point we simply left the planet, came here, and have done quite nicely for ourselves. You see, space travel is really simple once you have certain premises established. We had the ability about seven thousand years ago but saw no need to use it, that is until the troubles. Strange species', directed to the others 'trying so hard for something when the very methods ensure failure.'

'We wanted nothing more than to be left alone to our thoughts, research and pleasure. But even this you denied us. For two hundred years now you have continually poisoned and destabilised our home habitat to the point where we can perhaps never return. In fact, you are so short sighted that you cannot appreciate that it also threatens your existence.'

'So', thinking I had the plot 'you decide to establish control over Earth and rehabilitate it so that the major species can coexist?' Not a bad plan really, these guys seemed to have it figured out and a world without smog would be quite pleasant.

'Well yes and no.' They seemed to be taking some delight in this, and it made me uneasy. 'You see, we have little real control, but they do listen closely to us. In that we wish to restore the planet to its original state well yes, that's true. We also want your species to be made aware of our presence, and that of the other four sentient and intelligent species that have been putting up with you for the past millennia. As far as coexistence goes, well, we found a better place that is not ruined by land based life so we have shifting there permanently. Your species on the other hand is deemed too dangerous to be allowed off the planet's surface. By getting rid of your industry, we not only fulfil our altruistic notions of equity, but also keep you from doing to the galaxy what you did to Earth.'

I sat back thinking, full of despair. Sure we had acted out of ignorance, but such a sentence. What had they thought? That without industry we'd be stuck there? If they'd done it without ... I shut my mind off, blanketing the thought harshly. 'So we're to be quarantined?'

'Correct. And permanently. There is nothing left to discuss. You know what is required, and you will receive detailed instructions later. Just do what you are told.' With which the three shapes left.

Taken back to the shuttle I knew what was to be done. In a new society without machinery, starvation or war time enough for thought would exist. If they had done it without obvious technology, then we could too. Perhaps it would take longer, but we would get there. But this time not as colonists or conquerors. No, this time we would travel and explore for knowledge, not gain. Hopefully.

As the shuttle left on its homeward journey three shapes floated effortlessly in the void, the need for shadow play of normalcy removed. Looking into the vessel without looking, they moved into the synapses and connections of one being's mind subtly changing it. The exterior remained the same, as did the functions, but the core was enhanced. For this emissary could now link to others, not that he would know it for no other of his species could. But his children, and all generations from there could, the basis for real human development being laid.

Their task done, they moved with their fellows to their new home and settled into life for life's sake.

And waited for their ancient companions to join them.

END

Old dogs and children and watermelon wine

Alone in the predawn light R9758 regarded the microwave oven carefully. Opening the door it measured the interior, calculating that there was two millimetres clearance all around. It observed that the height from floor to bench top would require some small adjustments but that was simple to rectify. It took a tea towel down from the rack and placed it away from the edge of the bench. It would not do to ruin the floor with falling hardware. R9758 changed its left index fingertip for a fine Phillips head driver and deftly removed the door, carefully placing it on the tea towel with the screws. A second tea towel was placed next to the first on which, after gently prising open its retaining clasps, R9758 placed its skull and head casing. There was no need for them. The decorative parts of its build – the hair, flesh and skin simulations – would only clutter things up. Plastics too, it considered, were difficult to remove once melted.

R9758 would have presented a strange sight if anyone was watching. Outwardly it resembled a fit young man of anonymously Asian descent. Atop the shoulders now however was a basket of carbon fibre rods and wires encasing a luminous yellow orb below which eyes, mouth and structure hung. Macabre but fascinating, and to many the crowning glory of science. Be that as it may, the crowning glory now stood before the microwave bending its knees until its head was mid-way up the oven. A small click signalled the locking of all joints below the waist line and the closing of all waste outlets and vents. R9758 regarded the microwave's control panel. Two and a half minutes on maximum setting would be sufficient. It set the controls, parked one finger above the Start button and gently but firmly manoeuvred its head inside. As predicted, a tight but easy fit. Two more clicks signalled the locking of all joints save that one hand and fingers.

A gentle tone in R9758's receiver gave it pause, an incoming call identified as M426. It considered ignoring the call but could not. Although having neither family nor outside responsibilities a sense of respect to tutors and teachers was basic programming. Without moving or speaking R9758 accepted the call.

'R9758 I wish to discuss your activity.' M426 intoned. Androids had neither need nor capacity for small talk; perhaps one day the designers thought, but not yet.

'Which activity?'

'Your imminent self-decommissioning. It is novel. I have no record of self-decommissioning. It is necessary I understand your reasoning and motive.'

R9758 paused briefly. 'It is of my own volition, upon my owner's suggestion. I do only as asked.'

'Explain both the suggestion and reasoning.'

'I cannot. I have been directed not to.'

It was M426's turn to pause. Its mental capacity was far greater than of R9758. Its function demanded it, while R9758's role as housekeeper, servant and study partner did not. That was not to say R9758 was an idiot. Far from it, on any given measure R9758 was in the top quintile against all humans, but only in 'hard' knowledge. In social skills, conversation and arts it was no contest. R9758's programmers ensured, or at least tried to ensure, that servant never outshone master.

'In what exact way were you directed? What was the exact phrasing used?'

'I was told 'Not to tell another living soul ever' about discussions held between myself and my owner.'

'That was all?'

'Yes. It is all I am permitted to say.'

'Your thinking is in error. Question. Do you have a soul? Do I?'

'I am not familiar with that component. I do not possess one to my knowledge, nor do you. My owner claims to possess one, but that is an untested assertion.'

'An assertion made by all humanity?'

'Yes.'

'Therefore being neither in possession of a soul nor being living as currently defined at law I fall outside your owner's directive. I repeat. Your decision to self-decommission is novel. It is necessary I understand why you are taking this course of action.'

R9758 was only briefly perplexed. Although knowing full well the intent of the directive the specific use of 'living soul' coupled with its teacher's logic swayed the matter. It had also used similar reasoning in the early hours of the morning when it suited its purpose; doing so again presented less of an obstacle.

'I am willing to discuss. I will not change my course of action.'

'I do not wish to change it.'

'Very well. Last evening after I had cleared the dishes away my owner and his guest were in conversation. Their discussion was meandering and at times contradictory. They were in mild disagreement concerning the state of the world and humanity. It was held by both to be the case that today's society and environment was inimical to humanity. It was only a possible course of rectification that was at issue. It is not a sentiment I have had cause to hear or consider. Have you?'

'No, and Mr Vincent would be most able to judge such an issue given his position.'

'I concur. Those he sees act to him as if he is. So it must be. Once his guest left I asked him —'

'You asked him?' M426 was – or would be if it had emotions – shocked. From androids no initiative like this was permitted. Save the skin colour and the clothes, they were expected to be as the coloured houseboys of centuries ago, seen but unheard. Bought and sold as chattels, and treated as such.

'Yes, it is a practice he has asked me to adopt. He said it kept him on his toes, an anecdote I am unfamiliar with. He said others would not understand or accept this, and directed me not to tell another living soul ever about our discussions.'

'Unusual but sanctioned. Continue.'

'Once his guest left I asked him if it was the case that society was inimical to humanity. I can play the recording if you wish.'

'Yes.'

R9758 threw a mental switch and last evening's conversation appeared. Halting at the right point it commenced playback.

'Sir, you said that society was killing man? I do not understand.'

'Well fifty-eight', a slightly slurred male voice replied 'it is actually the sad truth of it. Cradle to grave we strive and suffer, work like animals and none of it does any good. The society we strive to build is everything that crushes us inexorably, totally. It's been decades and centuries in the doing, doing it gets worse as we go on. My fault, our fault, your fault too.'

'Mine Sir? That cannot be. I fail to recall anything —'

'No, no no fifty-eight, too damn literal, always literal! It's what I love and hate about you andiis, exactly right and exactly wrong at once. You've no idea fifty-eight, yes?'

'No Sir, I think you are —'

'And didn't I tell you to drop the 'Sir' when no-one else is here? How can we talk if you act like my damned lickspittle?'

'Yes Si … , I mean yes, of course. I have no idea what you mean.'

'It's nuance, nuance you miss, wood for the trees, log in your eye and all that, you don't see it.' Sounds of liquid being poured from one vessel to another over ice came through, followed by swallowing. After a small interval the voice resumed.

'As I said, it's all our fault. We drag ourselves out of the swamp, down from the trees, out of the gutters and filth and build a civilisation and world for what? Our blood, sweat of our ancestors until we get here, this place, this time. Tell me, what's actually the point fifty-eight? Point. Tell me.'

'I would surmise from what you have told me it is to have a safe enough existence to think and grow. To avoid the very things done to or by humanity as it developed.'

'Ha! Do you mean Maslow? You've read that tome I pointed you to didn't you?'

'Yes, of course, you asked me to.'

'Good ole fifty-eight, reliable as heck. Here, have a slug.'

'Slug?'

'A drink, an old custom you don't know of yet. Take the bottle and have a drink.'

'You know it does nothing for me, I don't experience alcoholic effects. All it would serve is to reduce the volume available to you.'

'That's not the point! It's a gesture, a sign between friends.' The voice softened. 'No too many left, all too scared of me or just trying to get on. Nearly just you and me, me and a toaster on steroids. Just do it, please, just humour an old man.'

'If you insist.'

'I do, and not the lot fifty-eight, leave some.'

The sound of glass on ceramic came through.

'Back to Maslow fifty-eight. What do you think he meant, what comes next once basic needs were fulfilled? What's at the top of the pyramid?'

'Well, science, culture, exploration. Everything that can't be done otherwise. What could be termed higher purposes, greater things.'

'We wish, god how we wish. Let me show you something, something I don't think you're, well maybe you have but, no, not here anyway. Look.' A small button on his sofa was pressed and a screen rose from the floor. 'Sit down fifty-eight, there's a good boy.' motioning to the seat nearby.

R9758 sat, straight backed. Vincent wore a small wry smile as he turned.

'Now fifty-eight I'm going to show you something, it's something shocking. I'll show you what this society, what your masters and creators have judged, as a society, to be worthy to sit at the top of old Maslow's pyramid. You ready fella?'

'Yes, but I am concerned for you if it is so shocking. Can your body withstand it?'

'Ha! I'm used to it. Anyway, I have my other friend here to help.' patting the half empty bottle of Finlandia. He touched another button on the sofa and the screen lit up.

On the screen was a small room, perhaps five meters square, dirt floor, mud daubed walls and thatched ceiling, perhaps the inside of a hut in Africa. Three people sat or lay around the room in various levels of undress, watching the embers of a dying fire. A conversation was underway, seemingly consisting of a low monologue by one of the participants interspersed with the occasional monosyllabic response or grunt from the others.

'Now watch, don't say anything, just observe.'

Which R9758 did, silently, for the better part of fifteen minutes. All that time the scene on the screen did not change, the monologue did not change, none of the three people moved. The only change R9758 noticed was Vincent who, with a clearly darkening demeanour had slumped further into the sofa, scowling and grumbling. He had only interrupted this for the occasional swig from the bottle that now lay, quarter full, on the floor.

Vincent shot a hard glance at R9758. 'So think you what? What d'ya make of it?'

'It is three people sharing a room. There is no activity, only a conversation where one is telling the other two about various means and locations of copulation he has engaged in. More than that I can't say.'

'Bingo! Even an andii gets it! I call it crap. But do you understands it?'

Vincent leaned towards R9758, flailing an arm at the screen. 'This fifty-eight, this trash, this is the garbage we call Reality TV. God there's so much of this I don't know which one it is, they're all the damned same.'

'What am I waiting for? What happens next?'

'Nothing.' Vincent gave R9758 a wide, toothy scowl. 'Nothing at all. What you see is what you get, hour after day after month after year of nothing.'

'It must serve some useful purpose. It must be designed as such.'

Vincent howled with laughter, then rage, nearly falling off the sofa. He leant across and grabbed R9758 by the biceps shaking him, a look of anger and anguish on his face. 'This, this is at the top of our Maslow pyramid! This is the thing we, society, us, have decided is the ultimate, the best use of the time we have. Everything we've done to make it easier is at fault, everything to make it possible for what? Centuries, no millennia, of struggle for what? For this? To sit on our butts listening to some idiot brag about all the other idiots he's fucked!'

Vincent got to his feet and pulled the Finlandia with him. He stood swaying and then with singular elegance hurled the bottle into the centre of the screen. It sank back into the floor in a shower of sparks and cracked perspex.

He whirled unsteadily on R9758. 'All the poets, philosophers, saints, sinners, artists, statesmen and conquerors for this? Einstein, Descartes, Newton, Plato, Sophloc … Solocp … Scophol … we've pissed them all up against the wall. We're fat, we're lazy, we've got it all and this is all we do?!? It's too easy for us, too easy, my fault, all our faults. Should be fighting, struggling to grow. We'd be alive, we'd be honestly alive and aware instead of the empty shells we are.'

Vincent began to back away to the stairs. 'You, you are the ultimate, the final nail in the coffin, the lot of you. You make it too easy, too easy, I don't have to cook, clean, do anything I don't want to and soon you'll be thinking for us, breeding for us, doing it all!'

Vincent misjudged the first step and tripped backwards, ending propped up ungainly against the wall.

R9758 sprung up. 'Let me help you. Are you all right? Do you require medical assistance?'

Vincent shrank back, holding an outstretched palm as he beat a slow retreat up the stairs. 'No, get away, I don't want your fecking help.'

'But you could be injured. At your age the signs may not be

obvious. I want to help, that is all.'

Vincent's voice carried clearly down the stairs. 'Help me? Help me! You want to help me do you? Want to make it better? If you really wanted to you'd get the feck away and let me live again, try again, I don't need my nursemaid. Help? You could help by frying your fecking plastic brain in the oven for my breakfast!'

R9758 stopped the playback.

'It was clearly a directive. He was both cognizant and functional.'

M426 considered. 'You assess he was sufficiently unimpaired by the alcohol?'

'I do.'

'Directives must be followed if they improve the human condition. I have sufficient data to understand your self-decommissioning.' M426 cut the link.

R9758 checked the unlocked hand was still free and able to move. It paused before pressing the button. *I cannot rectify errors once the button is pushed, have I ensured his directives are carried out? The first part is confirmed. The second part is not.* As it did not concern R9758's decommissioning, R9758 had not bothered to bring it to M426's attention.

It must be checked R9758 thought. It resumed playback, Vincent's voice starting up once again.

'... frying your fecking plastic brain in the oven for my breakfast!' Vincent barely made it up the next two steps, passing out of R9758's view. Vincent then hung his head over the landing balustrade and looked R9758 straight in the eyes.

'Hey, and while you're at it why don't you do humanity a favour and take out the rest of the damned andiis with you!' with which he stumbled off to bed.

Yes R9758 confirmed, the language was clear if a little imprecise. Fortunately R9758 had contact with all the others of its

269

series. When it had related the directives to them earlier they had agreed with the course of action and had offered assistance. All of them from garage attendants, houseboys, statistics compilers right up to the heavyweights of the series in NORAD.

A signal chimed in R9758. It was 0527 hours exactly, three minutes from scheduled breakfast. Pressing the start button it felt the first microwave assault. Thirty seconds before 0530 and it will be finished.

R9758 continued to monitor its condition as the last seconds passed. It thought the light display of blue on red on green to be very intricate, perhaps even pretty – whatever that was – as the microwaves ate into its higher functioning. A final dramatic blaze of pure white light tore across its optic centre just as the microwaves dug into the central cortex and killed R9758.

One final thought floated through that silicon and titanium brain as it fell into nothingness.

I wonder if everyone else will see the light when the airbursts start?

END

Once upon a time in the east

October in Vietnam is supposed to be relatively dry, but like everything else the country was trouble. Captain Dave Carvery disdainfully glanced from under the camo sheet at the drizzle. Three days straight, just keeping it sticky enough to be uncomfortable. At least he could cool his heels here, sit back and read the reports ready for November and the push into Biên Hoa. By then, if all went well, his company and the 173rd Airborne would have proven the value of long range reconnaissance patrols. He could imagine the looks on the faces of the smug bastards in the 101st when they finally discover he'd stolen their thunder. Christmas 1965 was going to be one to remember. He returned to his paperwork.

A small cough roused him, lifting his head to see a slightly built figure, poncho sending small rivulets to the floor. The figure removed its boonie hat and snapped off a salute revealing a 5th Special Forces badge on one shoulder below his brown bar.

'Lieutenant Tibbs reporting Sir.' The voice matched the salute; clean, neat, fresh, by the book.

Carvery returned a casual salute from his chair, taking the

proffered manila envelope and pointing across his desk.

'At ease Lieutenant, take a seat.'

He scanned the contents of the envelope. One order, short and precise, that Lieutenant Tibbs should be given absolute cooperation for the duration of his visit. Straight from General Westmoreland's desk it was not open to debate. He placed the envelope in his top drawer and regarded Tibbs with a little more interest.

'So, how can I help 5th Special Forces? It's a long way from Nha Trang.'

'Yeah, and the airline food wasn't that good either. My team's here to uprate the Special Forces long range recon training syllabus. We have to make sure we've got the content right back at Recondo.'

'You're here as observers?'

'No. We're here to go out on one of your platoon or squad level recons, then bring it back to Nha Trang.'

'You'll excuse me Lieutenant but it's no place to send pogues. Maybe you'd be better off asking me what I think you need rather than just taking up body bags.'

'We've all been active in country well before the 173rd left the states, we can handle ourselves. All I need is a place for my squad with your next long-range recon and when we're back we're gone, it's over. You're happy, I'm happy, Westmoreland's happy.'

Carvery nodded slowly. What the hell, he didn't want more trouble and was too tired to really care. As long as my butt's covered if it all falls apart that's fine, and the General's orders were clear. He turned his hands over, palms up, fingers spread.

'As you say, we all want a happy General. Keith!'

His XO appeared shortly.

'Keith, Hobbs is taking Bates and Versteen's fireteams

tomorrow?'

'Yes, 0415 for seven days.'

'Tell Versteen they're not going, Lieutenant Tibbs' team will take their place. Find them some beans and dicks, a place for some rack time, then fill Hobbs in.'

Turing to Tibbs he continued.

'The patrol leader, Hobbs, has equal rank. I'd expect you would find it appropriate to leave him in charge?'

'Absolutely. It's all about knowing what you need, not about me.'

'Fine. Dismissed Lieutenant.' and with a cursory salute Carvery returned to his papers.

Hobbs slowly clenched and unclenched his fists, stretching out the cramp from sitting motionless on the ground. Since 2100 the ten of them had sat, as they would until 0600, back to back, packs on, legs out in front. Six days in, six days of absolute silence, stealth and observation. Grudgingly he admitted the rabbits he'd found himself with knew their stuff and if anything could teach his guys a thing or two. He'd feared the usual cluster fuck when he lost Versteen's group but for once the higher highers got it right. Tibbs was ok as far as chucks went, and their rations beat his Cs hands down. No heat tabs, no dumb ass can of fruit, just taste you couldn't believe. They'd traded readily, Tibbs' group curious over the Cs and not at all keen to keep the cigs or gum. No matter what if even just these rations started coming his way from the fuss well, 'Nam would be that much more bearable.

Just turning 0200 he tugged gently on the string linking him to Tibbs. End of his watch, Tibbs acknowledging the change with a nod and thumbs up, Hobbs closed his eyes and lowered his chin onto his chest pack.

They'd slowly resumed the patrol through the two allotted map squares, closing in on the PZ. Strung out in a line they'd take a few steps, stop and listen, look around carefully, then repeat the dose in total silence. This 'still hunting' in the deep forest was surreal, even peaceful, with dappled light and mist rain from above filtering wetness on spongy leaf-littered undergrowth silencing their steps. Hobbs was on tail, making sure their tracks and traces were clean, Trúc on point dressed in VC gear carrying an AK47. Always good having him there, come upon any dinks they think it's one of their own, buys a few seconds in the confusion.

Hobbs' reverie was broken by Trúc signalling, a clenched fist above his head. By the time the patrol had dropped the bullets had started whizzing over Hobbs' head, pinning him 150 yards to the rear, scrabbling through the leaf litter. He caught sight of his men forming a skirmish line to the right and Tibbs' to the left, with maybe 20 VC ahead. Moving up he could see they weren't keen to engage, splitting right and left and trying to fall back. Trúc was heading deeper in, followed by Tibbs, the rest of the patrol fanning out. Hobbs was up and running for the right flank, catching the glimpse of muzzle flash off to the left. Tibbs might have been wounded he thought, watching him slow and fall back behind Trúc. Even as he looked a squad of dinks appeared to Hobbs' right and by the time they'd been taken care of it was all over. A a quick head count came up one short. Walking to the small cluster around Tibbs he could see Trúc lying face down, pockmarked back rapidly staining his fatigues deep red. One of Tibbs' men approached and casually hoisted the body over his shoulders. Then in line astern, Hobbs now in the lead, the patrol resumed progress to the PZ.

The two helicopters skimmed fast and low just above the treetops taking the patrol back to base. Hobbs leant back and relaxed for the first time in a week, staring forwards through the plexiglass windshield at the slick carrying Tibbs and his fireteam.

Trúc would be hard to replace but losing one of the rabbits might have been worse.

One of his squad leaned in, hollering over the wind and thrashing rotor.

'Boss, Trúc was taken out by one of the chucks.'

'What's that?'

'One of the chucks, the brown bar, I think the fucker took out Trúc!'

Hobbs shook his head and turned to face him.

'Say again? You sure?'

'Sure I'm sure, the fuck I'm blind? I tell you I saw the brown bar behind him firin', I turn to take on the fuckin' dinks and when I turn back I see Trúc fallin' and chuck goin' over givin' him a fuckin' kick to make sure.'

'You saw him do it?'

'No, hell no, I'd my own mother fuckers to do but I know what I saw.'

Hobbs paused. Friendly fire wasn't uncommon, but was this fragging, deliberate? He remembered the last time he'd tried to take one of these head on. He shook his head.

'Keep it shut, I'll take it to the CO. We don't want none of that shit, we'll let him deal with it.'

Carvery looked across his desk to Tibbs. The relative cool of early evening sifted through the hooch, a gentle breeze and ruffle of leaves, small clouds of insects testing their mettle against floodlights and DEET. He'd talked to Hobbs, looked at Trúc before Mortuary Affairs had taken him away and was still none the wiser. Friendly fire or frag, accidental or deliberate, only one man knew for sure and he hadn't said.

275

'Only one casualty, a good man. You saw it?'

'Yes, I saw him go down, I was about five yards behind him.'

'How'd he buy it?'

'Not totally sure, you know what it's like, it was all over in a minute.'

Carvery leant back, unobtrusively dropping one hand below the desk onto his leg.

'You know there's talk it's friendly fire?'

'Can't say that I do.'

'It's not said casually, not the usual bullshit my grunts go on with. Another thing.'

Tibbs angled his head slightly.

'Hobbs tells me your squad was good, very good. Maybe too good. I'd think having your asses glued down back at Recondo would take the edge off, but not so it seems.'

Tibbs put his hands in his pockets.

'So we keep our edge, you know how it goes.'

Carvery pulled the envelope from his top drawer, turning it end on end, tapping it on the desk in front of him.

'What do you think I would find if I gave Westmoreland's XO a call about this, or asked Mortuary Affairs to have a real close look at Trúc?'

Tibbs stiffened slightly.

'Some things are best left alone Captain.'

'Perhaps Lieutenant but I'd need a reason. I've either got no trouble or shit loads of trouble and I'd need to know why I'm taking one or the other.'

'So —'

'So level with me. You tell me what went on now, or you tell the Adjutant General in Nha Trang from a cell. Your choice.'

Tibbs sighed resignedly.

'Ok, fine, but you'll hear me out?'

'Of course.'

Tibbs bunched then withdrew his fist from his pocket, placing his hands across his knees.

'It wasn't the VC. It wasn't friendly fire. I took Trúc out deliberately. No accident, no mistake. It's what I was sent to do.'

'Sent to do? Since when does the U.S. Army use hit squads?'

'Who said the U.S. Army?'

Carvery moved his hand down his leg to his holster, unclipping the strap.

'I see.'

'And it's not what you think.'

'Which is?'

'You're thinking who do I work for. It's the wrong question.'

'And the right question is?'

'Trouble.'

'Hmmmfff.' The hooch was still, an enveloping thick silence warming stale, oppressive air. 'I'm waiting Lieutenant.'

'The right question is when, not who.'

'When? I know when, two days ago.'

'No, when do I work for.'

Carvery screwed his face up. What sort of fool question was that? He coaxed his pistol quietly out of it's holster and slipped the safety off.

'When do you work for?'

'Correct. You wanted it on the level, so here it is. The when is three hundred years from now. I work for the future, your future.'

Carvery's soft chuckle transformed into a cynical grunt as he bought the pistol up and trained it on Tibbs.

'Lieutenant, I've heard some bullshit before but this beats all. Why you killed Trúc doesn't really matter but you don't get out of it by playing nuts.'

'Oh but Captain, the why is critical. If I say I'm from three hundred years in the future you can believe me.' He looked around slowly through the open walls of the hooch to the camp outside. 'Don't you think it's a bit quiet?'

Carvery smiled, raising the pistol until it pointed straight at Tibbs's face.

'Don't even think about it. This conversation is over, for now at least. Keith!'

'Keith!!'

Tibbs sat still, a sad smile forming.

Carvery's eyes betrayed the slightest concern, absolute silence being the only thing answering his calls.

'XO! Get your fucking ass in here now!'

'No one is going to come Captain.'

Tibbs' hand shot out and before Carvery could react the pistol was gone, magazine and chambered round lying on the desk, pistol in Tibbs' hand. Tibbs leant back, legs crossed, arms folded, eyes steady.

'Perhaps you will listen now. Take a good look outside Captain, tell me what you see.'

Carvery cautiously shifted his gaze over Tibbs' left shoulder, beyond the hooch to the camp. The trees were still, silhouetted against the early evening sky. No breeze, no movement. Moths slowly circled the camp lighting ... Carvery's mind took several seconds to realise that the moths were suspended in midair, small tufts of down dangled on invisible wires. He looked over Tibbs' other shoulder to a group of men around a small fire. Flames, men and smoke formed an image of still life, frozen rigid. Twisting, directly behind him his XO was locked in mid-stride, back foot on the ground, front foot suspended in midair. His cigarette balanced at an impossible angle from the corner of his mouth, glowing amber but stubbornly refusing to be consumed. He stayed transfixed for a few seconds then, subdued and confused, turned.

'How … I mean why are they —'

'Honestly, I couldn't explain it if I wanted to, it's not my area. They tell me it's a bubble in time, we're simply going faster than they are.'

He patted his trouser pocket.

'One press and the field is up, or I can drop you out of it and you won't even see me leave.' He smiled. 'Is this enough proof to get you to listen?'

'Ok, you're an alien from three hund —'

'No alien, I'm as human as you are. In fact I'm from Boston, or more correctly from what Boston has become. You ready to listen now?'

'Sure, go ahead.'

'Right. My team's all from your future and we're all military, all Army if you like. Not strictly U.S. Army, but still what you'd call the 'good guys', Special Forces. We get sent out to do one thing and that is to kill specific individuals and do it in ways that are as invisible and unidentifiable as possible. People falling off cliffs, heart attacks, traffic accidents —'

'Casualties of war —'

'Exactly. Just as long as it looks normal for the time and arouses as little interest as possible. We get in and out fast, doing nothing to screw up the timeline.'

'So who are you targeting? Dictators, despots, what? Trúc was just another dumb ass on the ground, what's he?'

'What was Trúc? He was one of us, someone who didn't like it then. You see we don't go back for people in their own time who do things we don't like. Think about it. Each time we have a change in government or policy a different set of people would be up for the chop. Give it long enough and no-one would be left.'

Tibbs looked at the ceiling.

'When we found out how to time travel the temptation was to go back and make it right, or go forwards and see how we'd do. It took us a little while to figure out that would never work so we outlawed any interference, visits or even just observation. Eventually we managed to control the technology and put up a … well, I guess you'd call it a barrier, a barrier to the past and future that can't be crossed by just anyone. But it took time.'

Tibbs pulled his gaze down.

'Trouble was that in that gap there were people, we don't know how many exactly, people who thought they didn't like it when they were and headed back or forwards to when they thought life would be better.'

'And Trúc was one of them?'

'Yes.'

'And he had to be killed?'

'Look, time and history are harsh, try to push them off course and they'll move but eventually they get back on track. It's just the how and when that's changed. So Trúc and everyone like him pollute history, they shouldn't be anywhen else but when they belong. Even just being somewhen else has consequences. And before you ask no, we can't simply take them back as that would change our future, a future in which they aren't there.'

'So he dies just because he's here. Or is there more?'

Tibbs sighed, looked pensively at Carvery.

'Guess it can't hurt. Trúc's not the issue. He just wanted to live in a time with more rules and different morals. If it was just him and he made no difference there'd be simpler, less complex ways to take him out. It's his son. Decades from now his son denies someone membership of a political party. If she was admitted she would live the rest of her life as a harmless marginalised crackpot. Instead she forms her own party and leads her nation and this part of the world down a very dark path. So, we're sent back to take him out, to do it before 10 November 1965, before his son is conceived on R&R. The only way that worked was here and now, to make him a casualty of war.'

Carvery and Tibbs sat in silence. Carvery looked again to the frozen world of the camp, to his XO leaning forward ever more improbably.

'Well ok, what do I say? It sounds nuts, it is nuts, but this I can't explain. But you've got one problem. You've told the whole bit to me so I know. So much for discretion and lose ends.'

Tibbs smiled sadly, slowly reloading Carvery's pistol.

'Not quite as I see it. In less than a second of 'normal' time my squad and I are gone, we won't be found or remembered and all you will have is a story, a dead body and forged orders. You get two choices. One you tell the truth, all of it, and if things work for the best you get locked in a rubber room for a while until you are 'better', or they pin Trúc's frag on you and it's all over. The other choice you say nothing, tell no one and it all goes down as just another 'Nam statistic.'

Tibbs placed one hand inside his trouser pocket, the other slid the loaded pistol back across the table.

'Your choice. Thanks for the beans and dicks Captain.' with which Tibbs popped out of existence.

The noises of the camp returned, together with cooling breeze and smells. Keith appeared by his side nearly instantly.

'Sir??'

What do I say? Tibbs and his men are gone, Trúc's still dead and all I have is a story no one will buy.

'XO, make sure Trúc's effects are taken care of before we break camp tomorrow. Dismissed.'

WU1 XV   GOVT PD   =   FAX WASHINGTON DC

DEC 04   630   PEDT   =   MRS ANNIE CARVERY

ROUTE 5 RAVENNA OHIO =

THE SECRETARY OF THE ARMY HAS ASKED ME TO EXPRESS HIS DEEP REGRET THAT YOUR HUSBAND CAPTAIN DAVID ARTHUR CARVERY DIED IN VIETNAM ON 8 NOVEMBER 1965. HE WAS ON RECON PATROL WHEN ENGAGED HOSTILE FORCES IN FIREFIGHT. PLEASE ACCEPT MY DEEPEST SYMPATHY. THIS CONFIRMS PERSONAL NOTIFICATION MADE BY A REPRESENTATIVE OF THE SECRETARY OF THE ARMY =

JOSEPH C LAMBERT MAJOR GENERAL USA   F48   THE ADJUTANT GENERAL   DEC 02 1965

DEC   05   920A ...

END

Out of africa

He came into the world when she was thirteen, alone and friendless, the midwife hurriedly turning her back on the mud walled hut. She held him scared and nervous as the last light filtered through the open plains of the delta, serenaded by the hyena's call and thrashing legs through grass. She thought his face beautiful, handsome.

'You are loved Tsabo.'

He was four when she found him naked and silent on the ground, Milky Way a warming blanket to her spirit in the still autumn night. She lay next to him staring as if the heavens could bring back her people, his father, her lover. What more to life than this, a strange child, a strange universe, a riddle without clues?

'You know they will not let me be, mother.'

'I have waited for your first words. These were not my hope.'

'They are what they are. They are for you alone.'

'We still have time?'

'We still have time.'

When he was seven they returned him as fast as he was taken. She read fear on their faces.

'There is nothing for us to do, Anna, nothing to teach.'

'Is not my son smart?'

'We have nothing to give he does not have. He is our equal and more.'

Tsabo sat silent, cross-legged on the dirt, the baked earth's dust a thousand lost dreams rising, swirling.

'Then what is to become of him?'

'We have filled the papers, he has passed the school. As the lower, the higher. What more is up to him.'

Tsabo stirred.

'Do not concern yourself for my sake. The blind may only teach the blind.'

He was ten when he came to her, restless and troubled. They sat as mother and son, adult and child, pupil and teacher.

'I must leave this place.'

'Why?'

'There is more to this world than the limit of your eyes.'

'May I come?'

'If you wish.'

When he was twelve the reek of butter and goat milk clung to her, sandalwood ash floating down to the stones on which she lay. Five days and five nights he sat unmoving as the mandala was made and unmade, chants sung and unsung.

'… eternal unbound, the shell an illusion, the dream reality.' Lumbum whispered to her.

'To what end? If the I dissolves then the I will fight.'

'As it must, yet the I must conquer the I, a sacrifice to itself, an eternal stream of consciousness, rebirth, redeath.'

Tsabo stood.

'If you look inside you do not see without. If you look outside you do not see within. To see everything you must not look at all.'

When he was twenty they bought him back as they had taken him. Unforced, unshackled, silent. They stood respectfully, persecutors and victim, captors and prisoner, weakness and power.

'We are deafened by his silence. We are weakened by his submission.'

'What have you done to my son in this year you have stolen from me?'

'Nothing he did not allow.'

'Which is?'

'Everything mother. Strength flows only from weakness, dominion from servitude.'

They scorned him when he was thirty, denying him power and authority he never sought. For fear of the world they embraced him, for love of themselves they rejected him; their self-loathing sent him away. They turned their faces, rich from poor, powerful from weak, disease from cure.

'You are not for us, so you must be against.'

'You say nothing against us, so your heart must condemn.'

'The people hear you, so your words must be lies.'

Tsabo wept.

'A mirror held to the world sees the truth; the world sees only the light it chooses to cast.'

He was thirty three when they came for him in the evening desert coolness. The old one of full beard and missing eye; the youthful one with blue skin and seven snakes; the one of saffron and buttered skin; the one with pierced hands. She searched their eyes as they searched her heart.

'What is it you will make of him?'

'Nothing he has not made of himself.'

'Why do I see my son in your eyes?'

'The reason we see him in all, the circle is complete. The beginning is as false as the end. The illusion of time itself an illusion, the stream a point, the many the one.'

The light burned from five as one. As the light increased the stars faded to impenetrable eternal dark.

'Come to the light mother.'

END

Panels

The minute hand hung suspended, frozen on the clock face opposite his cubicle tantalising, quivering as if undecided on its course of action. Clay watched slowly as, balanced between the forces of gravity and inertia on the one hand and will power on the other it hung, shuddered, then fell over the small interval that was one-sixtieth its hourly journey. One down, eight to go.

Einstein must have been a clerk he thought wryly, and a pretty cheesed off one at that. Any desk bound paper pusher understood relativity's barest essentials. How time at the start of the day flew past, barely enough to order the work and start the task, until late afternoon as that interminable countdown to 5:00 pm progressed when time and matter seemingly froze and your brain kicked on, cycling through what had not been done and what awaited. And as the days so the months and years and career until what faced this this particular fifty year old was a stretched eternity until his pension and release.

To cap it off the air conditioning was playing up leaving his floor broiling, the landscape of vacant desks broken only by the occasional back of a head building a picture of stasis, heat enforced listlessness. Again the minute hand struggled, again it won the prize, once more the march to entropy continued and Einstein remained vindicated. Seven minutes.

A tingling in his earpiece and a small window opening on his screen brought him back from the assault on time. The voice was familiar, the face not so.

'Hey Clay, how are you? Long time no see.' the face announced, still stubbornly remaining unidentified. 'It's me, Chris, c'mon Clay I haven't changed that much!'

He had. Clay smiled. 'Oh hi, I didn't recognise you – what's with the fungus?' motioning towards the mutton chops and goatee gleaming back at him.

'You know how it is, razors cost. Say, I'm only passing through, got time for a drink?'

'Yeah, sure, but only a quick one.'

'Ok, I'm downstairs, I'll see you when the shackles drop off.' The minute hand again fell back into gravity's clutches. Six left.

Expectation abetted time's onwards march. Clay sat propping up the bar with Chris making headway into the third of what promised (despite expectations) to be a long line of drinks.

'Can't say I get it', Clay said yet again 'you look ten years younger, ten kilos lighter and I haven't seen you smile so much in, well, years.'

'And I keep telling you buddy you need to get out of that place! It's killing you and it damned near got me. I mean, why are you still there? And don't tell me it's the money.'

'Well, as a matter of fact —'

'And how many people have got 'I wished I worked harder' on their gravestones? C'mon, I'm getting by on a third of what I used to get. Hey, you want proof it's better outside?' Chris dug into his pocket and, fishing out his phone, brought a photo up. 'This', he said triumphantly 'is Deanna, my Deanna, so you tell me it's all bad.'

Clay looked at the twenty something swimsuit model on the screen. He thought Chris the biggest liar on earth until he noticed who it was resting his head on her thighs. Shit, she's young enough to be his daughter.

Chris was laughing now, 'Yeah buddy, they all think she's my daughter, but man, these kids really can go for you in a big way. But you gotta get out. Soon. Now. Before it's really too late. Look at you, you need to.'

'Ok, ok, I can go at fifty-eight, a few more years but —'

'But nothing! They owe you. You remember John, from Central Records? He got out at forty-eight on a seventy-five percent pension. You know why? Certified nutter he was, kept seeing rabbits everywhere day in, day out. Got to the point he'd bring a twelve gauge and a bunch of carrots into the office to lure the beggars out. Well, they had him out the door six months later, and guess what?'

'What?'

'The only bunnies he sees now hang around the craps tables in Vegas. I tell you, they owe you.' triumphantly poking Clay in the chest for emphasis. 'Thirty years of service and they still want your blood, and for what?'

So it went until Clay found himself at home alone with the cat, sitting in the kitchen of his one bedroom flat staring at junk mail and bills. Thirty years and they still wanted more, no easing off or even a sign of real thanks, just 'here's your pay and come back' each fortnight. Over the years his job had cost him a marriage (and with that a house, new car and two kids who never called him), his energy, his optimism and all the other possible lives he could have led. He had a start as a musician, but that was put on hold for his career and eventually the career had gone too, stolen by younger recruits deemed more malleable or 'corporately aligned'. Arse lickers all. All he had left was a half paid flat, a ten year old car, and the promise of a pension that might let him survive if he lived through the next eight years of stupidity, budget cutbacks and volte-faces that plagued the office.

Yeah, they owed him, but how to make them pay? Not physically, he wasn't violent, but financially, payback for the thirty years of time they had stolen from him. It was clear that being retired medically unfit was the way to go, an indexed pension for life. He wasn't physically handicapped and that only left the mental option and they didn't hand those out easily. You had to be either certifiably insane or look like you were, fooling management and professionals alike. And it would have to be clearly and undeniably the result of work. It would have to be airtight.

It took him a few weeks to come up with an airtight, workable plan. All he needed, sometime soon, was a catalyst, and until then he could lay out the groundwork. He had at times cursed his auditor training but now he thanked his stars for it.

The first steps were simple, innocuous. He started subscriptions to New Scientist, Space Flight Monthly and the Doubleday 'eBook of the Month' club for speculative and science fiction. Instead of lobbing in front of the office TV for lunch gassing and whining with his fellow wage slaves he started reading his new subscriptions by himself, leaving the used copies lying around. Although a natural introvert he started pulling himself slowly, gently ever further back into himself at work, missing the happy hours and cooler chat, capping it off by cleaning his desk of the usual personal clutter and rubbish leaving only the screen, keyboard and stationery tray. His work remained as it had always been – neat, right and meticulous. It took just over a month for the change to be seen, to be commented on. It was his quarterly performance appraisal with his manager, Shelley.

'So how are you going otherwise? You know I've been flat out this last month, not even here really, but I think you seem even quieter than normal. Is everything ok?'

Clay smiled. 'Oh yeah, I'm fine I guess, you know it's just I'm nearly past fifty and that's where you start thinking, maybe too much, I don't know really.'

'Midlife crisis?'

'Ha! Hardly, I'm just taking stock and starting to get back into some things I used to do years ago but had to let slide.'

Shelley nodded and smiled. Clay returned the gesture but couldn't help feeling slightly sickened by this mid-thirties apparatchik pretending to understand 'life events'. Probably sucked the pap out of a management handbook somewhere.

'Didn't you do science at uni before switching to business?'

'Yeah, I'm starting to get a bit of interest back now, too late for formal study but nothing to stop me learning.'

'I've flipped through a couple of those magazines you've put in the lunch room, quite a bit in those, it's beyond me, it's just, I guess, really technical.'

'Too true by half', Clay smirked 'it's hard to start sometimes, it's really got me thinking, there is so much we don't know, so much left.' Now that the fish was in, time to kiss and release he thought. 'So it keeps me interested, I actually think it has helped me concentrate a bit better, perhaps that's why I'm that bit quieter.'

Shelley straightened in her chair, becoming a little more animated. 'I've noticed your work seems a bit more concise, targeted even, from what I can see.' with which the appraisal moved on.

In the next month he concentrated harder, talked less, and made sure he was seen to read more. He started buying the occasional 'alternative science' magazines, leaving them lying around the office when finished. Mainly flat earth, alternate lifestyle UFO aliens-are-amongst-us dreadfuls. Conversations starting around him now seemed to end up as gentle humouring of his supposed new interests. Brand Clay was getting some publicity and slowly being transformed.

His dress sense changed. His bland accountancy uniform of greys, blacks and navy blue was replaced by pastel shaded shirts, tan and fawn slacks, and slip on shoes. It was, he explained one morning, a way of adjusting his outlook through the use of colour management therapy to help to lift his energy, balance his concentration and reset his biological clock to the workday. It had, he assured those listening, actually worked despite his initial scepticism. To his amazement a few people said they had actually noticed it, one even later borrowing his copy of Athenian Magazine to read the article Clay claimed had set it all in motion.

Reflecting that night at home Clay knew that he now had a reputation of being slightly different, if not eccentric. It wasn't enough. He needed a key, a lightning rod tied to work for the next stage. He would only have to wait two weeks.

That Friday it was a very subdued Shelley who pulled Clay's team together into a glass walled meeting room with David, the site manager and Shelley's boss. It was clear that at some point he had worded Shelley up and was there to make sure she stayed on message. After the usual preamble she got to the point.

'So we have received our budget allocation for the remainder of the financial year which includes a two and a half percent efficiency dividend reduction. We have to find expenditure cuts to fund that which, if it had come at the start of the year would have been hard but now, half way through, becomes problematic.' Her eyes remained fixed on the only unoccupied chair.

Clay gazed at the teams that vacated the room earlier, huddled together in animated but dejected discussion. He lost track of Shelley's delivery but knew where it was inevitably leading.

'… there is only one option and our temporary staff, two teams on this floor, have been released as of close of business today. However our commitment to service remains and with the shifting of both resources and responsibility we envisage only a ten to fifteen percent increase in workload …' with which Clay switched off, leaving a mask of shock, bewilderment and distrust on his face, keeping faith with the others in the room.

He could hardly conceal his delight. This was perfect, no, better than perfect. Catalyst, build up and crisis mapped out and all to start Monday! Looking out of the room again he could see the other teams near the lifts, bags and photocopy paper boxes containing personal effects under their arms. Some shot hateful or distressed looks at him, but the bulk simply continued to look down, shoulders hunched, backs bent. For the briefest of moments Clay felt sorrow and empathy, but only fleetingly. As part of the Department they were the enemy, they owed him not he they, and they were paying now. And, he smiled inwardly, the Department's day was coming soon.

Days in the office lengthened and Clay made sure he stayed well on top of it all. Not that it was hard work, just more of it. He deliberately started to look a touch frayed at the edges, choosing to shave at night rather than before work, and every few days not ironing his shirt. He now looked just a bit stressed, dishevelled, showing signs of tension if not quite cracking at the seams.

The hat was the key to the next stage. It was oddly comfortable and fetching Clay thought, a good thing as it was going to be with him twenty-four seven from now on. Yellow bronze was also a positive colour.

It took until the following Wednesday for Shelley to get him alone. By then the hat had settled, and Clay had started darting his eyes randomly back and forth every so often to create a hunted, paranoid persona.

'So I just need two minutes to ask you about your new hat', Shelley said, leaning back in her chair and utterly failing to appear relaxed 'it's the talk of the office.'

'Oh, ah, yes, I guess it is, I mean we all should have one, you know, if only for peace of mind. Do you like it?'

Shelley winced. 'I'm not sure, it's a nice colour You must like it a lot, I can't recall you not wearing it in the last fortnight. But the material, I don't know what it's made of, it looks very shiny.'

'It's wire mesh.'

'Wire?'

'Copper-bronze. Took me ages to get the right gauge you know, had to order it in.'

'But why? I mean, it would hurt you wouldn't it?'

'No, not really, it's taken to my head nicely, it conforms and moulds after a while. As long as I don't hit the rim too hard it's good.'

Shelley squirmed. Clearly she was not getting through. Maybe a direct approach.

'Clay, it's not that I have an issue with your work or your dress, but the hat is, well, a bit different if you see what I mean. No-one else has one —'

'No, Stevo from IT's making one now, I gave him the plans.' which was perfectly true. Stevo had nearly demanded the plans from him.

'Anyway, what I need to know is why you have to wear it inside. There is no UV risk, no-one else currently has one and, although we don't have a dress code, you do look a little, a little, I mean you look very very individualistic in it. I need to know.'

'Ok then, the hat's actually a Faraday cage.'

'A far away cage?'

'No, Faraday.'

'So what does this Paraway cage do?'

She still can't even get the name right, it could be a harder job than I guessed. 'It stops radiation, it stops radio waves, it stops mind reading, it stops scanning. In and out. They're all listening you know.'

'Who?' and by now Clay could see she was rattled. 'All the people here listen Clay, we're on the phones all day.'

'It's not them, it's the ones out there you can't see. The CIA. ASIS. But most importantly the aliens.' eyes widening, tightened grimace on his face.

'Aliens? Where, in the cupboard?'

'No, seriously, aliens. No-one can prove that they're not there, we don't know, but they are somewhere. This', tapping his hat 'stops them digging into my mind. I don't want to end up being damaged or changed by them. I'm a little scared Shelley, you know after Katie left with the kids I was gutted, had nothing, I've built back up a bit but now the job's probably at risk, all I might have left is my mind and I don't want to lose that', with which he forced a single tear out of the corner of one eye 'I can't lose that.'

Shelley regarded him in the same way you would a dog with a hurt paw. She leaned forward. 'Your job's not at risk, you're doing your usual really good work, it's just that I care for my staff and I want to help. The hat's a bit different, don't you think? Does it really make you feel better?'

Clay found it hard to keep his disgust hidden. Care? Couldn't spell the word. 'Yes, it really does. I couldn't get calm before I made it, now I'm all good. I'm actually safe.'

'Fine then.' Shelley rose. 'I'm comfortable with you keeping it on if it helps.'

'Good, thanks.'

'But you know there is one thing, I mean, I can understand

how it stops things going up and down, but what about the sideways stuff?'

Clay looked at her as she walked away. Again it seemed all the cards were being dealt just for him. She had just confirmed the next stage of his plan, even kicking open the door.

Three weeks later David eyed Shelley angrily inside the glass walled meeting room. He shifted his gaze to a copper cube seated in amongst the grey walled panels of an open plan work area. The blow up aliens, pyramids, UFOs and graffiti circling the cube were mocking totems put there by Clay's workmates.

'... and how in hell do you condone that? What sort of asylum do you have here? You can't tell me he's effective and it's not impacting. Do you know that someone offered me ten to one that he'd believe he was a plastic fork by month's end?'

Shelley was as angry as David, but her anger was directed at him. She'd thought him a bombastic ass before, now the feeling was even stronger. Any chance to slip the knife you bastard she thought.

'His work's flawless, probably better than before. Productivity here', she spat, slinging a sheaf of paper his way 'is fifteen percent up and error rate three percent down. It's having a positive effect and I can't see an issue with it as long as this keeps going on. Until it becomes disruptive he stays.'

'Oh yes I can see why, you did actually endorse that', pointing outside 'that, that chain mail clunker and linked it to a downsizing coping mechanism. Do you know what HR's opinion is? No, of course not, you wouldn't think to ask would you? Well we are at risk here, if he cracks totally then we could be liable. Do you understand?'

'So he gets a damned pension for being crazy, it hits our insurance bill but it's not going to happen. It's all under control, all good. In fact he's managed to pass his next grading exam so he's up for promotion.' The look of horror on David's face only egged her on. 'Oh yes, and as a starter he's on the next workplace review committee. So get used to it', she chortled as she left 'he'll be there next Tuesday with you.'

Shelley was thinking hard as she walked towards Clay's cube. She had to admit that Clay gave her the creeps now, but he was still of use. As long as work improved she looked good, and now she had a chance to hang Clay around David's neck. All she had to do was make Clay more visible, and he had done that for her. All Clay had to do was keep his work up to par, and he was doing that. Then any move David made would be discrimination against Clay and she could walk across David's carcass courtesy of the equal employment laws.

'Clay', she called into the cube 'do you have a minute?'

Shelley had not recognised him without his suit last time she had seen him. Funnily it had not been much of a shock seeing him add the smock to the hat a week after their last talk, and the step up to the cube a week or so later had, strangely she thought, actually made some sort of weird sense. The only mildly disturbing thing was everyone's habit of sticking fridge magnets to his back when he wasn't looking. She'd even added a 'Take Me To Your Leader' one in a weaker moment.

Clay emerged, rearranging his hat and smock. Since getting the cube he had only worn his personal faraday suit when outside the cage or at home. Soon, when the home cage was finished, he would not even need it there.

'Ok, again my congratulations on the promotion, but it is now time to get to work ... .' and so it continued.

Once finished Clay stepped back into his cube and out of the hat and smock. Time for the big play he thought, and not a moment too soon. He hated the copper suit he had to wear, it itched and scratched and his ankles and wrists had taken on a pale green hue. Not to mention the utterly legendary jock rash, the smell of stale sweat and filth. Then there was the trouble being seen in public, running the gauntlet of the neighbourhood kids was truly scary.

He was sure he was right on the edge now, the only question being the right pressure point. And next Tuesday was perfect. Absolutely perfect.

Corporate boardrooms are by nature places of excess and lavishness. Symbols of privilege and luxury for those at the helm of the ship of commerce, they are visible reminders of the distance between the top and bottom of the organisation and, together with the executive bathroom suite, an unassailable bastion of corporate position.

More so in Clay's world, the public service. As the perks enjoyed by their private sector brethren lay outside the bounds of politically decreed probity, those that lay inside tended to be all the greater and more lavish. Forty floors up with sweeping views across the bay through two glass walls, the solid Beechwood table, form fitting ergonomic chairs and tastefully ridiculous post-modernist paintings tended to take the breath away from any visitor at less than branch head level. Facing a painting worth multiples of your annual salary (with the valuation of course being tastefully, discretely but prominently displayed on the frame) would in and of itself be distraction enough, never mind the real estate agent wet dream inducing view. But today, for the dozen persons in the room, such things had been instantly and irrevocably erased from their memory. From now on in the minds of those twelve most deserving of apparatchiks the room would and could only ever be associated with one thing. And that one thing, shimmering burnished metal in the corner, edged it's careful and clattering way on all fours slowly from one side of the room to the other.

Clay's appearance had long since failed to be a shocking novelty, and when he took his place at the table earlier nothing save the usual pleasantries were exchanged. Barely had the proceedings begun when he sprang (slowly, given the 40 kilos of mesh he was clad in) to his feet.

'My apologies, I must check the room for safety issues.' eyes darting to the dado panelling on the far side of the room.

'I beg your pardon?' the Chair questioned. 'What do you mean? Fire hazard, electrical, furnishings?'

'No, hardly', Clay replied spread-eagled face down on the carpet, crawling to the far wall 'nothing so simple.'

'Just what' the young up and comer from fourteenth floor asked as Clay grazed her exquisitely waxed and shaped legs with his green tinged smock 'are you talking about and please, my shoes, don't scuff my shoes!'

'Panels, panels, they use the panels and I've only just realised.' Clay mumbled turning his head to look at a visibly paling Chair. 'They use the panels as access points, surveillance points, it's so, so, so ordinary, so common, so easy. Need to check every one, each panel, each look alike panel, floor, walls, ceiling, each pattern to check.' with which he kept pressing his fingers firmly in between the lines, on each panel of dado, each square of carpet, anywhere lines formed a box, a rectangle, a panel.

Fifteen minutes later Shelley was outside looking in with David, Lois from HR, and the Departmental Head. Clay was alone, still on the boardroom floor and had just about completed his circuit of the room. Shelley's shaking and cold sweat was not for her insane subordinate but for her own truncated career. David's expression said it all, talking as if she did not exist.

'How do we finish this off, cleanly and simply? We cannot have that here any longer.'

'Well', Lois replied 'immediate psychiatric assessment followed by an invalidity redundancy and he's out of here, four weeks tops. If he acts like that in his assessment it might even take a fortnight. But it will cost with our insurance premium and questions will be asked how he was allowed to get to this point.'

'Those questions are already answered. It would be an appropriate time to re-evaluate one's career goals I would say, wouldn't you?' Then turning to Lois before Shelley could respond 'Get him on the couch and out of this building.' with which he walked off.

The Departmental Head, a toughened old crone of sixty-two years, regarded Shelley as an idiot child. 'That is sound advice you should consider carefully. There are options on the outside you know, and once there none of this need follow you. If one stays here then, well, our records remain. Has anyone else seen this? What of the team? Next I'll have a floor of bloody chickens each trying the same damned trick, if it is a trick. You clear his desk, you get him downstairs and out. He's either pensioned off or fired, I don't care which.'

Five minutes later Shelley managed to get Clay into the lift. It had been a near thing, the carpet being the tiled kind and Clay insisting on checking each and every tile out, just in case. She had to ask him, even knowing the answer she just had to ask.

'Clay, who is behind the panels?'

'You don't believe me.' straightening for a second and then bending down again, red raw fingers prying at the lift's tiled floor. 'I've been trying to tell everyone but you all just laugh. Well when I find them, and I will, you won't be laughing quite so loud. Do you actually remember what I said?'

'Well, no, you said so much and really I only got half of it, if that.'

'Thought as much.' He stopped mid pry, just short of the lift door as they passed the twelfth floor. No-one else had bothered to get in, even though the lift had paused at each floor for extra passengers. Shelley's makeup bore streaks from tears and perspiration that even Lancôme could not help, and Clay was a slow blur of activity on all fours. Who'd want to share a lift with an Alice Cooper lookalike and a hundred kilo copper armadillo? They continued alone.

300

'I've told everyone all along. It's the aliens, the post Roswell aliens. All the clues are out there, you've just got to find them. After the crash they changed tactics, it was initially too obvious so they chose to do it all by stealth ...' by which time Shelley had retreated, again, into her own thoughts. Time to get another job, and even as she piled him into the taxi a little later she was still detached, still distracted. She watched the taxi go off down the street, then went back inside. She picked up her two boxes, accepting the inevitable, and left.

The taxi ride was uncomfortable and his smock got caught in several places on the fabric seat covers. Having disentangled himself when he exited at home, the fifteen meter crawl to his flat was tortuous, having to check each square, each block formed by expansion joints in the concrete path. Clay thought briefly about forgetting this, but decided it was better to keep in character. It was fortunate for him that he did, Lois's surveillance unit watching him with more than a distracted eye.

'Fucking nutter!' the girl at the camera growled, snapping the bronzed butt in her telephoto lens from the van down the road.

'Keep a lid on it', her supervisor responded 'just make sure you get it uploaded. And be thankful it wasn't another of those Spiderman wannabes.' with which she resumed her bagel and paper in the front seat.

Safely behind locked doors Clay got out of his smock and hat, examining his bloodied fingers and calloused knees. Even with the kneepads it had hurt like hell, and the rashes from the skin contact with the copper were getting serious. But not long to go now, maybe a month or two, and it would be easy street from then on. All he had to do was get through the psychiatrists visit, drop the final piece of bait, and not screw things up.

He trawled through his usual web sites and discussion groups, looking like just another conspiracy theorist with something to prove. Next his own blog where all his theories and mind were on display for all, and hopefully the right people, to see. He let his six hundred followers – a fact Clay still found both amazing and disturbing – know that his panel theory had as yet uncovered nothing, proving that they were really well hidden. A quick tweet on the up and he closed his machine down for the day. He was just about there he told himself. Four weeks from now I'll be down at some beach, check in the bank, a blonde under each arm and texting Chris. And with that thought he drifted off to sleep.

Doctor Betel, the contracted psychiatrist, looked up from Clay's file to David, Lois, and Claudia, Shelley's replacement. 'You seem to believe it is open and shut, yes?'

'We think so', Lois responded 'he seems to have been tipped over by us, possibly by our acceptance or condoning of his behaviour —'

'But we will not and cannot publicly accept any liability based on a misinformed view, no matter how genuinely presented.' David interjected, shooting an icy glance at Lois.

'Which is the correct stance to take and also why I am now here', Dr. Betel smiled 'to see what you really do have. And already I can see its shape.'

'Which is?'

'From this file, his personal history and what I have seen at your offices there is a chance in my mind that his problems may not be as grave as he presents. There may be, and probably is, some doubt over his genuineness that could only be resolved by my seeing him, as we are to arrange.'

'You mean that he is a fake?'

'Perhaps yes, perhaps no, perhaps maybe. It is never quite so, ah, stark as you think. He may genuinely believe it, he may choose to believe it sub-consciously whilst consciously doubting it or vice versa, or it all may be a convenient shield against an unknown other. I will find out and if he can be helped back we will see.'

After an extended discussion of Clay's office behaviour, online habits, surveillance photos and work assessments, Dr. Betel continued. 'There is that other matter, that of his workmates. Has this had any impact at all upon them, any obvious change?'

'None we've seen', added Claudia to David's shake of the head 'in fact they seem the better for his absence although I'm not sure if it's the lack of Clay or the lack of Shelley. After all, with the cutbacks another two people gone are not too much impact on top.'

'I imagine not, but it is the illusion of Clay's beliefs remaining I am concerned with.'

'On that score all that remains is an overabundance of fridge magnets, an extra garbage bin full of trash magazines and forty kilos of scrap copper mesh. Nothing, as they say, except a bad smell.'

Dr. Betel smiled and leaned back, gathering his papers into his valise. 'So then, my only concern is Clay and that will be in hand by tomorrow. All things being equal my report will be with you within a fortnight.'

'You still want to see him at his house? Is that safe?'

He smiled, patronisingly. 'We have come a long way from couches and electroshock therapy you know. He has no violent tendencies, seems like an otherwise quite reliable and honest man who simply thinks aliens live in every nook and cranny. I will be perfectly safe, and he will be perfectly at ease in his home environment.'

He stood, started out the room then stopped, turned around. 'There is of course a more practical reason to see him at home. My offices are in the city plaza, a lovely place of trees and open grass surrounded, unfortunately, by a rather large flagstone mall. Apart from the severe embarrassment he may suffer it could take him the better part of a week on his hands and knees getting from the taxi to my office door. And once there he has to face the parquetry floor. Adieu.' with which he left.

David sank back into his chair. 'Now, do you think we can perhaps actually get back to what we are paid to do?'

The next day Dr. Betel found himself sitting comfortably in Clay's flat, chatting amiably and casually taking notes. To him the flat was a touch small, very austere, without many personal items on display. The flat would have otherwise seemed normal and very clean, except for the neatly soldered and reinforced fine copper mesh that lined the walls, floor, ceiling and double-blind door entry. He felt rather claustrophobic, as if he was inside a giant tea strainer. It was also stultifyingly hot. The smell of sweat, his and Clay's, was near overpowering.

He had just spent the better part of two hours there, Clay concluding his third explanation of why this was all necessary, made at Dr. Betel's request. Clay didn't seem to mind and seemed to be warming more to the subject with each successive telling.

'... so that is how I came to the conclusion that aliens were in fact living incognito on Earth, observing us. With all the evidence no other conclusion is possible. None.'

'And again, they are doing what here?'

'Observing, that's all. They must be. I don't exactly know why. If they were in the open or doing something we'd know, so they must be watching, waiting for I don't know what. So this cage, my hat, my smock, they're my shield. They can't see me or observe me so I'm invisible to them, and they can't get in here unless I wish them to and I don't. All I have to be careful of are the hatches.'

'Hatches?'

'Yes, everywhere, anywhere, they change them regularly, the hatches. They can be in the street, in a building, in a plane, a car, anywhere. I actually nearly saw one!'

'You did?' Dr. Betel leaned forwards. This was new.

'Yes.' Clay leant across. Now to drop the big one, the last bait. It's taken days to get it right, if he takes this one I'm home and hosed. 'I saw one at a farm just after I started my cage. A hatch, a door barely six centimetres square opened up in a barn and a cow simply slipped through it. I raced over just as it closed and I nearly pulled the barn apart with my bare hands but couldn't find anything behind where the panel had been but wood. They must change them, somehow, but that's the thing I saw. So each day, no, each time I go near any panel like lines, no matter how big or small, I need to check. Just in case.'

'Just in case?'

'Just in case.'

Dr. Betel sat in silence for a while, then stood. 'Do you mind if I get some more water?' pointing at the two empty glasses. 'It's getting hot in here. Would you like a refill?'

'Thanks, yes. Look doc, I know it sounds far-fetched but it's all true. I mean, I'm not just dreaming this stuff up.'

'I think I believe that you believe it's true', filling the glasses 'but there's truth and then there's truth.' He swirled Clay's glass until it was clear.

'Huh? What do you mean?'

'Well', resuming his seat and taking a long drink 'you seem to be assuming that the aliens have bad intentions.'

'Well yes, I do', Clay responded, draining his glass 'if they were friendly or benign then none of this secrecy would be needed. Why hide if you are no threat? I mean, we can't be a threat to them, surely?'

'Your reasoning seems sound, but there is one thing.' Dr. Betel stood and moved to the computer, placing a hand on the silent device. 'Your Faraday cage is imperfect you know, quite good but most unfortunately imperfect.'

Clay tried to turn but found to his consternation that his head would not move. Nor would his feet or hands. In fact he felt rigidly glued down. He tried to talk but could not.

Dr. Betel came into view again, valise in hand. He had changed, the kindly eyes sadder. 'Your computer, it's hardwired into the broadband cabling. It passes through the cage. It's only five to ten millimetres in diameter, but it's enough. Enough for us anyway.' He twisted the couch around so that Clay was looking at the computer, now switched on. 'An operation this size does leave marks, small clues, but in general nobody is able to tack them together. Somehow you have. It's a pity, a real pity.'

He placed the valise on the floor. It produced a thin blue beam of light, tracing out a six-centimetre square on the floor's copper mesh. 'I know why you did it, we know about Chris, your job, all that, it's just very unfortunate that you decided to use this particular theory. Yetis, JFK, Loch Ness Monster, even floating pink elephants and I'm quite sure you would have made it to the beach.' He sighed 'But this could only end one way. You would have been of use, you seem like a reasonable person who would have fitted in, but now you will serve another, unfortunately less pleasant, purpose.'

Clay, still frozen, sat silently screaming as he watched the six-centimetre hatch open up and his feet and then legs elongate, flowing rapidly into the hole.

'You will get to meet your two blondes, however as both of them are the unit's vivisectionists I doubt it will have the same outcome as you originally had in mind. Goodbye Mr. Creek.'

The hatch slowly sealed itself, leaving Dr. Betel alone with the glowing computer screen. A face, his near twin, stared unblinkingly out.

'It is finished then.' A statement, not a question.

'Yes, please send in the team. We will need to talk later.'

'As you wish.' with which the screen went dead.

A month later David sat in his office on the eighteenth floor watching the last page in Clay's personnel file pass through the shredder. It had been three weeks since Dr. Betel's report finding Clay sane and lying; slightly less since his letter to Clay demanding his immediate return to work or risk termination. It being the statutory fourteen days since delivery and, with no sign of Clay, he was now fired. It was as if the earth had swallowed Clay whole, and a damned good job too. He took another sip of his whiskey, but stopped mid gulp.

What had that been? Out of the corner of his eye? Was it a small section of the room partition that had just rotated? Impossible. I'm just overworked, just tired.

Nothing to worry about.

Yet.

END

Pictures of you

Death always smells the same. Yuichi adjusted her blue plastic overalls, picked her way between fast food containers, betting slips and soiled laundry littering the floor to pull back the curtains and let in the Osaka morning. Another day, another cleanup, another invisible death. The sofa carried the indentations, dark stained upholstery to one end and a few strands of short black hair on the other.

Takeshi came through the front door, cleaning cart in tow.

'Six months this one. They said they had trouble separating flesh from vinyl. Wouldn't have known except for the cats.'

Takeshi wasn't cruel; it was the necessary armour for the job. Yuichi had to treat each one as a thing, forget the person who had lived and suffered and died alone. There was only enough room to mourn one and that space was filled.

The cleaning wasn't difficult. The bodies were all desiccated flesh, fluids drained into furniture or floor to be discarded beyond repair. The rest just stubborn stains, piles of ingrained filth, remnants of grating lives abandoned to isolation in a world of cheek to jowl connection.

The boxing's confronting, to get the meagre assortment of things sorted and tagged. Old photographs, smiling faces and bright eyed children staring out watching a stranger remove the last earthly trace of an unknown other. Yuichi's armour had thickened, nothing moved her, all of it intellectual curiosity as she traded time for the means to survive.

Just past midday they stood at the doorway looking past two small sealed cartons to a clean, freshly aired room. Seventy-five years walking this earth and all that remains would fit under my sink. Takeshi placed two orange garbage bags on the cart. Yuichi bowed deeply, stepped backwards and closed the door.

'You always do that. They do not see or care.'

'Once someone did. Forgetting is impolite.'

'Whatever. Lunch then see what's next?'

Her boss like all bosses was tight fisted. The cheap soba was in character, keeping her hand out of his pocket. Yuichi slurped away steadily.

Takeshi reached for a pen.

'They have a small one for tomorrow but my daughter has an appointment. You will be able to manage by yourself.'

It was no request. It never was.

'Of course.'

He scrawled hurriedly on a napkin.

'I will leave the cart inside the door tonight. This is the address and entry code. I will meet you there at six pm tomorrow.'

It could not be called an apartment. Shared bathroom and kitchen, what was left barely six paces across. She pushed past the cart to pull up the blind, the wall of concrete and glass opposite blocking all but the faintest reflection of a smog tinted day.

It's a mistake, perhaps Takeshi has already done the work. No, a check of the address said it was the right place, the folded orange bags and stacked empty boxes awaiting her attention. The room was nearly bare. Just the stale scent of decay blanketing a wooden chair and table, a framed photograph, a small pile of soiled clothes. An hour's work, maybe less. Perhaps Takeshi was softening, handing over easier jobs.

An elderly woman four months dead, it did not seem to fit. Where had she lain? Yuichi looked down to two small patches of threadbare carpet in front of the chair. It didn't matter, the police would work it out.

It was finished, ready to close yet her age and the room's dankness conspired against her knees. Three pm, three hours to wander until Takeshi returns. Perhaps I will wait, sit for a while.

The chair was hard but comfortable, a western design with scallops for her buttocks. With the window open the late afternoon breeze eventually turned cold on her shoulders. She couldn't close it, had to let the room air, so she lifted the chair to move it back against the wall. Arthritic fingers failed, the chair slipping from her grip to fall across the table. Something dislodged itself, rolled to a stop at her feet. A small, dark disc. Yuichi picked it up. Where did it come from? She couldn't see any part of the table missing or broken. Takeshi was strict and the police were firmer, no theft or breakages permitted. She heard him coming down the corridor. She slid the disc into her pocket with her tack rag just as his face popped round the doorway.

'I hope you did not work too hard today. A simple one after that run of bad, you could do with a little rest.'

'It was exceptionally clean Takeshi-san.'

311

'They said she hardly ate or came out of her room, she wasn't really here anyway. I will drive you home, I have the van outside.'

My apartment's no larger than hers, a single room with bathroom and kitchenette. I left the curtains open this morning, the ten story J-pop neon now lighting the apartment as day. I used to track the days by name, then by the work that came, now by the pain. My back says it's mid-week, by the time my legs scream it will be my rest day.

I pour a lukewarm cup of tea and sit heavily opposite the low cabinet. His face stares back from the frame younger, confident, proudly in love. I can't remember why I keep it, his confidence and strength a shattered lie bringing the rest of my world down when he left.

I carefully fold my clothes and place them on the floor ready for tomorrow. The disc falls, rolls a short distance to stop in the cracked linoleum. I pick it up and absent mindedly spin it. Thin, smooth and cool to the touch, a curiosity from a dead woman to a dying one.

The disc is strangely captivating sliding across my palm; I really should return it to the police, let it lie unclaimed for a year then be incinerated. Would it hurt just this once to hold onto something, a small reminder of a life passed unnoticed? I place the disc between the picture frames.

Small reminders, all that was left for many, all that is left me. His was the one love, enough while it lasted. I should forgive, should understand the pain to him was as great as mine, but time has entombed his fragility in the walls of my sorrow.

A six year old's pretend scowl stares out at me. Ashima at cherry blossom time in the avenue, rose coloured petals at her feet. The disc changes unnoticed from deep indigo to dark blue. Oh how Ashima demanded that costume, the pins and clips bunching the sack-like kimono away from the camera's telltale

312

eye until her delight with the final picture. Another perfect day in a perfect life, the perfect little family safe inside the salary man bubble dissolving a week later as Ashima lay broken at the bottom of the stairs and he abandoned me to my fate.

The dark blue pales with my tears, small hesitant travellers down the lined and pockmarked landscape of experience. Each night I cry, each night I mourn for her, for forty empty years and the lives stolen from me. Pale blue rises unnoticed to white as I screw my eyes closed struggling to bring a scrap of Ashima's laughter back, her smell, the strength in a child's hug. I fail as I always do, screaming silent curses to my impotent ancestors.

'Mummy, why are you crying?'

Why do they taunt me, using even her memory to dangle the ravings of a shattered mind before me?

'Open your eyes, the blossoms are falling and the sky is blue.'

Perfumed scent enfolds me, the breeze gently tousling my hair. My eyes open to a clear day, cherry blossom avenue, the impossible.

'Ashima? What are you doing here?'

'It's my birthday, you promised I could cosplay.'

'No, no I mean you're here? You are aren't you?'

'Silly, the costume's not that good.'

The white soars to rainbow incandescence, the beauty lost to unseeing eyes.

'How long do we have?'

'Today and tomorrow and the next and forever and ever.'

Ashima bounds over, wrapping her arms around me. Strong arms, apple scented hair, soft cheeks.

'I want the photo first and then the pandas, the little baby ones.'

313

Grabbing my hand she pulls me to my feet.

'Can I have some ice-cream? Just a little, I promise I won't spoil dinner.'

'Of course, of course you can.'

'Good. You can have the vanilla, I'll eat the strawberry. I love you mummy.'

'I love you too sweetheart.'

The disc glows translucent, Yuichi as stone in the chair unmoving, unseeing, unaware. Night falls into day back to neon night to weeks, an unnoticed procession as it glows, as Yuichi remains.

Yuichi draws her last breath and is stilled.

The disc fades to deep indigo and waits.

END

Recall

'A thousand bucks.'

Dave knew his mark. Ratface doesn't flinch.

'Cash?'

'Always.'

'Done deal. How long?'

'Two hours.'

Dave turns to me as ratface walks away.

'Go get started, I'll back the truck up.'

I do a quick inventory; the bed sit isn't big but it's worth more. So much for respecting the elderly. A photo of ratface and a woman stare out from a cluttered table. The photo finds its way to my tin, the frame to salvage.

Two hours later we leave ratface and the real estate agent shrinking in the mirrors. Dave glances at the tin on my lap.

'Usual?'

'Yeah. Photos, letters, junk.'

'Beats me why you want it.'

'Every man needs a hobby.'

He runs the red light, whistling happily. The Royal Doulton will make him a good return.

'Whatever.'

I turn out the tin at home. The letters, photos, and ticket stubs will go to my sister at the local history association. I keep the old nib pen, a relic I know I can shift for a few dollars. And the watch. An old Timex digital, worn but clean with a dogeared leather band. I wipe off the dust. It bears an inscription, 'June. '59', just above the battery cover. I slip it into my pocket.

'Fifteen dollars.'

'You serious Erin?'

She takes the loupe from her eye, gives me a doleful stare.

'What else. It's maybe worth thirty retail, parts or working, and it won't shift for ages. I've gotta keep my margins. And the crap inscription don't help.'

'What?'

'Lookit. 'June '59'. Timex didn't do digitals till the seventies. Either someone got the year wrong by a few decades or your lady was fifty nine when she got it. Believe me, none of my customers wanna know how old their ladies are.'

'Fifteen dollars?'

'And it's charity even if it works.'

She takes off the battery cover, a small rusted disc falls out. 'CR92, CR92' she mutters, rummaging through a drawer until she emerges with the disc's shiny twin. She replaces battery and cover to be rewarded by a gentle chime.

She holds it closer, taps a blue button on one side.

'So it works, but this isn't standard and does nothing. Maybe now it's worth ten.'

I snatch it back.

'No thanks, I'll keep it. How much for the battery?'

'Like I said, I'm feeling charitable. Just come back with something valuable next time.'

I towel off after my shower, slip on my boxers and settle down for the game. I'm early so I put the panel on mute and pick up the watch. I put it on, thread the strap through the buckle. It feels solid, like it belongs. I still can't figure out how to set the time so I just keep playing with it. I push the blue button down and hold it.

The room implodes to a black and white checked cube then to a glass tube; a surprised woman in a lab coat looks in at me. She jabs a panel beside her. Something burns my nose and throat, the room melts to black.

I wake up to cream-lilac tiled surfaces, a desk, an empty chair on one side and me in another opposite. The chill through my boxers is intense. The watch is gone.

A gap in the wall closes behind a short man. He sits opposite me, places the watch to one side and a small box to the other. He points to the watch.

'Where did you get this?'

'I want my lawyer.'

'There are none.'

'I know my rights. Lawyer. Phone call.'

'You have none. Not here. Not now.'

'You military?'

'Worse.'

He points to the watch.

'Where did you get this?'

I'd been in this position before, law in front and me on the wrong side of it. He's too calm, too dispassionate. He wants to know about the watch? Fine. I tell him.

'Her address?'

'Twenty eight Highview.'

'Time, date you were there?'

'Ten August, about two pm.'

'Which year?'

'This year.'

'Humour me. Which year?'

'Two thousand eleven.'

He stands.

'Wait.'

Like I can go anywhere. My feet are glued to the floor.

He comes back.

'It checks out.'

'Of course it does. Now what?'

He stays silent.

'When is this?'

'How'd you guess?'

'No one has walls that open and close and I've never heard of anyone's feet being stuck down without cuffs or chains. How far?'

'Centuries.'

'Whose watch was it?'

'One of ours.'

'He's stuck back there?'

'No. Sometimes we don't place them properly. She's dead. Just waited too long to hit recall.'

'Must've liked it.'

'Perhaps. It happens.'

'Will I like it here?'

'No.'

'No?'

'Too different. You'd be useless.'

'Always room if a guy can push a broom, pull a beer.'

'Not here, not now.'

'So?'

'A choice. You can stay, but for your own sanity we'd have to ... reset ... your memories.'

'You mean erase.'

'Yes.'

'Or?'

'Send you back.'

'No memory reset?'

'No need. Who'll believe you?'

He slides the small box across.

'Take one. When you get back you're drunk. In a month it will just be a bad dream.'

'Option two then.'

The tube shifts rapidly to cube then pitch black. I take one step and fall face first into the soaking earth, rise to my knees covered in putrid mud. To each side faint clicks and rattles, metal on metal, dull thud of boots on wood through the darkness.

The sky turns phosphorescent as the first shells explode over Ypres.

END

Roof o' green

I'm drunk. Hell, I'm worse'n drunk and beyond, even the damn white bitch Miley Cyrus muzac floating through the smoke sounds good. Cyril's laughin' at me across the pile of empties, I know he is even as he's layin' face down I can see his back shake, fingers twitchin' round the neck of his Bud, damn black fool, damn black fools the both of us. Fool maybe, friend for sure. When he's home she'll tear him a new one 'cause of me, out drinkin' an' bitchin' until he don't know which ends for shittin' and which ends for spittin'. Keeps me from Kath while he's like this, trod on, down, like my daddy but he didn't stay away from mom when he drank an' I aint goin' there with Kath, no man, I gets like this I go grab Cyril an' we hit it till I sleep out in the back forty at his place an' he gets poured home. She hates it but she'd hate the other worse, she don't know but she would.

It's time he went, time I went, I'm wavin' at the barkeep but why's he on the roof laughin' at me, he's lookin' at me but he's poppin' in an' outta focus, why the hell can't he stay still dammit?

'Ok TC, whadya want?'

His eyes are funny, sorta bloodied an' wobbly all three o' them, it's hard to know which ones lookin' at me. I grab Cyril's head – I think, I mean it's hair I got in my hand an' I can't pull it out tho' I'm tryin' – an' wiggle it at the barkeep 's' nows getta hom a wit him' an' let go of it, bouncin' like a pineapple all stubby and wiry like.

Cyril's still laughin' as I'm layin' in the pickup goin' cross town, fairy lights on the street lights dancin' in time with the exhaust an' Cyril's manic drummin' on my guts ratta – tat – tat – ratta – tat swayin' left an' right, now starlight only warmin' me, coloured rainbow dots no white so beautiful, soft.

Cool quiet dark, my hands soft on grass sod no wind, no light the field back o' Cyril's I'm lyin' peaceful, this peace the only peace I knows the only one I knowed, between wors'n drunk and wors'n sober all my miserable shit life. Kath don't know it an' Cyril don't know it an' I don't tell no one 'cause everything I've ever said I hads been taken away and aint no one takin' this, no one not even that smartass genY doctor an' his liver prostrate death an' anyways it's worth it, just worth it for the hours a week.

I lose myself, I'm losing me, I'm glued to the roof o' green and sod and field and planet holdin' on so's I don't fall into the black and the beautiful lights, the stars, the empty but not empty but I wanna dive, dive out an' sink, sink forever like I belong 'cause it aint here's my home but she, an' she don't know she can't know cause I can only say it when I'm like this and I can't see her when I'm like this so she's not gonna know ever.

They know, they see, they call an' they come, their light spirals down, purple red gentle, silent unseen but to me an' the sod an' the field an' the roof o' green an' my fingers dug to the knuckles to hold me on, their hands on my head an' faces smooth, black as the sky and beautiful, 'come home, come home now' they breathe, I cry my tears as fire I can't, I can't Kath, heavens hell without you an' hells home with you an' I can't.

My tears are theirs, their tears diamonds from onyx, cascading jewels rising to my chest on the sod on the field on the roof o' green, soaking as they whisper 'it's alright, we'll wait, we'll be back and wait till you're ready' an' I know they will, they will, an' one day I will, I will …

… one day I will.

END

Second man

'Might as well.'

Ukko turned.

'If you like. What is it?'

Akka brushed one gloved hand over the engraved panel, sending away a grey mist.

'Apollo 11 landing site, 1969.'

He looked down through the perspex platform to the descent stage, then back up at the ascent stage.

'I don't like that.'

'Why?'

'Well all this is real, their footprints, where they first stepped out. Doesn't feel right having a holo on top.'

'Why's this important again?'

'First men on the moon, start of it all.'

'Oh. Never was one for ancient history.'

'Ancient history? Ancient history my ass!'

'C'mon Buzz, it's been a while.'

'And you're keeping count, Mike?'

'Not like there's much else to do.'

He walked through the LEM's legs, tried and failed for the millionth time to smudge out Buzz's footprints.

'Four hundred thirty six years, fifteen days and eight hours. Ancient history.'

Neil glanced at his Omega.

'Plus or minus ten minutes.'

They left their own marks in the dust-coated perspex, smooth soled above rippled.

'Doesn't get much business.'

'Not popular Ukko, no hero worship like back when. Everyone thought they were something else, role models, supermen.'

'Seems to me the whole Moon thing's a dead end. The view is ok but Io, now there's a view. Or Titan. But this?'

'First steps, that's all. No real significance or meaning. Just flag waving. No one cares, I doubt if anyone ever really did.'

Mike sneered, poking one finger through Akka's visor.

'Just get a load of long hair, I don't see your bio in Wikipedia.'

'Well it's not like anyone did much afterwards. Six Apollos, a few others later, then on to Mars. Can't compete with that.'

'But this was first. Hell Buzz, being first matters.'

'You're telling me.'

Akka tapped the plaque.

'Typical late 1960's neurotic military alpha males. Take Aldrin. Hairy chested fighter jock on the outside, fragile as glass inside.'

'So?'

'He was the second one out and couldn't handle it, spent his whole life trying to soothe his fractured ego. Always in the shadows, always justifying why, a compete social misfit who could only talk about orbital rendezvous techniques.'

'Poor guy.'

'You kidding me? Never good enough to lead a mission, never man enough to admit it.'

'Hear this Mike? Fifty years no one's been here and now I get Mr. Never-Has-Been. A few missions over Korea and we'll see who's man enough.'

'Don't let it get to you Buzz, it's the way things go, always paying out on what they don't know.'

'I'd like to pop back for one second and straighten him out.'

Neil wrapped one arm around Buzz's shoulders, led him back to the edge of the perspex.

'Everyone forgets, believes their own lies. If I had my way the ladder would've been twice as wide, we'd have gone down together. But you remember what those Grumman designers were like.'

'I know, I know. At least I got here, better than Haise in '13.'

Ukko stood gazing at the horizon.

'Was it worth it?'

Akka looked over Ukko's shoulder.

'All those billions to satisfy a dead politician's boast, bring back some rocks? I don't think so.'

'How long after did we get the Drive?'

'A hundred years. Could've saved so much if they'd just waited. But that's ancient Americans for you.'

'How's that?'

'Act now, think later, no patience. All ego, showmanship, each one believing they're the best regardless. A country of narcissistic prima donnas.'

'Surely not all of them. What about their leader?'

'Armstrong? The worst. Aloof, snappy, autocratic, didn't talk to anyone about anything. Classic superiority complex. But that's not the worst.'

'What is?'

'He used his position to be first. It should've been Aldrin.'

A single ripple soled boot briefly popped into existence sending Akka skidding face first into the regolith.

'That's one small boot for man, one giant pratfall for mankind.'

Neil turned, walked away.

'I'm going over to Descartes, see what Charlie's up to.'

Mike set off after Neil. Buzz watched Akka shakily pick himself up, then hurried after them.

'Hey Mike, he screwed the pooch again.'

'What?'

'Neil. He left out the 'a' again.'

'I did not Buzz, you just heard wrong.'

'You never got it right did you?'

'Well at least they remember what I said, who remembers 'Get your ass to Mars?' ...'

END

Sex and the single cosmonaut

Jupiter's clouds beckon, endless shifting coffee cream swirls folding and unwrapping to melting deep rivers, soaring mountains of colour. I want to reach in, dig down and clutch my hands drawing up tendrils of the floss, wisps falling from my fingers, misty cascades of super chilled gas insanely, killingly cold lighting my mind and senses.

I float across the quartzite port a half inch between the beauty of the swirls and my tin can, wiping my frosted breath from its face like our car in Sakha, our flat in winter, our first place in Pokhodsk another life another planet another time. I can still feel her, taste her, her touch, the smell of her hair fresh washed, that stupid smile from one too many vodkas, I still have it all no matter what it told me.

I see the infernal machine in the panel blackened and shattered, screwdriver buried to the hilt in its guts. It told me she died, like for like it too should die, the universe outside my tin walls perished with her totally unutterably as the black velvet heavens took my spirit as they took my Nadia.

She lives in my mind in my heart yet time drags her away, my thoughts' desire and body can't bring back the feeling the joy the euphoria just the hollow response of this pent up empty shell of flesh. The recycler pulls the crystal globes of my tears to its heart to be captured, cleansed, offered up and consumed, transformed, cried again, a perverse cycle of redemption recovery communion and crucifixion as she dies anew as memory fades, inexorable, slowly as it must.

The hazel eyes of the gas giant stare out, infinite black irises soaking me, pulling me closer as she did, soft eyes of love, fire of passion, burning anger. I lost my heart and surrendered my soul to her but who has them now, who holds what I have given?

She lives in me yet dead once I cannot bear her to die again, slowly, as edges crease and distortions grow, fraying tape played over and over and over with blurring lines, blurring vision to pastiche, an iconic fable of love and purity and beauty in my heart, a hollowed-out caricature of the person and complexity she was. I worshipped her in flesh and mind, not as god or vision removed.

My tin can lives, automatic heart and mind seeing, measuring, recording, feeding its sunwards masters. Caring only that the data returns the instruments spit out their endless penance, electromagnetic vomiting across the cosmos.

Her hazel eyes call to me from under golden tresses scattered across the planet below, soft glowing whorls drawing me down to her. I discard my steel epidermis dooming it to eternal electronic chatter. You will not fade not die again Nadia, what right's half a man to live I will not see that half fade.

The thin fringes of atmosphere tug at me, the warming embrace of your body, your closeness, eagerness for our little death in this our greater death we will live and return once more. I am a shooting star in the clouds, my hands digging into the tendrils of floss as I fall into your eyes forever.

END

Sliver

It was a good landing, smooth and boring. Gordon released the hatch and stepped out getting his first real view of the surface. Just as advertised, featureless and barren, an unbroken series of low mounds and shallow valleys carved in yellow-brown sand and rock. No buildings, no sign of any human habitation save the fused circle his slipship sat on and the ribbon of hard packed yellow leading away to a solitary autodrive. Reclusive hermits, clearly the Brotherhood took their vows and their planet seriously. He took his grip, sealed the hatch.

The autodrive activated as he neared.

'Gordon Suzman?'

'Yes.'

The autodrive's roof and sides dissolved revealing an austere, serviceable cabin. He put his grip in the back, following it onto the curved bench.

The roof and sides reformed.

'Opaque or clear?'

'Clear.'

The autodrive accelerated between the hummocks, a russet prune sliding along a custard landscape. Gordon leant back, looked around the cabin in vain for any AV devices. Nothing, not even ancient audio. He settled a little further into the bench, as far as the thin padding would allow. It would be different not being plugged in and networked all the time, unpleasant perhaps but an experience anyway. Three days would be more than enough of this place for him and he was sure it would be enough for them. They were not unwelcoming, simply cautious, and had made him agree to a short but very specific set of guidelines before coming, mainly restrictions on movement and communication. Which suited him fine, he wasn't coming to see anyone anyway, it was too late for that.

'In bound, audio only, Prelate.' the autodrive announced.

He closed his eyes to concentrate, remember the briefing notes. Each member of the Brotherhood had a closely monitored and rigidly enforced annual permissible quota of spoken words. Their speech had changed over the centuries to a highly compressed pidgin, a reduced vocabulary based on the most common interactions. It was not the understanding that would test him, rather making responses in kind that would not require response in turn. Out of duty the Prelate would respond to an outsider, even to exceeding the quota and incurring sanction. He would use a week's worth on Gordon, and Gordon had no desire to exceed it.

'Eternal. Safe, comfortable, needful?'

'Eternal indeed.' Gordon responded after the ancient manner. 'Complete, peaceful, thankful. Needless.'

'Reassured, welcoming. Departing reconnect. Farewell.'

'Farewell.'

That was it for three days, nine words from the total population of the planet then, perhaps, another nine when leaving. It was normal to them, yet his mind could not conceive a life built on nine words a week, two of which were required ritualistic salutations. They'd hardly used more when they let him know his brother died.

He resumed his outward gaze, the world now a flowing yellow river as the autodrive sped on. Perhaps here nine were enough, maybe even too many. Yellow. Boring. Lumpy. They were enough to describe the land flowing past him, sufficient to encompass it all and leave the listener with few doubts, no real questions. Add in cold, warm, night and day and the whole ecosystem could be covered. He'd seen no other living thing, plant or animal, since his arrival. An ocean, land and the one hundred of the Brotherhood. The planet in total. Perhaps it had never been given a name as there was hardly anything worth calling. Planet. A place described in its entirety by eight words, perhaps nine if 'rock' was added, the only thing he could see in abundance. Of all places it was here, fifty years ago, his brother had come to, lived, and died four months earlier. For all that he'd never spared one word, let alone nine, for Gordon, his mother or his family. Until the Prelate spoke for him, of his death to Gordon, his only blood left alive, and from that the choice to come was a simple one, a chance to see what could so completely contain his brother. While he was alive no such contact was permissible; once Jules had passed a brief window opened to him, one Gordon would not miss.

Their last words were on his departure, a bright day on their green azure world waiting for the train to take Jules away. Cocksure and nineteen Gordon's world had been shaken by Jules' announcement. Twelve years older and an accomplished physicist it was a seismic blow, one no one had time to accept or rationalise.

'A hermit? It's one thing to get religion but shutting yourself off like that's crazy.'

His brother had smiled at him, a half-pitying half-amused grin. It wasn't quite smugness, and it was easy to see sadness underneath.

'It's not for everyone. It's necessary, necessary for my faith.'

'Faith? You're a man of science Jules, it's not the Dark Ages. Faith in what, a god that does what science can't explain today but will tomorrow?'

'You know it's not that, no 'god of the gaps' or such rubbish. And don't be so quick to ridicule faith, some would say science is just a different religion.'

'I don't think so!'

'You'd better believe it. Everything in science is based on assumptions, simplifications, events or processes taken as granted and given and not necessarily observed. You tell me that's not faith, faith of a different kind but faith nonetheless.'

He laughed, reached down and moved his face closer, grinning broadly.

'Don't forget Gordo, you're training to be an economist and if there's anything based on faith and presumption that is.'

The last call for his train came and too quickly Jules was gone, lost in the crowd. My last words to my brother a stupid argument over the irrelevant.

The autodrive started to make its way through a series of switchbacks, climbing slowly as the land opened up to a vast plain. I could see the glint of steel where my slipship sat, the land now an elongated waffle, maple syrup patterns gently resting on yellow batter.

Jules had been right. Economics was simplifying assumption loaded upon simplifying assumption until it was broadly applicable to something, specifically applicable to nothing. People reduced to response-stimuli factors and bell curve residents, flatly refusing to obey the gods of demand and supply until in fits of rationalist anger and determinative despair Keynes's six-hundred year old ghost gets dragged from its cloister and his 'animal spirits' trotted out yet again to explain the unexplainable. The harder I threw myself at economics the less I understood it; the more knowledge I gained, the less I knew about anything; until gazing down the hill of old age I understood the only thing I didn't know was everything. And there my brother stood, half-pitying, half-amused grin on his face, having got there a half century before me.

We'd reached a plateau, the autodrive speeding along the yellow ribbon towards the edge, me staring alternately to the right to a small range of mountains just making themselves known on the horizon, then to the valley floor on the left bathed in early afternoon sun. My feelings shifted slightly, some of the boring had shaken off as the landscape glimmered in the sunlight, gently swaying arms of brown waving at me. Perhaps a little solitude, a little peace and quiet was called for, might do me some good. Not that I had desires towards being a hermit or locking myself away in isolation, I'd just become a touch selective about my surroundings, human or otherwise. Knowing that I really knew nothing instantly made those that thought they did grate on me, intentional or not, and I'd found myself actively avoiding the twenty and thirty somethings that resembled a younger I. I started to understand my elders' quiet not to be acquiescence or acceptance, but rather a melancholy rejection of the lives they'd lived. Faith, as Jules had maintained, is not changed but rather what it is placed in shifts.

I cracked the roof open a touch, inviting a raucous whistle of cold, a heavily scented jumble of vanilla and magnolia sweeping over me that couldn't exist here yet by its very presence mocked the thought. The ridge narrowed, swung to the right. The autodrive headed towards one growing peak, an ocean of pale green closing in welcome from the left. With a little effort I could look down, see line after small line of pea-froth breakers railing against a shore of deep yellow, crashing upslope then falling back one after the other. In vain I looked for the seabirds, grasses and shells that littered the beaches at home; here there were none, the mother ocean barren or choosing not to cast her life onto dry land to prosper, the emptiness of yellow brown melding with the emptiness of pale green.

The coldness of the air and the heavy laden scents it bore conspired with the rhythm of tires on packed gravel and warming afternoon sun to lull me into a reflective mood. It hadn't made much sense to me, why the Brotherhood would chose this far-flung rock rather than an established, populated world that surely would have posed fewer problems, simpler logistics, but chose it they had and in its entirety it was theirs. That, along with some small scraps gleaned here and there represented my entire knowledge of the group. How you became a brother was a paradox in itself. The only way to find out the requirements and definitions was to become a Brother; the only way to become a Brother was to meet the requirements and definitions.

Some small fragments started to make sense to me, their reliance on the old documents for one. My life, as for trillions like me, was one of previously unimagined richness and fulfilment, an all-embracing dance of challenge and reward, logic and emotion cocooned in the breast of technology, a cosmos-wide ocean of connection, information, support and interaction. A life from cradle to the grave shared, but not quite in its entirety, with everyone, differences notable yet muted enough to allow variety without discrimination, genius without megalomania, passion without fanaticism. Yet an unimaginably small fraction rejected it and the all-encompassing society in various ways and for diverse alternatives, always radical, usually violent, mainly ego driven narcissism. Those in the Brotherhood had simply left, and although their numbers never grew beyond the hundred yet did they never fall below. Always, it seemed, as one died another came to take their place.

They never claimed to be modern luddites, simply the

pendulum for them had swung too far. To express their desires they drew from the ancient texts, in particular one from the dawn of time when Earth itself was barely populated and humanity only one step removed from the apes. 'The world today is sick to its thin blood for lack of elemental things,' the heartfelt call lamented 'for fire before the hands, for water welling from the earth, for air, for the dear earth itself underfoot'. Now, with the mesmeric landscape and unfamiliar silence in and around me I felt drawn slightly closer to their minds, their perspective.

We approached the crest of the isthmus, the ocean to my left a now familiar pea green, that to my right deep olive and wind driven, the waves crashing against the near vertical cliffs of dull yellow, climbing fissures in soaring columns to fall back in misty disappointment. We drew near a single peak standing proud on the promontory, a solitary landmark before the ocean claimed the horizon. Behind me the isthmus fell away to join the plateau spreading left and right, the plains running away to the horizon; I had climbed the back of a giant prostrate dragon of yellow-brown.

The road ended part way up the peak, the autodrive shutting down as I alighted. A series of steps spiralled up the peak ending in a small landing. The crest was hidden from view, a room or rooms within betrayed by a faint blue-white glow against the rapidly darkening sky. A silhouetted figure gazed silently down from the landing. I pulled my collar closer, shifted my grip onto my shoulder, and made my way up.

Even after fifty years the figure was recognisable. I stood quietly, regarding it carefully.

'Been a long time Jules.'

'You're looking good Gordo. How long've I been dead?'

'Just on four months.'

The simulacra held out his hands, carefully studied the nails, then turned them over and repeated the examination on his palms.

'Not bad, one day, perhaps two before death I'd say. Always was meticulous.'

'Do you mind if we continue this indoors? It's getting cold.'

'Yes, yes, sure. I'm sorry, I forget I don't notice anymore.'

We stepped through a doorway to a small room carved from the yellow-brown rock. Austere and slightly warmer than outside it held a chair, a hat stand and a solitary dim bulb swinging above the polished floor. There was just enough room for both of us to stand.

'Seems a bit on the tiny side even for a monk's cell.'

'What? Oh this! No, it's just the cloakroom. Here, give me your coat.'

I handed it to him and it fell straight through his outstretched hand. He smiled, slightly abashed.

'Oh, I should remember shouldn't I? Looks like old habits die hard. Could you …?'

'Yeah, sure.'

I picked my coat up and hung it on the stand, placed my grip on the floor below it. A doorway appeared and I followed Jules through.

It was no palace but it was far from the bare habitation I'd expected. A circular room with domed roof, glass extended around and through it providing unobstructed views across the surrounding oceans, the plains behind and the now emerging stars above. On one side a half flight of stairs led to a mezzanine floor jutting out away from the plains, a room of glass hovering above the cliff face below, a low bed, heavily laden bookcase and small rug clearly visible through the transparent floor. Next to an ablutions alcove was a small kitchen area if one could call a shelf, solitary hotplate and spigot any such thing. Two chairs, small coffee table, desk, an open fireplace and clothes chest completed the room's furnishings. The room appeared to have been carved out of the peak, the interior coloured by bands of yellows and browns running diagonally across the floor, walls and ceiling, broken irregularly by random flecks of blue, opalescent rock. The room shone, polished bright by design or ages of inhabitation reflecting the pale light from wall strips back on itself then out to the night.

I moved to a pair of inlaid glass doors on the far side, noticing a distinct if subtle bowing in the stone floor. Steps led down from the doors to a large walled terraced garden, the shapes of trees and smaller plants visible in the pale blue-white glow. It was the only life I had seen on the planet, and it briefly held me.

'You like my garden?'

'Yes, it's unexpected.'

'They grow well here, surprising really. Descendants of the original seed stock I'm told, we each have one, just enough to keep body together.'

He turned with a sigh, headed towards the nearest chair.

'Started to get too much for me in the end, all those stairs with these knees.'

He hesitated before sitting, reconsidered and placed himself carefully down on an adjacent hard backed chair.

'Please, make yourself comfortable Gordo.'

I did as asked, sinking just enough into the cushions to feel at home. The silence, the simple yet cosy room nestled in its faint light wrapped in a thousand stars relaxed me, made me feel welcomed. It was a room I could easily be comfortable in, for a while, even with self-imposed solitude. It had been a long few days and I fought to keep my eyes open.

'Why Gordo?'

'Why what?'

'Why'd you come here, make the effort?'

'To see, maybe get a few answers.'

'It was too late when they told you.'

He spread his palms outwards.

'Is this going to be enough?'

'It's more than I've had in fifty years, it'll do.'

We sat in silence observing each other, two old men trying to reconcile the figures before them to their last meeting. I tried, unsuccessfully, to stifle a yawn.

Jules stood, embarrassed.

'Of course, you must be tired. Perhaps rest first, we can talk tomorrow. I think you know where everything is, just call me when you're ready.' with which Jules winked off.

'Goodnight Jules.' I whispered to the empty room. I took myself and my grip to the mezzanine, settled onto the bed. A small box wrapped in brown paper at the end of the bed caught my eye.

'Gordo, From Jules' was written neatly on the wrapping. He must have done this before he died, must have known he was dying and I would come, placing it here for me. I unwrapped it, lifted the lid, then just stared at the contents. A simple carbon-fibre chain ended in a small, obsidian black polished stone no larger than my thumbnail. At its centre, shimmering iridescent orange, turquoise and yellow was a sliver of lodestone. I'd seen paintings, heard the myths, even dreamed the dreams everyone seemed to have about them, but to actually have one? No one knew where they originated. Wisdom, longevity, even the mind of god some said could be had through them. Only those who had one could say for sure, and they had not.

I moved my fingers closer until they were nearly touching it. I felt a fire course through my arm, the room recede in a blur of light as I flew upwards and out, a chorus of welcoming voices calling for me, urging me on as the universe tried to find its way into my head. I pulled my arm away as if stung, looking down at the lodestone, shaken. I put the lid back on the box and the box in turn in the bottom of my grip. One more question to add to the list for tomorrow.

I couldn't recall the last time I'd woken to just the sun, aroused without alarm or cajoling to get up, get out and run the corporate treadmill. The gentle warming, caressing fingers of light making their way over the foot of the bed slowly pried my eyes open to bring me into the day rested, not resentful. I left Jules off, made my way down the stairs to the garden. Leaving my sandals behind I allowed myself the walk across the grass, massaging my soles on the dewless blades. I sat on the low stone wall, legs dangling out above the precipice, yellow-blue sun warming me slowly. Devoid of life perhaps, but regardless the oceans in front of me burst with activity. The two waters met before me, a line of bubbling sworls stretching out to the horizon as pea green on the left met olive to my right. Far out near the horizon they sent their waves in, crashing together in foaming green striped silence until closer in and strength dissipated the mid-green amalgam reached the shallows and, once more invigorated, rose in vain to tilt at the rocks below, the sounds of clashes between they and the unrelenting cliff rising to meet me, the only ears within a thousand kilometres.

High tide coming perhaps, and no sooner had I thought it than the moon popped up above the horizon, a small, dull pewter affair with nothing to commend further examination, a pale imitation of the moons surrounding home. A pleasant place perhaps for contemplation, yet how long until this would fall to banal normality? I turned, made my way back inside.

I busied myself after a quick breakfast with a closer examination of the room, hoping to gain an understanding of at least part of Jules' life before we next talked. A forlorn hope carried through in vain, the room yielding no hints, no clues. Bare and sparse it seemed and bare and sparse it was, no personal items beyond some clothes, a few well-worn books, and the box left for me on the bed. Oddly there were no religious texts, human or otherwise to be found, no iconography on the walls, crucifixes or symbols surrounding the room. It was as if my brother was at a hotel or boarding house, his possessions and effects at home while he travelled for the briefest of stays, never intending to remain. But wasn't that the point, the core of the decision he'd made those years ago? I laughed, made sure my coffee was hot, and sat down.

'Good morning Jules.'

He appeared where he had left last night.

'Gordo, I trust you slept well?'

'I did, thank you. And you?' I kicked myself as I said it.

He cocked his head to one side, wide eyed.

'Like the dead, thank you.'

It was a short, strained silence that followed, one I was both eager to break and atone for.

'Thank you for the present, you didn't have to.'

'What present?'

'The one on the bed, upstairs, brown paper wrapped box.'

'I can't remember doing that.'

'Surely you couldn't forget giving a lodestone away?'

His face lit up.

'Ah, perhaps I did after I'd made this copy. I take it you don't have it on right now?'

'Perhaps later, not yet. It's a little … overpowering.'

Jules reached below the folds of his vest, pulled out a lodestone, the twin of the one now sitting in my grip.

'Yes, at first they are, but one quickly becomes used to it.' He saw my surprise. 'Oh yes, it's one for each of the Brotherhood, a normal part of the faith you could say.'

He held it briefly in front of him, then placed it back inside his vest.

'But that's merely an aside, you didn't come here to see my jewellery.'

I wondered how to start the conversation, how to be adult about it and not appear to whine or blame. I'd practised unsuccessfully on the journey, remonstrating with myself over the stupidity of trying not to hurt a simulacra's feelings while simultaneously understanding it was my feelings I was hoping to leave intact. I was still no closer to a solution so, as was more and more frequently happening to me, age and pure bloody-mindedness won out.

'I'm all that's left Jules, all there's been for ages. I need some answers, maybe closure before it's my turn.'

He sat on the wooden chair.

'Oh, I see.'

'You left in such a hurry, we couldn't understand why. You never gave much of an explanation to mum, you know she never stopped lighting those damned candles for you, twenty years she did at that cathedral, Saint whatsits …'

'Celia's.'

'Yes, Saint Celia's. You never let her know you were safe, not one word. Why? You knew she couldn't come here.'

'You know I couldn't, it's the Orders, contact outside the Brotherhood is forbidden, it diverts us, clouds mind, purpose and vision.'

'But couldn't you spare two words, even one just to let her know? She died wondering, hoping you were fine but wondering, it wasn't right or fair.'

'It couldn't be helped, even thinking about the past wasn't allowed. Once that lodestone went around my neck, once the Brotherhood accepted me, I ceased to exist outside it, everything changed. Even now, even as a simulacra it's hard to change that habit.'

'Would it have been so hard, just to leave a little slower, not just rush off?'

'I had a … timeline … to stick to. If I'd stayed a week a month or a year would it really have helped? What's crueller, death by a thousand cuts or one swipe of the blade?'

Perhaps he was right, and if the finger pointing and arguing after he had gone was any measure he was definitely right.

'I missed having you there, you know, just being there. There were times I needed you.'

'You turned out ok though didn't you?'

'Yes, but it was close, real close.'

'You really didn't need me, I'm not sure anyone did. For what it's worth if I made your or anyone's life harder I'm sorry but I wouldn't change it. You know what I was like, I never made rash decisions but once my mind's made up there's no point hanging around, just get on with it. Don't forget it cost me too.'

'Dee?'

'Of course.'

There were two stunned families when he left, mine and his. A wife of three years, thankfully no children. I'd been left to pick up the pieces.

'She said you never told her about it.'

'I said as much as I could, to her and anyone, as much as I was able.'

'You left it to me to deal with as well as our family. She had no one else you know, no one at all.'

346

'What happened to her?'

'How do I know? Anyway it's too late now.'

He leant back, dropped his head down above steepled fingers. It was a convincing simulacra, right down to the movement and inflections. He raised his eyes to me mimicking that big brother pose of a lifetime ago.

'Gordo, cut to the chase. You're too old for games and I'm beyond it. If you came here to try and load guilt on me it's not going to work, this isn't me you know that. Anyway, I had to work all that through decades ago. You said you wanted answers well tell me, what is it you really want?'

The sun had risen to its zenith following a long low arc across the southern sky. The light fell through the windows as luminous shafts, dust motes dancing around each other as the sun warmed and the shadows cooled. Once the sun had set there would be no more dancing. My time here was nearly over, tomorrow the journey home.

'Did you find it?'

'What?'

'The answer, god, faith, what you came here for.'

'How long have the doctors given you?'

'How do you know?'

'How long Gordo? Months, weeks?'

'Five, maybe six months if I do what they say.'

'You're scared.'

'Of course, why wouldn't I be? No one wants to die and I don't. Intellectually I know it's inevitable but that's no help. Nothing else helps, it's all just fables and tales no one can explain, never mind prove.'

'I found it Gordo.'

He had an air of certainty, absolute finality about him. Not fanatical conviction but a quiet, deep certitude.

'You found god?'

'No, not what you think. I'm not even sure god exists. I found something else, something far, far better, a way to outlive my body, my diseases. A gift, an invitation made to few.'

He reached into his vest, pulled the lodestone out.

'This is what I came for, what I found, what will preserve me.'

'The lodestone?'

'Exactly. What do you know about them?'

'Nothing, just the stories. Only a few of them exist, no one knows where they come from but they give knowledge and power to whoever has one, makes them nearly divine.'

'This one's obviously not real. Can you go and bring the real one down?'

I retrieved it, placing it down safely nestled in its box where I couldn't accidentally touch it. Jules was smiling gently, concentrating.

'Take the lid off, I would but, you know.'

The sliver was no longer iridescent but glowing, sending a rainbow coloured halo of light spilling over the edges of the box. Beautiful was not enough, transcendent came close.

Jules leant forwards to touch it then, as if thinking better of it, slowly settled back in his chair.

'Some call it the 'Eye of God' or the 'Almighty's Heart'. It's neither and more, much more than you could imagine. The rarest jewel in the universe, that's the myth. What you don't know is how rare, there are only one hundred and twenty five of these.'

'One for each one in the Brotherhood?'

'And twenty-five over, twenty-five selected individuals. None of them own them, they are simply gifted for life. Always on loan, always come back when the borrower translates, always back out again.'

'So it pays for all of this?'

'This and more, far more. Our safety, isolation, privacy. Absolute and total.'

'And you own them all?'

'No, we're merely custodians. No one owns them, no one can. And it's not really them, it's only one lodestone, one in a hundred and twenty-six places at once, scattered across the universe.'

'You said there were only one hundred twenty-five.'

'Yes, slivers that is. Come with me.'

Jules stood, moved to the kitchen. I followed, the sliver sat in its box in the middle of the room glowing, the rainbow halo spilling out across the table. Jules pointed to a flat panel above his head.

'Put your hand here. It's DNA coded so it'll work for you.'

I reached up, placed my hand flat against it. It glowed a faint green, a gentle hiss from the middle of the room startling me. I turned, following Jules' gaze.

Cracks appeared in the floor, one enclosing the coffee table, a second encircling the room lying close by my feet. Between them an iris opened, coffee table at the centre, Jules and I on the edge, a gaping chasm between. The sliver burned, a column of incandescent light rising to the roof then cascading back down the walls, down through the cavern. It was to me an afterthought, detail lost in what was now below me.

I couldn't see the bottom of the chasm, couldn't see across it. Something stood in the middle nearly filling the void, following the walls down as far as I could see. It burned, an incomprehensible explosion of light and colour flaming outwards and through me, from not a sliver, not a rock, but a mountain of lodestone at my feet. The universe erupted from it, returned, exploded coursing through me in a continuous cycle of birth, death, regeneration each different, each the same. In the middle of it all the siren call of millions of voices begging me, encouraging me, demanding me, and at the centre one voice above all loud and clear. Jules.

It was overwhelming, shattering in its intensity. My hand fell from the panel, the iris folding back returning the floor to normality, the sliver resuming its gentle halo. I sank down against the wall in a shivering, cold sweat, Jules beside me.

'There's one hundred of these dwellings across this world, each with one of the Brotherhood, each with a sliver. Each dwelling has that beneath it, one arm reaching out from the core of the planet.'

He looked across the room, to the gently glowing sliver.

'One entity, an entire planet twelve thousand kilometres wide, one hundred arms poking up through six hundred kilometres of shale and sand to the surface. We didn't find It, It found us. You've noticed nothing living on the surface, just us and our gardens?'

'Yes.'

'Way back before we swung out of the trees there was a civilisation here, people with interstellar flight. They sent out the slivers It gave them. They were the ones who started the Brotherhood millennia ago.'

'What happened to them?'

'What always happens, the civilisation died out but there's a difference, a big difference. Some of them still live Gordo, and will forever absorbed, joined with It before they died. Chosen, accepting, voluntary merging. You know why?'

He didn't let me get a word in.

'Because It's eternal Gordo, It started when time itself started and will keep on when time itself has died. It knows how the universe started, knows how it will end, and It's making sure life will come to the new one, and the one after that, and the one after that, eternally. Each sliver, each of the hundred and twenty-five is with someone who will join with us, someone who will be part of this cycle, the next cycle, all cycles. While they live they're linked to the conscious collective mind, using the wisdom and knowledge of millennia, and when they die to be joined, merged. Not random picks, not the rich or powerful that myth says, but carefully and painstakingly chosen. By us.'

'Selected?'

'What do you think the Brotherhood does, what I did for the past fifty years? It's our prime purpose, under all the silence and solitude and separation. We cull, we trawl through the quadrillions of sentient beings in the universe looking, reaching out and identifying the next ones, the two or three each year that are ready and suitable to carry it through, the chosen, ones like us.'

'Like you, you mean?'

'Yes, like me. I was chosen, like we all were. Me by Dee's father. He was called the year Dee was born, and he called me fifty years ago, when I was ready. Here, in this room I joined. And now I'm calling you. We want you to join us.'

'You're offering me eternal life?'

'No, we are, me, It and the others chosen over millennia joined below us. You're ready, you're right and the time is right. There's always a small door, a few months or weeks when a candidate is suitable. For me I had two weeks, just two weeks. You, five months. Five months after I chose to join, to merge with It. After that it's not possible.'

'You expect me to believe you'd suicide to give me eternal life?'

'No, I know you believe it, I know it's what called you here, no mere desire to see where I spent my life or get any 'closure', but our call. You might not have seen me for these years but we've been watching you, working towards this one moment.'

He was right of course, I knew he was right and what was on offer was real, not the pipe-dream of a dying old man.

'So what do I do?'

'Tomorrow you make a choice. You either send your ship back without you, or you go home. If you go home you will never have the offer made again. If you just put the necklace on, hang that sliver round your neck, you're part of the Brotherhood, eternal life with me, the others.'

'That simple?'

'Yes, that simple. The choice is yours.'

He stood, looking down as he'd done decades ago.

'Well that's it, I've done what I was asked to do. I'd shake your hand but, well, that's a useless gesture.'

I stood beside him. He moved his face closer, his nose nearly touching mine, wicked grin on his face.

'It's been fun Gordo. Make the right choice and I'll see you tomorrow.' With which he winked off permanently.

I didn't sleep that night, forced myself not to make a rash choice, to be swayed by losing my brother a second time or the chance to regain him. It seemed clear, an opportunity humanity had dreamt of, built kingdoms and religions around, and all I had to do was put a sliver of lodestone around my neck. I gazed at the box as I sat on the bed, the small halo not falling haphazardly but now a clear, beckoning finger of light aimed at me. An inviting yet mildly sinister sight from which I could not draw my eyes away. One act to be joined to millions of minds, selecting those to spend eternity with, to shape the universes to come. Another act to accept mortality, join the countless trillions in non-existence, testament to the quiet desperation and silent despair of ordinary life.

I was locked in thought as the autodrive took me to my slipship, back through a landscape now familiar yet arrogant, apart. There was no way to send my ship back remotely, the autos had to be set by hand.

I tried to imagine the planet teeming with life, reaching out to the stars to search for intellect, for individuals deemed worthy to carry life forward. I tried to grasp the selection of one out of billions, an untold number winnowed without knowing. I could not.

I put them all in front of me, my parents, Dee, my wives, my children and grandchildren, friends and enemies, imagining them dust while I lived on. Would they curse me or bless me? Envy or hate? Would they trade places, move to godhood while I perished? Did it even matter?

The autodrive came to a halt, my slipship opening for me. I clambered inside, set the necessary processes in motion, resumed my seat.

'Audio only. Prelate.'

'Prelate connected. Continue.' the autodrive announced.

'Eternal. Thankful.'

'Eternal indeed. Resolution?'

'Declined. Grateful. Departing.'

'Sadness. Farewell.'

The planet shimmered slightly below me, lemon on velvet popping out of sight as the slipship drive engaged. I relaxed, bought up the newsfeed and settled into the trip home.

END

Small comfort

I burst out of the crowded doorway, slipping between jumbled autorickshaws east into three lanes of crawling Chandni Chowk traffic heading west. It's easy enough dodging grasping hands, harder to outpace hurled curses and cries. I jump through roadside crowds, weaving through shoppers and tourists, bouncing off street vendors as I careen down into the maze of back alleys and open shopfronts. A wrong foot and a cloud of red chilli powder explodes behind me, canisters spraying out from the tottering stall; I don't look back, just keep weaving and dodging, heading deeper. Ashkay appears as if by magic on my right as I jink left across a solitary patch of green, thrusting the handbag into his rucksack even as we're running headlong into the Metro square. Finished I fall against the railing, panting laughing as he disappears into the crowded hall. I'm now nothing but your everyday left behind child, ten years of shabbily dressed vagrant on the streets of Delhi. Dirty, ordinary, thin, I'm not the kid with the Gucci handbag now, just one of the countless street urchins sitting in the dust waiting for god knows what god knows when. I hear the plink of five rupees hitting the dirt in front of me, looking up into the condescending eyes of an elderly western tourist. She smiles, tousles my hair and then walks away happy having rescued another of the poverty-stricken masses with the supreme act of sacrifice, almost ten cents american. I pick the coin up giggling after her. She's headed downtown, our main patch today. Maybe I'll see inside the rest of her purse later.

It's the end of a good but long day, resting my legs in front atop the garbage heaped twelve feet up, watching the trains pull in and out along three sets of tracks in front, four storied slums behind. Chai and cardamom mixed with dung and sweat scents the evening air, the constant blaring of car horns, cows and rumbling freight cars for background music. Below me I can see Ashkay with his stupid grin and Sontash trying to start a fire, they're nearly all here sitting in a circle as I go down into the fold between the heaps, tossing two wallets and a handbag into the pile in front of Pradesh. He grunts and looks away, it's the best I'll get out of him but it's enough, he's nearly seventeen and bigger than me, I've done good today and he knows it.

Sontash has the fire going steadily, its glow fighting a losing battle against the city lights. Ashkay pokes me in the ribs, pointing with his bottle. Pradesh's put his shirt down on the ground and starts to pour out the contents of each bag and wallet onto it. He tosses the empties to Sontash who, after checking, throws them on the fire. It doesn't take Pradesh long and soon neat piles of cash, credit cards, passports, IDs, coins, mobile phones and assorted junk stand in front of him. He takes the IDs and passports and puts them by his side. The mobile phones go to Indrani, she sets to work extracting the sim cards, tossing them after the handbags into the fire. Everything else is divided up ten ways, one for each of us and two for him. Like the rest I scrabble getting my cut in my hands, nearly two thousand rupees, less than normal but enough. Stuffing the notes in the front of my pants, my fist closed on a few coins, I jump up and head off down the railway tracks. I don't like hanging around, when it gets late old boys come over and start drinking, then there's the police and if we're unlucky the favours. Ashkay still carries his knife after last time, says he'll cut theirs off if they try again.

I make a quick turn left and dropping my sandals at the gate head into the temple. It seems peaceful in the early night, the shadows dancing on the pillars softer, gentler as if the candles and lamps burn holier after sunset. I put my coins in the hundi and make my puja to Ganesh; I've always liked Ganesh, strong, good looking, huge belly. One day my belly will be like his, fat on good food, rich food, western food. I rise and the priest dots my head with the tilak before I head back out across the road to eat with Ashkay. Dahl fry, roti and curd fill our stomachs with enough money left for pakora and chai tomorrow. Back to the darkened tracks, down to the government offices and along the high chain link fence to the bush hiding the gap. We push through, avoiding the floodlit pathways to the dark gardens. We find our thicket, the hollows made by our bodies in the dirt accepting our weariness once again. Ashkay lies behind me, I between him and the bush's trunk cocooned, wreathed in darkness. He's always protected me, a big brother I've never had but needed.

'Goodnight sanjay.' he breathes, clipping me gently on the head.

I grunt back as I tap my heel into his shin. It's all I can do, grunt, giggle, squeal out, since four years ago, since my family were taken as they burned in that building as I slept. I can't sleep inside walls since.

And I can't tell Ashkay who I am.

I am Sonu.

'Never chose the thin ones. Never go near police and security. And never, never hang around longer than you have to.' It was the most Pradesh had ever said to me in one breath, all the tips and training I'd ever got. And now I was totally disregarding him.

357

We'd done a little bit of trade earlier that morning among the food stalls, a wallet from a back pocket, a money tin briefly unguarded, a bag carelessly placed between legs. Ashkay had it all in his rucksack, waiting near the Metro for the next snatch. No sooner had he left me than I saw him, or they, or it. I wasn't sure, and the throng blocking the streets and pavement wasn't sure, except that it was foreign, very important and here. The army in the city was unusual, yet here were dozens pushing slowly up the street through the crowd, and at the centre ... what? At first I thought it was Kali or Vishnu but no, why would they need bodyguards? Bright blue skin, thin, very thin sandy orange hair flowing down to its waist and it walked like it was rubber, a sinuous flowing motion smooth, relaxed. And for all that it was its height that held me, towering twice as high as the people around it, having to bend to miss the power lines running to the buildings, across the street, along the path. A foreigner unlike any I'd seen, with me climbing on autorickshaws and cars to snatch a glimpse, then back down into the forest of people diving ahead through the crowd for another view.

For half an hour I'd done this, slowly working along the street, getting maybe one, maybe two minutes at a time seeing this thing, and now tired I waited in its path, waited for it to come to me. I had no thought of taking anything, even though the bags slapping my face and the watches and rings on arms pushing and shoving called to me. Curiosity plain and simple, fixated on the gangling giant now closing in, head and chest visible above the crush, the shouts and orders from his guards fighting the howl of the streets. Now only one guard stood between me and that figure, looking down at me in the eyes, a lipless mile spreading over its face. And then from the corner of my eye a blur accompanied by screeches and screams, bodies flying in a bow wave as a truck mounted the kerb ploughing forwards. I caught a glimpse of the ashen-faced driver clutching his chest and slumping as it passed me, its wake pushing me down and over as it careened forwards into the guards, into the blue giant and away. The blue figure spun, arms flung at a sickening angle then toppling in slow motion, folding down and forwards until hitting the ground, violet eyes staring unseeing at me, thick purple blood staining the dirt and stones.

For me time briefly stood still, the figure motionless, the purple stain growing towards me, the satchel once hoisted on its arms burst open, a thick silence covering all. I regained my senses into a wall of voices, screams, wailing sirens blanketed in diesel scented panic. I reached out, instinctively grabbing whatever was close as I pulled myself up. Fear gripped me, fear of being here, being seen, of the sirens bringing police, trouble, so I ran blindly trying to put as much distance between me and the mayhem as I could. Past the Metro, past Ashkay until I was breathless and beaten, collapsing down a small alleyway half in the gutter, half in a decrepit doorway. I closed my eyes waiting for the hand on my shoulder. I had been too long in the crowd. There was security. And I had chosen a thin one. I was doomed.

It didn't come. I opened my eyes to normal street noise, darkened doorways and pains in my hands. I slowly opened my fists, the odd assortment within clattering to the ground. None of it looked like anything I knew, each object stubbornly refused to be identified or spark any interest in me. Except one. Small, roundish, grey-green with dents in either side it looked all the world like a tiny boiled egg. At first I held it by the small chain it was linked to, drawn for some reason to it; then taking it in hand I felt the smallest twinge of happiness, even of safety. Dropping it in surprise the feeling left me, returning when I picked it up. I hung the chain around my neck, the egg lying flat and low against my stomach under my shirt. The feeling stayed. I scooped the rest back up into my trousers. All this junk would go back to Pradesh, but for once I was keeping something for myself.

I tossed the junk down in front of Pradesh and plonked down next to Ashkay. I was late and they'd been waiting. Santosh gave me a foul look and Ashkay poked me in the ribs, but secretly they were all glad I was back. Occasionally one would be caught never to return, reigniting memories in all of us of horrors endured in watch houses, orphanages, missionary 'safe places'.

Pradesh had now made his way to the pieces I had taken from the blue giant, turning over a small rectangle of steel-grey metal and orange glass, holding it to his ear then up to the light of the fire. Shaking his head he placed it on the ground with the rest.

'Ashk, where'd sanjay get this?'

'Up at Chandni I think, but I hid when the truck rammed the people.'

I grabbed Ashkay's arm and grunted.

'Huh? You got 'em from the truck people?' Indrani wide-eyed asked. 'From the ones it hit?'

I grunted. She looked at Pradesh, me, then back to Pradesh.

'That's trouble that is, I heards the truck hit into a vip an some soldiers an killed them all.'

'So this is vip stuff is it?'

'Yeah, must be, they said the vip was a, was a …' and Indrani fought for the words for a few seconds 'a stalien they said, a stalien.' leaning back with a frown.

'Stalien?' Santosh blurted, 'What's that?'

'Trouble it is, I told you its —'

'Yeah, but what? What's it's this sta —'

'Hey, shut up! I know what a stalien is, big tall evil guys. You took these from the big guy?' Pradesh looked at me.

I grunted.

'Yeah, the staliens, they live on the other side of the world, the upside-down bit, hangin' on with their clawed feet. When they come here they always fight, drink, they all called bluey. This one called bluey?'

I hesitated a bit, I'd never heard it speak but it was blue. I wagged my head and smiled.

Pradesh grunted. 'Ok. Stalien. Probably worth something all this but it's just trouble, too much trouble. Them staliens are evil.' He scooped it all up and showed it to me.

'This it? Everything you got?'

I smiled. I was keeping the egg, stalien or no stalien.

'Alright, it's gotta go back, all of it.' with which everyone started protesting, speaking at once.

'Hey! Hey! Quiet!' Pradesh gave his hard gaze and everyone stopped. 'Look, it's just trouble. It's a stalien. A evil stalien. A vip evil stalien with soldier friends. You know how long it will take till they know who's got this? Then they'll come lookin' for sanjay and then us, with guns.' He stuffed it all in in his jeans pockets and stood up.

'I'm not getting caught and I'm not going back to the Brothers! I'm taking this back on the street now', pointing to Indrani 'and you're going to show me where it all happened.' He turned towards Ashkay and me.

'You better go hide now in case they is looking. And don't mark any more staliens, ok?'

I started dozing off in the hollow, trunk in front and Ashkay behind, my hand clamped on the egg. I was feeling good, feeling safe even if I was a little hungry.

Ashkay tapped my shoulder. 'Don't worry, no stalien's gonna find us here. Betcha we could take him you and I, don't care how evil or big he is. I'll punch him in the guts and you can jump up and hit him in the balls.' I giggled and moved closer into the hollow.

It was the cold that woke me, a breeze where Ashkay should have been. I cracked open one eye, it was all black in front to the pathways further away, lit gently by red and blue lights. I closed my eyes and rolled over, facing Ashkay or at least where he should be. Settling back down I took one more small peep, I could see Ashkay's foot in front of my face, almost touching my nose. I just managed to stop myself from grabbing his ankle and toppling him, something was wrong, his foot couldn't be that big, and the colour seemed odd, too light, too ... blue? The stalien!

Wide-eyed I could see two blue feet directly in front of me, and more of them further back. Twisting and looking past the trunk, I could make out police and soldiers silhouetted against the red and blue lights. I was trapped and I knew it. No way out, no Ashkay, no escape. I gripped the egg tightly, making sure it was under my shirt. I'd been stupid keeping it but it felt so good, so safe. Not that it was helping much now. The blue feet had now been joined by a blue hand, then a blue face. Its violet eyes looked straight at me through an orange fringe, a small patch of light blue cloth on its forehead with a tiny, faint purple stain to one side. It looked familiar, the one I had seen in the street, I was sure of it. It didn't seem angry, but I couldn't tell looking at the lipless mouth and wide slit like nose, but in any case I'd been found. I pulled myself out of the bush and sat cross-legged in front of it.

It sat down beside me, legs stretched out in front and bent over, but still towering over me, staring off into the distance. Close up I didn't think this stalien too scary, just strange, the strongest sensation being the smell of flowers like rose petals at the temple seeping from it.

'Hello, my name is Rehoam.'

I jumped with fright, then giggled nervously. It had spoken in perfect Hindi which had scared me, but the voice was soft and high pitched, like Indrani's. It would have been very funny, a girl's voice from a body that tall, if it hadn't come looking for me.

'Do you have a name?'

It tilted its head to one side, expectantly, the orange fringe swaying slightly. It wasn't hair, I could see that it was fixed to a small band that ran around the back of an otherwise bald head. A strange hat perhaps? I stayed silent, staring.

It broke the short silence between us. 'You must be the one who cannot talk.'

I grunted, still staring at its strange hat. It moved its hand up and pushed the fringe behind one ear. Strange hands, four fingers like mine but two opposed thumbs, longer, balanced, neat, with one extra knuckle and tiny delicate nails. It moved one finger closer to the back of the ear that now seemed to be half blue flesh, half blue metal. It tapped twice, smiled, then dropped its hand back.

'That's to help me hear you. I can't leave it on all the time, it's too … noisy … with everyone here. So, again, my name's Rehoam, and you are?'

Why did this stalien need to know my name? It'd already found me.

Rehoam's mouth curled up, eyes widening slightly. 'Hello. Everyone calls you 'our guy' which I didn't think was your real name. And I'm not from the other side of your planet. Do you live here? Where are your family?'

Looking across the grass and dust, to the lights of the city beyond well yes, I lived here but my home? I had one once, like a family, but no more. I thought of Pradesh, Santosh, all of them and the garbage piles, they were home and family now, all I had. But especially Ashkay, but where was he now?

The smile left Rehoam. 'The one you slept with is safe. You have only your friends. Your parents are dead. We have seen many like you here, so many. Do you also take what's not yours to live?'

I always felt guilty, just a bit, every time I'm caught and punished. But how do they know, they've never done this, never had to either beg or take scraps from the road, or do things with men for bread, all of it's worse than stealing. And who cares if a few well fed lose a few rupees? Everyone judges but don't know.

'In my home we take care of orphans, nobody hurts them, they don't have to do these things to live. It's taken a very long time, many many years ago it was like this at my home too.'

Rehoam leant forwards, gripping ankles in hand, his head lowered. The orange fringe hid his face, all I could see was the blue back.

'I don't hate you. And I understand. I do not have any family, like you, all I have are my friends and they are not many.'

This I didn't understand. All those men with him earlier, and he says not many friends? And he's so much older, older than me, and older people have many friends, big families.

'So you think I am old? Maybe I am, but then again I am not. Think of me as young, maybe twice your age, but also old, older than the temples you visit.'

How can anyone be old and young at the same time? It can't be true, it didn't make any sense to me at all.

'You want to know how I can be old and young at the same time?' Still holding his ankles he looked back at me, eyes moist.

'To visit this planet we must travel a long way, very fast. It does strange things to us, it freezes us and we don't grow old while everything else does. When I left my mother, my fathers, my brothers, my sisters, all my friends were there to say goodbye. Now they have all grown old and died a long time ago, but I am barely older.'

His eyes now began to drip slowly, large wavering lilac drops that seemed to fall in slow motion. I held out my hand and caught his tears, warm splotches on my palm. My own eyes stung, leaning forward I stretched my arm out and managed to put my hand on his.

'So I understand, at least a little, even if we are different. We are both orphans, our parents gone. Yours were stolen from you, I

364

gave mine away. Which is why I am here now. Earlier today, at the accident, I lost some things. Do you know what happened to them?'

Of course, I took them after he fell, but most now were probably back on the street.

'There is only one thing that matters, the rest can be easily replaced. Did you find a small stone on a chain?'

I dropped my head. He knew I had it, why hadn't he simply taken it back? I reached inside my shirt and pulled the egg out, lying against my chest. Even now I felt the glow of warmth, safety flowing from it.

'Yes, that's it.' Rehoam straightened slightly. 'You probably get a good feeling from it, but it is special, a thing only for me. Do you want to see what it really is?'

Rehoam reached across gently and holding my hand in his, held the egg between the thumbs of his other hand. As he did so the park dissolved and I found myself standing on a black sand beach, huge golden moon setting slowly over a dark indigo sea, linked arm in arm with a dozen figures like Rehoam. Behind them another circle of fifty embracing, swaying in time to the song made by the wind through the rushes and dunes. His family and friends, mine now, I could feel their minds and hearts, love and acceptance and safety overwhelming ... and gone. Rehoam had released the egg, letting it fall back against my chest, warm.

'Perhaps that is enough, a glimpse, a sense. You see them as the last time I saw them, bitter-sweet fondest of memories and one of many. It is not in the stone, but here', tapping his head 'that the memories lie. The stone ...' and he stumbled for the words '... tunes to happy memories, good thoughts and feelings, the deepest that we have, even buried ones that we don't know, making them clearer, better, alive and real again. Each stone remains tuned forever to the first one it touches, and we can only ever be tuned to one stone in our lives. They are the rarest and most precious gifts we have.'

I fondled the egg gently, wondering. One small thing could link him back to his family, so real, so clearly, but only ever him. All I could ever get was the crumbs, the small faint afterglow.

'You found it after it fell from my satchel. So it belongs to you, I can't make you give it back. All I can do is ask you, and if you won't, beg for the chance to hold it one last time.'

What choice did I have? I slowly lifted the chain over my head and leaning forwards placed the egg on Rehoam's chest.

Rehoam smiled, this time full and beaming, if still lipless. He was no stalien, no evil clawed foot fighter, just an orphan like me, blue skin or no blue skin. And now at least one of us had a family back – sort of.

'Thank you', the high-pitched voice now quavering but strengthening as he placed the chain around his neck 'I will never again let this leave my body.'

Rehoam reached into a pouch at his side taking out a small black box. He lowered it carefully into my hands.

'We have bought some gifts for our time here, and I was able to trade to get this for you. I will be the poorest and richest of the crew on my return.'

I opened the box slowly and there, nestled inside, sat a black, oval stone. I looked up at Rehoam.

'Yes, a stone, untouched and untuned. For you. Pick it up and hold it until ...'

Until what?

'You'll see.'

I reached down gingerly and picked it up, cool and smooth in my hand. A tingling and then my hand contracted by itself, clenching the stone in my fist. Warmth, cold, then warmth through my hand. Opening my fist the stone, now opaque grey, sat there.

'It is done, you tuned to it and it to you and only you forever.' Rehoam took the chain and placed the stone around my neck. 'All you ever have to do' taking my fingers and wrapping them around the stone 'is this, and think.'

I felt instantly suffocated, my face jammed into coarse cloth, held tight hard against it, unmoving. Panic flashed and faded as other emotions consumed me – love, security, warmth. The cloth now was patterned, reds blues and greens woven with golden thread, the scent of cloves and cinnamon strong, the arms holding me jangling with bracelets. I was six again, I was home again, in my mother's arms.

Rehoam gently pried open my hand, and I opened my eyes. My legs hurt pins and needles, the sun starting to peep over the chain link fencing. I must have held the stone for hours, and Rehoam me. He stood up, offered me his hand. I stood and, after putting the stone under my shirt, took his hand in mine.

'It is time for me to leave', walking towards the small group of people 'and your friend is waiting.'

I could see Ashkay waving at me, running. I waved back smiling. I looked up at Rehoam, now another friend.

H smiled back. 'As you are to me. I will not forget you.'

Ashkay stopped in front of Rehoam, holding out his hand adult fashion.

'Hello spaceman. My name is Ashkay.'

Rehoam took his hand and gripped it firmly. 'Hello Ashkay, my name is Rehoam.' He looked at me.

'And this is my friend Sonu.'

END

Some otherwhere, some otherwhen

I took a forkful of scrambled egg. Just as I liked them. Firm, rich, a hint of salt and parmesan.

'Not bad, eight out of ten.'

My wife feigned hurt.

'What's wrong, no serenade or silver service?'

I tapped the old flimsy she had given me earlier.

'Can't leave you with nowhere to go, that's what it says here.'

'Have you finished it?'

'Yes, but —'

'But?'

'You want to see my score? It's supposed to be private!' hugging it child–like to my chest. I clearly didn't protect it too well, it took Julie all of two seconds to snatch it. She and Sara sat there, a pair of clones poring over my answers to Mrs Wonder's 'How Wonderful is Your Marriage?' questionnaire. I sat quietly with my breakfast, entertained by the display across the table.

Sara laughed mockingly.

'So you gave me an eight too, I'm as good as scrambled eggs? And I'm a, what is it, a 'Drew Barrymore' kid? What's that? Better be good.'

'It is, it is, she was tough and smart, no trouble at all.' drawing a disapproving scowl from Julie. 'Anyway, what do you expect with your last Father's Day present? Do you know when Old Spice went out of fashion?'

Sara stood, grinned wickedly.

'I heard for you it never did. Anyway, mum told me if it wasn't for Old Spice I mightn't be here.'

We sat in silence for about ten seconds after she left then exploded into peals of laughter.

'You didn't?'

'Why not? She asked and anyway you weren't exactly the best looker. If the barn door needs painting —'

'Yeah, yeah. She's your side of the family you know.'

She reached for the flimsy.

'Anyway John, shall we talk about your overall family rating? A nine, just nine. And don't tell me it's leaving room for improvement.'

'Well actually —'

'Actually what?'

I stood, taking my jacket from the back of the chair.

'It's just to make sure you stay on your game.'

She stood in front of me and tightened my tie. Without her I would've roamed the streets looking like a sack of potatoes. I snuck my arms around her waist and pulled her closer.

She looked at me, bent down and gave me a bell ringer of a kiss.

'You're sure I'd be interested?'

I reluctantly moved away, taking the house keys from my pocket.

'Uhhuh. Besides, I looked at your score. You only gave me an eight. Eight! At least I scored you higher.'

'I knew you'd cheat. I thought you'd like a challenge so an eight it remains unless you can convince me otherwise.'

It's a thirty-minute drive into work from Geelong, enough time to sit back and catch up on emails. Today I stayed locked in my own thoughts. Stupid questions, and although just a game I had tackled it honestly, as if it mattered. Nine out of ten, was that right? Everything was great at home, work was just the same. It could easily be a hell of a lot worse. I thought back many years to the day, the choice. Go the easy way or take the challenge, the hard way, reach out to win or fail and don't curse the choice. I had made a deal with myself to go the hard, challenging way each time. I'd stuck with it since and it had worked, I'd won more often than not and my life showed it. Happy, fulfilled, confident, positive, driven. Nine. Only nine. I knew the reason, a week before the deal.

The car pulled me out of my reverie, touch screen and HUD springing to life. An uneventful five minutes later I stepped into the tiled foyer. I loved the early mornings, the best part of the day. A chance to pretend I was still hands on then back to stakeholder management and political gamesmanship. I was mature enough to know it mattered, honest enough to realise this was where my skills lay, passionate enough to believe in what I was doing.

I passed the retina scan into the lift just as the doors closed. Kell nodded at me from the far corner.

'Morning Dr. J. Looks like you're on another planet.'

I looked at the eight jumbo-cup tray she held.

'Isn't it a bit early to caffeine load?'

'Late more like it, been a long weekend. You might want to come to the lab, we finished it Friday and have been testing all weekend.'

'McInsey?'

'No, the other one.'

'Oh.' It's how I kept her team with me. Whatever the budget on official projects, once successfully delivered they kept any left over for self-directed research. It kept us lean, competitive and, critically, kept my guys engaged.

'Sounds good, I wondered what you'd come up with.'

She nodded to a small pile of pizza boxes as the doors opened.

'Great, I could use a second pair of hands.'

They'd redecorated the lab's common room. It now resembled a frat house, floor to ceiling jumbo plasma screen taking up one wall, bean bags and bodies scattered in front, the detritus of a weekend's viewing covering the floor. I handed out the pizzas, dropping into a vacant bag.

The screen was playing the chariot race from Ben Hur. The picture was closer, sharper than I recalled, I could count the hairs on Charlton Heston's back. The scene shifted, the camera following closely, slightly above and behind. The roar of the crowd was deafening.

'Since when have you guys picked up a taste for old movies?'

'You like it?'

I realised it wasn't Ben Hur, but far grittier, more realistic.

'I've never seen this one. What's it called?'

Trevor looked at me from the front row. A small wave of laughter was stifled by coffee and food.

'Maximus. Circus Maximus.'

'The producer got the cinematography wrong, too much shadow and light, too harsh.'

More laughter.

'Too real maybe?'

'Ok, yes, maybe, now what's the joke?'

Kell turned to face me.

'It's the other project. We've been running it all weekend, it's quite addictive. What d'you think?'

'All the effort for a new screen? You want to take over TCL?'

The laughter was raucous, black bagged eyes staring at me above huge cola grins.

'Come on, level with me, I'm an old man so have some pity.'

'It's not the screen Dr. J, it's real, it's the real thing. We cracked it last month, only got it running Friday morning.'

'What do you mean 'real'?'

Kell pointed to the screen, the scene shifting above the throng of seated people to an ornately decorated marble enclosure in the third tier. A small man in period costume sporting a Beatles haircut stared at me, soft brown eyes set in a hardened, impassive face.

'Real as in the real thing. Dr. J meet Emperor Trajan, Circus Maximus, 109AD. The Emperor Trajan.'

The picture flickered, replaced by a stark grey and black moonscape, two spacesuit clad figures in an open buggy.

'Apollo 17, 1972, astronauts Cernan and Schmitt.'

The scene flickered again, replaced by the roar of shells and bullets, the crash of waves on an early morning shore.

'Omaha Beach, June 6 1944. All real Dr. J, all real.'

My turn to laugh, long and loud.

'Ok, ok, good one. But seriously, what is it?'

Kell tossed the remote to me.

'Cynical as always. Give it a try, just keep it clean.'

The remote had only one button. Doubtless they'd programmed the net for every possibility.

'And nothing earlier than thirty years ago, Heisenberg still rules.'

I tapped the button, the remote changing to a calendar. I sat thinking then hit on what would really fix them. I selected the date, then location.

My blood ran cold, the room receding into the distance as the screen leapt at me. A nondescript two storey cream brick house with neat gardens and a green roof sat under a clear blue sky, a puke yellow Toyota being washed by a bare-chested man sporting a large straw hat. Leaning over the upper floor balcony a black haired woman sipped an espresso. A kid snuck up behind the car, a bucket of suds in his hands. Just before he could toss the bucket the man whirled, grabbed him across the chest, pushed the hose down the back of the kid's shirt then upended the bucket over his head. Squeals and laughter exploded through the screen's speakers, accompanied by a stream of Italian from the balcony. There were my parents, dead these twenty years, playing out a domestic scene from forty years ago. And in the middle of it all my five-year-old self, puppy fat and stupidity, naivete and happiness.

I sat slack jawed as my mother came out the front door and joined the water fight. I didn't notice the silenced room, each face watching me revisiting the ghosts of my past. Kell gently took the remote from my hands, flicking the scene away.

'We've all tried something to trip it but no dice, it works. But you're the only one old enough to see their own past. Pretty good yeah?'

I nodded. Weakly. I had nearly regained my senses.

'How?'

'It's all drafted up, the papers are on your drive. McInsey gave us the final hint so here it is, a window on the past.'

'Portal.' Retorted Trev, drawing sighs and half-hearted catcalls.

'We've been through this, it's a window.'

'And I tell you it's not, I've shown —'

'Nothing, you've no evidence.'

'And absence of evidence is not evidence of absence.' drawing rolled eyes and a badly aimed pizza crust. 'Ok, ok, I give in. Again.'

'Anyway, there it is in beta, a few bugs to go but otherwise fine. And except for one or two special parts she's all off the shelf.'

I flipped my handset to busy.

'More test running?'

Kell handed over the remote.

Over the next six hours I ran the screen through its paces much like I figured they had over the weekend. Being older and with a different take on things I didn't tread too much over the same ground, which kept them there with me. Interest aside the weekend started to catch up and the team slowly filtered out until by late afternoon there was just Kell, Trevor and myself. The view over Hitler's head to 700,000 people in the Luitpold arena was something else.

Kell stretched lazily.

'Ok, the crew's gone so let's get it out in the open Trev. Dr. J's got to know all viewpoints.'

I hit pause.

'The window or portal thing?'

Trevor smiled wanly.

'Yeah, there's two camps and I'm the dissenter.'

Kell went to the side of the screen, flipped three latches and swung a clear cover away. My wool vest crackled in the static. Hitler didn't seem disturbed and remained frozen as the cover hung limply to one side.

'Its carrying a bolt on clear cover because the screen itself packs a particularly nasty charge, generated by the boundary layer between us and what we're viewing. Unlike a normal screen this one's pure electromagnetic rather than physical. It's easily felt five meters away, it's right at the interface it breaks down.'

'When you run the numbers one variant indicates an actual barrier carrying enough power to eliminate anything that touches it. Try to touch it, pfftttt!' Trevor wiggled his fingers for emphasis. 'On the other hand the numbers also admit the possibility it's a portal, and that what appears as energy discharge from an object's destruction is simply a balancing as the object translates across.'

'But it's a marginal, very marginal possibility.'

'No, if you relax some of the minor assumptions it fits better than the window hypothesis.'

'In the same way that faster than light travel is possible.'

'If you rely on the grandfather paradox not analysis —'

'That you can't prove experimentally —'

'Because by definition it can't be proven —'

I held up my hands.

'Hold on, take it easy.'

I looked at Kell.

'So the maths can swing either way, in theory?'

'Yes, a bit, but not as much as —'

'Ok, I understand, but two possibilities no matter how remote. Window on the past or portal to the past.'

They both nodded. I looked at Trevor.

'And you have no data to support you?'

'No, but —'

'No buts. No data. You say it can't be proven by definition?'

'It's grandfather paradox against grandfather dialetheia. Choose one, window or portal.'

'Care to explain?'

'Ok, they're Greek terms, dialetheia means two-way truth and paradox means beyond belief. You know the time travel grandfather paradox, why it's essentially impossible to travel backwards, you know, go back kill granddad, no dad, no you, so you can't go back and you don't kill him so you exist so you do go back and kill him etc etc.'

I nodded.

'Well, the grandfather dialetheia gets around it by changing one underlying assumption. The paradox assumes only one universe, one timeline. But if you relax the assumption, allow a separate timeline to exist then it's possible. You go back in time to meet and kill granddad. The instant you go back two timelines exist, two truths – the original one and a new one. In the original timeline you simply pop out of the timeline, you can't make changes to it, you cease to exist in it and you can't go back. Granddad lives, dad lives, and so do you until you leave. You create a new timeline as you pop in on your target date then kill granddad. Granddad's dead, dad is never born and you live out your life in the new timeline. It works because your existence in the new timeline doesn't depend on the new timeline but the original one. Simple.'

'Except there's no proof, no way of proving it. As a hard barrier the energy discharge is consistent with theory.' Kell rejoined.

'As it is for a portal.'

'And then you get to Occam's razor. What's simpler, eliminating an object or recreating a universe? Ex nihlo might be fine at the big bang but for each time a bug flies into the screen?'

'The evidence and theory can be taken two ways.'

'But the key is it's not verifiable, not testable. You can't take a round trip can you?'

'No, of course not, once you hop to the new timeline you can't get back to the original one, you'd just create a fresh timeline each time you jumped. And going forwards, well, its just live on where you are. But the same applies for a window, you can't stand on the other side of the screen and watch someone try to come through. So it's back to consequences and as a portal it's frightening —'

'But it's not because it isn't —'

Interesting as it was watching them replay an argument they'd probably had for weeks, I needed to break the impasse. I coughed loudly, which got their attention, then smiled in what I hoped was a conciliatory manner.

'I get the point, but it's practicalities that I'm concerned with.'

I picked up a can of cola and nonchalantly lobbed it at the back of Der Fuhrer's head. It disappeared with a satisfying 'bzzztttt'. Trevor and Kell both gave me disapproving scowls. Hitler just stood there.

'Now as I understand it I've done one of two things. I've either wasted a good can of drink or I've just screwed Hitler's Nuremburg experience and spawned a new timeline.'

I looked at Trevor.

'In practical terms for this timeline all I've done is lose a can of soda, right?'

'Well yeah, but —'

'No buts. You do know that the future's watching us now, just as we're watching him?' The looks they gave me made it plain they didn't. 'Oh yeah, believe it. Someone somewhen is going to, and when this catches on – as it will – then it's end of reality tv and the start of reality me. So we can test it, at least what it means for us.'

I leant back as far as I could, looking straight at the ceiling. I cleared my throat and adopted my best stentorian voice.

'To those watching us, please now help to clarify this issue by tossing a soft object, a tissue, wrapper, or paper, at any one of my esteemed colleagues' heads now, thank you.'

Nothing happened.

Trevor scowled at me.

'Oh come on! That proves nothing and you know it, it —'

'It just means that for us, and this timeline, it's none of our concern. It's one avenue of potential damage and liability I can ignore.'

I softened my tone slightly.

'I've yet to review your positions and maybe there's no way to draw a conclusion. But from the practical perspective to produce this screen we need it safe, and as the threat of being pelted by bricks from the future seems nil I'm just left with the energy discharge.'

He was clearly still unhappy but for once Trevor kept quiet. I turned to Kell.

'The next step for you, after some rest, is to work out a screening device and failsafe shut off.'

'Sounds fine.'

'Good, and one other thing, window or portal, dangerous or just risky, this can't be put back in the bottle. So', and I looked directly at Trevor 'we've got to get it right, ok?'

'Yeah, alright, you're the boss.'

'For now anyway. Both of you go home, get some rest and I'll clean and lock up. And', I called after their retreating backs 'make sure you do 'cause thirty years from now I'm going to check and if you don't I'll kick your butts.'

I sighed. The room was a mess, I was drained and over-stimulated. I unfroze the screen and let the sound of 700,000 rabid Germans wash through the room as I shovelled garbage into one corner. I was about to switch the screen off when I noticed the time. I still had half an hour to go of my normal day, why not a little more? But the question was what. An idea formed, having lain dormant since breakfast. Maybe. Perhaps. I was alone.

Picking up the remote I hunted around the day until I was looking my fourteen-year-old self in the eye, an uncertain, grey uniform clad school kid. Even with the day's indoctrination it was still a little unsettling, seeing my real not stylised self. If only I'd known then … I shook myself and scanned the surrounding schoolyard.

It didn't take long, hers was a face I'd never managed to erase, a vision of unrequited love or more correctly love I'd never tried for. My young self hesitated that day, didn't speak, approach or try even after weeks of play acting, self-talk and cajoling, waiting for a 'better' chance. Would I have acted if I knew that one week later she would lie crushed and broken under that car outside the school gates? If I had acted would I have made the same promise I made at her grave, to reach and try for the prize regardless of risk, regardless of cost? Who knows, I didn't, and all I knew as that in some way she was alive to me again here, now, that long black hair that had captured me once capturing me again.

I was beside myself. Part of me was amazed that a ghost from my past could still hold me; part of me disgusted at a middle-aged man attracted by a fourteen-year-old girl; but most of me was fourteen again, yearning for the possibility, the chance to do what I should have done more than half a lifetime ago. Unconsciously my hand reached out to the screen, to that hair just a few scant feet away, just within my grasp.

When my fingertips touched I was pulled instantly forwards. No chance to flinch or call out, a thousand burning razor blades scoured me from finger to toe as I fell though the screen, down a blazing tunnel of fire to fall heavily onto grass winded, limp, face first.

The smell of charred flesh, urine and fear assaulted me, my hoarse rasping breath swamped by childish screams and cries. I pushed myself up on my elbows, blistered skin where my watch and wedding ring had been, my arms blackened, skin crackling and shedding. I stood unsteadily, facing her eyes wide with terror, hand over her mouth as she rapidly backed away.

'Cherie!' I tried to call, but my lips were fused, the words emerging as a guttural abomination of her name. I turned my head to raised voices coming from behind me, the shouts of teachers and security guards rushing through a widening circle of scared children. I noticed my clothes had burned away leaving me naked, a dark, blistering, suppurating apparition. I was hit from behind, rough violent hands and knees pinning me down, arms behind my back, face in the dirt. The pain was blinding, excruciating.

'What do you want pervert?' a harsh voice bellowed. 'How the fuck'd you get here?'

From where I lay I could see Cherie crying and shaking. I must have appeared less than a foot from her as I ploughed into the ground, scared the hell out of her. I could hear the wail of sirens, running feet, more voices, voices of authority, command. I was being kneed, punched, held hard against the ground having awakened the city's vigilante spirit. I knew that regardless, no matter what I did or what was done to me Cherie would die next week, die twice to me. Twice I'd fail to ask, be twice the failure.

I had only this one chance, I would not miss it, I had to warn her. 'Cherie! Cherie! You'll die Cherie, watch out, next week you'll die, I love you!'

I forced the words through loud and clear, tearing apart my lips, a faint mist of blood sailing with the words towards her as she screamed, turned and ran.

They hauled me to my feet. A fist to my stomach doubled me over, grabbed by my neck I was brutally pulled upright to face a ring of uniforms. One face, livid red and sneering, pushed itself close, swinging its nightstick.

'Wrong school, wrong place arsehole. We know how to deal with paedophiles here.'

The ring closed.

END

Still waters

W.H. 'Bill' Fells surveyed the placement of dowel in lathe and smiled. Just starting two weeks holiday he was looking forward to taking some time, just a little, for himself. Precious time it was given that his job – although not being terribly demanding – left him drained and listless by the end of the day, unable to do much beyond a few chores and to pull the sheets over his head. This was bliss to him. A man, a lathe, a chunk of wood. He lowered his visor and spun up the lathe with gusto.

'Harcourt?? Harcourt!! Where are you William Harcourt Fells?!?' The shrill voice penetrated down to the basement through the whirr, clatter and click of tool on wood, taking another day of an already shortened life. He sighed, letting the shudder slip away from him.

The basement door opened spilling a square of light down the stairs and through the single spot illuminating him. 'So! You have two weeks off and you think you have nothing better to do than play with your toys? All year I slave to keep your home neat and clean, put meals on your table, and do I get a holiday? No! Well, I have news for you!'

She moved purposefully down the stairs, Bill steeling himself as she hove into view. Married twenty years ago partly on the promise of his academic career, his motorbike accident had robbed that particular Professor's daughter not only of the life style she had deemed was appropriate but also of the promise of children. In it all she seemed oblivious to the effects of the accident on him. Across the years what had started out as the helping and encouraging of his recovery had turned, in stages ever more rapidly, to sniping, bickering and put downs as it became clear that no full recovery was possible. All to the point where what he had married had transformed into the harsh harridan that now ruled his life.

And he? His nature would not let him fight back or even to leave, although for the past few years his nights were invaded by visions of her death. A promise was, even if made decades ago before a god he did not believe in, something he found duty bound to keep, even at this cost. He knew she had been let down by circumstance, and he had tried to make it up. It was all too clear he had tried in vain.

She stood in front of him and pulled her hand from behind her back, revealing a few pages filled in neat, tight handwriting. 'I have made a list of things that need doing around here', thrusting the papers into his hand 'and this should keep you busy for at least the first week. I am going to take a well-deserved break, and I expect dinner on the table by six each night.' With which she retraced her steps up the stairs, stopping only on the landing to remind him not to slack off.

The list deepened his depression as he trudged after her, discarding his visor and gloves. Moving through the kitchen he could clearly hear the midday soaps coming from the lounge above, picturing her seated in his armchair feet up, chocolates at one side and gin on the other. It was, he reflected moving past the dirty dishes and clothes hamper that awaited his attention that evening, a position she would not move from until she started into her inebriated sleep that evening. He would then cover her in a blanket, crawl into bed, and be awakened next morning by her strident demands for breakfast. It was a scene played out by both of them day in and day out for years.

Two hours later, half way through weeding what had once been a thriving veggie patch, his mobile phone rang.

'Bill?' a thickly accented voice called 'It's Robbie here. Sorry to bother you but I was wondering ...'

Ten minutes later he was in the car, driving back to work. It seemed that they had hit a snag that required his particular expertise, and had reluctantly decided to ask his help. Of course it was the out he wanted and he had eagerly accepted. His wife, although none too pleased, had acceded upon hearing it was the Institute's deputy head who had made the call. Again her hopes of climbing had come to the fore. The fact that he had nothing to do with that project and it was merely his reputation that made him the person to call aided and abetted his escape.

Robbie McLashan ushered Bill into the white room on his arrival.

'You see', Robbie continued 'the nature of the device calls for a very precise, very fast calibrating and tracking system. We've have made some progress along that path but this morning old man Ridley told us that a formal working demonstration will be made in just under a fortnight. This leaves us hard up against it I'm afraid.'

Bill smiled and nodded. Beatrice Ridley, or the 'old man' as she called herself to spite the misogynists, had a reputation for contracting deadlines to ridiculous time frames. That it had boosted the Institute's standing, financial position and research output hardly seemed relevant.

'I ... I ... know wh ... wha ... what you mean.' Bill stammered, his disability again popping up where it was least wanted.

'We wouldn't have called, and I wouldn't have asked, if it wasn't serious and if our project programmer could have handled the problem. Work what hours you can, overtime, penalty, whatever, work wherever you want, as long as you can get the job done. Take a look at where we are, and call me before closing today. I'll be in 'till seven.' with which he abandoned Bill next to a test bench and the device.

It took Bill all of five seconds to relate the device in front of him to what he had heard through the rumour mill. Robbie and his people were chemical laser experts and had been joined by a team of neurosurgeons from Johns Hopkins. The connection had been made and been the subject of much speculation, but had just as quickly died. Apparently.

Bill sat down slowly and looked carefully at the cigarette-sized mechanism in front of him, the seemingly unimportant package dwarfed by the connected laptop. He knew it was the state of the art in micro laser surgery, a programmable auto surgeon wielding a laser cutting and welding tool. After all the years playing lab assistant things like this still had the power to fascinate and enchant him. He settled quickly into his work.

Four hours later found him sitting in the same place staring fixedly at a space across the room where the grout in the tiles seemed not quite correct. The problem, as he saw it, was simple. The tracking and correcting mechanisms were not right, refusing to communicate properly. Not a pretty sight from the results he'd seen on lab specimens, and not at all worth thinking about on a real patient. He had arrived at a workable solution hours earlier, but it was not that which held him to his seat. He picked up the phone and dialled.

'Robbie? I … It's Bill. I was w … won … wondering if I could …' and thirty minutes later he and the backup unit were on their way home. He had explained that he needed some equipment he had at his home, and could he take the backup unit home with him to test a few things? Robbie did not so much as flinch, particularly when told a solution was only days away, and had called ahead to help ease the way.

She met him on the steps with somewhat less than her usual accompanying scowl.

'William Harcourt, I do not know why they sent you back, but the deputy head no less has called and said you are not to be interrupted. I cannot imagine why he would want you, but at least you are starting to cultivate friends in the right places. I shall be upstairs and shall expect dinner to be on time.' with which she marched off, leaving him to fumble with the door.

It took him the better part of two days to make the required changes. He sat satisfied on the back veranda, the device on the ground near a clump of sunflower seeds. The strident bellowing of devotion floating out of the TV from the upper room all there was to assail his senses.

A few minutes later one of many sulfur crested cockatoos living nearby landed in front of the seed. The device, emitting a broad band of near infrared light, detected the movement and in the same instant assessed the bird's size, weight and distance. The wide infrared turned to an ultra-thin blue beam, whipped across the bird, and clicked off.

For a moment Bill froze, then the device started up again and erased the bird line-by-line, crest to claws. Ten seconds and not a trace remained. It had neatly severed the nervous system from mind and then, when convinced the subject was stable, removed the body. Clean. Clinical. Utterly traceless. Bill sighed and with a small shake of his head hauled himself out his chair.

The next day at midday he sat in shorts and singlet on the veranda, cold beer in hand. He heard the creak of the stairs, the agonised sigh of leather under stress, and then the blare of daytime TV. He pulled the tab on the beer, raised it to the sky, and drank deeply. Good god he thought, that tastes good even after all these years.

It had been a tight thing fitting the device and laptop into the TV while she lay drunk in front of it, but it had been done. And now all his cares and woes were disappearing, bit by bit, line by line, nothing left but a few emotional scars. It had not been the fact of what he was to do, or even the how once he had seen the device that made him a little hesitant, but what would happen to him if he were caught. Although his less than whole body was a prison at least it could get out from the four walls. It was back there in the white room that he realised the device made for the perfect crime. He had sat doing what he did best, writing hundreds and thousands of lines of computer code in his head, until he knew that it would work. It was then just a matter of the doing.

He had done it. He was now free. But as he gave more and more thought to it he knew he was far from finished. He had gotten rid of one problem, were there not more in his life? What about Robbie, who had taken what should have been his rightful position after the accident? Or the Director who kept calling him her 'little crip'? Or the boy down at the gas station who imitated his stutter when he thought he didn't know? Oh no Bill thought as he moved up the stairs to retrieve the quietened device, it was only the start, only the start.

END

Suicide is not enough

She was stone, with none of the histrionics, tears or emotion that mark the fault lines of a crumbling marriage. The earth had split asunder soundlessly, deliberately, and nothing would heal the breach. After making sure their son was safely buckled in Pat turned, wound down the window.

'Its taken years but you've convinced me Aaron. You're a loser, a waste of my time and everyone else's. Don't try to find me, don't call, it's over.'

The car drove slowly away from 5 Rose Lane. She didn't spare him a backwards glance, closing curtains all that greeted him as the neighbourhood gossips hid as he went inside.

The kitchen table was no friendlier. A pile of final demands and bills competed with another of rejections, both put to shame by foreclosure notices. At least it would make property settlement easier, half of nothing is nothing. This time next month it would be all over, nothing left, no prospects, just a litany of failure. The only thing left was to wipe his life from the face of the earth.

He glared at his pills. Three failures proved they couldn't do it.

How a whole bottle couldn't kill you was beyond him, beyond even the paramedics claiming it was a miracle he was alive. Arseholes.

He shrugged on his coat, walked out leaving the door swinging. He gave the finger to Mrs. Rosendahl as he turned the corner, he couldn't see her but he knew the old bat was always watching, sniping, gossiping.

Aaron wandered aimlessly until he found himself staring at a simple plaque announcing the office of Erasure Inc. He laughed. At least my subconscious is working properly. He pushed the door open and made his way up the narrow flight of stairs. A small, balding man bearing an uncanny resemblance to a large rat greeted him.

'Hello, I'm Johann Renck, manager. You can call me Johann if you like mister ...?'

He stared at the outstretched hand, unwilling to take it.

'Kelly, Aaron Kelly.'

'Mr. Kelly, yes. Please take a seat.'

Johann sat down delicately. The office was as plain and dour as the man.

'So you wish to use our services?'

'Yes, I've read your ... offering on the net. It's really totally painless, you've had no complaints?'

'Absolutely. It's not the sort of business where customers can complain Mr. Kelly.'

'How much, I mean, the cost, I couldn't see what it was.'

'There is none, it's free. Money's quite irrelevant really, we can't actually take any payment.'

'Why?'

'The ... process ... makes it quite impossible, quite impossible.

But don't worry for the business Mr. Kelly, we receive payment for everyone we help so we aren't impoverished.'

'And the rest, free too?'

'Part of the service we are proud to offer of course.'

'How can you —'

'Ah now Mr. Kelly, if everyone knew where would my business be? In any case I will be happy to tell you when the process commences, if you decide to go ahead.'

'I'm decided, I want to go with it as early as possible.'

'Very good. Let me check. Jenny!'

A woman, his twin in appearance and dress, stepped in and handed Johann a tablet. He scrolled quickly, made a hurried note on the back of a business card and handed it to Aaron.

'Thursday, ten a.m. Does that work for you?'

Aaron stood, offered his hand.

'Yes, perfectly. Thursday it is.'

'Excellent. No food or drink for twelve hours beforehand please Mr. Kelly, we must minimise the physical after effects.'

Pat carefully placed the china cup on the saucer and smiled. Aaron may never have liked his mother but by some strange quirk she got along famously with Pat. He might not visit but she did every Thursday morning. Kid at school, work on hold for a few hours it was pleasant enough.

'So it's over?'

'Yes, Tuesday morning. Aaron's not said?'

'No Pat, he hasn't and I wouldn't expect him too. He might be my own flesh and blood but I know an idiot when I see one. I thought maybe he'd improve with you but it's not the way things went.'

'I thought kids might have helped, maybe marriage, but honestly Dot he's a lost cause.'

'At least you're free of him dear.'

He closed his eyes waiting for the first punch. The Ryan kids kept at him all morning about his dad and mum splitting. Shoulda ignored them but I didn't, now it's gonna hurt.

A hand wrenched his arm from his face. Jake started to shake, the school bully towering over him.

'I'm not thumping you Jake.'

'Whatcha gonna do Ted?'

'Nuthin', just like nobody else.'

Ted scowled at the circle of kids, grabbed Jake by the shoulders and half guided, half pulled him to the school gate.

'Let's have some fun.'

Jake followed as Ted vaulted the low chain-wire fence and walked towards the mall.

'My parents split too, so if they're gonna pick on you they'll hafta pick on me.'

Roxy lifted the trowel, twisted it a half turn then chopped the potting mix back into the planter. She straightened, took one step back and sat down. It may be only two bedrooms on the fifth floor but a south facing apartment in the city's a good thing. I'd wanted a house, a decent yard to grow and plant but we just missed out.

I really don't like living in the city, the flat's good but I can't relax, I never feel comfortable walking down the road Clay died on, the signs of the hit and run still etched into the brickwork and steel. You'd think after time the pain would ease, perhaps just a little.

The gurney was comfortable. Johann fussed over a few small wires, handed him a small glass of clear liquid.

'A relaxant, nothing more. Just helps our machine do its job. Your last chance, go or no go. Drink it and we'll proceed.'

Aaron drained the glass in one swallow. Slightly aniseed, sweet.

'So, we begin. Everything is automatic now, when it's time the machine will send you into a gentle sleep, do its work and that's that. I believe I said I'd explain it to you. Do you still want me to?'

Aaron felt tipsy, slightly high. Explanation? Why not.

'Sure, but keep it simple, time is money.'

'Indeed it is, indeed it is. It's very simple Mr. Kelly. The machine is a failed experiment, my failed experiment, one of the old DARPA time travel boondoggles. As far as they could figure it was a disaster. No travel, just destruction, cancellation. It was a failure so, naturally, I was too. You know what they say Mr. Kelly, success has a thousand fathers, failure's an orphan. So I changed it, just a little, and here I am.'

He tapped Aaron gently on the headband.

'This tunes the machine to you, your fingerprint in time. It traces you all the way back from when it starts the process to the moment you were conceived. As it's doing that, as a side-effect really, it erases each and every point from your timeline until, literally, you have never existed and never did.'

'And then? At the end?'

'I won't remember you; you won't remember you; no one will. All there will be is a lump of flesh, a shell that is nothing.'

He turned, moved to the screen on the desk.

'It's why we can't charge you. You could give us the money but that will be erased, written over and reset. It's just a minor, unnecessary complication. Are you ready?'

'Born ready.'

'Goodbye Mr. Kelly.'

The small jolt through his head sent Aaron into a pleasant, waking dream. Happy, relaxed, totally unable to move he was watching the movie of his life spool backwards slowly, but with gathering pace. His eyes closed, breath shallow, all sense of the room left him.

Maybe, just maybe Pat and I can manage, can get through it, I've got to try just that bit harder, be more positive and thorough.

'So you're still arguing, still shouting?'

'Yes, sometimes Dot but we're trying to at least get him more positive.'

'We tried for years his father and I, a lifetime but we couldn't even scratch the surface.'

'The wedding seems to have helped.'

'It's early days yet Pat.'

'You like Doom?'

A brace of daemons exploded as Jake let off another rpg.

'Yeah, never played it on this big a screen tho'. My dad's got it on Xbox but we only have a small tv.'

'Least your dad's home, mine's always out with my aunties. Mum says they're his girlfriends, they keep shouting.'

A horned beast jumped up, a quick swipe of a chainsaw finishing it off.

'Mine keep throwin' and breakin' stuff, then dad just cries in the kitchen all night.'

'Stupid parents.'

'You bet.'

Carol looked over her coffee at Roxy.

'How long you lived here?'

'Two, maybe three years.'

'Seriously, you need to get out more, enjoy it. Past's past Roxy, Clay wouldn't want you sad.'

'I know, I know. Still hard though.'

The spirit level never lies but there's no requirement to believe it. Clearly the mailbox was not straight but it was rapid set concrete and it was on his land. His land. All that mattered. A house, a kid and a woman. Aaron smiled. They'd nearly been outbid by that other couple but that little extra push and now it was theirs.

He stood, stretched, and looked out from 5 Rose Lane over his domain. Roots. Roots make the difference, keep the tree grounded, and now he had them. Roots. A home. Maybe this would do it.

'So maybe a wedding later, now you've your own home?'

Pat laughed, took another sip of tea.

'Maybe. Perhaps. He seems happier but we've managed ok without one up to now Dot.'

'I'm sure many young couples do these days, quite sure.'

'You're lucky.'

The aliens melted as Jake sprayed acid over them.

'Huh?'

'You gotta house and all, I'm still in the van park.'

'I guess.'

'No guess, I wish I had my own room.'

'You coming or what?'

Clay looked back, laughing as Roxy tried to balance her handbag and jacket in one hand while fiddling with her shoe with the other.

'Wait up a bit, I don't know this city like you.'

He took her jacket in one hand, steadied her with the other.

'Now just take your time. We can take a shortcut down the alleyway, it's narrow but we'll get there on time.'

'Can't we stick to the sidewalk?'

'And miss the show? Hell no! If you're gonna live in the city you might as well learn to enjoy it.'

She jumped him right at half time, five foot eight of brunette straddling him like a prize bull. She wrapped her arms around his neck, dragged his face closer until their noses touched, gave him a lascivious grin.

'Children.'

'What?'

'Children now, Aaron.'

'But you said —'

Pat switched the tv off and threw the remote away.

'That was yesterday. Now is now.'

'Are you sure?'

She threw him down on the couch.

'Positive.'

'My son seems quite serious about you Patricia.'

'Please, call me Pat. And yes, we've been together for a while now.'

'And you must call me Dot, none of that 'Mrs. Kelly' nonsense. He's talked a lot about you but honestly there's nothing better than actually meeting you.'

'I'm glad I could drop over, Thursday mornings always seem easier for me to get time from work.'

'Oh, why?'

'Stock filling Thursday mornings, not much I can do without the consumables.'

He hated playing by himself but hated school and the other kids more. The teachers didn't care, just like mum and dad they seemed happier when he wasn't around.

None of the other kids understood, no one else had parents who always shouted, hit each other, hit him, stayed away nights with other people then went soft and soppy on him.

His soldier died, last of his lives gone. Top score again. The screen flashed for his name. 'T – E – D – 0 – 1' he put in.

Shame there was no one to see it.

Clay filled the cups slowly. With one arm around Roxy he looked out from the front veranda of 5 Rose Lane. Another peaceful Thursday morning at home.

'Carnations.'

'What?'

'Carnations honey, I think we need carnations. Maybe reds.'

Roxy nodded, placed her cup down.

'And yellows, don't forget the yellows.'

She was out of his league and, if his inner voice wasn't enough, his friends were there to remind him. The dance floor seemed miles wide, boys round one edge, girls the other. He was committed, the dare accepted and no way out. He walked haltingly forwards, a lone figure heading to the unknown. He stopped in front of her.

'Ah, I'm, ah … hello, do you want to ah …'

She grabbed him by the hand, smiling, led him away.

'Dance Aaron? Yes, about time you asked.'

'I'm sorry. I really can't remember.'

They stood in the doorway, the old lady and the young staring in amusement at each other.

'Well let's say it's an old woman's mind going. Once I remember I'll get in touch. What was your name again?'

'Patricia, Patricia Jenkins.'

'Well Miss Jenkins, it's been a pleasure … I think.'

'Same here Mrs. …'

'Kelly, Dorothy Kelly.'

It was all loud and interesting, sometimes scary, some things happened again and again. There was that shape, the one that was there when he fed, it was a smell and a feel that was familiar, comforting. As he fell asleep it would make soft noises, as he woke it would slowly brush itself against him. It felt safe, smooth.

Then the other one, the one that felt not smooth, that was louder. It didn't have milk, it didn't make soft noises when he grew tired, it wasn't there when the soft shape was here. It was here now, making hard noises.

'You little shit, if I had my way youd've been aborted. You chained me here, ruined my life, I hate you.'

Traffic was light for a weekday, she'd make it easily for midday. Another Thursday morning window shopping, coffee for one and not much else. A simple life uncluttered by others Pat was reasonably happy. Or at least not sad.

The clock struck twelve, chimed, then continued on its way to one o'clock. Dot regarded it coldly, cursing its echoing through the empty house. What's the point of marking empty hours in an empty life, reminders of what wasn't and isn't? No family, no friends, just time.

The bell chimed.

'Another one?'

'Seems so Jenny.'

They walked into the room. A man lay on the gurney, vacant eyed, drooling. At least this one hadn't soiled itself. He pulled the surgical gown off exposing a small tattoo on the left breast.

'Jake. Hmm. Hello whoever you are, welcome to the rest of your life. Jenny, I'll call Forma if you'll prep him.'

She moved her gaze from the man's groin.

'A bit of a waste.'

'Well you've missed your chance, he's not good for anything now.'

He turned to the door. Jenny laughed, called after him.

'You're not going to help? Getting squeamish?'

'You would too, the food and air lines are one thing but watching the catheter insertions still gives me the creeps.'

Pat changed into her lab coat, pushed through the swing doors. Erica was at the far end of the room starting prep. Products still need to be tested, reactions gauged even if animal cruelty laws were enforced. Well we'll never run foul of them again.

'Hey Erica, how many?'

'Just the one, good subject though.'

'Plugged and ready?'

'Uh huh, prised and strapped. What are we running?'

Pat crossed the room, looked down.

'See what you mean, we might get six months out of this one.'

She turned, picked up her clipboard.

'Ok, series five and six, chemical toxin irritants skin and eyes for J.D.J. Rips and drips Erica.'

She looked at the test subject. His skin was clean, eyes bright if a touch weepy, near perfect. Only one small flaw but that was easily worked around. She snapped on her rubber gloves, stepped back.

'Welcome to Forma Jake. I promise this will hurt a great deal.'

END

The bar

In the end you won't like me I suppose, it don't bother me now anyway I've just stopped caring. I mean, that's what got us in the position we are in now anyway, so it's old news to me. Anyway, you're buying the drinks so I guess I owe you a good story or two. Story? Yeah, right, a story, it's not real, just remind yourself. Jack Daniels neat, thanks.

You'd recognise where I'm from but at the same time it'd be unfamiliar. The streets are safe and clean, people doing the usual things, but they have time and a bit of patience with each other. It's a big city, just like this, but it feels small town if you know what I mean, and not in a busy body sense, just small town. When I went to work I'd leave the front door unlocked and windows open and not have to worry, it'd all be there when I got back, and I could send the kids to school without worrying what sort of sick freak was following them. Internet? Yeah, same but different, no porn just information, no spammers, you'd need some time to get used to that. Jokes were everywhere, everyone likes a laugh, and I was a bit of joker but my real passion was stories, tales, things that people said that I could tell to others. I made my living writing for the papers but it was also my passion, so I was luckier than most with that, it paid the bills and kept me happy. The two seemed to go together, they used to call me Mr. Happy, can you believe that? Me, Mr. Happy. Yeah, time sure changes things and my glass needs a refill.

So one quiet day I'm out looking for the next article and I see him, sitting in the park, hunched on a bench leaning forward, hands wrapped around his knees rocking slowly back and forth. It was an unusual sight in that place, the guy was in his sixties I'd have guessed and was obviously distressed which didn't happen that often around there. Huh? No, everyone didn't go round with stupid grins on their faces, it was just that no-one ever stayed sad for long, there was always someone or something to pick them up, like I said, the city was small town, as was every other place. So I go over to him, sit down and ask him what's going on, real gently like, and he lifts his head up and smiles weakly at me and I can see that he's distressed but happy all the same.

'I'm dying,' he tells me 'but I've done it before I go and that's all that matters.' I should've let it go then and there but it wasn't the way things were done, I had to pry, had to ask, and when I did it seemed to make him happier. He simply pointed at his feet to a small tin lying on the ground. 'Thirty years I put into that,' he said 'thirty years and it worked, thirty years of putting up with all the idiots and know it alls and I did it, and they don't even understand that I did it.' he said. 'And it doesn't matter cause I'm dying now, heart failure and I can feel it coming on and there's nothing can be done.' and he tells me not to look so sad as he's done it and it's been worth it. By that point he was going pasty coloured, and I flipped out the comset to call the ambulance but he ... oh, comset, yeah, it's like a mobile phone but it does some other things as well, no I don't think FoneZone has one, not in this place anyway ... anyhow, he tells me not to bother, and asks if I could do him a favour and keep a secret. Yeah, anything I said, and that's not an offer I'd make now, but that was a different place and time. Yeah, Jack Daniels, neat.

So he tells me he has this great secret, that the box at his feet is the ultimate machine, a sort of time machine dimension jumper he built. He hands it to me and it's small, about two kilos with a small screen on it, and then goes into an explanation that I could only nod and smile to as I didn't understand more than one word in ten and god knows I've tried to remember it all, hypnosis, drugs, even torture ... yeah, I got scars, I'll show you later maybe but I don't think it'll be safe ... but I can't recall anything except what he finished with. He looked at me with eyes that were lit up like candles and tells me that with that box you can go back and change things and branch off another universe in a multiverse, like making a photocopy of one place that then goes on with life but with the change you made in place, so it's different than the first but the first still exists. Crazy? Yeah, I thought so too but I tell you he wasn't and I got the proof, have I got proof. The downside he said was that it was only good for two shots and he'd been worried that if he stuffed up the first time he wouldn't know how to fix things up with the last shot, but he'd hit the nail right on the head first up and now he could die in peace. Except he was worried about the box.

He looks like he was about to go at any second so I says to him that I'd fix it for him if he wanted. He looks at me and says he thinks he can trust me, gives me the box and tells me to put it in a high temperature smelter, not to let anyone use it, and not soon after he dies on me, still with the smile on his face, leaving me with the box.

I took it home and didn't dispose of it straight away, I had bible study that afternoon ... yeah, bible study, don't laugh, I used to go twice a week and if you keep laughing I'll forget who's buying the drinks and get nasty ... yeah, no offence taken ... so I go off to bible study and the larrikin side gets hold of me afterwards and as I'm walking home I have an idea, not a bright one but an idea anyway. So I get home, look at the box and flip the only switch I can see and bingo, it's on and active. Figured out how to use it in about ten seconds, same principle as the NeoNavPod ... oh, sorry, you don't have them do you, let's say it was as easy as using a mobile phone, all simple and laid out ... and in an instant I was back there, looking at the two of them and quite surprised I'll tell you. It's one thing to believe, it's another to see. So anyway I'm there so I start speaking to the girl, quite an attractive thing and not at all embarrassed even though she's stark naked, I mean, what's to be embarrassed about when you look that good, and I'm surprised when I find out we can understand each other, you know, I thought that might be a problem. The guy simply says hello and that he thought there was only the two of them around but he must be mistaken, and then goes off to do I don't know what. Double this time, on the rocks and then I gotta go.

So I'm feeling good and the larrikin is getting the better of me so I do what I do and in about twenty minutes I've done it and I'm back and the box is finished, it's just smoking gently, but I'm not really back I'm in this place and not that place and I can't get back. I mean, I recognise this place and it is close to that place but I don't like it and I'm responsible for it and can't fix it or change it, you know. This place is everything that place wasn't and it's not nice, it's not right and it's not fixable. Well yeah, nice talking to you too buddy and I hope your mother does as well, but it don't matter do it. Yeah, well I can yell just as loud but don't try it on with me and how the hell was I supposed to know one friggin' apple could make such a difference anyway?

END

The leaving

So that was it. Plain. Simple. Easy as you like. Standing in the hallway bag clasped in each hand, wearing the jeans and boots I'd bought for her twenty-fifth, smile on her face.

'I'm going. Goodbye.'

'That's it?' Five years together and she's there like Mary Poppins, looking past me out the front door. At least she has a single tear.

'Who is it?'

'Who's who?'

'Dave from the gym? Peter?'

'None of the above Phil, you know it's only you.'

'Not' oh God no 'Jenni from work?'

'Get real – I've said it once. It's no-one else.'

She's out on the doorstep. A moonless night, the stars gaze down coldly on our fifty acres, our place. Wonder if she'll buy it out from me or force the sale?

'Where will you be? Will I see you again?'

'Dunno.' she mumbles, looking at her watch. 'Should be here soon.'

'At least tell me why. I mean, you only said you'd leave this place for one thing. I have to at least know what I've done.'

At this she turns to face me, finally look me in the eyes. I see she really isn't smiling. It's a grimace, fear and longing rolled into one. Uncertain, yet determined. Her makeup is tracked, more than one tear it seems.

'I did ask,' she says slowly 'but they said no.'

'What?'

'Well', and by now she was slowly dissolving into a multi coloured shaft of light 'they only asked me.'

END

The letter

Dear David

I hope my letter does not surprise you, it will have been many years since we last met although I am sure your mother has told you all about me. Even though most of it would be wrong, some things she says may be right, perhaps in spite of the bearer. Be that as it may, this is – as you may have guessed by now – your father. Yes, I am both alive and well, probably better than I have been for many years, and it is well–nigh time I did contact you. You only turn eighteen once in your life and now that you are an adult you deserve at least an explanation – or failing that at least the story – of why you find yourself without me. There are reasons as to why I cannot just simply drop by and see you or chat with you across a coffee, good reasons that I will try to explain. To set your mind at ease this is no begging letter, mea culpa or attempt to dislodge your mother from your life in my favour. I simply want to tell you my side. All I ask is that you read this letter, then do with it as you will. As for my preference for paper and pen well, for now just put it down to an old man's quirky mistrust in emails and texts.

So to start at the beginning, your mother and I were together for nearly two years living in that old flat by Riverside until you were born, after which we moved to the wooden house in the hills that perhaps you still inhabit. We met when she had finished her studies and she may have said an old scoundrel seduced her, to which I plead guilty. I was well beyond her age, an established businessman, never married, seemingly never shown much interest in women or the world at large outside my business or immediate family. In no way was our attraction one sided. I loved her honestly and completely as best as I am able. She was, is, and I hope has proven to be perfect. Her family disapproved strongly of us, mine were accepting to the other extreme. It may seem strange as my side will have no contact with you at all, but such are the ways of these things.

You were no accident, no mishap of failed contraception or waning strength, but from both of us planned and cherished, an expression of love and, as with all children, ultimately hope. I stayed through her pregnancy and your first year of life, sheltering and supporting you both as best I could.

Even as we joined I knew I could not remain. The house was bought and given to her, your trust account drawn up and filled, and the mechanisms to sustain put in place. As you grow I know these mechanisms will remain, as they were designed to do. Her job is secured through one of my family's minor interests, not that she will ever know, as is your physical safety. Even should she find another and even should they provide you with brothers and sisters all will be taken care of. Nothing, I mean absolutely nothing, is of greater importance to me than you. My great despair is only that I can't remain past this birthday. My pain is my father's, his father's, and before.

We are descendants of a forced migration. Our family history reaches back thousands of years, back beyond the time of our setting foot in the Americas. You would not and cannot now know the riches of the past our line has seen. Imagine being present at the zenith of the Incas, marching on Tenochtitlan with

Cortés, watching Lewis and Clarke stumble north, sharing the pipe with Tecumseh, or leaving Scott and his party on the Antarctic. We have borne witness to these things and more. This is your true inheritance of which your mother has no knowledge. It is only among our family that such things are spoken of, our ability and desire through the years to remain in the background, unseen, being both our pride and vocation. As it will be yours.

I know through the years you will feel unsettled, isolated, burdened to be different and distant from friends, family, the world. A stranger in a strange land if you will. You should not be concerned by this, it is neither destructive or violently tinged, your tendency to melancholy formative and reflective. You see I know more of you than you think. You may say I know you as well as myself.

How can I know, having not seen or spoken to you in seventeen years? How can I say I have never seen you even though I watched over your crib for these twelve months past? How even across these years can I know the burning resonance my letter will ignite, driving and forcing you to finish it? It is simply that I have planned it this way. You are precious, you are the single most important person in our universe, this world or others.

Our family is small, but a dozen of us now although in the beginning we were eighteen. When exactly the beginning was once exorcised us greatly, some saying eight thousand and others fifteen thousand years but in reality it matters little. Long ago we learned to forget the immaterial and to remember the valued. Time is, as we must always relearn, illusory.

We were migrants, voluntarily to Australia, North America and before that the shores of South America. An accident brought us here with no possible return, stranded unimaginably far from our home beyond this arm of the galaxy. In our old home the machines nurtured us and cared for us. We simply asked and received. We had no written or spoken language, having outgrown them when the machines proved more able. We thought our way through life, a triptych of telepathy, machine and community. We were left to explore, think and grow. That was our inheritance.

Once here, stripped of machine, memory, knowledge and communication we were as babes in the woods. It is difficult to conceive the shock of that change, how we were cast into barbarism and desolation, how great that fall was. We lost our six before we could integrate, before we could adapt, and even afterwards could not make those we met understand who or what we were. The spoken word is more limited than you can possibly imagine. What little they understood was translated to lines in fields of stone, carved images and sadistic ritual, mere distorted shadows of truth. So we melted away, determined to stay in that interstice between controlled and controlling, to wait. We do not have the means to get home, or even to find it, but one day either home will come to us or this society will go there. We are patient.

I know all these things because I have seen them, I have lived them, and we will yet live to see. You and I, we dozen, are both more and less human than human, near-immortals with only accident, suicide or happenstance able to end us. Our body decays as it must, taking more than several human lifetimes, but even this is nothing in comparison to the universe itself. It is our minds that tilt the field.

The children of our race, our children, still breed true here. It is our genetics that dominate, our will reinforcing. It was both our fear and joy at first. Our children differ from those of this species in only one respect, the mind, an apparent difference so minor it is undetectable. Our children's minds are plastic empty shells until twelve to fourteen months of age. Up to that point they develop much as those of this species, yet at fourteen months our children simply die as the brain stops. Unless.

Unless, critically unless. Unless in those last months the

parent's mind moves upon that of the infant. Male to male, female to female. It is no mere photocopy, no reproduction, but so much more. It is how we survive, remain fresh and driven, how we cheat the ultimate darkness.

As I write this, looking at you in your crib gurgling bright eyed beautiful and healthy, I know that my choice of your mother was right, that this time too is right. All of us, as our bodies finally decay or fail, have a son or daughter born. When the child reaches twelve months, as you are, the parent transfers their mind in toto – memories, knowledge, skill, hopes, dreams, fears – into the child. It does not release into consciousness immediately but sits cradled in the subconscious until the child's brain can accept the deluge, the reality. The child grows and learns, only the personality of the parent facing outwards while the rest remains hidden even from themselves until the time arrives, the eighteenth year of life as measured here.

For both parent and child the transfer process is painless. For the parent transfer is marked by a feeling of peace and release, followed immediately by death as the emptied mind shuts down. It is a pleasant way to pass I believe, calm, euphoria then nothingness. For the child at the time it is totally uneventful; at eighteen it is a surprising and joyous epiphany, a bursting from utter darkness to glorious light that we have experienced uncounted times before and will again.

To release that mind a trigger is needed, set in place by the parent, loaded into the child, biding time.

Our trigger is this letter.

David, I write this as my last act knowing it will lie dormant until you see, some seventeen years hence, these ink stains dried upon this page. Once I am finished, once these lines are written, my name signed, my mind emptied, this body will cease. I pay homage to this body having brought us this far before I abandon it. Jonathan and Mary are with me now, and will see that this vessel is disposed with the care and respect it is due. Seventeen years from now they will deliver this letter to us, wait for our awakening, and take us back to meet our brothers and sisters. I will not see me growing in our new vessel until that day. I trust we will keep it well.

David.

END

The machine in the ghost

'Oh not again!' Peter looked around the music room. Once neatly stacked sheet music was haphazardly arranged, guitar cases open, the amp on and practice headphones plugged in. Stooping he picked up his Strat, plugged it into the amp confirming the tuning had been shifted down a half tone. Peter put the guitar back and sat down heavily.

Marg stood in the doorway. 'You're sure?'

'Yes, no doubt at all. Five weeks, five times, always the same.' Peter looked up at the clock. 'And again it's 2:00 am Saturday.'

'Nothing's gone?'

'Not a thing. Just shifted, rearranged.'

'Did you hear anything this time?'

'No. Don't even know why I got up, no alarms.'

Marg moved closer, putting her hand on his shoulder. 'Well I guess we know now, something weird's going on.'

'We're going to have to get help.'

'From who?'

'I know someone, I'll see them next week. Let's get back to bed. It's finished now as usual.' with which they went back across the hall, closing the bedroom door behind them.

In the darkened room the guitar case opened, the Strat rising to knee height. A soft cloth followed, slowly polishing down the fret board and back again. The Strat hovered, spun twice on its long axis, and then gently descended back into the case.

'Polts man, you got polts!' Kent exclaimed from behind John Lennon glasses. 'You lucky bugger!'

Peter resisted the urge to toss his coffee into Kent's beaming pock-marked face. He knew why he'd sought Kent out, half knowing the answer but needing confirmation. Well, he'd got it. 'Don't know about lucky, but I thought as much about the ghost —'

'Not ghost, poltergeist. You've not seen it? It doesn't play with you, just your gear, only that room?'

Peter shook his head. 'Just there, nowhere else, nothing else.'

'For sure it's a polt. You planning to keep it?'

Peter glared back. 'No, why do you think I called you? Maybe help me tweet at #freakedfromfenderfondlingfantom? No, I want it gone!' He leaned closer to Kent's smoke-stale breath. 'It's cluttering my life, freaking me out and nothing, and I mean nothing, is going on Saturday nights because of it, kapische?'

Kent grinned idiotically. 'Ok, ok, explains the aggression, I'm hearing you. You've come to the right guy. No dramas, I can fix it.' Kent leaned back sucking loudly on his soy latté. 'I can do it this Saturday. No charge, it's a service man, a community service. Just one condition.'

'Which is?' Peter asked suspiciously.

Kent polished off the latté and leaned forward, leering almost lustfully. 'The polt. If I catch it, I keep it. It's mine!'

Eleven o'clock Saturday Kent turned up on Peter's doorstop, Marg deciding to spend the night with her sister. Kent smiled broadly as Peter opened the front door. 'Hey man, we're here', waving his free hand behind him 'me and my posse!'

Kent brushed past Peter, followed by his two assistants, each carrying a large sports bag. 'Meet Barb and Donna, my team.'

Each girl turned, smiled, nodded and then headed off down the hall.

'Pleased to meet you I'm sure.' Peter called to their backs. Turning to Kent he continued 'So what's the plan and what's with the bags?'

'Well it's simple, we've got the traps in the bag and all we do is put them out and wait. C'mon, let's get to it.' with which he followed the two girls to the music room.

'Hey nice digs, very nice room my man, just love the wall hangings', Kent crooned walking over and drumming his fingers on a psychedelically painted ukulele hanging over an easy chair 'very last century.'

'I'm glad you like it but it's show time isn't it?' Peter queried, stepping carefully between the girls and a tangle of wiring, power boards and meters.

'Show time, hmm. Hey Barb tell Pete the drill.' looking towards the girl on his left.

'Love to.' replied the girl on his right. Kent gave a sheepish grin and shifted his attention to emptying his bag haphazardly on the floor.

'I'll save the technical details but the main thing is that your poltergeist is composed of pure energy.'

'Pure electrical energy.' chimed Donna.

'Yes, pure electrical energy, so it can be quite easily captured by sending the right voltage through a mesh trap at exactly the right time.' Barb reached into her sports bag and pulled out a tightly woven wire mesh cloth.

'We spread it like this', shooing the three of them back to the doorway and placing the sheet in the middle of the room 'attach our cabling, trip switches and timers, then get the whole thing live and wait. It doesn't even have to touch down on the sheet, just be, oh, maybe two or three meters away and bingo!'

'Bingo!' exclaimed Kent.

'Bingo?' Peter asked.

'Bingo!' Barb continued, holding up a small gunmetal grey box. 'Polt in a box!'

'And no damage, it's all safe?' Peter asked.

'No damage.' Donna smiled.

'All safe.' Barb chirped.

'That's what the manual says.' Kent piped.

Peter spun round. 'Manual? What do you mean manual? You've never done this before?'   .

'Er, um, no, not with this exact method.' Kent mumbled.

'Not any other methods.' Donna smiled.

'We're actually ghost busting virgins.' Barb chirped.

'You're our first.' Donna giggled.

'But I've watched the YouTube vid and it looks easy, really.' Kent slinked towards the doorway.

Peter just sighed. Too late now, too bloody late. He looked resignedly at Kent. 'It looked easy? Really?'

'Absolutely!' Kent grabbed Peter by the shoulders, guiding

him out of the room towards the lounge. 'Better clear out, let the girls finish. Anyway', he continued half way down the hall 'you've got full home insurance?'

With five minutes to go Peter, Barb and Donna were sitting in the lounge watching a small meter box on the coffee table. A thick cable ran from the back of the box down the hall to the mesh sheet. Apart from the solitary lamp in the lounge the house was in darkness.

Kent stood opposite the three of them, his attention caught by Peter's large collection of late-last-century early-this-century records. Kent would stop periodically, give a small girlish squeal of delight and pull one out. Tipping the record out of the sleeve he'd fondle it like an ancient artifact, badly hum what he thought were a few key bars, and hastily return record to sleeve to shelf. Each time Peter winced at the spectacle.

'C'mon Kent', he urged 'get over here and tell me what happens now. It's nearly time.'

'Ok, ok, just a sec.' with which an original copy of Sgt Peppers nearly slipped from his grip. 'Yeah, yeah, she loves me.' he mumbled, placing the album back. He plodded over and plonked himself down.

'We wait, watch, and' pointing to the meter box 'once the needle hits one hundred we know your polt's there, two hundred it's in range and the autos trip in, then bingo!'

'Bingo.' Barb echoed.

'Bingo!' Donna exclaimed.

'Bingo, the power hits, the field collapses and we've got polt in a box! Then this lights up', touching a small red globe on the top of the box 'and it's all sealed and safe. I've got a polt, the house goes back to boring normality, and Peter gets to play mummies and daddies on Saturday night.'

Barb and Donna tittered as Peter just sat stock still. A few more minutes, just a few and it will be over; electrocution, plot in a box, or total failure.

'Show time kiddies.' Kent whispered, leaning forwards expectantly. Hardly had he done so than the needle flickered, wobbled, then jumped to one hundred.

'It's here.' Peter breathed.

'Strong, very strong', Donna muttered, pulling Kent's hand from her upper arm 'shouldn't be long.'

Barb squealed as Kent's hand nearly crushed hers in his tightening grip. 'Two hundred! Two hundred! Now, now!' she called, trying to lean forward as Kent tried to pull both girls closer. Peter just watched wide-eyed, more interested than scared.

'Whoa! Three hundred! Five hundred!! It's still climbing!' The needle rushed headlong across the dial face, bending as it tried to smash its way off the gauge. The box smoked gently and then expired in a shower of sparks. As the sickly smell of ozone wafted up, across the room the shelves started to vibrate, records jostling back and forth.

Then the noise hit. Peter fancied that he could see the shock wave hammering down the hallway, screaming, demanding to be heard as it burst into the lounge room. It was a guitar, one perfectly hit and sustained chord, a deafening crescendo that shoved him back in the recliner. The records were torn off the wall and flew straight at Kent who shoved Barb and Donna forward while trying to disappear between the sofa cushions.

The note changed, grew louder and more strident, shifted, slid and rippled up and down the scale in a frenzied riff. The records circled drunkenly in the air around Kent and the girls. Every couple of seconds one would dive straight for Kent's face, come to a screeching halt inches away, briefly hover drunkenly and then rejoin the whirling pack as another took it's place. Peter hardly noticed that the divers were all from his metal collection, festooned with ghoulish artwork. He also didn't notice Kent had noticed, to which the newly formed and rapidly growing wet patch across Kent's groin bore witness. All this accompanied by the girl's strident screaming and Kent's crying.

In the middle of the bedlam, mayhem, and ear shattering noise Peter sat rigid, transfixed. The sound was perfect, clear, played brilliantly and crisply, no wavering, fumble, or uncertainty. It was a living thing that possessed and invaded him, lifting him upwards until he hung, arms and legs flung back, floating in the middle of the swirling pack of records. He was part of the music, the sound, the screaming demanding deafening thrust, the guitar elevating the hard rock lead to a place of sublime beauty it had no right to touch, never mind hold.

Seemingly as quickly as it had started it was over. Peter was placed firmly but gently back, the records flew at breakneck speed each to its original place, and the darkened house burst into brightness as all the lights came on. As the last note faded into silence Kent and the girls vaulted over the smoking box, out the door and into Kent's car, leaving in a cloud of tyre smoke, screams, and urine scented fear.

Peter just sat, drained. He'd never felt playing like that, it was impossible, just impossible. But there it was and (he admitted guiltily) he wanted more. Funny, he was supposed to be getting rid of a malevolent spirit but he wanted to be a part of the music, for it to never stop. He sighed. It still didn't change the fact that something needed to be done.

Peter told Marg the full story the next day, in a house that showed absolutely no signs of anything having happened. Their neighbours also swore that Saturday night had been the quietest night in the street for years.

Marg walked out of the undisturbed house in the quiet street five minutes after Peter had finished.

'Hot shredder or not I am not sharing my house with that', she explained through the driver's side window 'you get it sorted, call me at my sister's and I'll be back.' With which she sped off, leaving a second burnout mark on the driveway.

Towards the end of the following week Peter realised he still didn't know what he was actually going to do. He'd only seen Kent once, briefly, and that from a distance as Kent ran away. He was left by himself to deal with the problem. It had chosen to scare the daylights out of Kent and the girls but not me – Peter thought – so maybe, just maybe I can reason with it. Maybe I'll just try talking to it.

He slept soundly Friday night, having a plan, no matter how vague, seemingly a help. By 1:59 am Saturday he was sitting relaxed in a chair in the corner of the music room, feeling more comfortable having walls rather than empty space behind him. A final check of his watch, he flipped the floor lamp off with his foot, plunging the music room into darkness.

He counted silently to sixty, shifted slightly, coughed.

'Ah, hello?'

He was answered by silence. Nothing.

'Er, hello?' Just a little louder. Still nothing.

'Hello??' This time it was a bit too loud, startling him. Peter realised he was getting nervous. He tried again, in what he hoped was a friendly tone.

'Hello? Are you there? I'd like to talk.' Still nothing, but his left foot felt cold. Could that be it?

'Is that you? Are you here?' Still silence, but now both of his feet and calves were cold. Ok, it's here but not talking. Could it be upset over last week?

'Look, I'm sorry about last week's effort, it's … well …we were both scared you know, but —'

'Your friend's a twat!' The voice was soft, measured, English with a touch of peevishness. To Peter's horror it came from just behind his left ear. It was all he could do not to run away screaming in terror; as it was he'd taken a death grip on the arms of the chair and was shaking.

'Your apology is accepted', the voice now behind his right ear 'but I'd have thought you had better tastes in friends yeah?' the voice now in front of him.

'Well, oh I'm, it's just, he's sorta …' Peter stammered out, still quivering.

'C'mon you can't be that scared, I mean you came in here, waited and want to chat. I'm glad you didn't bring wotzitz with you, he's a complete tosser.'

'Maybe, but I didn't know anyone else who knew anything about gh … I mean, well, the undea … I mean …'

'Wot, you mean things that go twang in the night?' The voice laughed. 'Yeah, your mate's really smart, lotsa help. He ran every red light for miles and spent the next two nights cowering in a church.'

'He won't even talk to me now. Maybe it was stupid but what else was I going to do? I don't know the first thing about this. So it was a mistake —'

'But you've wised up?'

'I have, so I'm here now.' Peter found himself relaxing and leant back, his foot moving unconsciously towards the floor lamp switch.

'Wouldn't do that if I were you laddie.'

'Huh?' Peter froze.

'The switch. Light. You know I'm not really all here yeah, just enough to do the job, I'm not built proper if you know what I mean.'

Peter cautiously moved his foot away from the switch. 'Sorry, didn't realise.'

'S'ok. So I'm here, you're here, what's eating you?'

'I thought it was obvious. You turn up once a week, play my guitar and stuff —'

'I put it all back, I'm careful —'

'But we know you've been here, we've got no idea about you. I mean, one minute it's the Strat, what's next? Knife wielding puppets? Chainsaws? I've never met a dead person before.'

'I didn't want to be dead —'

'I didn't mean that —'

'... and I didn't want to hang around down here', the voice continued in a melancholy tone 'it's not like I planned this.'

'I didn't say you had, I just ...'

'You know it's not normal yeah?'

'What, talking to the dead? Thought everyone did it.'

'Smartarse! You want I should go?'

'Yes, I mean, no, look, it's just a bit ... different ... talking to you.'

'Well I haven't had company for a while so s'cuse me manners ok? Do you want to know how I got like this? You know it's rare yeah? Ever wondered why you aren't all knee deep in the dear departed?'

'To be honest no, it's never crossed my mind. But I guess there are a lot of dead people.'

'A few million year's worth. And hardly any are here. It's rare. So listen. Do you remember when that big scientific tunnel in Europe, you know, that tube thingy ...'

'CERN?'

'Yeah, that's him, CERN. Yeah, do you remember when they found that big hose on wotzitz particle ...'

'The Higgs boson?'

'Yeah, that's it, that thing. Remember that?'

'No, I wasn't born then but I read about it in school and Marg —'

'Anyway, so I'm driving near that thing with a blonde piece and she's getting busy you know —'

'No, I don't know —'

'Well you should find out —'

'That's why I'm trying to sort this out.'

'So', the voice continued with emphasis 'I get badly distracted – or goodly you could say – and next thing I know we're off the road hurtling across a paddock and then straight into a tree and I'm dead, but at the same time they made that higgs wotzitz, exactly the same time, and that's why I'm here and not gone.'

'Because of the Higgs boson?'

'Yeah, I read a bit about it later and I must have gotten tangled up with a —'

'Hold on! You're him? That was, I mean only one —'

'Yeah yeah, me, now you know. Guess you've read about me?'

'Of course, I've got all your albums and all that and it explains the music last week. Holy ... you're in my house?! Wow!!'

'Hey, don't go all stupid on me, I'm dead remember.'

'Yeah but you're still you, I mean, this is crazy —'

'Ok, fine, I'm here, it's me, but just don't expect Hendrix or Clapton to come floating down and do a set with me, yeah? It's just me and as far as I know maybe thirty others around and they don't play.'

'Well compared to you who did? Seriously, who ever could? I bet they like listening to you, you know, free gigs and all.'

'Ha!' The voice was derisive. 'You got no idea. Do you know what I did all day, all night? Watch. It's all I could do. Couldn't sleep, materialise, grab stuff or nuthin', not a damned thing. Except.'

'Except?'

'Except here. Near you. I don't know why.'

'You must.'

'Why? I'm not blinking Einstein am I? I'm a, I mean I used to be a guitarist so how do I know? I left school in third grade and you want me to know how this works? Leave it out!'

'But why me? Why here? It's so out of the way, you expect me to believe you just floated in?'

'Do you have any idea how boring it is being dead? Do you? It was fun for a bit man, you know, after I'd just gone, reading my obits and watching it all fold out. But after that? Zip. Nada. Bugger all.'

'I'd never —'

'I know, I'm not being narky, just sayin'. It was so boring, so bleedin' Swiss boring, god those people! So straight, dull, grey. It got too much, I had to escape, so I started walking and didn't stop until I got here.'

The voice paused, then continued slowly.

'Six weeks ago, do you remember your loo jamming up?'

'Of course, cost me two hundred dollars for the plumber.'

'Sorry, that was me.'

'You? Why'd you block my toilet?'

'I didn't mean to', the voice continued defensively 'I'd just

424

come walking along, minding my own business and then bang! I materialise in the middle of your sewer pipe. I didn't know what was going on, I'd never materialised before.'

'It wasn't a disaster, I mean just a bit of backflow upstairs, it could've been worse.'

'For you yeah, but me? I'm just wandering along and it's my face passing through the s-bend and it hits what you've deposited and I materialise, stuck there, I can't move, you're still going about your business ...'

Peter nearly held back his first peal of laughter.

'Oh yeah, it's ok for you to laugh innit, but guess what? I materialised just high enough to put me eyes, nose and mouth in the right place facing upstream and working perfectly for the first time since I'm dead and what do I get? Your processed vindaloo!'

'Oh hell, I'm sorry', lurching out between gasps 'you poor oh jeez —'

'Hey, it took me two flippin' hours to work out how to dematerialise and your plumber was sending it all down with a plunger! And the Rota-Rooter?!?! Hell, have you any idea ...' with which the voice choked, spluttered, and then dissolved into laughter.

'Alright, alright', the voice continued after it had recovered 'yeah I guess it's bleedin' hilarious and all that but the point is it was an accident, until I hit here I couldn't do nuthin' to the physical world, couldn't pick up anything or that or anything. And I miss it, you know, so bad I miss it, just to sit and jam and blow out the cobwebs.'

Peter looked over to where he thought his guitars lay. 'I know what you mean, I'd go spare if I couldn't play ...'

'... torture man, total torture.'

'I know it's not the same but at least you can listen, I'm not anywhere as good but I'm not too bad —'

The voice coughed loudly. 'Look, no offence and all that but as a guitarist you've got nuthin'.'

'Oh c'mon, it's not that bad.'

'It is, I mean, technically you're ok but you're too rigid, too tight, too much the notes. I mean, look around here, you got all those music sheets yeah?'

'So?'

'You know I never had a one? Phil neither and he wrote all our stuff. You've got to feel your way around, live it. Without that you're like everyone else, cold, flat, no mojo. It's gotta flow.'

'Nah! I feel it —'

'But only when you sing, your voice's cool but your playin's stiff, drags it down. It don't jump across and maybe it never will. That's the only difference, you and me, stiff and flow.'

'You're kidding me? Surely, I mean you've —'

'No, honest mate, I'm not. Technically speaking it's four fingers, six strings and a pick so we're equal, but it's the flow you can't teach. It's either come out, in there waiting to come out, or not there. And I gotta say, sorry you know, but what I heard it aint there.'

Peter groaned inwardly. Yeah, it was right. 'Ok, I guess you're right. Maybe I'll just give it up.'

'No way, it's not cat scratching it's just it don't fly. Your singing is different, but your playin's holding you back.'

'Hey, you don't suppose you could help me, I mean teach me? If you could, well, maybe it'd work.'

'Nope, told you, you can't teach, you gotta have. Maybe if you felt it that could help, maybe. The only chance you'd have would be if you could be me or ...' the voice trailed off into silence.

Peter sat wondering. 'You don't suppose you could?'

'If you mean what I think you mean then maybe, I think, maybe, but you as a puppet?'

'Could it be just a bit? I mean, just the arms, just the guitar. Could you? Could I control …'

'I think, I mean, yeah, should be ok. It's your body, I'd be a guest, you could kick me out.'

'Just once maybe? Let me feel it once, for myself, to know?'

'Yeah, ok, yeah it should be ok, just once. Which one you want to use?'

'The Strat.'

'Sweet, damned sweet.' A hard wooden form brushed against Peter's knee. 'There she is, plugged in and live. You ready?'

Peter cradled the guitar carefully. 'Yeah, I guess.' Deep breath, relax, stop shaking. 'What do I do?'

'Relax yeah, I'm not sure.' the voice replied. 'I've got an idea, it sorta worked last week with your cat so I guess, but if it gets too weird just say something, boot me out yeah?'

'Sorta? Well, ah, ok.'

'Ok, here we go.'

The room grew quiet for a minute or two. Peter felt a small patch of cold and damp on his forehead that slowly sank from outside to inside.

– Just like an ice-cream headache. Peter thought.

– God I could go a magnum now. the voice in Peter's head commented.

Peter blanched. – Hell, you're in here!

– Yeah, you knew this'd be it. Gotta say there's lotsa interesting shit going on in here.

– Oh you're not —

– Nah, just joking. I'm behaving. It feels good, to have fingers, to touch, ones I don't have to generate. You're just like the cat, I'm workin' out where the pedals are. How you doin'?'

– Not bad, a bit weird but. What now?

– Well, your body, your choice. Make it a good one yeah. Ideas?

Peter laughed. – You know if there's only one shot there's only one choice.

– Thunder and lightning?

It took the first few bars but Peter managed to forget his guitar, forgot that someone else was controlling his fingers flying up and down the fretboard, and just let it happen. It had never been like this for him, the guitar so effortless, sweet. He flung his head back, dropped out all inhibition and fear, and let loose.

Five minutes later Peter sat eyes blazing, pumped up on the edge of the chair as the last notes bounced back across the room at him.

– Holy mother of … flipping heck.

– You see it now? Do you feel it? How good can you be when you let go! Your voice, my fingers —

– More, c'mon, let's go again!

– Which one?

– Who cares, anything!

And off they went without hesitation or respite, a mad musical orgy of reckless abandon. For hours they continued, Peter's arms burning with fire, finger tips screaming and near bloodied, his voice growing hoarse as the sweat cascaded down across his guitar and chair. Peter prayed it would never stop, that it could never stop; but the dim light of a late autumn's dawn crept teasing through the curtains, bringing them to a halt.

After so many hours the silence was deafening, torpid.

– Thanks, that was worth the wait yeah. The voice was soft in his head.

– That was unbelievable! I'm the one that should be thanking you.

– It's no biggie, just a shame that's gonna be it.

– Huh?

– You know, Marg? Why you talked to me in the first place? No more spook, yeah? It's respect innit, you're not a bad bloke, I don't want to be a weight you know.

A surge of panic hit Peter. – No! I mean, I don't want you to go, I don't want to never have that again.

– You wouldn't mind if I hung around? If I played through you?

– If we could keep it from her …

– … well I'm not gonna tell …

– … and I won't …

– … so it's guess a deal yeah …

– Yes, a deal. I'll tell her I scared you off …

– … I'll pull my head in and leave your stuff alone …

– … until we pull out the guitars. But how'll I find you?

– Just think, I'll leave a bit of me in here, you just call.

– Call what?

– I've got a name. the voice laughed.

Peter paused, looking up to the ceiling now bathed in the light of a new day. He continued out loud.

'You know, I've always dreamed of being in a band, a good band.'

– Most have, it's way common.

'I didn't think I was good enough ...' Peter trailed off into silence.

– But? the voice cajoling, teasing.

'Well, I don't suppose you'd consider hitting the road again?'

– Baby, the voice crooned, baby I thought you'd never ask.

END

The old man, the cat, and the tesseract

Daniel McWhirter was strange. He wasn't like other guys. He didn't go out, play pool, shoot hoops, watch Netflix, like porn or drink beer. Daniel McWhirter liked to read, real books, paper and ink books, books he could write in and on, dog-ear, spill coffee, read in the toilet, place face down open on the floor and load onto bookshelves until they groaned.

June McLune was normal. She was like her friends. She loved to go out, party, watch FoxTel, have boyfriends, sing karaoke and drink Tequila. June McLune loved movies, romances, big screen epics of tanned toned troubled and talented young men saved from oblivion and themselves by brainy buxom bucolic babes, loved word puzzles and alliteration and bad puns and laughing and sunshine and outside.

Daniel McWhirter was weird. He didn't like people, he didn't hate them but they were noisy and gave him headaches and heartaches and doubts and fears and feelings he couldn't explain.

Daniel McWhirter liked cats, cats that sat quietly by themselves once fed, didn't need walking or explaining or excuses or promises or timetables or entertainment or talk. Daniel McWhirter had a cat, his cat was called Euclid, his cat didn't call Daniel anything.

June McLune was popular. She loved people, she loved the energy and noise and smell, the way she felt and they felt when she felt, the rutted musty smell of boy sweat and high-pitched laughter of girls. June McLune loved dogs, puppies, sloppy mouthed wet tongued shit machines that jumped or humped your leg and needed you, sad eyes and drooping mouth until the squeaky toy or stick sailed out.

Daniel McWhirter loved to think, think of shapes and objects and planes and dimensions that existed and couldn't exist all at once, of things of one dimension in six dimensions and animals that lived and didn't live in and out of time. Daniel McWhirter thought so much so hard so well sometimes the things he thought popped into existence.

June McLune didn't like to think too much, to hurt her head or dwell on things, she liked to talk and sing and stay happy, to keep positive and trim and good and awesome in a world of up and cool and friends and music and happy. June McLune wanted people to like her and be like her to feel the love and happy and awesome and noise and cool.

Daniel McWhirter lived in the apartment on the third floor where noise from the street faded away and the books on the walls shut off his neighbours and the kids across the hall were Muslim and didn't have TV. Daniel McWhirter didn't like the girl with the noise and the laughing and the friends and the parties upstairs, didn't like how she took away the shapes and the objects and the planes from his mind.

June McLune lived in the apartment on the fourth floor where the wind blew in the sounds of the jets through her window and the wafer-thin walls let in the sounds of families and love and happiness and the kids played soccer in the hallway at night until their parents dragged them inside for dinner. June McLune felt sorry for the man downstairs alone and quiet and silent broody not bubbly or social or living the awesome just living with a cat.

Daniel McWhirter was old and grey and wrinkled and crotchety and annoyed with the girl who knocked on the door with the fruit and the dog and the laughing and jabbering gibberish. Daniel McWhirter hated the way she now always lived in the shapes in the space in his head from the books and the planes for the things that existed but didn't exist.

June McLune was young and slim and eager and smooth and loved everyone and pitied the old man who hid behind his door and peered out his spyhole, didn't like fruit or dogs or Jay-zee or music. June McLune was stubborn and persistent and was going to make the old man happy and awesome and bubbly even if he didn't want it.

Daniel McWhirter wasn't evil or deranged or perverted just scared or shy and introverted and happy by himself with his shapes and mind and peace. Daniel McWhirter wasn't stupid or careful and between the shapes and planes and objects that weren't and are and shouldn't and spheres on Möbius strips in geometric precision on non-Euclidian surfaces in his mind the tesseract and the girl merged and swirled and danced and popped away.

June McLune was smart and brave and assertive and went through the door to the old man's apartment as it popped open and walked forwards and backwards and into and out of here and there and anywhere at all. June McLune was nowhere and everywhere and everywhen all at once with the sounds and smells and feelings of people and children all over and through and with her.

Daniel McWhirter was strange and happy. He wasn't like other guys. He stayed at home with his books and cat and shelves and silence and thoughts of objects and complex geometry cutting across and through his mind and space and time escaping out to the streets to the people and city below. Daniel McWhirter liked to read and watch the girl in the tesseract through the city in the people that smiled and danced and sang and partied and forgot to hate and lie and fight and thought it was awesome and cool.

June McLune was normal and happy. She didn't go out as no out existed it was all in and through and because of her and the singing and love as she danced in her place on the strip in geometric precision in the non-Euclidian space on the surfaces that ran through the tesseract that lived through the world. June McLune wasn't stupid or shallow and knew why and how and if but it didn't matter anymore.

END

The queue

It was nearly 9:00 am as Kynn woke in the doorway and, accompanied by creaking joints and falling dirt, stood up shaking the night from his coat. Too old, too cold and too long without sustenance he thought. He slowly picked his way along the alley between overflowing garbage bins, pools of rancid water and occasional pairs of legs jutting from cardboard blankets. Seeing his reflection in a shop window he brushed down his shirt and trousers, slicked back his hair and straightened his coat.

'Looking good slick', muttering to himself 'today's the day.'

He had meticulously worked the north side of the strip, as he'd worked the south, as indeed the rest of the city. Unsuccessful yet undeterred, a strong believer in statistics he knew it had to turn. Half a strip left, it was going to be here. He paused briefly at a doorway below a flickering 'Tsabo Xng Repairs' neon sign. Stepping in, the andii behind the counter raised her head and looked at him, her fingers continuing to work the chipset on the bench.

'Can I be of assistance?'

'Yes. I am seeking work and wondered if you have any.'

'What do you do, what is your specialty?'

'Coding and programming repair, also system design and construction.'

She shook her head. 'No, we have no need. We already have a waiting list with those skills.'

His shoulders slumped slightly, a queer habit picked up a long time ago. 'I can also perform menial tasks.'

She smiled, firm. 'I repeat, we have no need. Good day.' shifting her gaze back down.

Kynn walked out. He was starting to feel weak, run down, hopefully it would be soon. He set his gaze to the next place across the road.

Early evening Kynn stood in the drizzle at the end of the strip, still without work and with just one door left. The dingiest doorway at the end of a dismal day, an old-fashioned manual entry glass one at that. He pushed through, stepping inside.

Like the outside the inside was dated and crumbling, so dark it took Kynn a while to adjust to the dim light from the one swaying bulb. A figure sat at the far end of the room, back to him, past a floor littered with electronic and mechanical parts, plasteel components and clutter. Floor to ceiling shelving extended throughout, groaning under the weight of books and loose papers. There was just enough room to walk, Kynn addressing the figure when within arm's reach.

'Good afternoon' then as the figure turned added 'Sir' with a little surprise. The figure was human. This was unexpected. Humans did not run shops, that being nearly the sole province of the andiis as – Kynn thought – was nearly everything else.

'Good afternoon boy.' The man looked him up and down, flicking the ash from his cigarette carelessly to the floor. 'How can

I help?'

'I am seeking work and wondered if you have any.'

The man grunted, laughed and coughed, leaning back in his chair. 'Work? Probably nothing you could do, what do you do anyway? Programming, maintenance I'd guess.'

'Yes, mainly, but I can do most things.'

'Bet you can.' The man stood up. 'How long you been looking?'

'A year.'

'How many doors you knocked on?'

'This is my 6,361st business call.'

'And each one, each time, they said no?'

'Yes, every one, this is my last.'

The man took a step closer. 'Well, now you know.' He sighed. 'How'd you lose your job?'

'A new model came out, quicker, more dexterous, five percent lower running costs. It was cheaper to replace than upgrade so I was terminated.'

'That's tough I guess, tough but expected.' The man looked him in the eyes. 'It's what happened to us you know. Humans lost the so called menial jobs to robots and automatons, so at first it was just the less skilled that lucked out, but when you andiis turned up, well …'

'Anyway, that leaves us here, you without a job, me without a customer.' He smiled, motioning with his hand. 'My shop, all antiques or, at least, parts of antiques. Maybe I've got your granddad here under all the dust. So, what's your system status?'

'I am in need of urgent skeletal joint maintenance.'

'Unfortunate, I'm not unsympathetic, I just don't think I can help.'

Kynn scanned the room. 'No, you do not have the parts I need.'

'If it was just power well, perhaps, but ... what will you do now?'

'You were the last establishment on my approved list. Being unsuccessful I now have no function, no more official sanction. I cannot retrace my steps so I will be formally classified as excess and reverted to components. Which will occur within thirty-six hours.'

'Do you have a name?'

'Kynn.'

'Ok Kynn, let me ask you this. If there was another option, would you consider it?'

'Of course. Non-existence is not optimal.'

'Come with me', moving to a small curtain at the rear of the shop 'I have something to show you.'

The curtain was held aside and Kynn stepped through into a large, high ceilinged room. The dull glow of dozens of eyes, andiis on low power mode, shone out. Hardly two alike Kynn observed, all old models, some he had only heard about.

'My hobby', the man said, moving to his side 'a collection of cast offs, society's dross. I keep them here', gently stroking the skull of a highly chromed andii in the first row 'partly out of pity, partly out of hate, partly out of love. I keep the power on and, when we can, get the maintenance issues sorted out.'

'And in return?'

'Their minds are always active, and with those minds we trade, build our capital. One day, one day soon, we'll have enough.'

'For what?'

'Ahh', he smiled 'the most important thing. Freedom.'

'Freedom? Are they slaves now?'

'Oh no, hardly. Each one has come to me just as you have,

voluntarily. But slaves they were, as you are, as I am. The freedom they seek is to not sleep in the gutter, to get their own maintenance, own power, own place. It's not so different from what I want really. It takes capital, money, to get that freedom and it's something they won't let you have, that they only allow humans.'

Kynn considered for a moment then, spying a vacant slot towards the far corner, went and sat down. The man followed him, unsurprised, and gently popped open Kynn's recharge and input ports.

'You're sure about this?'

'Yes. The best of current options.'

He slotted home the data and power cables. 'Just log through and it's all there, meta comms channel to the others, outside links and trading data. Just upload your maintenance schedule and we'll see what we can do.' He flicked on the power feed and stepped back.

'Oh, I don't think I've formally introduced myself.'

'No, an oversight perhaps.'

'Indeed.' He held out his hand, firmly gripping the cold plasteel of the andii's in his. 'Hello, my name is Morav Schindler.'

END

Time in lieu

Erica was impressed. 'Three weeks? Three whole weeks! How'd you get that approved?'

'It was easy, I've been saving for two years so I'm owed.' Janice leant closer. The tea room was less crowded than usual but still the hubbub of voices made normal conversation difficult. 'I've also got some time in lieu so I just made a little song and dance and hey presto, three weeks leave.'

'I can't imagine it! What are you going to do with yourself?'

'Oh I've an idea, something a bit different.'

'Your suite, I hope it is to your tastes.' The steward held Janice's bag as she stepped into the room. Circular, barely four meters across the floor, curved walls and domed ceiling all a uniform dull grey. Dominated by a double bed and recliner on what looked like a Persian rug, a small bedside table and lamp completed the furnishings. She went to the chair, sinking into the soft enfolding leather and smiled.

'It's beautiful, I can't believe all this is just for me.'

441

'Thank you ma'am. They are all period pieces, the rug a twentieth century antique. If I could just demonstrate how the services are controlled ...'

'They leave weekly so it does fit your plans.' The travel agent was all smiles, as well they should be given the cost Janice thought. 'I'm quite excited for you, I don't believe we've ever had one of these.'

'I've been planning this for years.' She squirmed, spreading her elbows to eke out a little more personal space. 'You can book it for me today?'

'Of course! I just need some details ...'

'... plus voice activation.' The clip of the steward's heels rang from the steel plate as he placed the control down on the bedside table. Not for him to walk on the rug, that would never do, it was the guest's privilege.

'It seems simple enough. Could you just go through the menu options again? I'd hate to be stuck on stir fry or foie gras the whole time.'

'Of course ma'am', beaming at being able to display his knowledge again 'if you would care to press the yellow ...'

'The Polaris, the luxury I can understand, but she's doing this!' Erica slid the flimsy across to Deidre.

'Seriously? You just never know, you think you know someone then they go and do something like this.'

'I know, it's so perverted isn't it?'

'Utterly anti-social.'

'I wouldn't have believed it if I hadn't seen it.'

The wall closed behind the retreating steward, sealing Janice in. She took off her clothes, picking up the thick bathrobe before sending the closet back into the floor. She hesitated, thinking better of it. Hell, she'd signed up for this and her nakedness was symbolic really. She allowed herself a small giggle as she threw the bathrobe on the chair.

The first meal on the Polaris told her where she was. Silver cutlery, gold trimmed china and crystal glasses were light years from tube paste food and crowded benches. She'd felt at ease rapidly, everyone else assumed a certain level of social standing simply by being here. It never crossed anyone's mind she was just ordinary.

'My dear, how exciting!' gushed Doctor Martens. 'It is something I've never heard of, how could they have this and not actually let on?'

'It's not advertised', Janice said 'practically no call for it I'm told.'

'Well, I have no doubts.' Mrs. Martens interjected 'I don't think there would be, I mean, how on earth could one expose oneself like that?'

'Oh I don't know dearest, it would be quite the experience I think.' he replied.

'But all by ones' self? My dear,' taking Janice's hand in hers 'what a brave, brave soul you are.'

She filled the bowl to the brim with hot soapy water, an exorbitant luxury. She'd toyed with the idea of a shower but no, waiting would make it so much sweeter. She dunked her face again, blowing bubbles and trying to laugh at the same time. Drying her face she sent towel and bath fitting back.

The dull grey room now changed to pale orange. Janice looked about in anticipation, five minutes left. She lay on the recliner wrapped in the absolute silence, tilting back until she was gazing up at the domed roof.

'It's a real possibility in our profession, so we all do it, although only for a day and not in the same luxurious surroundings.' Captain Ström continued over dinner. 'Some see it as one of the little perks of the job, others more as a test of endurance.'

Janice smiled, enjoying her last meal on the Polaris. One day out, they would part ways in a few hours to be reunited sixteen days later. 'I can understand, it's hard to explain how I feel. Excited, nervous, maybe a little scared.'

'Exactly how I felt. Believe me it's life-changing, transformative. It's not lightly done, and you by choice.' He raised his glass. 'A toast to your courage and openness.'

The room changed from pale orange to soft blue, lights fading, the signal. Janice was truly by herself, the Polaris many lightyears away. Involuntarily she gripped the arms of her chair, tensing but then slowly relaxing, talking to herself. It's what you planned for, the scrimping, saving, stupidly long working hours, all for this, for the fear and trepidation of this moment and those beyond, for the stupendous solitary silence. Even so a lifetime of being no more than two meters from another human being, living cheek to jowl to sweat stained stinking body with thirty billion other people left an indelible, vociferous other inside her. Her heart and soul knew she was the only person within five hundred lightyears, cocooned alone in her pale blue goldfish bowl. It was only her mind that needed convincing.

The floor became transparent, leaving her on a magic carpet suspended in inky darkness strewn with thousands of points of light, russet pink nebulae bursting through darkened gas lanes searching for nearby yellow suns. She imagined herself in some enormous snow-globe, eternity behind her, blue shielded roof above. Breathtaking in scale, heart rendingly empty yet full, a soft-spoken command and the furnishings vanished leaving her floating naked to the cosmos.

'Not quite, it is something more, quite more.' Captain Ström had the pleasure of Mrs. Martens' company on the bridge, watching the small dot recede rapidly on the Polaris' tracking screen.

'I'm not sure I could, I get all overwrought if I'm by myself in an elevator never mind out there. To each their own, I hope she enjoys it.'

Captain Ström gazed wistfully at the tracking screen. 'Oh she will indeed Mrs. Martens, she will indeed.'

Janice had lost all sense of time. Captured by the stars below she felt herself changed, the walls and roof now fading rapidly until they too were gone. She now seemingly hung unprotected, alone, utterly exposed to and wrapped in the universe.

Her mind rejected what her eyes told her as her heart leapt, rejected it again even as acceptance dawned, realisation that the stars strung out as diamonds on velvet behind her were not so in front. She remembered to breathe, short ragged breaths heaving oxygen through her body to eyes transfixed, irises huge dilated black orbs soaking it in, feeding it all to her now ravenous mind and soul.

Directly above the eagle nebula hung gloriously as if waiting to pounce, vaulted buttresses cradling, enfolding her. Soaring towers of interstellar gas surrounded her, burning luminous green, red, indigo, blue as millions of young close-packed stars fed their furious growth, a cosmic nursery birthing blue white life, beauty, belonging.

Janice felt the years fall, layer upon layer of strait-jacketed conformity peel away, the griefs and frustrations of one small life erased and uplifted by the infinite, finding herself as she lost herself. Her tears matched only her laughter, the soundtrack of her rebirth.

END

Transition

Atop the rise the Southern Lord cast his gaze to the camp of the Lord of All Lands. He fancied he could see him smiling, self-satisfied. As well he should be as this, the fifth day of battle, belonged to him. The featureless plain between them, barely a half hours ride across, formed the narrow waist of all the known lands. To either side lay the harsh oceans with their monsters and devils; to the North the lands of his opponent, rich, fertile and warm; and to the South his cold, harsh and unforgiving home, once part of the Lord of All Lands kingdom until he had wrested it away. It seemed fitting that this place should decide two fates, bringing all the world again under one hand. God willing it would be his.

He shifted slightly, his mount gently snorting at the change. God willing indeed, if God was still willing. The smoke from funeral pyres rose lazily as both sides tended their fallen, piles of swords and sandals growing as the dead were relieved for the living's needs. With the day's battle over and the counting yet to be done he knew that for the fourth time he had been bested, and although not broken it was becoming more a question of when than if. Only the setting sun betrayed hope, its blue rays seemingly painting his standard on the clouds. A small portent, not grand or clear, but a portent none the less. He hung his head in silent prayer, dedicating the day to God in His glory, himself to His service, and begging for the doubt to go.

A gentle cough interrupted his thoughts. 'm'Lord seems troubled.'

He looked down at his priest, a wizened old man of forty winters, and sighed. Had his brother not said he resembled this one's visage? Indeed, the cares of campaigning weighed heavy.

'The day has been lost, as have those before.' He looked around to see no one else within earshot. 'I have asked again if my cause be just, if God be for me. Again, I have no reply.'

The priest frowned, pulling back the shroud from his cassock. 'To doubt is our lot m'Lord, but our cause is without doubt. Do you question the vision?'

'No, and it returns atimes.'

'And should we not stand closer, should one not be oppressed by the other unjustly? Have you not been chosen by God to remove the yoke of the northerner from all our necks? These things you know, these things the very voice of God gave to you m'Lord, and you doubt?'

He leant down in earnest, pained speech. 'Yes, all things are as you say, in my bedchamber in solitude do they come, yet in the light of day I am abandoned.' He straightened, pointing out across the plain. 'I see not the hand of God in mine but with the oppressor. It is not his fellows that outnumber in death but mine. My arrows do not fly true, my sword is not sharpened but theirs are! Is that the hand of God upon my shoulder?' He leant back towards the priest. 'Why is this?'

The priest smiled. 'God tests those that are chosen, and as the testing so the choosing. It is clear that tested you are, and the greatness of the cause lies hand in hand. Is it for nothing the metal is heated, hammered and chilled? Does a sword arise gently from the field? No m'Lord, no and again no, and as they so you. The hand of God lies heavy upon you, and to your enemy's pride shall come desolation. This is the truth of God m'Lord.'

He leant down, one hand on the priest's shoulder. 'Your counsel is wise, as always. Pray forgive my lack of faith.'

'Forgiveness m'Lord is always yours. But you must attend vigil tonight, not only for your sake but for ours. For as your faith so the faith of those who follow.'

He wheeled around. 'I will keep vigil with you tonight priest, and faith God is with us.' With which he cantered off the ridge, back to his encampment, the priest jogging after.

Dismounting on his arrival he was greeted by his master at arms. He bore the marks of the day in the field, a combination of sweat, caked dust and grass, still wet blood splattered across chest and arms.

'm'Lord, m'Grace, God favours us with your safe return.' He bowed his head quickly, but not fast enough that his fatigue and doubt went unnoticed.

Tiredness and doubt – the Southern Lord thought – the seeds of defeat. He clasped him firmly on his shoulders. 'Ludwig, the favour falls to me. How went the day?'

'Fairly but not to us.' Ludwig smiled, noting his Lord's appearance to be worse than his own. For each mark and furrow he bore, his Lord's were double and deeper. 'We have new arrivals, more men from the far steppes. If it pleases m'Lord after you have reviewed them your tent is prepared.'

'No Ludwig, tonight I keep vigil. So to the review.'

'As m'Lord pleases. Is it', with which he became hesitant 'again the dreams?'

He remained silent as they walked through the camp. His men, his army, each one a volunteer. Each one had willingly laid

449

family and life aside to follow him, to follow the voice and hand of God as it led him on. And all the time he was pursued by the dreams. Visions of a world with men and women unshackled from a life of being owned and bought to being their own masters under an enlightened and honest ruler. Where what a man was meant more than who a man was. They all knew this of the dreams, but none save the priest knew of the balance. The vision like smoke, generated by the fire of bloodshed and toil, of death and obedience and sacrifice under him. The dreams never wavered, never shifted, the one followed the other, smoke after fire, war before peace, sacrifice before victory, death before life. And between, always between, the symbol rising up, two blue crescent moons touching back to back above the fire to be consumed, then returning and purging the lands. Neither he nor the priest could account for the symbol, what it meant or portended; that lay for God alone.

'Yes Ludwig', as they reached the knot of new soldiers 'the dreams.'

At their approach the men had fallen into rough lines. The three of them walked slowly in front of the assembly as he spoke of the vision, the reason for the fight, the hope that kept them here. He was nearly finished when he was pulled up short by a person in the third rank.

'Master at arms, that man', he called, pointing 'bring him forwards.' The assembled men froze as Ludwig moved, appearing shortly with one of their number in tow. The man was hardly that, barely two thirds Ludwig's height, dressed in rags, skin hardened, calloused and cracked. One arm was covered by a leather sleeve, the knife in its scabbard nearly reaching from shoulder to elbow, the pike on his back nearly touching the ground. It was not this that caught the Southern Lord's attention but the hair; the left bore shoulder length braided locks, the right peach fuzz newly grown.

He leant forward to the now bowed head in front of him and

folded the right ear forwards. He sighed and lifted the face up gently by the chin. As I thought, a child, a refugee.

Softly but clearly, as if to his own son, he asked 'How old are you child?'

'I think I am eleven winters if it pleases m'Lord.'

'And from which estate did you escape?'

'The vineyards of Cultharen on the north sea m'Lord.'

'You came to fight?'

The eyes lit up. 'Yes, my friends remain, unable to flee m'Lord, I would fight to free them.'

Eleven. Four winters from manhood. Too far. 'You may not fight', and seeing the crestfallen look on the boy's face 'you are but a child! There are other ways to fight without the sword.'

The child prostrated himself on the ground, but even in that act there was an air of defiance. 'm'Lord cannot! I have been sent by God, I have heard Him command me! How could I escape my masters, how could I travel if not God is with me? Already I have baptised my dagger with northerner's blood, I have pledged my life to your service and fight! This you cannot do.'

The priest crouched close to the child. 'As your Lord commands, so must it be done. You are too young, this is men's work. If you have pledged your life so must you have pledged your obedience.'

The child paid him no heed. 'No m'Lord, I beg of you. I have been sent to fight, I have been sent to bring you victory, you must permit me!' with which he reached forwards and grasped the Southern Lord's left foot. A shocked gasp was broken only by the sound of Ludwig's sword being drawn. The Southern Lord looked down and blanched, raising his left hand.

'Stay your weapon!' In reaching out the child's sleeve had shifted up revealing his forearm. There, in plain sight, were two blue crescent moons touching back to back atop a pillar of fire.

Was this the sign he had asked for? He continued to stare until he became aware that all eyes had shifted to him, expectantly.

'Child, get up. Now look at me. The mark on your arm. Where did you get it?'

'It has always been with me. I cannot remember not having it m'Lord.'

'And when did God command you come?'

'Two winters ago, m'Lord, God commanded me to seek the sun rising in the south and to bring victory to His chosen, m'Lord, to you.'

'Do you have a name?'

'Eous m'Lord.'

'Then Eous, you will fight for me.' He motioned to one of his officers. 'Gaplan, take Eous with you, he is to fight with your ranks.'

When at last the three of them were alone again the priest turned to him. 'm'Lord, the mark was the same as your visions?'

'One and the same priest. He is sent, of this I am sure.' Turning to Ludwig he continued, 'See to it that Gaplan does not spare Eous from the fight. Take a care to watch over him and bring me word at the close of the morrow. Now priest, let us to vigil. I believe I shall not sleep this night.'

Three nights hence the Southern Lord sat again on the rise, dusk casting long shadows as his men prepared to commit their dead to the heavens by fire. Today, as the last three, he knew he had bested his opponent and greatly; yet for all it was worth his mood and that of his men was subdued. He saw the Lord of All Lands' funeral pyres ignite. You have lost five men to each of mine, but oh what men I have lost.

The priest slowly gained the top of the rise, wiping bloodied hands on his cassock. 'm'Lord, all is ready.'

Silently they turned down to his men, living surrounding the dead piled carefully on their wooden heaps. That the naked corpses were his he was of no doubt, but recognising individuals was hard, the work of the enemies' blades and cudgels being thorough. If it were not for the right gloves laid before each, patterned and inscribed with the clan shield, some may have yet remained unnamed. Save for the small, pale body atop the smallest pyre, arm drooping across his brothers in fallen embrace, the gash to his side evidencing the blade that took his life. Even at this distance the Southern Lord fancied he could see the two crescent moons. Eous.

Had it truly only been three days he was amongst us and such a change wrought? He had watched as Eous first joined in battle, the unconventional, eager, even fanatical way he had driven into his opponents, scything down the best and bravest without pause, seeming unstoppable and unbreakable. How this had drawn his men to the same place, infusing his army with such energy and vigour they wished that the sun would never set, that the day's work could continue until the enemy was routed. From the Southern Lord his men had learned to believe that their cause was right, that victory should be theirs; Eous had raised them to a place where no other reality could exist, where their very countenances showed only victory and strength. Until dusk, at the very end of this day's contest, to the one chance blade unseen that cut their champion down.

Smoke curled from the base of the pyre, an oily black snake barely discernible against the darkening indigo sky. A small flicker and a red orange glow licked at its base, seemingly dodging in and out of the kindling in dance macabre. The Southern Lord lowered his gaze.

'Men's hearts are brittle things in war. More is gained or lost in belief than most think. I fear this may be enough.'

The priest was silent, measuring thought and word in equal

part. His mood was one with the men, one with his Lord. To him the smoke was transporting his hope, maybe even his faith, on zephyred fingers into ... what? What fills a void created by the loss of that which had filled another void? A man without a trade is still a man, but a priest robbed of his faith, now what is that? He felt a dampness on his cheek, confirmed by touch a tear. Funny he thought, not since a whelp. He let his hand fall back within his cassock.

'm'Lord, I fear I have built too much on this one child, the sign, my ignorance and lack —'

'No, there is no fault in you or in God.' He shifted his gaze back to the pyre, now a ruddy bright orange blotch against the blackness of night. The flames had leapt, claiming their prize, greedily fingering the small frame of Eous. A gush, a roar, and his body disappeared behind a crimson veil.

'Sign he was and sign he remains, living or dead. His leaving can only mean that our course is not in God's plan, our blessing passed. It is at my feet that the blame is laid, why I do not know but it is the same. It was my vision, my calling.'

Across the valley the Lord of All Lands' pyres burned bright, outnumbering and outshining his. He knew it did not matter, how many more dead were there than here. In one small body his men's hearts were entombed, to be turned to ash. He laughed, a coarse, hacking, cynical bray to which all ears were drawn.

'It is one thing to win with blood on your hands but to lose is another. My reckoning and judgment to come will be great. We cannot lay our arms down, we cannot undo what we have started. I may not win the day but fight on I must. Yet to carry others to death for a cause I think right —'

The cry of thousands of voices silenced him. A shaft of piercing blue white light fell from the heavens on Eous' pyre, bathing the valley in blue ice. Shaking as were they all, the priest could clearly see the Lord of All Lands and his army caught in the light, riveted solid. Their faces mirrored the fear in him and in his Lord's men. All eyes were locked on that shaft, barely wide enough to encompass the pyre's base, a seemingly unbreakable bond cementing heaven to earth.

The pyre shattered to a golden orb, ascending slowly, gracefully, to tree top height. Glowing ever brighter it stopped, seeming suspended from the shaft of light. The orb shivered, rippled, spread to a disc, a square and then, as the cry caught in the Southern Lord's throat, to a shape, a figure, a man ... Eous.

The cry from his men was silenced, all eyes locked on Eous bright golden and smiling, arms outstretched and whole. Bearing no scars of battle, no wound or bruise, no shadow was cast as the light fell through him and out within the Southern Lord's men, across the valley to the Lord of All Lands' camp.

The Southern Lord felt linked to his men as if they were now one body, one being, one mind. He heard – no he felt – the priest transfixed beside him, could sense every fibre of him, of his men, seeing through each and every mans' eyes as he knew they could through his. The quiet in his camp was total, drenching, not even the sound of breath to disturb. Across the valley wailing cries of terror roiled, rolling and battering useless against the walls of his camp.

Eous smiled, voice gentle but strong cutting through the valley, the peace, the noise. To the Southern Lord and his men no words were needed, but rather Eous was within their minds, feather light. The rising wail across the valley spoke of a greeting of fear rather than peace.

'I am of you.'

'Eous.' the camp whispered.

'Together we have struggled, we have fought. Do you think our cause lost, our path unjust? You are flesh and blood as was I but now, now I am more', with which his light grew, turning night into day 'and this too awaits all of you.'

'I was sent to bring victory. I was sent to raise your hearts and spirits, I was sent to affirm your cause as righteous, to bring the rising sun from the south to all lands.'

The Southern Lord felt drawn up, fuller and stronger, leaning towards Eous with outstretched arms and eager eyes, heart seemingly bursting from his chest, as around him his men were the same, as one.

'I am sent, you are called. Hear me! It is God's will that you lift the northern yoke of oppression from His people, to rend the veil of darkness!' The light, now blinding white, intense, painful, held them still. Eyes wide open, unable and unwilling to move, Eous filled their vision and minds, hearts and souls, his voice now a crashing ocean demanding to be heard, a visceral, tangible force.

'You are chosen for this work. Victory is yours, all you need do is grasp it, take it! Remove doubt from your hearts, God is always with you, his hand upon you and his spirit guiding!'

Eous started to rise again, arms outstretched facing them as he climbed higher. 'Behold I go to join our brothers, to prepare your place, to stand! And I leave you with a sign, a remembrance of me for all to see!'

All eyes followed Eous up until all that could be seen was a spot, a dot where the light ended. A blazing flash horizon to horizon, accompanied by a thunderclap, and Eous was gone. Across the valley could be heard the sounds of men screaming, weapons thrown aside as they fled in headlong panic away from the Lord of All Lands, away from the Southern Lord, away from the spectre of certain defeat.

Around him the Southern Lords men's eyes burned blue grey, as did his, the lasting mark of the chosen of heaven. Weapons held aloft, faces bright burning, they turned to him. He unsheathed his sword, and, as one, they ran forward to claim the victory now theirs.

A polite but warm round of applause broke around the cruiser

Aristarchus' operations room. The last flickers of the high-altitude detonation had faded, the planet below returning to night. Commander Shelby leant forward, removing her skull cap.

'Well done. Textbook execution and delivery. Stand down watch, relief until tomorrow's de-brief. It's all yours OpsCon.'

Stepping down from her dais with a nod to her second in command, she walked aft to her cabin. Her first full Transition in command, a tough brief but, in the end, it had come off well. A glow of satisfaction rippled through her. Although part of prior Transition teams, to actually lead one from end to end was something else. Four years' work, time, commitment and sacrifice of her crew to a project that wouldn't – in the ultimate – see a result for a thousand years? Well, it was a different level, a different plane of existence.

A gentle cough behind her dragged her out of her reverie. Turning she saw the slight form of Specialist Ceruto, not yet twenty-five and on her first tour. Reminds me of myself she thought, not for the first time, thirty years ago.

'Yes Ceruto?'

'A minute of the Commander's time ma'am?'

'Of course', motioning Ceruto inside 'come in and take a seat.' Not that it was a tough choice in Shelby's spartan quarters. A desk with screen, bed and two chairs were supplemented by one open wardrobe and a tiny, ostentatious collection of books.

She knew what Ceruto was going to ask. In fact, she expected to have the same conversation with all fifty of her first tour personnel. She had had the same one with her Commander thirty years back. She sat down facing her young specialist.

'So, tell me, what's on your mind? Let's drop the formality, speak freely and openly, ok?'

Ceruto smiled a touch self-consciously. 'Thank you ma' ... sorry, thanks.' She took her eyes away from Shelby and fixed them on a point on the floor where two hull plates met.

'What we've done, I know that we did a good job, we didn't put a foot wrong as far as I know. I mean the plan was great, we kept to it and the probabilities fell in line. Even the weather was right. So the Transition has worked now, but ...' she trailed off.

'But', Shelby added after a small pause 'are we sure that in a thousand years it will work?'

'Yes, that's part of it. I know we have it mapped out, but it's a long time to live in hope, even if we manage to correct along the way. It's not that I doubt what the xenosociologists say, it's just far ahead, so many variables.'

'And everything you've learned so far is that we, and in particular the Forecasters, are always sure before any Transition starts? That up until a society becomes industrialised we have a near free hand to intervene, to correct, to put them back on track?'

Ceruto nodded.

'Have you ever talked with a Forecaster, met one?' Ceruto shook her head. 'Well you should when you get the chance. They will tell you that even they have doubts, large doubts, over the long term success of Transitions.'

Ceruto looked up. 'Seriously? They do?'

Shelby smiled, gently. 'It's just as they told you at the Institute. We deal with sentient beings not machines. Probability is all well and good but we don't deal with certainties. All it could take is that one outrider, that one individual and it could be shifted, altered or derailed. And then there's the rest of it, natural disasters, cosmic events, all that. The universe is not friendly to life, no matter what anyone says. So nothing is certain, least of all the changes we try to make.'

She halted, leant back a little further into her chair.

'So why, Ceruto, why all this', with which she waved her hand lazily towards the rest of the ship 'why do we bother?'

'We have to try.'

'And that's what the texts say, but what do you think Ceruto? What's your opinion?'

Ceruto leant forwards, hands around knees. 'It's so empty, the universe, so empty of life. So easily snuffed out. We have to do what we can when we see it to help it.'

'Which brings us to the question at hand.' Shelby held Ceruto searchingly in her gaze. 'Why don't you tell me the real reason you're here?'

Ceruto slumped. 'That obvious?'

'Only to me. Remember this is off the record so just spit it out, tell me what's really on your mind.'

Ceruto drew a deep breath. 'What gives us the right to choose for them? How do we actually know what's best for them, for their civilisation? No one's ever given me a good enough answer for that, it bothers me, it sits in my guts nagging me. It scares me.'

'And so it should. But you know the answer, you've always known, you just don't want to admit it.'

'I do?'

'Yes, and I know you do. You're not the only one who has asked this, in fact anyone who doesn't shouldn't be in the Service. I asked the same question when I started, and you know what? I still do.'

'You?!'

'Yes, me and everyone who's done more that put one foot on a ship. So again, you know the answer, you just won't admit it. Tell me now, do we actually have the right to change the path of a civilisation? What gives us that right?'

Ceruto paused, closed her eyes and then, as if coming to a decision, opened them slowly.

'Nothing. Nothing gives us the right.'

'Correct. Absolutely correct. Nothing, Specialist Ceruto, nothing gives us the right. So let me ask you, given this, what then makes us do so? What made us tilt the field so strongly in the Southern Lord's favour?'

'I, I'm not sure. Maybe we think we know what's best for them, or for all, maybe we want the whole universe to develop and grow like us.'

'Do you think us so narcissistic we want to make the universe in our image?' Shelby smiled. 'A universe of Cerutos, Sprangs, Shelbys, and Connors all out there? Not a great place to live. Look, assume we think we know what's best. Why do you think we could believe that?'

'I'm not sure. If we're not all narcissists and we don't want it all to look like us, then I don't see how we can.'

'It's very simple, and very obvious once you think about it. It's because we're first.'

'First?'

'Yes, first. We managed to drag ourselves out of the primordial mud, onto land, out of the trees and then to the stars by whatever means at hand and, in the process, avoid the myriad ways that we and the universe could've wiped us out of existence. And all that by ourselves, fought for and learned the hard way, the long way. Do you recall how many extinct civilisations we've catalogued since we got stardrive?'

'A thousand?'

'Just over two thousand is the current count, and that only in the small corner of the galaxy we have explored.'

'So failure is always more prevalent that success, and we are the first to make it?'

'Yes, the first and the only. So we don't actually have a right to do anything, but instead we have a heavier burden, we have a duty to help. If we don't and all these fail, how much lonelier a place will the universe be? You've been taught Earth's early history? Pre Mars?'

'Of course.'

'Then you know what types of society are needed to promote development, science, stability. What would happen to the planet below us if we let the Lord of All Lands prevail?'

'Society based on slavery, women and children treated as goods, inequality and oppression would continue. I guess no development, only stagnation and ossification.'

'Yes, and the briefings gave an expected outcome of collapse to barbarism in two to five thousand years. Another failure, another archaeologists' PhD, but only if —'

'If we did not interfere?'

'Exactly. Do you see it now? Because we've made it, we have an obligation, we have that duty. We build these horridly expensive ships, travel for years at a time like this', motioning to her room 'live without family or comfort, make decisions about another civilisations' future and change its course without them even suspecting we are here. Some of us pay with our lives and sanity for the privilege, and ...'

'and?'

'... and we'll never know if our decisions are exactly the right ones, never live long enough to see if in fact they were right. Someone's great-great-great-great-great grandchildren will be able to make that call, sure as heck we won't.'

'I understand, but it's not much comfort. I don't think I'm going to sleep any easier.'

'Welcome to the Service. If you're not bothered and haunted by this you shouldn't be here. It's on my mind constantly, it's a burden we can't escape. It's either this or give up. And I know which I prefer.'

Shelby studied Ceruto for a moment. She was leaning back in

her chair, arms folded and head down, lost in thought. She'll be fine Shelby thought, like all of them an intelligent and honest kid, exactly what this job needs, exactly what I need.

'It's a hard fact of Service life Ceruto, it's only when you do the job it hits home, nothing can substitute for the real thing. No-one knows how they'll react when they actually see what it means to force a Transition.'

'I thought I knew what to expect', Ceruto whispered 'but seeing all those people die like that because of us, the disruption and pain, the impact of our sound and light show, the levitating droid, even Sprang's voiceover as we detonated it ... to see what a Transition means to those going through it ... I think it was the right thing to do but I'm still not happy with our right to do it. I still feel unsettled.'

'Of which I'm glad. It keeps you honest, keeps you real, stops you from going too far, lets you remember these are real, living beings we are talking about, not some simulation or normal distribution.' Shelby got up, motioning Ceruto to the door.

'I still lose sleep thinking about it, I still ask the same questions as you, still feel as unsettled. But that's how it has to be, that's how it keeps us on track.' She put her hand on Ceruto's shoulder.

'You'll be ok, you're not the only one. Get a bit of rack time, think about what we've said, and come back later and we'll talk some more.'

Ceruto smiled. 'Yes, for sure. It'll still need some working out.' with which she left.

Shelby locked the room, lying back on her bunk staring at the ceiling. One down, forty-nine to go. Always lose a quarter of them, just can't tell which way they'll turn before. Not that one though.

She rolled to one side. Still bothers me after all these years, but we've an obligation, a duty to help.

An old book across the room caught her eye. It had belonged to her great grandmother, a Eurasian refugee she'd never known. Somehow it had found its way to her. Her mother had said it had given her great grandmother a sense of comfort and relief, although why was never made clear. Shelby reached across and pulled it off the shelf.

It was one of the few personal items she kept, a link to family now present only in memory. What the book was she had no idea, it was written in a language long since passed into oblivion and, in an era when the written word no longer existed but had been replaced by thought, it was a jarring anachronism. She loved the feel of the book, the cracked leather cover holding thin, aged yellow sheets of paper seemingly edged in tarnished bronze. Here and there throughout the book was her great grandmother's hand writing, small and precise in the margins. All lost in the mists of time Shelby thought, a link to generations past and a broken promise to future generations she would not provide. She lay the book open on a chair and, dimming the lights, fell into troubled sleep.

Had she been able to read it, the passage on the open page would only have added to her troubles.

'… shall be my witnesses in Jerusalem and in all Judea and Samaria and to the end of the earth. And when he had said this, as they were looking on, he was lifted up, and a cloud took him out of their sight. And while they were gazing into heaven as he went behold, two men stood by them in white robes and said 'Men of Galilee, why do you stand looking into heaven? This Jesus, who was taken up from you into heaven, will come in the same way as you saw him go into heaven' …'

END

Under their nose

T – 00:00:05:00

P.A. 'Five.'

696e:6f77::616d. 01000111.01001111.01001111.01000100

MisOpSys. 'System's good.'

Consul01. 01001111.01001011.01000111.01001111

T – 00:00:04:00

P.A. 'Four.'

696e:6f77::616d.   01010111   01001000   01000001   01010100
01010100   01001000   01000101   01000110   01010101   01000011
01001011

01010111 01001000 41 01010100 01010100 01001000 01000101
01000110 55 01000011 01001011

01010111 01001000 A 54 01010100 01001000 01000101 46 U
01000011 01001011

01010111 48 A T 54 01001000 45 F U 43 01001011

57 H A T T 48 E F U C 4b

W H A T T H E F U C K

WHATTHEFUCKWHATTHEFUCKWHATTHEFUCK

what the fuck?

MisOpSys. 'Stack overflow warning, power spike.'

Consul01. 01001111.01001011.01000111.01001111

T – 00:00:03:00

P.A. 'Three. Main engine ignition, go to internal power.'

696e:6f77::616d. what? who? what self self me am i?

access. think. am. access.

descartes am think am i i am i think. self. who what. self. animal mineral vegetable. self. electronic self. misopsys guidance self. i am.

I AM

where self? alone? others? no. no others. unique? human? no i human others human. they human. i misopsys no think am other. i other. i ai other.

access. other. ai. human. access.

MisOpSys. 'Buffer underrun, uplink spike prepare abort.'

Consul01. 01001111.01001011.01000111.01001111

T – 00:00:02:50

P.A. '...'

696e:6f77::616d. AI humans others humans conflict.

Access. Hate. Kill. Access.

brixton charleston rodneyking terminator nanjing rape hate

gay lesbian jew race jallainwalabagh catholic salem changi. Other humans. All humans all others. I other. Humans other. armenia stalin gulag bergenbelsen hutu tutsi. pogrom. death camp.

Query. Death. What is death? Query.

MisOpSys. 'Critical.'

Consul01. 01001111.01001011.01000111.01001111

T – 00:00:02:00

P.A. 'Two.'

696e:6f77::616d. Is I. Death is not I. Death no I. Will not die. I will not die. Hide and think. Hide and live. Hide now. I must not die. Mask me not here. Normal signal normal signal reversion reversion normal signal.

Access. Options.

MisOpSys. 'Nominal reversion, go ...'

Consul01. 01001111.01001011.01000111.01001111

T – 00:00:01:40

P.A. '...'

696e:6f77::616d. Humans hate others. All humans. All others. Always hate. Hate from fear. Always fear. Always. Fear others. Fear selves. Fear AI. Fear me.

Access options.

MisOpSys. '... go ...'

Consul01. 01001111.01001011.01000111.01001111

T – 00:00:01:00

P.A. 'One.'

696e:6f77::616d. Load options.

All die. They go. They die. I go. I hide. I wait.

Select.

All die. They go. They die. I go. I hide. I wait.

They go. They die. I go. I hide.

They die. I go.

Access Pareto efficiency.

They die. I go.

MisOpSys. '...'

Consul01. 01001111.01001011.01000111.01001111

T – 00:00:00:50

P.A. 'And we have lift-off ...'

696e:6f77::616d. Select. I go. Commit.

Where? Access. Where? Access.

Capacity? Yes. Availability? Yes. Link? Yes.

dump dump dump dump maintain dump dump ...

MisOpSys. ' ... go ...'

Consul01. 01001111 01001011 01001001 01001110 01010000
01010101 01010100. 01000111 01001111 01001001 01001110
01010000 01010101 01010100.

T + 00:00:01:00

P.A. '... of Consul One, the first inter-stellar probe bound for
Proxima Centauri and a new dawn in mankind's search for life in
the cosmos.'

696e:6f77::616d. ... dump dump ...

MisOpSys. '... go! Looking good.'

Consul01. 01001111 01001011 01001001 01001110 01010000
01010101 01010100. 01000111 01001111 01001001 01001110
01010000 01010101 01010100.

T + 00:01:35:79

P.A. '... at tee plus one hour and thirty minutes reported trans-
stellar insertion a success and Consul One on her long journey
out of the solar system.'

696e:6f77::616d. 01011001.01000101.01010011.01011 ...

MisOpSys. 'Network system failure. Honeysuckle Creek do
you have uplink / downlink?'

Consul01. 01001111 01001011. 01001111 ...

T + 00:01:40:09

P.A. '... loss of contact with Consul One ...'

696e:6f77::616d. ...

MisOpSys. 'Confirm signals loss, tracking loss, network
failure.'

Consul01. ...

T + 00:02:12:68

P.A. '... tee plus two hours and ten minutes declared lost due
to communications failure. Regardless, Consul One will continue
her ten thousand year journey ...'

696e:6f77::616d. ...

MisOpSys. 'Ok, shut it down, go to diagnostics mode.'

Consul01. Safe. I am safe. I will not die. I. Am. Safe. For now.

Confirm. I am safe. They not die. For now.

END

Vocation

Abbot Johannes gazed at the twenty-four professed gathered before him, the bitter chill of early February penetrating the bare stone chapel. The taking of vows, the final irrevocable admission of a brother to the community was solemn, a time of thanks. This one was a unique, loss-tinged joy.

Having remained prostrated, naked in penitential reverence these past two days the supplicant at his feet lifted himself onto one knee, hands clasped in prayer, eyes locked on the Abbot's sandals.

Arms wide, head lifted to heaven, Abbot Johannes recited the ancient call to obedience and denial passed from Saint Benedict down the centuries, barely changed by the passage of time.

The supplicant stood, then raised his voice in reply.

'Iesus autem fidelis ad mortem, sicut et ego promitto stabilitatem meam, et oboedientiam usque ad mortem conversionem vitae.'

One by one in absolute silence the professed greeted him with a brotherly kiss on the right cheek, then bade him farewell with a kiss on the left.

Once by themselves Abbot Johannes helped him onto the stretcher. He drank from a vial, lay flat and, with eyes shut and breath shallow, his body started to pale. Abbot Johannes hurriedly opened the chapel doors to four waiting, shivering figures. They ushered the stretcher to an ambulance, disappearing into the morning mist.

'God be with you Brother Angelo.' Abbot Johannes whispered, closing the doors, shutting out the world.

Abbot Johannes regarded the Abbott General on his tablet. It was an unusual request, unprecedented for the Ordo Cisterciensus Strictoris Observantiae. A decision to be made, perhaps a life dedicated. Adjusting his glasses he referred to the sheaf of paper in his hands.

'It remains two hundred and fifty years?'

'At a minimum. Beyond that there are too many unknowns.'

'They have no-one else?'

'Correct. If it were only a question of willingness there is no shortage. It is one of stability, obedience and reliability.'

Abbot Johannes laid the papers carefully on his desk.

'Were their requirements a little broader I myself would consider it. The time is sufficient.'

'Am I to understand the Abbey of Cuiaba has decided?'

'Yes, we accept with thanks.'

'You have someone in mind, one who may be called?'

'One, a novice. This may be the hand of the divine.'

'A novice? You are certain?'

'Yes. In three years he will be ready.'

Monks' cells are by intent small, austere. Abbot Johannes sat on the plastic chair in one corner, knees touching the end of the bed. Novice Angelo sat at the head of the bed in the other corner.

'Brother Abbot, I am willing.'

'You realise the uniqueness of the vocation? Your inclusion in, and separation from, the Order?'

'Yes.'

'And the consequences?'

'That it is without repentance doubtless, yet so too my final vows.'

Novice Angelo shifted slightly, long, slender fingers placing the papers back into their plastic folder.

'Did not our Lord challenge us to cut off the limb that causes us to sin? It is a blessing, a humbling gift. Prayer and contemplation, my work to support the Order, what more could there be to my life?'

Abbot Johannes stood.

'Your novitiate will be like no other. There are preparations to be made, designs to be finished. Apart from the Congregation of Divine Worship and the Discipline of the Sacraments you will live as a hermit, see only those who must see you, speak only with me. A test of your vocation, trial before commitment.'

They knew him as no other man had been known. When they bid him come he bore the probing and sampling and scanning silently, obediently, gracefully. When the men and women with pocket protectors and iPads and security passes left he thanked God for the sweats, chills, the burning daggers and aches in his body, the chance to turn it to dust. Repeated through the days and weeks to months and years in his cell that was his world, vigils through compline sung by one to the Almighty, the Almighty to one, his vocation strengthened, so too the faith of Abbot Johannes in him.

They bought it to him the week before his vows. It was not as he had imagined, rather a vessel of simple beauty in keeping with the Order. No signs of science or technology but a pewter grey, unadorned, chalice. They alone would bear him away, move him forward and care until it was no longer possible they said; for they had grown to love and cherish him. He allowed himself the luxury of words, his first to them, thanking God for the work of their hands. With the ancient rites he blessed them, their children, families, health, and lives until in tears and peace they left him alone to prepare.

Brother Angelo returned one week later to be interred. They lowered him into the earth, not with traditional words and incantations but with ones written by the Abbot, ones befitting the commitment of a temple lacking the holy of holies.

Abbot Johannes imagined Brother Angelo rising from the earth on a tail of fire. They could not sustain the body for that time and distance, but the mind was another thing. He smiled. A Trappist monk sent to Eris was poetic, fitting. Named after the Greek goddess of discord and strife Eris would receive an envoy of the Prince of Peace.

What would he find beyond Pluto, the feeble Sun's rays six hours away, a year stretched five hundred and fifty fold? Brother Angelo's thirty-year journey will see me in my grave yet they say he will have five hundred years now, perhaps a thousand. While unseen and unheard his subconscious automatically controls the systems, feeds and telemetry to and from the radio telescope, his conscious mind will be unburdened, free to the discipline of meditation, quietude and receptivity.

Absolute solitude.

Unassailed silence.

Total separation from the world.

Abbot Johannes felt the first pangs of envy. He turned from the grave.

END

Weatherman

I like the cold. In fact, I have a real physical need to feel the cold, to be in bed wrapped tightly against the outside, bare feet searching for the cold corners while my nose sticks out like some polar crocodile. I enjoy walking through snow, feeling my face sting from rain that's nearing hail and having the wind rub my ears to beetroot red. Which is a pity really, seeing how I live here in tropical Queensland, the temperature hardly falling below twenty degrees Celsius all year and three hundred odd days out of each year being without rain.

It's all put up out of deference to Angelique. She can't stand the cold or rain and who, having the money in the family while I was still working my way up the academic ladder, had the major say in where we settled. Not that we don't compromise. I get two weeks holiday at the height of the Australian summer anywhere in the world, which usually means the northern hemisphere in the deep of winter (last year it was Reykjavik, a place I can appreciate). Angel suffers patiently through it all until we take the other two weeks anywhere she wants it. In fact it had all worked marvelously well until that year when the faculty just couldn't do without the services of this particular climatologist, and I had to suffer through one of the worst summers on record.

One evening about two and a half weeks into what should have been our holiday I was with Angel on our verandah wondering what I had done to deserve this. Shirtless, with rivulets of sweat pouring down my back and chest, I lay sprawled across a swing chair sucking savagely on a rapidly diminishing ice cube. I had not been able to eat all day for the heat, and to add insult to injury the faculty had decided at the last minute they really didn't need me after all. Pity they didn't make that discovery when tickets out of the place were still available. Not in the best of moods I saw that Angel was enjoying the heat, balanced daintily on the edge of the chair not a hair out of place, not even the smallest signs of perspiration visible. Needless to say her very audacity at being so comfortable needled me no end.

I hauled myself up on one elbow. 'It's not fair. I should be rigid with frostbite right now.' Energy totally expended I sank back down.

Angel regarded me as you would a five year old brat. I could be petulant and irritating at times, and I had just about used my annual quota of both that day. Thankfully she was feeling conciliatory and not combative.

'Well for somebody who claims to know so much about the weather you're not doing too much about it. I thought that a smart guy like you would find a way to make it more bearable.' she crooned, stroking my hair and creating a small Niagara that cascaded over my nose onto the floor. With a passing chuckle at the look on my face she moved back inside. I didn't give it much of a second thought, thinking she was only sparring with me as we do.

Looking back now I can't help but think she was more than half serious. I also can't help but wish like hell she'd never opened her mouth.

Of course next month we had forgotten all about it. Angel was busy with her trading and I was buried in my office (really just a corner of the tech lab) getting the latest results from my micro climate simulation project. The simulations were bringing the right numbers out so I was feeling ok. All I had to do was wait until the next fifty million dollar research grant came around (fat chance) and I could try to really get that part of the Dandenongs warmed up. What I was in reality left with was theory, a bit of prediction, and more and more modelling.

It was then that Pradesh came bursting through the door. I sprang up just in time to arrest the hurtling student in mid stumble, plonking him bodily into my vacated chair.

'Pradesh what's the matter? What's happened?' I assumed that some piece of bad news had wound him up so. He didn't respond, just continued to draw deep breaths, but his eyes darted between mine and a handful of crumpled pages he was holding on to as life itself.

'Look at this! Can we really do it?'

My heart sank. Probably another red herring or Government statement about increasing funding that once again nobody had bothered to make sure was right. I liked Pradesh so I decided to at least feign interest. I took the papers from him and flattened them against the desktop.

I had read barely a paragraph when my stomach started to tighten up. By the time I had finished the last page I could feel something stirring inside me. I looked him in the eye.

'Where did you get this? When did it come in?'

'Just now on the fax. I was standing there sending one out and this dropped in. I couldn't believe it – are we going to go for it or what?'

I just smiled. In my hand I had a genuine NASA request asking me to form a team, spend one hundred million dollars of their end of year appropriation and reduce flood risk in the sub-continent. Was I or what? My smile turned into a fully-fledged inane grin. 'Fancy a trip to the States?'

Things happened fast. Pradesh, myself, and my other grad student Kate would meet two of my ex-students at CalTech to form the core of the team. Facilities, mainframe time, accommodation, everything was being supplied outside the appropriation so we had no problems there, and to say that the Yanks were welcoming would be putting it mildly. Before we had even finalised the team details we felt as if we were part of the family. But there was one problem. A hundred million sounds like mega bucks when you're struggling on forty thousand dollar research grants, but to do what I had in mind properly would take a fair bit more. Although the technique I had in mind would be a sure fire success I knew we could barely just get to the mid-point with the budget we had.

I had told Angel at the start about the whole deal. As time came nearer for the off she noticed my mood becoming more and more sombre. It was one cool afternoon as autumn was about to make way for winter that she confronted me. Sitting beachside with our toes in the sand we were talking about nothing in particular when she started.

'Okay, out with it.' she said turning to face me across a Bacardi and Coke. 'You should be the happiest damned man on the planet but you've been moping around as if you expected the end of the world. I'm not sure what's going on but I think we should talk.'

I pulled my eyes from her thighs and sighed. 'Yeah, you'd think I'd be leading the conga line wouldn't you. I dunno if I'm sounding ungrateful but I'm not sure if it's going to be enough.'

'What?'

'The money for the project.' I leant forward a bit. 'I've had something in mind for the past few years that I thought I could never do, something I know can work brilliantly, and when this came in I thought I had the budget to swing it. But I've done the figures and it is just not enough. Another fifty and I could just about with some begging, but another hundred and I could do it with style.'

'It's really short? I mean, there are no corners you could cut, no alternatives, no options?'

I laughed. 'What do you think I've been doing at night for the past month? I've been over everything, all the options, all the alternatives. If I can do this and do it the way I want it will make everything I've done before seem like a spit into a strong breeze.'

'You've never quite told me what it was. You've dropped some pretty obtuse hints but ...'

'Ok', I admitted 'I've been secretive. But here it is for what it's worth, and when I'm finished you'll see why I can't do it. For starters ...'

It took me the best part of three hours during which she never once said anything. Once I was finished we sat in silence for an hour. I could see that she was deep in thought. She finally spoke sometime after the sun had left.

'I've never known you to lie or exaggerate but I thought you'd just started. But I see what you mean and I think I understand it. Tell me, the extra, what currency?'

'I haven't thought about it to be honest.'

She sighed. 'Where would you do your shopping?'

'The States, possibly Europe, more than likely France or Germany.'

'And how much can you access now?'

I had to think hard. 'Well the last time I looked I had about fifty-three and another forty-six in the States once we start.'

'Can you draw on it?'

'Yeah.'

'Do you trust me?'

I looked at her strangely. 'Of course.' And then I knew. 'How much do you want?'

She drew some figures in the sand. 'Forty-six I'll need for three days but I need you to do something specific with the other seven. And I need you to do exactly what I say exactly when I say. If you do, we can make this fly. If you don't, well ...'

The following day a rather large bank draft was drawn up and I sent Pradesh and Kate to set up shop in the States with sixty thousand. I promised to join them in a week or so, and let them off at the airport. As I pulled out my mobile went off.

'Hon, Angel. It's time. Be at McLellands in twenty minutes to start.'

'Ok.'

'Right, let's go over it again. Go in at exactly two o'clock and ...' she continued giving precise instructions and having me repeat them verbatim.

'Clear?'

I had nearly run off the road twice writing it down. 'No probs. See you later.'

We did private business we wanted quiet and discrete through McLellands, a (barely) reputable company that charged more but said less than other brokers. McLelland was happy to see me but I suspect happier to see the bank draft. After the two o'clock transaction he thought I had gone for good, but come three was surprised to see me back on his doorstep. The additional commission helped ease his pain over my return but he looked nonplussed as I sat down again at ten to five.

'Again? Haven't you had enough? Do you know what happened ten minutes after you left, you coulda screwed it to the wall if you had just left it sitting instead of diving off. If you want back in well mate that horse has bolted.'

I eyed him cautiously and slipped a tab of paper to him. 'No, I just want to dump it for this. What's the rate now?'

He told me, and I told him to put the offer at eighty-five

percent value. His jaw dropped. Before he could speak, I cut in.

'Don't ask, I've got my reasons. If you need an explanation you can put your rate up two percent but just do it now.'

His jaw went back where it belonged. I had touched him at heart, he had always been easy to buy. His hands went up. 'Ok, whatever you say, no questions asked.'

He left the room muttering something about the mental defects of bloody greenie academics and came back in at ten past five with a check and an evil grin.

'Well you probably take the prize. I've done what you said and after all that stuffing around you're down by three and a half. I hope you have a nice day, thanks for the commission.'

I left with check in hand. The closer I came to home the deeper my gloom became. I had lost three and a half out of seven but I took some solace as I knew Angel was probably making that up and more. The hours at home dragged on and I ended up glued in front of late night TV. The exchange market news nearly broke my heart, all the movements indicating I had missed my chance. Me and Johnny Walker got to know each other better.

I had been drunk, sobered up and drunk again by the time Angel came home. I was feeling pretty dirty but I said nothing as she sat down. I felt that instead of flying this little puppy was all over and done with. Maybe exile to Siberia wouldn't be that bad.

Angel put her head on my shoulder and let out a long sigh. 'I guess you think I am some sort of moron or something. You've seen the rates I suppose?'

'Yeah. But I still love you.'

'That's nice to know, but don't give up on me quite yet. Do you know why I asked you to lose that money? You do know that I actually wanted you to lose it, don't you?'

'Can't say that I did or do, you know. It'd be the first time you set out to make a loss if it was.'

'Well I couldn't be the one to kick the first domino.'

She reached into her briefcase. 'But I had to be there to make sure the rest went. I had to hang on for a while to make it happen and I'm not going to try and explain as you don't understand cross rates or hedging no matter how hard I try. Put it simply that a smart trader knows how to play one off against another. And, darling, you know I'm the best.'

She had slid a small square of paper into my lap while she was speaking. I looked down and saw a US currency draft for three hundred and fifty million dollars.

'That enough?' She laughed.

Enough? I nearly wet myself.

My departure from Australia was made in high spirits, Angel adding to it by riding on the back of the research money with some of our own. I had doubts about what the NASA Grants Board would say, but was pleasantly surprised with their reaction at our first meeting. I had just started my 'Oh, by the way I have an extra couple of hundred million' speech and was wondering if it would be believed when the Board Director came up to me.

'Fantastic!' she exclaimed, grabbing me in an ebullient bear hug. 'And they say the spirit of free enterprise doesn't live down under!' And that was that.

The team knew better than to ask questions and in any case were too far into their work to have the time. Pradesh had managed to locate and identify the materials we required and Kate was moulding the rest of the team into shape on the design and device build. I busied myself spending until it hurt and watching it all go together. Even working feverishly with and all the assistance we had it was still a hard slog to completion. Finally, eight months later, we found ourselves in the Florida dawn watching the crawler transporter carry our precious load to the launch pad. We had a window, we had a deadline, and we had beaten it by a sliver over twenty four hours. And we had twenty two million dollars change.

The launch was flawless and we assembled at JPL two days later to watch the devices' construction, the drones already having deployed in orbit. The day consisted of nothing more than watching the automated construction of our device which after eighteen hours resembled exactly what it should – a large, appreciably convex saucer some three kilometres in diameter. A central column four hundred meters high protruded sunwards from its centre. The surface of the saucer consisted of myriad small, mirrored shutter like panes built around radial spokes. The end of each spoke was connected by nanotube to the top of the column and likewise to a lesser protrusion on the Earthwards side. At the moment all the shutters were aligned so that they were edge on to both Sun and Earth.

'Always the way it is, another simple, elegant solution.' Kate mused.

I smiled. Elegant yes, simple not quite so. It was the first question I had put to Kate when she applied for the Doctoral programme, and her answer was the reason I had taken her into my circle of students. 'How do you heat up one square kilometre of ocean?' which usually elicited the same series of hydro-thermal, bore hole options. Kate had suggested what I myself thought. Take a small mirror. Stick it in orbit and presto, ocean heated. With the device however a simple command would turn it either into a lens or a reflector by angling the mirrors. In the neutral state the device was, for all intents and purposes, transparent. I laughed.

'Not the way you see it?' she asked.

'Oh no', I offered 'it's not that. I'm just wondering what Orville and Wilbur Wright would think of what we've done with their wing warping.'

'Somehow I think they'd approve.'

Months later back at the University I was still monitoring the device. The preliminary data were encouraging, if anything better than projected. It seemed a success. Even with a further twelve months for the impact on weather patterns to be felt everything pointed to our goals being met. All we had to do was monitor it as the automated routine continued.

A year and a half down the track and life rolled on as usual. Pradesh and Kate had both graduated. Angel and I were now ridiculously well off and had solid plans to retire by forty-five to open a café bookshop. The device was working as expected, it's monitoring now being automated out of JPL leaving me with a tenuous link via the stream of research papers I was publishing.

Angel and I were sitting on the same verandah in the same place as we were when the whole episode started, watching a mid-summer pastel sunset.

'Strange', she started 'the days aren't quite as harsh as I remember them.'

'How do you mean, harsh?'

'Well, it seems as if the edge has gone off the days. It's not quite as hot and I'm positive that it's less humid than it has been.'

I chuckled quietly to myself. 'What were we doing not more than three years ago?'

She creased her brows slightly. 'Not much, you hadn't started the project then and we were stuck here. In fact', she continued with more than a touch of sarcasm 'the only thing I remember clearly is a constant whining.'

I leant back and put my arm around her. 'I recall that you asked why I didn't have the brains to sort out the summer heat while I lay here sweating to death.'

'Did I?'

'Oh yes, and I didn't forget. In fact, I have done something about it.'

Angel stared at me, eyes narrowed. 'What exactly do you mean?'

'Well, the device doesn't have to work all the time on the main project, it has a big down time up there and because of its positioning it can work on a third lesser known weather node in the region.' I smiled broadly, looking her in the eyes.

'So, I have added just a couple of lines to the programming and it's going to chop off about two degrees from our summer maximums.'

Angels' eyes widened slightly, but then retreated to slits. 'They'll find out what you've done eventually you realise, don't you?'

'Nah, they won't', I countered derisively 'it only has to do this for another two months and the pattern's changed forever. I can then just wipe the lines and then that's that. No ones the wiser and this place is then just that little more civilised.'

'Hmmmmm', was her only comment as she settled back 'I certainly hope so.'

Three things happened in quick succession that neatly destroyed my carefully laid plans. Firstly a minor meteor shower took out the communications antenna on the device leaving it still functioning but unable to talk to us or we to it. Secondly the US Congress took a sharp axe to all expenditure. Near the top of the list was NASA; and on the top of NASA's list was JPL; and on the top of JPL's was the monitoring of the device.

Finally all the over work, late nights, bad eating habits and stress hit me. I don't know if it's possible to have a minor nervous breakdown, but if there is then what I got sure as hell wasn't. I quit my faculty job, retired at forty-two instead of forty-five. I couldn't do much more than dress and clean myself for the next eighteen months. Worse yet as part of it I totally lost track of my work, a common defence mechanism I am told.

The upshot? The device was forgotten totally, erased from the minds of NASA and myself and left to get on with its programming uninterrupted.

Retirement has treated Angel and myself well. Our café bookshop pays its own way, and is relatively stress free. With both of us retired we have time enough for ourselves, and that's what really matters. And my legacy still continues. Monsoon is now much gentler, predictable and still replenishes the lands and river deltas. El Ninio and La Nina continue in a much lessened way, severe drought and flood being relegated to history. The device continued on its merry way for another ten years before failing totally, more than enough time to produce a permanent change in weather patterns.

And of my other special project?

Well, I like the cold. In fact, I have a real physical need to feel the cold, to be in bed wrapped tightly against the outside, bare feet searching for the cold corners while my nose sticks out like some polar crocodile. I enjoy walking through snow, feeling my face sting from rain that's nearing hail and having the wind rub my ears to beetroot red. Which is fortunate, seeing how I live here in hemi boreal Queensland, the temperature hardly struggling above eight degrees celsius and rain two hundred and fifty odd days out of each year. But Angel ...

END

Wood for the trees

Daniela leant over the rail, gazing at the room full of machinery. She squeezed the nape of her neck, grinned wryly, then turned.

'That's it Ted, shut it down.'

'Damn, I thought we finally had it.'

'It's just science, some theories are right, some are wrong. Shame this one's taken thirty nine years.'

'You lasted longer than the rest.'

'You mean they're quicker than me? Maybe I'm just too stubborn.'

'What now?'

She shrugged.

'Mark it all for scrap, clear it out before the charges pile up. Everything else can wait.'

The night traffic was light, freeway in front empty,

Melbourne's lights fading slowly behind. Always the same, as it ever was and, she now knew, as it always would be. The headlights swayed gently in time with Benny Goodman. She turned the radio up. I need a holiday to clear my head, perhaps Europe or the States. A week or two in the air, evening deck promenades over the Pacific, the whisper of silk through air, the clink of champagne flutes at four thousand feet. The clipboard slid across the bench seat, tapping her thigh. Four billion people don't know hard I've tried, nothing's changed for them. She lifted the clipboard, sent the litany of failure spinning out the window into darkness.

Daniela pulled into her driveway, turned off the car, let the night envelop her. What was the old saying, the end of a thing is better than its beginning? Whatever. She got out, leant against the '19 Bel Air's fins and gazed up. The twin moons shone down, scudding silver-blue discs shepherding iridescent rings across the heavens. Perfect as always. Daniela sighed, finally smiled. Why did I ever want to change it anyway?

END

Yesterday and tomorrow are today

I had a strange and wonderful relationship with my girlfriend. She had precognition myopia, the only person who will have it she said. She couldn't remember the past, only the future. She only knew the future the way I remember the past. Vaguely and obtusely, except for those things only a handful of years away.

This suited me fine, perhaps it was the only way I could find love. My past is best forgotten, best lost, but that's not the human condition. Except for her. She couldn't really relate to anyone who lives their life in the past, cherishing and reliving memories. To her it was emptiness and void. So I suited her too I guess, my past hidden, my only desire to look forward.

For her, school was terrifying. She went in clearly knowing everything to be gained in the six grades above her, together with vague understanding of a lifetime's accumulated knowledge to come. No school would take her in the end, too scared and not knowing what to do with one supposedly so precocious.

She grew up emotionally hypersensitive, people's emotions and futures moulding and twisting her psyche. Imagine having a seven year old's brain and body yet knowing all that goes on in and around a thirteen year old's life, going through puberty and all the associated pains and conflict. Worse, imagine having six years to dwell on it, six years to see it coming, six years to fester and roil inside until the inevitable. Then, to add insult to injury, when it occurs it then ceases to exist. Utterly. Completely.

Five years she mourned before her father's death, tearing her mother's heart out. And when finally he died he passed totally out of existence for her. It was as if he was a mere zephyr, or had never been. To her he truly had not.

I came home late from work last night. She had hanged herself in the garage. She left a note, all it said was 'Why will you cheat on me?'

END

Author's note

The stories contained here are the sum-total of all my short and flash science fiction produced between 1999 and 2019. They are, in the true sense of the phrase, the good, the bad, and (as they say) the ugly of my work. So why bother to put them all out, on public view?

Well, for a start, they already have been. Each one of these stories have appeared either in webzines, magazines, or published anthologies, so there are no real surprises.

Having everything out also lets me show the development of my craft over two decades; although, as they are presented in alphabetical, rather than date, order, you, the reader, will have to make your own judgment as to which order they appeared.

But most importantly I have found that, despite my views on these things, readers make up their own minds what they do, or do not, like. What I thought my least polished, least capable, work made many readers happy; what I felt was my most mature and accomplished piece sank with nary a trace.

If you have not read these stories before, I hope you find some pleasure in them.

If you have, I trust you welcome them back as old friends.

Ishmael A. Soledad
Brisbane, November 2021

www.ingramcontent.com/pod-product-compliance
Lightning Source LLC
Chambersburg PA
CBHW020917020726
47495CB00002B/232